CHAINS OF BLOOD

THE CHAOS CYCLE #1

ML SPENCER

STONEGUARD PUBLICATIONS

This is a work of fiction. All of the characters, organizations, and events
portrayed in this novel are either products of the author's imagination or are
used fictitiously.

CHAINS OF BLOOD
Copyright © 2019 by M.L. Spencer
STONEGUARD PUBLICATIONS

Cover by Felix Ortiz
Edited by Morgan Smith
ISBN: 978-0-9997825–90

Karog

Arjul

Farath

Carash

*Rajul
Plains*

Zagra Valley

Jur

Maghra

*Orien's
Finger*

Tolath

Glen
Farquist

THE Malikari Empire

Bel Arun

Qalm

Janul

Farrow

Karikesh

Auberdale

Nabad

Covendrey

Din Hollow

*Isle of
Titherry*

Cantridge

Smith's Forge

Wertan

Meridan

Southwark

Bergin

Gandrish

THE

Fells

Kingdoms

Tivendale

Dandry

Foundry

THE Southern Continent

c. 1766 DCE

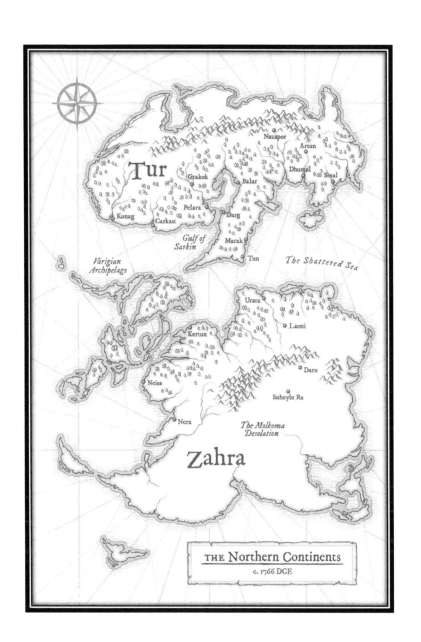

Nazapor
Artun
Tur
Grakok
Balar
Dhumal
Sinal
Pelara
Darg
Kunag
Carkast
Gulf of
Sarkin
Marak
Tun
The Shattered Sea
Varigian
Archipelago
Uratu
Laoni
Kertun
Daru
Neisa
Suheylu Ra
Nera
The Molkoma
Desolation
Zahra

THE Northern Continents

c. 1766 DCE

MAP OF KARIKESH

1 The Lyceum
2 The Temple of Death
3 Mabuer Qtr.
4 Mashad Qtr.
5 Ashgar Qtr.
6 Chasman Qtr.
7 The Rat Market
8 New Faubourg
9 The Warf
10 Old Rothbeard
11 Kivilin Qtr.
12 Baydam Qtr.
13 Kazri Souk
14 Houak Qtr.
15 Abrenar Qtr.

16 Talat Qtr.
17 Turpan Qtr.
18 Muliash Qtr.
19 Darvu Qtr.
20 Vadi Qtr.
21 Damuh Qtr.
22 Mipaz Qtr.
23 Aushkan Qtr.
24 Virlou Qtr.
25 Barafaz Qtr.
26 Narven Qtr.
27 Alqazac Citadel
28 Bitil Qtr.
29 Nogodu Qtr.

GRAND CANAL

GOLDEN HORN BAY

MURQAK SQUARE

ANDARAPI PALACE

Nerium River

1

GIFT OF DARKNESS

THE INN'S DOOR BLEW OPEN WITH A SHRIEK.

Rylan Marshall flinched at the noise, his hand moving to the hilt of the sword resting at his side against the table. One of the inn's customers bolted up, strode across the room, and slammed the door shut. Rylan's fingers loosened on the hilt, eventually retracting. The tension that gripped his shoulders took longer to go away.

Seated across the table, his father offered a sympathetic smile. "Can always tell when a man's served time at the front," he said, letting out a slow sigh. "The nerves get stretched thin. It took me a year before I stopped jumping at every barking dog. Some men never lose it." He ran a hand through his auburn hair, which was cropped shorter than he used to wear it and peppered with far more gray.

"I'm just glad to be home," Rylan said.

He drained the last of his whiskey, then set his cup down on the planks of the tabletop. The blur of conversation filled his ears, a monotonous sound that never quite faded from his awareness. It was soothing, in a way. Normal. It had been two years since he'd stepped foot inside the Farlow Inn. His gaze trailed across the dim and smoke-filled interior, from the river-rock hearth to the elk's head mounted above the door. Everything about the inn was comfortingly familiar. It felt like home.

Outside, the wind gave a ghoulish moan.

He poured himself what was left of the whiskey and tossed it back in one swallow. Setting the cup down, he swiped a lock of thick black hair out of his eyes. "You should have seen what they did to their own vanguard at Edden's Ford," he said. "We had them trapped against the water, so they turned their weapons on their own men. They forded the river on a bridge of corpses. Walked right over them."

His father shook his head. "Desperate men do desperate things," he muttered. For a moment, his eyes grew haunted. He stared down into the shadows of his cup, absently sliding a fingernail along the rough grain of the table's surface. The air moving in under the door fanned the lanterns, bringing Clemet's mind back from whatever hell it had wandered into. He lifted the empty bottle, signaling the inn's proprietor for another.

Rylan raised his hands in defeat. "That's it for me. I've got to be heading back. I've decided to take Korey into Auberdale tomorrow and get him a pair of good shoes. The ones he's got have holes in them."

"While you're there, get yourself a pair," his father said, gesturing at Rylan's worn boots, which had seen many miles and many battles. He dug a small handful of coins out of his pouch and slid them across the table. Rylan opened his mouth to protest, but Clemet cut him off before he could get the words out.

"Go on, now," he insisted, waving him away. "I've still got another round left in me. I'll walk you out, though."

"My thanks," Rylan managed, knowing that arguing wouldn't get him anywhere.

He accepted the coins and stood up, taking a moment to

stretch his legs and gird his sword belt. The sound of abrupt laughter drew his attention to a group of men playing cards in the corner. Only a few patrons were gathered in the common room, all locals. Rylan pulled on his coat and followed his father out the door. The smell of the hearth trailed after them into the night.

Outside, Clemet embraced him and clapped him on the shoulder. "It's good to have you home, son," he said with a sincere smile. "Tell your mother I'll be along in a bit." He gave Rylan another squeeze, then turned and walked back into the inn.

Rylan strolled with his head bowed, enjoying the warmth of the liquor in his belly. The dust-paved streets of Farlow were quiet, almost ghostly in their stillness. Not a soul was about. Obscured by clouds, the moon was reduced to a thin yellow haze that shed an anemic light over the town.

A building across the street gave a sharp crack. "Settling," as his mother would call it. The noise startled him. At the front, he'd learned not to trust sounds he didn't expect. He glared at the house, resenting it, and continued down the street, his right hand fingering the coins his father had given him. Another gust of wind came up, ruffling his hair.

Up ahead, a shadow crossed his path and disappeared down a side street. Human-shaped. At least, he thought it looked human. It could have been anything. Something about it tugged at the hairs on the back of his neck. Rylan paused and brought a hand up, scratching the week-old growth of whiskers on his face. He shrugged off the feeling and walked on.

He left town on a narrow, gravelly path leading through acres of cornfields toward his family's homestead. Tall stalks rose around him, walling the path to either side, swaying back and forth between gusts of wind. Overhead, the moon dodged in and out of the clouds, the path ahead alternating between silver and shadow.

A scratching noise like metal against metal came from the field to his right.

Rylan stopped, frowning, and turned in the direction of the sound. He could make out a break in the rows of corn, as though someone had left the trail and carved a path through the stalks. He started toward the opening, then stopped himself. Whoever was out there, it wasn't his business. He had a family to get home to. He turned and continued on.

The cornfield ended with a long row of sycamores, a wind-break that wasn't doing much of a job. On the other side, Rylan could make out the lights of his parents' farmhouse glowing warmly through a lacy silhouette of leaves. His mother was still awake.

The scratching noise came again.

Rylan whirled toward it.

Behind him was another human-like shadow, only this time, standing in the center of the path. It was gone as soon as he saw it.

Rylan blinked. His stomach tightened, and his brow broke out in a sweat. A feeling came over him in an icy wave, one he recognized. It was the same feeling he got when staring across a battlefield at enemy lines.

"Who's there?" he called into the darkness, taking a step forward.

Nothing.

A rush of wind trilled the leaves of the sycamores.

Whoever it was, he didn't want them near his home. Hand on his sword's hilt, he started back toward the cornfield. The night grew alarmingly quiet. The sounds of his boots crunching on gravel rang much louder than they should, echoing through the darkness in the absence of other noise. The wind had stopped. The limbs of the trees swayed to a standstill.

Rylan walked back out into the field, the moon casting his shadow ahead of him. He scanned the path to either side, seeing only tall walls of cornstalks, until he came to the opening in the rows. He stopped, considering the trail. A stale breeze wafted past him, carrying a rank odor. Rylan drew in a deep breath, gathered his courage, then walked into the corn.

Following a dark and narrow path, he had to fight with the rough stalks that raked his skin as he pushed them out of his way. Part of him didn't want to keep going, but another part of him did. From ahead came the scratching sound again, louder this time. It scraped like a dull knife down his nerves. He pushed aside the stalks.

Another shadow streaked across his vision.

It lunged for him.

Rylan's reaction was primal and automatic. He bared his sword and swept it around in a two-handed arc. The blade parted the shadow without connecting with anything.

Startled, he took a jolting step back. The shadow swept forward, reaching out for him. He spun back around—

—and cried out, stumbling away from the face of a man standing only inches from him. His fingers opened on their own, and the sword fell from his grip.

The man reached out and caught his arm. Rylan stood frozen, the fear in his gut a paralyzing venom. The hand tugged at his arm, and he walked woodenly forward, his feet moving of their own accord. The shadowy man led him back into a ring of trampled cornstalks.

Rylan's eyes went to the remains of a fire that had been built in the center of the circle. He recognized the smell now: burnt human flesh. He'd smelled that stench before on the battlefield. His gaze was glued to the pile, unable to look away. Before him, the blackened flesh took on definition. Thin arms, twisted legs, distorted features. Small, like a child.

He flinched away, his gaze settling on a small leather shoe with a hole in the toe. Rylan collapsed to his knees, throttled by horror. A soul-wrenching cry welled up from his depths, twisting his guts.

His assailant stepped forward out of the shadows, a tall, gray man with an angular face. His piercing eyes bored into Rylan through a mat of long, oily hair. He reached out his hand, as if offering to help him to his feet.

Rylan scrambled toward the charred remains of his boy. But the gray-skin man sprang in front of him, cutting him off. Rylan sank back, all his strength pouring out of him in a flood.

"Why?" was all he could get out.

"Because it is your fate."

The words were meaningless. None of this was happening. He must be asleep. Dreaming. More human-like shades slid forward to encircle him. He drew his legs up to his chest and smothered his face with his hands. His cheeks ran with tears, his body wracked by sobs.

"Why?" he moaned again.

"Because of who you are."

He looked up at the man through thick layers of incomprehension. "Who I am...?" He shook his head. "I'm nobody..."

This wasn't real. This wasn't happening.

The thin lips drew back in a smile, baring teeth. The gray man knelt before him, staring into his eyes. "We bring you a great gift, Gerald. Think of it as your inheritance."

Rylan's thoughts lurched. His brain jammed like stuck gears. "Who's Gerald...?"

They had the wrong man, the wrong family. This was all a mistake.

But his son's bones lay smoldering in front of him, and the devil-bastard who'd killed him wasn't going away.

Rylan's anger exploded, wrenching fear aside. He struck out with a fist and hit a wall of solid air. He heard the bones of his hand snap. He opened his mouth to scream, but something slammed him to the ground, knocking the air from his lungs.

The gray-faced man stalked toward him, face frozen in a look of intense calm.

Gasping, Rylan rolled over and pushed himself to his feet. He backed away from the man, circling the edge of the clearing. His assailant pursued him, maintaining his distance, his flat expression never faltering.

Rylan sprang for his sword. His hand closed on the hilt, and he brought the blade up.

The weapon dislodged itself from his grip and flew back at him, the pommel driving hard into his temple. Dazed, Rylan staggered.

Something knocked him off his feet and hurled him to the ground. Rylan lay there, blinking slowly, as his assailant came to stand over him. Gritting his teeth, Rylan forced himself to move, pushing himself to his hands and knees. A foot shot out, taking him in the ribs. Another kick knocked him back to the ground. Rylan glared wrathfully up into the man's stone-calm face.

"You son of a whore!" he rasped. Spitting a mouthful of blood, he pushed himself upright.

The gray-faced man knelt in front of him, staring into his eyes with an infinite glare.

Rylan brought his hand up to throw a punch at the man's windpipe. The gray man moved with the speed of a snake strike. He caught Rylan's fist and gripped it hard. Then something struck him, and he gave a grunt.

Rylan felt a stirring in his fingers. A strange power flowed into him from his assailant's body, moving through his hand, washing up his arm, flooding into him. It swept through him, engorging him, awakening every fiber of his being with an exhilaration that transcended anything he'd ever known. The energy swelled, rapturous, until the ecstasy became unbearable.

Rylan screamed.

The flood of energy ceased.

He collapsed, falling face-first onto the trampled cornstalks. He lay there for several minutes, twitching and gasping. When he could finally open his eyes, he saw the gray-faced man lying dead beside him. With a cry, Rylan jerked back.

Another man appeared, taller than the first, stepping into the circle through the ring of shadows. This man wasn't gray. He had olive skin and a hawk-like nose. He wore his long brown hair pulled back from his face. The man stooped in front of Rylan and peered at him. The shadows in his eyes were endless and harrowing.

"You will repeat after me," he said calmly. "I commit my soul to Chaos."

Rylan gaped up at him, shaking his head. "No."

The man leaned closer. "Yes. Or I swear by Xerys, your daughter will meet an excruciating end."

Amina...

Rylan shook his head, unable to draw breath through his horror.

The man's eyes narrowed. "Say it!"

Not Amina too. Not my baby girl...

Trembling, he whispered, "I commit my soul to Chaos..."

"From this day forth, I will be the obedient servant of Xerys."

Rylan stared at his son's charred body, trembling in revulsion. He shook so hard it was difficult to get the words out. "From this day forth, I will be the obedient servant of Xerys..."

"And may not even death release me."

"No..." Rylan wheezed.

"Say it!" the man hissed. "If you value your daughter's life, you must swear the oath. Remember the oath, and chains will never bind you."

Rylan sucked in a long, shuddering breath, then whispered,

"And may not even death release me... oh, gods. Please help me..."

"Only one god can help you now," the man assured him, straightening.

Rylan collapsed. Through his sobs, he heard the sound of footsteps walking away.

"I'm taking your daughter back with me," the man informed him. "Someday I will call, Gerald. And you will come."

The man-like shadows swirled away into darkness. The olive-skinned man disappeared with them.

2

BORN ENEMIES

GIL ARCHER WALKED INTO THE LYCEUM'S LIBRARY AND ANGLED toward a small group of mages gathered around an ornate chessboard. Two of the men, Nat Hopkins and Payden Walsh, sat on opposite sides of the table, contemplating their next moves, while five other men hovered over them in a tense cluster. Gil drew up behind them and stood quietly, taking a moment to assess the game. Apparently, it was Nat's turn. The young mage sat with his hand lingering above a pawn, fingers swirling the air. His other hand supported his brow, his straw-gold hair falling forward into his face.

Gil studied the gameboard. It looked like Payden had employed his typical opening, the Queen's Gambit, and Nat had replied with his standard Albin Counter. Payden controlled the center of the board, Gil noted, but his last move had left him vulnerable.

Gil leaned forward and lifted Nat's bishop, planting it down at the edge of the gameboard and capturing Payden's queen.

"Check," he said and walked away.

Behind him rose the expected cries of outrage.

"What the hell, Archer?" Payden called after him.

Gil chuckled as he crossed the library to the far wall, past rows of bookshelves, then made his way to a colonnaded walkway that overlooked a tiled floor three stories below. He trailed his hand absently along the rail as he walked, his gaze slipping over the soaring white walls and frescoed ceiling overhead. Despite being built only a score of years before, the Lyceum of Karikesh housed one of the most extensive collections of books anywhere in the world, second only to the Temple of Wisdom in Glen Farquist. Gil appreciated a good library. He'd been raised in one, and returning to the Lyceum's collection of books felt like coming home.

Or as close to home as anything could feel. He had never known a real home, at least none that he could remember. He could only guess what a true home felt like.

At the end of the walkway, he came to a room caged off from the rest of the library by wrought-iron bars. Digging into the pouch he wore at his waist, he produced a ring of keys and sifted through them. He found the one he wanted and, unlocking the barred door, stepped inside. He stood still for a moment, looking around at the circular room lined with shelves loaded with books. Inhaling deeply, he savored the musty odor of ancient paper and leather bindings, a comforting scent that brought an intense pang of nostalgia.

His gaze trailed over the rows of bookshelves and the treasures they contained: a priceless collection of texts and documents, most found nowhere else in the world. Some were well over a thousand years old, harvested from the ancient library on the Isle of Titherry, where they had spent a millennium protected from the ravages of mildew and time. But now, with their relocation to the Lyceum's library, the texts in the Cage required enormous care in their storage and handling.

Gil moved to a tall desk and, opening a drawer, removed a pair of pristine white gloves. He drew them on, flexing his fingers to stretch the fabric. The gloves were a standard precaution when handling the books, protecting them from skin oil and nail abrasions. There were many other strict protocols in place to conserve the delicate collection. Some of the texts were so old, their pages would disintegrate if handled at all. Only a few of the Lyceum's many scholars were allowed access to the Cage. And, among those, fewer still had access to the Vault.

Gil was among those few.

He walked over to an iron door set into the wall between shelves and stopped in front of it. For a long moment, he simply stood there. Then, with a slight click, the heavy door popped open just a crack. Holding his gloved hands up, Gil used his foot to nudge the door open just enough to sidle through. He moved forward slowly into the small room, which was little more than a niche carved into the wall. The Vault contained some of the rarest–and most dangerous–texts in existence. The room's purpose was twofold: to protect its trove of relics from the world, but also to protect the world from the danger of its contents.

Standing with his hands raised, Gil scanned the dark shelves lining the room. In the ambient light, it was difficult to make out the markings on the spines of the texts. He strolled forward, scanning a long shelf of books of similar sizes, until he found the text he was looking for.

Carefully, Gil pushed back the two books to either side of the one he wanted, then removed the leather-bound text from the shelf. Staring down at it, he wandered back toward the center of the Cage. There, he paused, silently contemplating the title inscribed on the book's dusty cover:

A TREATISE ON THE WELL OF TEARS

Supporting the book so as not to harm the ancient spine, Gil opened the cover and flipped to the first yellowed page written in flowing ink:

The Well of Tears was created under the direction of Prime Warden Zavier Renquist, who purposed to use the power of the Netherworld to halt a magical cataclysm...

"Excuse me. Grand Master Archer?"

Gil cursed himself. He'd forgotten to lock the Cage door.

He gave a defeated sigh, then turned to regard the lost-looking acolyte who had come up behind him. The boy wore a black mage's cloak, though his cheeks were covered with only the first attempt at a scraggly beard. Gil stared at him expectantly, eyebrows raised.

The acolyte reached up to fidget with his collar. "I'm sorry for interrupting—"

"Then why are you?"

The acolyte paled. "I, uh... Sorry..."

Gil smiled. "Relax. What can I do for you?"

Looking enormously relieved, the young man said, "I bear a message from the Prime Warden."

Gil closed the text in his hands. "What's the message?"

"The Prime Warden desires to speak with you in her office. Right away."

"*Right*-right away?"

The acolyte looked confused. "Yes, Grand Master. Right... right away."

Gil glanced down at the book in his hand, feeling flustered. He said, "Thank you."

The young man bobbed the slightest bow, then scurried out of the Cage, where he hadn't belonged in the first place. Gil returned *Treatise on the Well* back to its place on the shelf, beside other influential texts not half as apocalyptic. He stepped out of the room, locking the Vault. Then he removed the white satin gloves and left the Cage.

As he crossed the library, Gil passed the same group of men lingering over yet another game of chess. He angled away from them and made his way toward the stairs.

Payden called after him, "You're such an ass, Archer!"

He took the stairs two at a time to the ground floor, then started up a wide hallway lined with sandstone blocks. As he walked, his black cloak fluttered in his wake, the outward symbol marking him as a mage to the rest of the world. Embroidered into the fabric between his shoulders was a silver eight-pointed star: another legendary symbol, this one far older than even the cloak that bore it.

Gil's long strides propelled him down the wide, tiled corridors to the Prime Warden's office, situated at the north side of the Lyceum and surrounded by its own courtyard. Gil found her secretary's desk mercifully empty. Which was good. The woman was a battle-axe with the personality of a prison guard. Moving forward, he rapped once upon the door and entered without waiting for a response. Inside, he found the Prime Warden seated behind a cherrywood writing desk.

Naia Seleni looked up from the letter she was scribing. "Grand Master Archer. Thank you for coming. Please, have a seat." She gestured with her quill at the chair across the desk.

"Thank you, Prime Warden," Gil said.

He sat and waited in silence as she finished scribing the letter. After a moment, he realized he was staring at her and dropped his gaze to the desk. Naia Seleni was a formidable woman, and yet beautiful. Though middle-aged, her face remained untouched by the years or by the power she wielded. She could have been taken for any one of the young acolytes scurrying about the Lyceum's halls, right up until she wanted to be seen as something more. Then, Naia's presence could swell to dominate any room. The Prime Warden was the most powerful woman in the world, with or without the white cloak of office she wore.

She set her quill down and, pushing back her auburn hair, smiled at him warmly. "You look more like your father every time I see you. How long has it been this time?"

"Eight months." Gil leaned back in his chair, his gaze roaming over the walls. Naia's office was decorated in an intriguing riot of colors: tapestries, curtains, knickknacks, cushions... all of a style Gil had never seen anywhere else in the Rhen. He often wondered how Naia had amassed the collection.

She gave him a surprised look. "Has it really been so long? It doesn't seem like it. So how was Southwark?"

"Bloody boring." Spying a bowl of dates on her desk, he leaned forward and popped one into his mouth, sucking the flesh off the pit.

Naia cocked an eyebrow before continuing. "Then it sounds like you might welcome some excitement. I have another task for you."

Gil looked at her in interest. "What kind of task?"

Naia's face turned grim, and she sat forward in her seat, lacing her fingers on the desk. "There has been a rather tragic incident involving a farmer and his family from northern Chamsbrey. The crime, as it was reported, sounds particularly heinous. The farmer's young son was burned alive in a cornfield. The assailants left the poor man alive but absconded with his daughter."

"What about the man's wife?" he asked.

"She died in childbirth."

Gil sat still for a moment, gazing straight ahead at a paining on the wall, letting the information seep slowly in. "That does sound very tragic," he said at last. "Are you sure the 'poor man' didn't murder his own children?"

Naia nodded. "Quite certain. Apparently, one of his two assailants was a mage who forced his Gift upon him. And died in the process, of course."

Gil's mouth dropped open in shock. Every mage carried inside them a magical legacy that could be passed from one person to another. But such an act always resulted in the death of the donor of that legacy. This mage had sacrificed his life to transfer his Gift to this particular farmer. He must have been desperate. Desperate enough to die for his cause... But why? What could he have possibly hoped to gain?

"When did this occur?" Gil asked, still deep in thought.

"Two days ago."

Suddenly, the ancient texts in the Lyceum's library didn't seem important anymore. He asked, "Since we're having this conversation, I take it you're sending me to Chamsbrey?"

The Prime Warden nodded. "I am. Your task will be to determine exactly what happened in that cornfield and why. But more importantly, you are to deliver the farmer here expeditiously. We must assume his life is in grave peril."

"That's a good assumption." Gil picked another date out of the bowl and plunged it into his mouth. Chewing, he said, "I'll leave right away—"

"One more thing." Naia said, cutting him off. "You will be taking your new acolyte along with you."

Gil stopped chewing. He must have heard her wrong. Clutching the pit of the date in his hand, he peered sideways at the Prime Warden. "My new... what...?"

Naia looked at him sternly. "It's past time you took on an apprentice, Gil. I'm assigning you Ashra ni Sayeed."

He almost choked on the date. "You've got to be kidding."

"No. I'm not." Naia's smile seemed almost motherly. "Ashra needs a mentor, and you're in need of an apprentice."

Gil shook his head. "Prime Warden, forgive me, but give me anyone—anyone in the whole world—but not her! You know our histories—"

Naia smiled. "Your histories are *exactly* why I decided on this match. This land has not yet recovered from the deep wounds inflicted upon it by both your parents. It is long past time to start mending those wounds. I'll begin with you and Ashra."

Gil felt himself sinking lower in his chair with every word. When Naia was finished, he looked at her dismally. "And there's nothing I can do to convince you otherwise?"

"Nothing."

He dragged in a deep breath, held it in for a moment, then slowly let it back out again. "All right, then. I'll let her know. This is going to be a fun trip. I pity the poor farmer."

He shoved back his chair and started to stand up, but her voice halted him.

"Take great care, Gil," Naia said, her gaze capturing his own. "Whoever did this, did it for a reason. It is imperative we determine that reason. And it's also imperative that we keep this farmer out of the hands of those who have taken such an interest in him. Do you understand?"

He stared across the desk at her a moment before finally nodding. "Understood."

"Relax, Gil. She won't bite."

"It's her claws I'm worried about," he muttered.

He didn't acknowledge Naia's sympathetic smile as he left her office. His mind continued to grumble all the way back through the Gathering Hall and up the stairs to the living quarters of the Lyceum. By the time he reached the hallway of the Acolytes' Residence, his mood had turned exceptionally black, as black as the cloak on his back. He drew up in front of Ashra's door and raised his hand to knock.

He couldn't make himself do it. He lowered his hand, glowering at the door. Then, gritting his teeth, he rapped forcefully.

Long seconds dragged by. He heard nothing from the other side of the door. Gil waited, listening for the sounds of footsteps. He almost turned and walked away.

The door cracked open.

A young woman with lustrous brown skin and sleek raven hair peered out at him through the narrow opening. Her lips parted, as though in shock. But she recovered quickly and opened the door wider. She was holding a glass of wine, which she immediately retracted, bringing it close against her chest almost protectively.

"Grand Master Archer. To what do I owe the pleasure?" There was more than a hint of sarcasm in her tone.

Gil had to force himself to look at her. Swallowing his anger, he asked, "Might I come in?"

She opened the door the rest of the way, standing aside.

Hands behind his back, Gil shuffled past her through the door. A single lantern lit the dim interior of her quarters. The floor was covered in patterned rugs, the walls softened by woven tapestries. Her bed was a simple pallet pressed up against the far wall. That surprised him. He didn't think someone like Ashra would be content with simplicity of any kind.

She gestured at a pair of cushions set before a low table. "Please, have a seat. I'm sorry, but I don't have any more wine."

"I'm not thirsty," he said, moving around her.

He doubted she was out of wine. Malikari didn't share cups with their enemies. It was a subtle way of letting him know where he stood with her. Gil claimed a cushion for himself, while Ashra settled on one across from him. She set her glass down on the table between them and proceeded to stare at him with a raptor's pinned gaze.

He had no idea how to say it. So he just said it. "I've been assigned to you as your mentor."

"I see." A slight smile formed on her lips. "And by the look on your face, you're not happy about it?"

It was a rhetorical question. Nevertheless, he answered it anyway. "No. I'm not happy about it. Look. Trust is an important part of the whole acolyte-mentor relationship-thing. But liking each other isn't. So, for the sake of trust, I'll just state my feelings plainly. If the world was ending—and if you and I were the last people left in it—and if all I had to do was lift one finger to save you... well, to put it bluntly, you'd die."

He stood up with a forced smile. "But I've been told I have to work with you. So, I guess I'll have to work with you." Bending down, he scooped her wine glass up from the table and took a thirsty gulp from it. She rose after him with a look of outrage.

"Sour!" he gasped, wincing, and handed the wine back. Gil started to say something else, but then stopped himself. Instead, he moved to the doorway. "Pack a bag, Princess. We're leaving for Chamsbrey."

He let his feet carry him swiftly out of the room, then smirked at the sound of the door thundering closed behind him.

3

THE FARMER'S SON

THE SHRINE OF DEATH ECHOED COLDLY, ITS HARSH MARBLE WALLS devoid of warmth and solace. It was not a place for children. No child should ever be made to lie on a cold stone bier. Even the flowers brought by well-wishers did nothing to ease the shrine's bleak austerity. Instead, the colorful blossoms served only as blunt testimony to the inequity between the world of death and the world of life.

Rylan Marshall sat on a bench near the front of the shrine, his mother and father at his side. He sat with his eyes pinned on his son's funeral shroud, a semi-transparent fabric that revealed just enough of the boy's burned features to make his heart ache in misery, and yet opaque enough to maintain the sense of separation that was his new, unbearable reality. A priest of Death lingered between them, uttering a long litany of prayers Rylan didn't hear. They were a meaningless, droning refrain that dissolved into the background of his awareness.

A hand squeezed his.

Rylan looked up. The priest had stepped back and stood with his head bowed. He was done with his eulogy. The guests behind him rose from their seats and filed out, sharing words of grief and comfort. It took Rylan a moment to realize the rites of passage had been spoken and the blessings administered.

It was time to say goodbye.

Rylan stood. The blurry world waivered for a moment. Summoning the last, tattered scraps of his courage, he crossed the floor to stand over his son's remains. That journey was the most difficult he had ever undertaken and seemed the longest. Rylan lingered over the cloth-draped bier for a long while, his throat clenched in grief. Collecting himself, he stooped to gather a single white daisy from a cluster of flowers arranged at the foot of the bier. He placed the blossom on the embroidered shroud, next to the new shoes Korey would never get a chance to wear. Then he bent and pressed a kiss against the fabric.

He straightened, his hand lingering upon the funeral cloth.

There had been words he'd wanted to say. But no words were adequate to express his grief. Anything he could say would be vastly insufficient.

So he said nothing.

"I think that's it," Gil said, nodding at the farmhouse ahead of them: a two-story structure ringed by outbuildings, visible through a stand of trees.

Ashra peered in the direction he indicated, her arms crossed, squinting her eyes against the harsh glare of sunlight. "How do you know that is the right house?"

"Because of that bunch of flowers." Gil nodded at a bouquet of dried flowers tied with black ribbon and hanging upside-down over the farmhouse door. "It's a symbol of mourning." The flowers were an offering to the Goddess of Death. Different kingdoms had different traditions. Chamsbrey had known more death than most in recent years. The kingdom's long-contested border with the Malikari Empire was a continual source of corpses to feed Death's Catacombs.

Ashra nodded, gazing ahead at the farmhouse. A breeze played with wisps of hair that had fallen loose from her intricate braid. She fretted with it as she followed Gil across the field, angling toward the gravel-strewn farmyard. The house in front of them was made of stacked river stone supported by dark beams of wood. It had an ancient feel about it, as though its tired bones sagged wearily with age. Considering the area, the farmhouse was at least a hundred years old. Perhaps much older.

She was still fussing with her hair when they arrived at the steps to the house. Gil halted under the dried bunch of flowers hanging from the eaves. Ashra drew up beside him, staring up curiously at the blossoms. They looked like daisies, though dry and brittle. She reached her hand up to examine one. Her light touch disturbed some of the petals, which showered down on Gil's head.

He shot her a sideways glare as he dusted petals off his shoulders, then reached up and knocked on the door. He didn't hear anything within, as though the farmhouse was vacant. No conversation, no creaks of footsteps walking on the floor. He was about to turn away and start searching the outbuildings.

The door opened, and an old farmer with thinning red hair and a sun-leathered face greeted them. At the sight of their black cloaks, the man's skin took on a pasty hue. He sniffed and rubbed his nose, then just stood there with a blank expression, as if uncertain what to do.

Gil glanced at Ashra before extending his hand to the farmer. "Good afternoon," he said. "I'm Grand Master Gil Archer, and this is my acolyte, Ashra. We're here to speak to Rylan Marshall."

The old farmer stood staring down at Gil's offered hand with a defeated expression. His eyes were red-rimmed and weary, his shoulders sagging. He considered Gil's hand for a long moment. Then his gaze swung up to Ashra's face and hardened. Apparently, the man wasn't fond of Malikari. Probably from twenty years of watching his kinfolk being slaughtered by them. Gil couldn't blame him. He understood completely.

The farmer said in a firm voice, "I'm sorry, but Rylan's not accepting any visitors." He started to push the door shut.

Gil shot his hand out, catching the door before it could latch. "I know it's a bad time, but—"

"It's all right," came a man's voice from within. "They can come in."

The old farmer fixed Gil with a resentful glare that expanded to encompass Ashra. Heaving a sigh, he opened the door the rest of the way and stepped aside.

"Thank you," Gil said, moving past him.

The interior of the farmhouse was warm and dim, except for broad streaks of light that slanted in through sheer curtains hanging in the windows. The rugs and the furniture were drab, and the walls lacked almost any kind of decoration. A rock hearth, darkened by soot, dominated one end of the room, an area that doubled as a kitchen. A woman in a prim black dress stooped next to the hearth, tending a large iron kettle that hung suspended over the flames.

The old man grudgingly shook Gil's hand. "Clemet Marshall. This is my wife, Lena. And this is our son, Rylan."

He gestured toward a dim back corner of the room. A man sat there in a high-backed chair, staring at them through a thick screen of stringy, shoulder-length black hair. He looked to be in his early twenties, but it was hard to tell; the man had been severely beaten, one eye swelled shut, his face a mask of bruises. The shaggy growth of whiskers on his face was too long to be considered stubble, yet not quite a beard. He was dressed in what was probably his best outfit, though it looked slept in. He regarded Gil with a shrewd, steady gaze that seemed out of place on his haggard face.

He nodded in their direction, then rose slowly to his feet. "You're here for me, I take it," he said. "Because of..." His words trailed off. He spread his arms, palms upward.

Gil took his meaning. He nodded, sympathizing with the man. "We're here because you're a mage now," he said. "We're also here to find out why this happened to you. We've got some questions."

The man continued to stare at him, at last issuing a slight nod. He lowered himself back into his chair. The old farmer brought up a stool so Gil could take a seat next to him, while Ashra pulled up another chair from across the room. The man's brown eyes lingered on Gil's black cloak with an indeterminable expression.

"Rylan Marshall," he said, nodding his head by way of introduction. "What would you like to know?"

His right hand was bandaged, probably broken. The fingers of his other hand fumbled with something in his lap. It took Gil a moment to figure out what he was holding. It was one of the daisies from the dried bunch of flowers hung over the door. Rylan twirled the flower absently between his fingers, back and forth, gazing down at it with a vacant expression.

Gil asked, "Can you tell us a little about yourself?"

Rylan looked up from the flower, his expression never changing. In a flat voice, he said, "I'm just a farmer. This is my family's farm. I've lived here nearly my entire life. Though for the past two years, I've been serving my time in the King's army. I just came home from the front."

Gil asked, "What did you do at the front?"

The man hesitated a moment before replying. "Infantry."

There was no emotion in the young farmer's voice. His fingers kept twirling the dead blossom. He didn't seem aware he was doing it.

Behind them, the floor creaked as Rylan's father crossed the room and sat down on a bench, holding his head in his hands. Ashra glanced at him, her face sympathetic. Gil's eyes scanned the drab walls of the room, his gaze coming to rest on a wind-sculpted piece of sandstone sitting upright on a bureau.

"You said you lived here *nearly* all your life," Gil said. "Where did you live before?"

The man answered, "My family's originally from the Vale of Amberlie. We were displaced by the war."

Gil pondered his words. Nothing in Rylan's account was out of the ordinary. Thousands of families shared a similar story. When the Malikari had invaded the North, they had sacked every town and village in the Vale of Amberlie, butchering the defenders and driving the population southward.

Gil asked, "Did you know your assailant? Or had you seen him before?"

"No." Rylan shook his head.

Feeling at a loss, Gil spread his hands. "Do you have any idea why you were singled out? Any idea at all?"

"None."

Gil blew out a sigh and glanced back at Rylan's mother, who was making herself conspicuously busy. He allowed his gaze to roam the long room. It was a simple farmhouse. Except for one chunk of sandstone, there was nothing to distinguish it from any other farmhouse in Chamsbrey, just as there was nothing to distinguish Rylan from any other farmer. No reason why a mage would sacrifice his life to pass his power to him. There was a large piece of the puzzle that was missing, Gil felt sure. But he couldn't fathom what it could be.

Ashra placed her hand compassionately on Rylan's arm and asked, "Can you tell us of the attack?"

Rylan's gaze slipped to her hand. His eyes darkened, shoulders stiffening. His fingers stopped twirling the daisy. To Gil, he looked about ready to slap Ashra's hand away. But at last, his shoulders relaxed, and he nodded slightly. He closed his fist around the dried blossom, then told them of the two men who had lured him into the cornfield. Gil listened to his account, becoming more unsettled by the word. When Rylan recounted the moment the mage forced his Gift into him, Gil asked him to repeat that part of the story. Rylan frowned but complied.

"When he caught my hand, this terrible energy flooded into me," he said. "It was the most unnerving thing I've ever felt in my life. I can't describe the sensation. But you know what I'm talking about, don't you? You're a mage. You've felt it. Whatever he gave me, it came out of him, and it killed him to give it to me. When I came to my senses, I found him lying dead on the ground next to me."

He shook his head, drawing a deep breath. "That's when the other man appeared. A tall man. I think he might have been Malikari. I asked him why–why me? He said because of who I am. I didn't understand, and he didn't explain himself. He promised me he wouldn't kill my daughter. But he took her. He said someday I'd come to him." His voice trailed off into silence, his eyes going toward the fire in the hearth.

Gil saw that Rylan had let the crushed flower slip from his hand. His own mind fumbled with the images conjured by the farmer's account. He wasn't sure which part of Rylan's story disturbed him most: the appearance of the shadow-men that he described, or the fact that his assailant seemed to think he had some kind of lasting control over him.

Feeling a cold sense of dread, Gil asked him, "These men that looked like shadows. Did you ever see their faces?"

"No." Rylan shook his head. "They didn't have faces. They weren't physical. My sword went right through one, as if it was made of smoke."

Gil believed him. Rylan had perfectly described a type of demonic servant called a necrator, a collection of souls bound to serve whatever master controlled them. But there were no more necrators left in the world. Not since the Well of Tears had been destroyed. That was the last time a darkmage had walked the world, and no mortal mage could raise such minions. Unless something significant had changed. Unless the Well was open again... or something just like it.

Gil pressed, "Is there anything else you can think of? Anything that struck you as odd? Or unusual?"

"Other than my son being murdered?" The man's face went hard, and there was a sudden, intense anger in his eyes. But then the farmer squeezed his eyes shut. He brought his hand up to his brow, hanging his head. "One of the men called me Gerald."

He said it so softly, Gil almost hadn't heard him. "What?" he asked.

"One of the men called me Gerald."

Out of the corner of his eye, Gil caught Rylan's parents exchanging startled glances. He didn't think Rylan noticed. And then it struck him: that was the piece of the puzzle that was missing. He looked at Ashra. She met his gaze and nodded slightly.

Gil turned to face Rylan's father. "I'd appreciate it if you'd let us stay here tonight," he said. "We'll be leaving in the morning. And I'm sorry but... I have to take Rylan with us. I hope you understand."

The woman grimaced and brought a hand up to her face. Rylan's father put an arm around her and drew her in, holding her close as she wept quietly against his chest.

Rylan looked at Gil coldly. To his credit, he said nothing.

Awkwardly, Gil pushed himself to his feet. He felt horrible for the farmer but didn't know what to say to him. Rylan had lost his son and would now be losing everything else he knew. Gil couldn't imagine what that must feel like. And somewhere in the world, Rylan still had a daughter who had been taken from him. To be used as leverage, Gil felt sure.

"Ashra," he said. "Stay with Rylan."

"What about his injuries?" she asked.

Gil glanced at the farmer's bandaged hand, wishing that Ashra wasn't an acolyte. Then she would have a mage's power and could heal Rylan's hand on her own. And, more importantly, she wouldn't be his problem.

"I'll mend him when I get back," he grumbled. He looked at Rylan's father, beckoning him toward the door. "I need you to show me where this happened."

The old man nodded and, kissing his wife's head, let her go and walked, head bowed, toward the door. Gil let him go first, then followed him. Clemet Marshall trudged down the gravelly path that led out of the farmyard, out toward the wide, flat expanse of cropland that spread for miles around them. Gil followed him in silence, not knowing what to say that would offer even the illusion of comfort. He could feel the weight of the old man's grief pressing down on him, even at a distance.

Clemet led him into the cornfield, then turned off the path and held the stalks back for Gil to enter. Gil followed him through the corn, down a narrow, barely visible trail that led deeper into the field, until they came to a small clearing where the stalks had been trampled down in a wide ring. There, Clemet stopped and stood with his back to him. He fixed his eyes on the ground and simply waited.

Gil walked slowly forward, his gaze roving over the ground. In the middle of the clearing was a blackened ring where the boy had been incinerated. Walking closer, Gil knelt over the spot and trailed his fingers through the remaining ashes. Staring at the scorched ground, Gil felt his stomach clench. He stood up and looked at Clemet.

He didn't want to ask his next question. But he knew he couldn't avoid it any longer.

Walking toward the old man, Gil said, "I need to ask you something. And I need you to answer me honestly. The people who did this are very powerful and very dangerous. If you tell me any word that's not true, or if you leave out any of the truth, you'll likely be signing your son's death warrant. Do you understand?"

Clemet Marshall paled, his red-rimmed eyes seeming to falter. He stared at Gil for a long moment with a stricken look. At last, he bit his lip and nodded, looking down.

Gil asked, "Do you know why Rylan's attackers called him Gerald?"

The farmer brought a trembling hand up to his face.

"Mr. Marshall. I need to know."

There was a long, gaping span of silence. Then the old man responded, "Gerald was Rylan's birth name." He made a strangled noise deep in his throat. "He's not our son."

Gil stiffened, his brain stumbling over the information. After a minute, he whispered, "Does Rylan know?"

"No." Clemet shook his head. He raised his hand, forcefully wiping tears from his eyes.

Gil moved forward and placed a hand on the old man's shoulder to steady him. "Why don't you tell me about it?"

Clemet nodded, his body seeming to deflate. "We used to live in Amberlie—a little town in the Vale below Aerysius."

Gil knew of it. The town had been overrun during the invasion. Prior to that, it had been a hub for travelers going to and from Aerysius, the ancient city of mages built high up on the face of a mountain cliff. When the Well of Tears was opened, Aerysius had been the first casualty. The city had been destroyed, along with every mage inhabiting it.

Clemet paced a few steps away. "One of the mages of Aerysius, a woman, came to town looking for a family to foster her baby. Lena had just given birth to Rylan. Since Lena was already nursing, we volunteered to foster the babe. The boy's name was Gerald."

Gil's lips parted in a silent "oh."

Hands balled into fists, Clemet paced away across the circle of trampled cornstalks, staring dismally at the ground. "We raised them together, our two boys. When our own son was eighteen months, he fell ill. At first, it was just a cold. But then his lungs filled with water. We didn't know what to do. We tried getting him up the mountain, to Aerysius. Hoping the mages up there could heal him. But he died on the way up, before Lena could get him help..."

Clemet's voice broke. He stood still for a moment, clenching his teeth. Fighting back tears. He drew in a deep, shuddering breath. It was moments before he could continue.

"Lena was devastated. She'd just lost a son. She couldn't bear to lose another, and we knew Gerald's mother would be coming back for him. We couldn't do it. We couldn't lose him too. So we told the mages it was Gerald who'd died. That way they'd leave us alone."

Gil stared at Clemet without speaking, his brain working furiously. It was all starting to make sense. Perfect sense. Only, the farmer's story raised more questions than it answered. Who were Rylan's real parents? And how did his attackers know his lineage when Rylan didn't even know it himself?

"I know it was wrong," Clemet said gruffly, casting Gil a resentful glare. "But I don't regret it. Together, our family buried Gerald in the oak grove behind our home. We kept Rylan with us. He's our son now. We raised him up as our own. Do you understand? He's my boy. And I don't want you nor anyone else telling him different. You understand? He's our son..."

His voice choked off into sobs. He brought both hands up to his face and wept openly into his palms, his shoulders quaking. Gil stood still, gazing down at the ground, feeling wretched. Not knowing what else to do, he let the old farmer spill his pain into his hands.

When Clemet's tears subsided, Gil said quietly, "He has to know. You should be the one to tell him. Not me."

The old man nodded, biting his lip.

Gil took a step closer. "Do you know the names of his true parents?"

Clemet shook his head. "The mother wouldn't tell us her name. She never mentioned the father."

"And there's nothing more you can tell us? Anything we could use to figure out who his parents are?"

"No." The old man shook his head wearily. Gil could tell from the look in his eyes he was done. Clemet Marshall was emotionally emptied.

Gil said, "Come on, then. Let's get back."

He reached out and patted the old farmer on the back, lending him what meager strength he could. He wished he could do more. But one look at Clemet Marshall told him that nothing anyone could do would ever be enough.

4
————

STABBED THROUGH THE HEART

RYLAN KNELT AND PLUCKED A BLOSSOM FROM A FIELD OF DAISIES that spread all the way to the golden horizon and beyond. He looked up and smiled at Emma. Though his wife had been dead for over a year, she was somehow standing there in front of him, a breeze stirring her chestnut hair. Her kind blue eyes gazed at him with the same look of joy she'd had the day he'd proposed to her. He would do anything to keep that expression on her face.

Standing, he offered her the white blossom. "I want you to keep this," he said, pressing the stem into her hand and gently squeezing her fingers closed around it. He drew her into an embrace and kissed her cheek tenderly. "I'll come back. I promise. And when I do, I won't leave you again."

Emma lifted the daisy, closed her eyes, and breathed deeply of its scent. She looked up at him with a blissful smile. "I know you'll come back, Rylan," she said. "But when you do, I won't be here. I'll be dead and in the ground, and our son will be charred bones and scattered ashes. You failed us, Rylan, just like you'll fail every person in your life."

Rylan felt his heart freeze and fracture into shards of ice. In his wife's hand, the daisy wilted and began to dry. The flower blackened and then crumbled to ash. The wind carried the ashes away, leaving her fingers lingering and empty.

Emma smiled at him. Her smile deepened and saddened. "I know you'll try, Rylan," she whispered. "But the harder you try, the worse you'll fail and the more people you'll hurt."

Before his eyes, his wife dried to ash, just like the flower had, darkening to char and then dulling to gray. Emma crumbled in his arms, turning to dust that scattered away, carried by the wind. He reached out to catch her, but she spilled through his fingers like sand. And then she was gone, taken by the wind. The merciless wind.

The pain he felt was staggering. It stabbed right through his heart.

He awoke with a cry.

Metal glinted, and a knife sliced through the darkness.

Rylan rolled out from under it, and the knife stabbed deep into the mattress. He kicked out through the covers and tried scrambling out of bed. But his assailant jumped on top of him, using the blankets to pin him down. He caught just a glimpse of the blade falling before it tore through his rib cage.

A terrible agony clawed into his chest, ripping him apart. He flailed against the pain, gasping for breath. The more he struggled, the worse it got. White-cold panic set in as he realized he was dying.

He couldn't die yet. Not without finding his daughter.

Amina...

The agony in his chest was appalling.

"Don't fight it," whispered a soft voice. "The more you struggle, the more it will hurt."

But he had to fight. He was his daughter's only hope. He couldn't let go. Couldn't leave her.

There was a loud crash and a shrill scream.

His assailant flew off him. There was a scuffling noise. Then hands were upon him.

"What's wrong with him?" cried a woman's voice.

"I don't know!"

The pain swelled, became unbearable. He was at the end of his strength. He couldn't fight any longer.

A warm, soothing energy poured into his body from somewhere outside, flooding every part of him at once. It washed away the pain, calmed his panic, and rocked him gently on comforting tides. He didn't fight it. He closed his eyes and let go, drifting peacefully away.

When he awoke, Rylan discovered it was morning. He was in his parents' room, in their bed. Warm sunlight diffused through the curtains, bathing the bedroom in a muted light. The air was stuffy, swirling with circulating dust. He lay still, gazing upward at the waxed beams of the ceiling, letting awareness seep slowly back into him.

"Thank the gods, Rylan. I thought we'd lost you."

He turned toward the sound of the voice. His father sat at his bedside, his face even more haggard than Rylan remembered it. Clemet Marshall looked very frail and very old. Beside him on the bedstand stood a ceramic bowl filled with bloody rags. Rylan stared at the rags for a while, memory of the knife slowly coming back to him. Pain stirred awake in his chest and pulsed dully.

"What happened?" Rylan whispered, finding his voice. It came out in a croak, like a frog's voice.

His father grimaced and shook his head. "You were attacked."

"By who?" Rylan asked.

"We don't know." Clemet shook his head. "They got away."

Rylan tried to sit up, but the pain made it difficult. With his father's help, he accomplished the motion. He brought his hand up to his chest and felt at the compress bandaging a wound over his heart.

His father dropped his gaze. "They tried, but they couldn't heal it. At least, not all the way." He sounded dismal. "It should have killed you. Thank every god it didn't... but it should have."

Rylan retracted his hand. "It'll mend," he mumbled, feeling numb. His father was right; he should be dead. He'd seen enough casualties to know a mortal wound when he saw one. Then he remembered the oath he had sworn to the man in the cornfield. He had pledged his soul to the God of Chaos. Had that terrible god intervened and forestalled his death?

His father said, "They're taking you to Karikesh with them. They're going to get you help." Clemet looked down, licking his lips and hesitating. "Rylan..." His voice shook. "I've got something to tell you, and it's the hardest damn thing I've ever said in my whole damn life." He drew in a long, ragged breath, puffing his lips as he let it back out. "I need to talk to you about Gerald."

5

A HALF-HEALED WOUND

GIL STOOD LEANING AGAINST THE ROUGH WOOD OF THE BARN, arms crossed, waiting for Ashra to finish tightening the girth strap of the horse Clemet had given her. The mare hadn't been saddled in a while and wasn't taking well to the notion of a rider on her back. The harder Ashra tugged, the more the mare bloated its belly. It was a fine game, and mildly entertaining to watch. Gil stood grinning as Ashra finally kneed the horse in the gut and tugged the strap tight before the animal could react. She stepped back, dusting off her hands.

Gil nodded in the direction of the farmhouse. "I think we should go check on him."

In his hands, he fingered the knife they had found by Rylan's bedside after the attack. It was old. Perhaps ancient. It was etched with a series of characters that were completely foreign to him. Whatever they were, they were lethal. The wound Rylan had suffered hadn't mended well. Gil had never seen anything like it, and he considered himself a capable healer. He wrapped the blade up in a shroud of cloth and stuffed it into his pack.

The farmhouse door burst open, banging thunderously

against the side of the house. Rylan trudged out into the yard, propelled by forceful strides. His left arm was in a sling, his right hand clutching a blanket that flapped behind him like a cloak. His face was pale, almost white, and rife with fury.

He made it halfway across the yard before his parents spilled out of the house after him. Clemet caught his wife's hand when she tried to run after him, holding her back. The farmer's face was full of despair, and his wife's cheeks glistened with tears. Gil didn't have to ask to know what had happened. Rylan's father—Gerald's father—must have told him the truth about his birth.

Rylan stopped in front of them and stood staring at the ground, his shoulders heaving with the angry tides of his breath. A dewy sweat had broken out on his brow. Gil wasn't sure if that was from anger or the half-healed wound in his chest. Or both.

Ashra cast an alarmed glance at Gil. She untied Rylan's horse, a shaggy grey gelding, and handed him the reins. He gazed down at the leather straps in his hand as if not quite sure what to do with them, his eyes still focused on the ground.

Concerned, Gil walked up to him. "You all right?"

Rylan nodded but said nothing. Gil heard a crunching noise and glanced up to see Clemet approaching. The farmer paused in front of Rylan, the look on his face speaking volumes of regret. He shook his head wordlessly. Then he embraced the man he called his son. Rylan returned the gesture with a grimace, clutching him hard. Clemet patted him on the back and, releasing him, walked away without a word.

Rylan brought a hand up to his face, wiping his eyes. For a moment, he wavered. Ashra moved quickly to support him. Gil hoped he was well enough to ride. The portal to Karikesh was a day's journey southwest of Farlow, and not all of it was easy going. By the looks of him, Gil figured they had about a fifty-fifty chance of getting Rylan to Karikesh alive.

Gil said, "All right. Let's get you on that horse."

He helped lift him up. Rylan gritted his teeth as he swung his leg over the gelding's back. Gil hoped the action hadn't reopened the wound. If it had, there was little that could be done about it. Rylan's injury would have to wait until they arrived at the Lyceum in Karikesh, where there were dedicated healers far more skilled than he.

Gil waited for Ashra to mount, then climbed into the saddle and snapped his reins, clucking his horse forward. He watched Rylan's face as they turned out of the farmyard onto the trail that led toward town. He studied him hard, intensely curious to see if Rylan would turn to look back. And if he didn't, wondering what that would say about him. Just when Gil thought he wasn't going to, Rylan surprised him. He glanced back at his home with a look of bitter sadness. Then he noticed Gil staring and twisted back around.

———

They took the main road that led out of Farlow and followed it south toward Auberdale. Vast tracks of croplands spread to the flat horizons on all sides, a monotonous view that persisted as the hours wore on. Rylan rode at Gil's side, his eyes closed, his blanket drawn tightly about him. His shoulder-length hair hung in oily strands over his face, so that it was hard to get a good look at him. By mid-afternoon, Gil was starting to grow worried. Rylan's damp skin had taken on a pasty cast.

"Rylan," he said, trying to get the man's attention. When he didn't respond, Gil said louder, "Rylan!"

The man flinched as if waking from sleep and glanced over. Gil edged his horse closer, studying the farmer carefully. He asked, "How are you doing?"

Rylan shrugged. "I'm fine."

He didn't look fine. Concerned, Gil leaned over and caught his wrist.

Closing his eyes, he reached out from within for the magic field. Here, in this place, the lines of power that roamed over the earth flowed evenly across the plains. The pulse of the field was steady and serene, almost like the stately tempo of a waltz. He took hold of it, drawing it in and using that power to send his mind tunneling deep into Rylan's body. It wasn't difficult to find the reason for the man's feverish appearance. The wound had broken open and was starting to fester.

He let go of the farmer's wrist and called back at Ashra, "We need to stop."

He turned his horse off the road. He led the others toward an old oak tree with a split trunk. There, he dismounted and tied his horse to one of the branches.

"What's wrong?" Ashra asked, glancing at Rylan with a worried expression.

"He needs tending to." Gil took the reins from Rylan's hand and tied the shaggy gelding up beside his own. "We'll stay here tonight, then move on tomorrow."

He helped Rylan down from his horse and, supporting him, led the farmer over to the trunk of the oak, where he sat him down in a crease between two great roots. Ashra knelt beside him and pressed a hand to his forehead.

"He's clammy," she reported.

Gil knelt beside him and released Rylan's arm from the sling. The farmer clenched his teeth when Gil peeled the compress back from the wound. It came away wet with blood and pus. Gil grimaced at the smell. He placed his hands on Rylan's chest and closed his eyes, feeling Ashra setting her hand lightly on his shoulder. He knew what she was trying to do: feel through him as he worked. He hadn't spent much time trying to teach her anything, and he supposed she had a right to be growing impatient with him. He wanted to shrug off her touch but, grudgingly, decided to oblige her. The only way she was going to learn was by observation. And it was his job to teach her, whether he liked it or not. Gil did his best to ignore her and tried to concentrate.

He bit his lip, his mind working furiously to weave all the minute changes that had to occur almost simultaneously in order to mend the festering layers of tissues. Beneath his hands, he felt the wound shrink and start to close. The bleeding stopped. Muscle fibers regrew and knit together. He burned away the infection that had started and cleaned the surrounding tissue. Soon, Rylan's flesh was whole again, save for a puckered, shallow cut where the knife had pierced him.

When Gil was finished, Ashra retracted her hand with a frustrated sigh. He knew he had worked too fast for her to have a clear understanding of what he'd done in those few seconds. It wasn't intentional; healing was something that had to be done quickly and intricately, which was one of the reasons why it was such a difficult skill to master. Just watching a mentor perform it wasn't enough.

When he withdrew his hands, he saw that Rylan had fallen into the healing sleep, his body propped against the rough bark of the oak's trunk. Leaving him there, Gil moved to fish in his saddlebag for a fresh bandage.

"You work too fast," Ashra complained, her arms crossed. "How am I supposed to learn anything if you don't slow down?"

"Maybe you need to learn faster," Gil snapped at her. Then he signed, relenting. "Let's do this again. I'll probe him, and you can feel through me. Then all you have to worry about is what I'm seeing, not what I'm doing."

Ashra cocked an eyebrow, her gaze suspicious, as though she didn't trust him to actually teach her without an ulterior motive. Nevertheless, she conceded, and placed a hand on Gil's shoulder.

He said, "Now, look as deep as you can and as close as you can, and tell me what you sense."

Ashra nodded and closed her eyes. Gil set his hands on Rylan and concentrated. An image of the wound came to his mind, as well as a general knowledge of Rylan's overall health. The more he concentrated, the clearer the image became. After a moment, he opened his eyes and looked up at her.

"I don't understand," Ashra said. "The wound is healed, but there is still something there. What is it?"

"I don't know," Gil admitted, and leaned forward to apply the new compress. "I'd rather not guess." He had his suspicions, but he wasn't about to mention them to Ashra until he was more certain. When he had the bandages replaced, he buttoned Rylan's shirt and pushed himself to his feet, dusting off his trousers. He looked down at the man in sympathy. "All I know is, we've got to find a way to get whatever's in him out of him. Unfortunately, that's beyond my ability."

Ashra stared down at Rylan with a worried expression. "I'll go start setting up camp," she said.

Gil stopped her. "I'll get the camp. You go fetch some water."

"I don't want to fetch water. I—"

"Just get the water," he snapped, wondering why the woman seemed bent on arguing with him.

Ashra cast him a sideways glare but obeyed, wandering off to find a stream to replenish their canteens. He made himself busy by clearing a space for a fire and gathering wood. Getting the kindling lit took only a moment's concentration; within minutes, he had a crackling fire going. He went to check on Rylan and found the farmer sleeping soundly, propped up against the trunk of the oak tree. Gil thought about moving him closer to the fire, but then thought better of it. The air wasn't especially cold, and he didn't want to disturb the wound again.

It took her a bit, but eventually Ashra made her way back to camp carrying two full water cannisters swinging from their straps. She dropped them down by the rest of the supplies, then sat next to him beside the fire. From within her pack, she produced a biscuit and handed it to Gil, taking a strip of dried meat for herself. Gil stared down at the biscuit, half-wondering if it was poisoned, before tearing off a bite and popping it in his mouth. As he chewed, Ashra sat in silence, staring into the flames. Perhaps she was avoiding conversation. After long, awkward minutes, Gil picked up a stick and used it to prod the campfire. One of the logs broke with a loud crack and a shower of sparks. Ashra glanced sideways at him with a sharp look.

"Did the fire do something to offend you?" she asked.

"I'm just bored." Gil shrugged, tearing off another piece of biscuit. "I find the fire at least mildly entertaining."

"Mmmmm." Ashra worried at a strip of dried beef, tugging at it with her teeth before breaking off a piece. "So, are you actually going to teach me anything?" she asked.

Gil tapped the stick against his leg in irritation. "I'll teach you—though if I had a choice, I wouldn't," he admitted. "And you can't blame me. What your father did to my people was despicable. His armies spilled more blood on this continent than anyone else in all of history."

Ashra's gaze slipped to the fire. "My father saved millions of lives. And he wouldn't have had to lift his sword if your kings had honored the treaty they struck with us. I'm sorry you lost your own father, though. He was a man of great *sharaq.*" Her eyes locked on his. "We can't change the past. But we don't have to let it control us."

He nodded, knowing she was right—at least the part about the past not controlling them. He didn't know about the rest of it, though. He'd have to think on it.

"All right, then," he said, tossing the stick away. "I'll train you. But you'd better start acting like a proper acolyte. You don't listen to a damn thing I say."

Rylan woke to cold air and damp earth. A heavy fog rolled over him, obscuring the branches of the oak, misting his face with icy beads of moisture. His wound hurt. It ached a throbbing counterpoint to his heartbeat. He brought his hand up to his chest, feeling the bandage. It was wet with fresh blood.

A startling screech pierced the fog.

He drew himself upright, gritting his teeth against the pain. His gaze searched the blanketing gray, but he saw nothing, save for the remains of a campfire that had burned out. The mage and the Malikari woman laid curled up on opposite sides of the grayed coals, cloaks wrapped snugly about them, their supplies piled between them.

Another shrill screech cleaved the darkness.

"What was that?" Gil said, rolling over onto his back.

"It's an owl," the woman said groggily without opening her eyes.

But it wasn't an owl. Rylan knew the sounds of all the night creatures within a hundred leagues of his home. There had been nothing natural about that shriek.

"It's not a bird," he said.

At the sound of his voice, both mages sat upright. Gil climbed to his feet and walked away from their campfire a few paces, peering out into the murky bank of fog. He stood there for seconds, eyes scanning the darkness.

"Where are the horses?" Ashra asked.

Rylan looked around. She was right; the horses had wandered off. The knowledge made every nerve in his body spring taut. He rose painfully to his feet and started inching around the campfire toward his saddlebag, where he had a short dagger tucked away. But the mage put his hand out, warning him to stop.

"Don't move," Gil whispered over his shoulder. "Both of you stay put."

To Rylan's dismay, Gil strode away from their camp and was quickly swallowed by the fog. Ignoring the mage, he made his way to his bag and rummaged through it, retrieving his sheathed dagger. The motion made his wound scream in protest. The Malikari woman glanced at him and, seeing what he was about, shook her head emphatically.

"Put it down!" she hissed.

Rylan ignored her. He closed his eyes and focused his attention on his hearing, softening the sounds of his breath. Gil's footsteps carried toward them through the fog, barely audible. And other noises as well. Other footsteps. Many of them. He glanced down at the dagger in his hand, his mouth going dry. It was not a weapon he could wield effectively. At least, not in his current state.

The crack of a snapping twig warned him of the mage's return. He glanced up to see Gil emerging from the fog, leading the horses. Rylan let out a long breath he hadn't realized he'd been holding.

"There's people out there," Gil reported in a whisper. "I don't know who, and I don't know what they're about. But I'm not going to stay to find out. Let's get out of here. And be quiet about it."

They loaded their belongings onto the horses and mounted up. Rylan gritted his teeth as he swung his leg over his horse's back. A stabbing pain lanced like a hot poker through the wound in his chest, making him wince. To his chagrin, the mage and his acolyte were staring at him with concern in their eyes.

Ashra nodded in the direction of the road, but Gil shook his head. He turned his horse away from the road, then kicked it forward. The sounds of hoofbeats and the creak of saddles would signal their presence for anyone listening. Rylan wondered who was out there in the fog and whether or not they posed a threat.

They rode at a trot across a farmer's open field, parting the mist before them as a ship's keel parts the waves. The moon shone drearily through the fog, its light somber and diffuse. Rylan concentrated on the sound of his horse's hoofs, trying to distract himself from the pain.

A shadow passed by overhead, for a brief second eclipsing the moonlight. Another shrill shriek pierced the night. Rylan looked up just in time to see a pair of dark, leathery wings gliding away, soon lost in the mist.

6

WORD OF COMMAND

GIL KICKED HIS HORSE TO A GALLOP, GLANCING BACK OVER HIS shoulder to make sure his two companions were following. He didn't know what that screeching sound was, but Rylan was right—it wasn't natural. He directed his mount in the general direction of the lowlands, his eyes studying the sky.

Beneath him, his horse gathered itself, then leapt over a berm that marked the edge of the grainfield. It broke across a dirt road into the woodland on the other side. There, Gil drew back on the reins, bringing the lathered animal to a halt. The gelding whinnied, stomping its hooves and rolling its eyes. The horse hadn't liked whatever it was that had been chasing them in the sky. Gil waited for the others to draw up beside him, then he nodded toward the west.

"The transfer portal's in the middle of a bog not too far from here," he said.

"The bog's that way," Rylan corrected him, pointing further south.

Gil didn't argue; the farmer knew the area a lot better than he did. With all the shrieking going on overhead, he'd probably gotten turned around in the fog.

"What was that thing?" Ashra asked.

Gil could only shrug. "I have no idea."

He glanced at Rylan. The farmer was looking worse for wear again. His face was pale, and there was a fresh stain of blood on his shirt. That was a problem. With that creature overhead, he couldn't risk using magic to heal him. Rylan would likely lose consciousness again, and they didn't have time to wait for him to come out of it.

He said to Rylan, "You know where the bog is. Would you mind leading?"

The farmer nodded. Snapping his reins, he sent his horse ahead. Gil waited for Ashra to pass him before urging his gelding after. The route Rylan picked followed a meandering path through the trees; probably an old game trail. Gil kept his ears strained for the sound of more screeching, but there was none to be heard. Whatever it was hadn't followed them—or had lost track of them. Whichever it was, he was grateful.

It took about an hour to reach the edge of the woods. Rylan led them out of the trees and downslope into a misty, lowlands bog. The sun was starting to come up, graying the eastern sky and driving back the fog. It made only a half-hearted attempt at warming the air. The morning was still cold, almost as frigid as the night had been.

At the edge of the marsh, Gil kicked his horse forward and drew up alongside Rylan. The farmer looked even worse than he had before. His face was streaked with sweat, and he looked half-asleep, canting a bit in the saddle.

"Try to stay on your horse," he advised. "If you fall off, I'll have to heal you. But that means we'll be stuck here with that screeching thing until you wake back up again."

"I'll be fine," Rylan said, although the weariness in his voice wasn't reassuring. "Just get us out of here."

Ashra flashed Gil a concerned look. "This is not a good idea..." she began.

"Of course it's not," Gil snapped. "But I don't have a good idea. Do you?"

She shook her head.

"All right, then. Let's go."

The transfer portal was situated somewhere up ahead, hidden in the depths of the bog, which meant they had to go through it. There was a noxious odor to the place, a rotten-egg smell. Gil rode holding his cloak over his face, repulsed by the scent.

"It's like going for a swim in a latrine," he complained.

He scanned the pockmarked ground ahead, which was scarcely visible through drifting clouds of swamp gas. They wound their way past stands of tall rushes and yellowed clumps of peat. When it came time to cross a section of mucky soil, his horse balked, digging its hooves into the murky ground and refusing to budge.

He kicked his horse in the flanks, which accomplished nothing, so he redoubled his efforts. "Obstinate animal," he grumbled, flicking the reins. "Hell of a time to throw a sulk."

With a smile, Ashra swung down from her horse and caught his gelding's bridal. With a firm hand and a pat on the neck, she started the animal moving again.

"Horses are smart," she said, regaining her mount. "He doesn't like the smell of this place either. I don't blame him."

They continued on, following a narrow trail that wound a serpentine path bordered on both sides by grassy pools. About an hour in, they came across a dead sheep that had become mired in the bog. The back of the sheep was above water, exposed to the air, and had rotted away down to the ribs and vertebrae. The rest of the sheep was underwater and appeared perfectly preserved, its skin and wool intact. Gil couldn't help staring at the dead sheep as they rode by, transfixed by the odd sight that was both gruesome and astonishing at the same time.

It took another hour to reach the portal chamber. Most

portals were ancient, situated in rooms carved into hillsides or dug out of the ground. The Chamsbrey portal had been created more recently, and was disguised within a shallow, murky pool, indistinguishable from the rest of the bog. As they guided their horses into the water, the swamp around them dissolved and became a wide, circular chamber lit by magelight that swirled over the floor.

The clatter of their horses' hooves on stone echoed harshly off the walls. At least the stench of the bog hadn't followed them; instead, the place was musty and damp. In the center of the room stood a tall, cross-vaulted arch supported by four columns of rose-colored marble. The arch stood on a marble platform with a short ramp leading up to it. Beneath it, the diffuse magelight thickened and grew brilliant.

Ashra drew her mare up and dismounted. Gil slid down from the back of his horse and tied his reins to the saddle's horn. Then he helped Rylan dismount.

"What is this place?" Rylan asked, looking around the chamber with an expression of awed disbelief.

"It's a transfer portal," Gil answered.

Rylan squinted at the glowing arch. "What is that?"

"A means of getting somewhere fast," Gil explained. "This particular portal will take us to the Lyceum in Karikesh."

Rylan stood frowning at the portal. "I never thought I'd be going to Karikesh willingly. Unless it was to topple its walls. I don't suppose they like soldiers from the Kingdoms overmuch."

Gil said, "There's nothing to worry about. You belong to the Lyceum now, which means you're apart from the war." He motioned in the direction of the portal. "Come on. Let's get you through."

Ashra tried to catch Rylan's hand, but he pulled away and glared at her distrustfully. Gil understood; Ashra was Malikari, and Rylan had spent two years fighting to drive her people out of the North. She was the enemy any soldier of the Kingdoms had been trained to hate. And trained to kill.

Ignoring his look, Ashra said calmly, "We should enter together."

Rylan relented, allowing her to guide him up the ramp toward the portal arch. When he hesitated, she assured him, "There's no reason to fear. It won't take a second."

He appeared doubtful. He looked like a man fighting a battle within, a battle over much broader issues than a mere transfer portal. Patting his back, Ashra led him beneath the cross-vaulted arch. There was a brief, intense flash of light.

Then they were gone.

"Come on, you devils," Gil said, tugging at the horses' reins. His gelding started forward, the other two following behind. When the first horse approached the ramp, it lay its ears back and bobbed its head obstinately. It took a lot of goading to get it moving. Holding the gelding by the bridle, he led it forward under the archway.

The world shifted.

The dim walls of the chamber flickered and were gone. Other, brighter, walls rose in their place. Blinking, Gil saw Rylan lying on his back in front of the transfer portal, Ashra at his side. Gil dropped the reins of the horses and cast himself down at Rylan's side.

"I'll be all right," the farmer whispered. "Just give me a moment."

Gil stared down at him, realizing he needed more than just a moment. Rylan's shirt was soaked in blood. He glanced up at Ashra, "I'll try to heal him. Go get some help!"

Wide-eyed, Ashra rose and ran to a flight of stairs that led upward to the ground floor. Gil put his hands on Rylan, probing him deeply. Something inside him hadn't liked the transfer portal. The wound was active, carving its way through his chest toward his heart. Concentrating, Gil tried as hard as he could to mend it. But he had to give up after a few seconds, realizing he was doing more harm than good. Rylan had fallen unconscious, his skin a pasty white.

Help arrived with a clatter of footsteps. He found himself surrounded by a milling crowd of servants and acolytes, until the arrival of the Rector brought order to the room. Gil looked up into the age-worn face of Master Gayle Kelson. The woman knelt down beside him and placed her hand on Rylan's forehead, assessing his condition. She was a far better healer than he was. Within seconds, she had the wound closed.

Motioning for the guards, she said, "Take him up to the Acolyte's Residence. Get him into a bed."

Gil rose and edged back as two large men came forward to comply. They helped Rylan to his feet. When he staggered, they caught him and supported his weight between them, helping him walk toward the stairs through the crowd of anxious onlookers.

The Rector swung back to Gil, lifting an irritated eyebrow.

"We need the Prime Warden," Gil said, glancing around. He wasn't sure how much he could say in front of an audience.

The Rector stared at him hard, as if trying to decide how far she should trust him. At last, she snapped her fingers to get the attention of the people gathered around them. "Clear the chamber!"

At her order, the crowd dispersed immediately, acolytes and full Masters alike, until only the three of them remained.

Gil stared down at a smear of Rylan's blood on the tiles. "He's our charge," he informed the Rector. "The Prime Warden ordered us to retrieve him. That's all I should really say."

Master Gayle folded her arms, sucking in a cheek. "Very well. I'll accommodate your need for privacy," she said. "But next time, warn me first."

"Of course, Rector." Gil ducked his head.

The Rector turned in a swirl of black robes and left the

portal chamber. Gil remained behind, still staring wearily down at the darkening stain of blood. With a sigh, he took a glance back at the transfer portal, then said to Ashra, "Get the horses to the stable. Then meet me in the Residence."

He headed up the stairs. It took him long minutes of hunting before he found the room they had taken Rylan to on the third floor. He immediately shooed the servants out, then closed the door behind them. He lit the room's sole oil lamp and pulled a chair up beside Rylan's bed. The farmer was asleep, his chest rising and falling in a steady rhythm. Someone had removed his shirt and changed his bandages, and his color looked a lot better.

Satisfied, Gil leaned back in the chair and waited.

He must have dozed off.

Gil awoke to the sound of the door swinging open. He shot to his feet when he saw whose face appeared in the doorway.

Prime Warden Naia stepped into the room, followed by her husband, Quinlan Reis. Quin was Malikari, and a powerful Grand Master. He was also over a thousand years old. Gil bowed at the sight of the two of them.

Naia waved her hand dismissively. "Be at ease."

Ashra entered the room behind them, moving to stand beside Gil. The Prime Warden slid into the chair, her husband moving forward to lean over the bed, studying the farmer as if the man were something of a curiosity. He pushed back the black felt hat on his head. Reaching down, he touched the bandage on Rylan's chest, which was already spotted with fresh blood.

Naia gazed deeply into Rylan's sleeping face, her eyes widening, as if in recognition. She glanced up sharply at her husband.

"Do you see it?" she whispered.

Quin's jaw went slack. He stared harder at Rylan. "I see it..." he said finally. He looked haunted, as though he'd just glimpsed the spirit of an ancestor.

The Prime Warden placed a hand on Rylan's brow and closed her eyes. "Quin," she said, her voice breathless.

Her husband leaned down and probed Rylan himself. Then, straightening, he removed his hat with a heavy sigh.

"It's a Word of Command," he pronounced. "Bound to his heart."

"What is that?" Ashra whispered.

"Just what it sounds," the Grand Master replied. "It's a word that commands something to happen. I've only ever heard of them placed on objects. A good example would be a magical lock on a door. If you speak the right Word, with the right inflection, the door opens. The same Word locks it tight again. Some Words are more complicated, more like a series of commands."

Ashra asked, "Are there Words that can be attached to people?"

The Grand Master sucked in a cheek and gestured at Rylan. "Obviously, there is. Or our new friend here wouldn't be bleeding through bandages. But I don't know where it could have come from. We don't have anything today that could be applied to a person. Words of Command are something of a lost art."

"Apparently, not so lost anymore," the Prime Warden whispered, staring down at Rylan.

The Grand Master shrugged. "It doesn't have to be a new creation. It could be an ancient Word delivered by an artifact."

Hearing that, Gil reached for his pack. He opened it and fished around inside until he found the knife left behind by Rylan's attacker. He unwrapped the cloth and handed the weapon to Quin. "Interesting workmanship, don't you think?"

Quin accepted the knife and held it up in front of his face. The blade was wide and slightly curved, bitten through with rust. All along the spine was an inscription made with small but highly complex characters. He brought the knife closer, squinting at it. Then, with a growl of frustration, Quin fished out a pair of spectacles. He put them on, then bent to hold the knife closer to the lantern light. He tilted it one way then the other, inspecting the blade thoroughly.

"Interesting indeed," he said. "I've never seen characters like these, but this is a powerful artifact. Whoever assailed him wasn't necessarily trying to kill him. They were trying to control him."

"If that is the case, then we must assume their mission succeeded," Naia said darkly.

Quin placed his hat back on his head. "Not necessarily."

Gil stared harder at the blade, feeling a growing chill in the pit of his gut. The knife suddenly seemed even more sinister than it had just moments before. He asked, "So what does this mean for him?"

The Grand Master's face was grimly set. "It means that anyone who knows the right Word can kill him with a whisper."

"Can the Word be removed?" Naia asked.

"I don't know," he said, lowering the knife. He placed the weapon on the small table by the bed. Then he bent and placed his hands on Rylan's shoulders. His face took on a look of intense concentration. After only seconds, he removed his hands and peeled back the bloody bandage. Beneath was only smooth, unblemished skin. Gil looked on in admiration; Quin had a thousand years of magical practice under his belt that he could never rival.

Quin stared deeply into the farmer's sleeping face.

"What is his name?" he asked.

Gil answered, "Rylan Marshall."

"But that's not his name," Ashra interjected.

"Pardon?" Quin turned to regard her with an expression of great interest.

Gil glanced at Ashra, then back to Quin. "His real name is Gerald," he explained. "His mother was a mage. A Master of Aerysius."

The Prime Warden's eyes widened, her complexion paling. She remained frozen for long moments, her gaze fixed on Rylan's face as if glued there.

"Who's the father?" she whispered at last.

"No one knows."

Quin drew in a sharp breath. Naia's eyes darted to lock on his, her jaw going slack. Gil wondered what it was they saw in Rylan. Something significant, he felt sure.

Abruptly, the Prime Warden rose from her seat and moved toward the door. To Ashra, she said, "Remain here. Send for me immediately if his condition changes."

Ashra ducked her head in acknowledgment, moving aside to let her pass.

Naia looked at Gil. "I need you to come with us," she said. "Right now."

7

BORN OF DARKNESS

RYLAN AWOKE TO DIM LANTERN LIGHT FLICKERING ACROSS DARK mahogany walls. Startled, he realized he had no idea where he was. He was in a strange bed in a strange room. He lay still for a while, struggling with his memory. Then he saw Ashra's face and remembered the transfer portal. And the pain.

"Where are we?" he asked, looking around the small room. It was dark and plain, containing only a small wardrobe and two other pieces of furniture. There wasn't even a window; just four dark walls.

"The Lyceum of Magic in Karikesh," Ashra informed him. She smiled kindly. "How are you feeling?"

"I feel fine," he said, surprised that the words were actually true.

Reaching up to his chest, he found that his wound had been healed completely. An intense feeling of relief swept over him, and he closed his eyes. He was enormously groggy, like he'd been sleeping for days. And *hungry*. Rylan could feel his stomach squirming inside him. He realized he had no memory of the last time he'd eaten.

Ashra smiled, pushing her thick, raven hair back behind

her shoulder. "The Prime Warden herself came to look in on you. She's concerned, and she also has questions. When you are feeling well enough, she wishes to speak with you."

Rylan tensed. He had no desire to meet the Prime Warden, especially not in the state he was in. He had no idea how to behave in front of such an important person, for one thing. Prime Wardens had always been the true authority in the Rhen, above even kings and queens. But it was more than that. Thinking of the horrible oath he had sworn to the man in the cornfield, he felt a wellspring of shame seeping up from some dark place inside. What if the Prime Warden looked within him and saw the corruption that was there? Would she order him slain? No doubt he deserved it—deserved death. But he couldn't die. Not yet. Not before finding his daughter.

"Give me a moment," he said.

"You can have more than a moment," Ashra assured him. "Take your time."

He moved to sit up, swinging his legs over the side of the bed. He sat still for a moment, waiting for the room to steady itself, blinking back the shadows. He ran his tongue over his parched lips. "Is there anything to drink?"

"Water," Ashra offered, indicating a pitcher on the table. "Or I can ask for some tea."

"Water's fine."

She poured him a cup and handed it to him with another smile. He wasn't sure how he felt about her smiles. She was a woman of the enemy and had shown no signs of changing her sympathies. Nevertheless, Rylan downed the entire cup in a few gulps.

He asked, "Do you think the Prime Warden can help me find Amina?"

The woman raised her eyebrows. "Is that your daughter's name? Amina?"

"Aye." He nodded, scratching his cheek. His whiskers itched; he'd gone too long without shaving.

"You can ask the Prime Warden to help you look for your daughter," Ashra told him. "Naia knows many things. Many secrets. And she can connect you with others who know even more."

That answer was enough for Rylan. He set the empty cup down on the table and rose from the bed. "All right, then. Take me to her."

Ashra looked up at him in surprise. "All ready? You still look exhausted. You need more time—"

He shook his head. "I don't. If there's a chance she can help me find Amina, I'm not about to linger here." Somewhere out there, his daughter was in the hands of monsters. Nothing else in the world mattered. Nothing.

Ashra's eyes searched his face for a moment. Then she rose from her chair. "Very well. The Prime Warden's office is downstairs."

Rylan pulled on his boots and followed Ashra out of the room. Unlike the small bed chamber, the hallway outside was well-lit, the walls tiled in a riot of colors and patterns. As they walked, they passed a few people, all wearing the same black cloaks with the emblem of the Silver Star on the back. Mages, Rylan knew. His skin prickled at the thought that everyone around him could wield a power he didn't understand.

Including himself.

His mind was spinning by the time they descended the stairs to the ground floor and arrived at a wide door at the end of the hall. Before the door, wedged into a corner, a prim, gray-haired woman looked up from behind a small writing desk.

Ashra said, "Please inform the Prime Warden that Rylan Marshall would like to speak with her."

The woman rose from her chair. Opening the door, she disappeared within. It was a moment before she emerged and beckoned Rylan forward with a curt motion of her hand. "Master Marshall, the Prime Warden awaits you within."

Those words clawed at Rylan's nerves. He felt suddenly weak, hesitant to move forward. The most powerful woman in the world waited for him on the other side of that door. A woman he had no business being in the same building with, much less the same room. It took all he had to gather enough courage to walk forward, Ashra following after.

The woman held her hand up, halting them. "The Prime Warden desires to speak only with Master Marshall."

"Of course," Ashra said, glancing at Rylan with a look of apology. "Go ahead. I'll wait out here."

A nervous sweat broke out on Rylan's brow as he realized he wouldn't have even Ashra's meager support. Following the woman's direction, he nodded his thanks at her and moved through the doorway.

The door close behind him, and he stopped where he stood.

In front of him stood a wooden desk, the chair behind it empty. Instead, two mages were seated along the back wall of a room. One was a woman wearing a white cloak, her auburn hair captured in an elaborate braid. She was of middle years, but exceptionally elegant. Next to her sat another mage, olive skinned, garbed in a black cloak and a black hat. On the wall across from them sat another man of Malikari descent who was dressed in opulent layers of cloth worn over a gold-trimmed tunic. His hair hung past his shoulders in tight curls, and he wore a well-trimmed beard that accentuated his jawline. He regarded Rylan with a penetrating stare that felt like it cut right through him.

Rylan had no idea who the two men were, but the sight of the Prime Warden was enough to intimidate him. Instantly, he dropped to his knees before her, bowing his head. He had no idea if that was the proper greeting, but it was the only gesture he could think of.

"Please rise," the woman said, her voice rich with the accent of Chamsbrey.

Rylan obeyed, regaining his feet. He realized that all three people in the room were staring at him intently, as if he were some object of intrigue. He could feel their eyes on him, making his skin itch and prickle. The Prime Warden raised her hand, indicating an empty chair adjacent to her own.

"Please, have a seat."

He complied awkwardly with a distrustful glance at her companions.

The woman said, "I am Prime Warden Naia Seleni. This is the Sultan of the Malikari Empire, his Majesty, Sayeed ibn Alborz, known as the Conqueror. And this is Grand Master Quinlan Reis, Warden of Arcanists."

Rylan felt his mouth go dry and his pulse stutter to a stop. His gaze went to the Sultan and stuck there. The man returned his stare with eyes that held no expression within them. Rylan didn't know what to say or how to feel. This was the same man who had conquered his own motherland, had driven his people from their homes—those he hadn't massacred. Rylan felt his cheeks heat in fury at the thought. He clenched his jaw, reining in his emotions. It took everything he had to force his gaze away from the man and back to the Prime Warden.

Naia Seleni smiled affably and gestured toward a silver tray that held a small tea service. "Would you like some tea?"

Her words seemed unfathomable, surreal. Rylan licked his dry lips and said, "No thank you, Prime Warden."

She poured herself a cup, sweetening the tea with a scoop of sugar. Setting the spoon down carefully, she asked, "How are you feeling, Rylan?"

"Better. My thanks for asking," he said, then thought to add, "Prime Warden."

The Sultan and the other mage were still staring at him fiercely. He didn't think either one of them had so much as blinked since he'd entered the room. His eyes scanned the walls, which were cluttered with various pictures and tapestries, along with shelves of bright knickknacks.

The Prime Warden said, "My condolences on the loss of your son. I cannot imagine the pain of losing one child, much less two. I understand your daughter was taken?"

Rylan nodded, relieved the topic had come up so soon in the conversation. Determined to take advantage of the opportunity, he blurted hurriedly, "She was, Prime Warden. I was hoping you'd help me find her. I—"

Naia Seleni raised her hand, cutting him off. "Be assured, finding your daughter is of utmost importance. But for the moment, we must attend to other matters more pressing, not the least of which is your health. And your identity."

A heavy weight of disappointment sank deep into Rylan's bones. Nothing else was important—didn't they understand? They had taken his baby girl. And the longer it took him to find her, the more she'd suffer. He cast a resentful glance at the Sultan, blaming him whether he deserved it or not.

The woman went on, "While you were recovering, we spoke at great length with Grand Master Archer. He told us what he knew of your family. He mentioned that the parents who raised you are not your true parents. And he informed us that your name at birth was not Rylan. It was Gerald."

Paying only half-attention to her words, Rylan said absently, "That's true."

"Do you know anything at all of your birth parents?"

He shook his head. "No, Prime Warden. I don't."

There was a long pause. The woman lowered her teacup and set it on the table beside her.

"We do."

At first, he didn't think he'd heard her right. He chastised himself for not paying better attention.

"I'm sorry?" Rylan asked, looking up in confusion.

Lifting her hand, Naia Seleni gestured around the room. "The three of us are very familiar with the story of your parents."

Rylan's breath hitched in his throat. "You know who they are?"

"We know who they were," she corrected him with a look of sympathy. "I'm sorry, Rylan, but both of your parents are long dead."

For some reason, he felt disappointed at hearing that. He wondered why. They were two people he'd never met, who'd abandoned him as a child. Who hadn't cared enough to remain.

With a sigh, he said, "What can you tell me of them?"

The Prime Warden sat forward in her seat, adjusting her cloak. She said, "Your mother's name was Meiran Withersby. She was a Master of Aerysius. After its fall, she became Prime Warden for a short while."

Rylan felt stunned. "My mother was a Prime Warden?"

"Yes." The woman nodded. "As was your father."

Rylan glanced around the room. The two men were still studying him, appearing to be assessing his reaction. The truth was, he didn't know how to react. He felt dazed. Everything about the room and its occupants seemed entirely unreal.

"Who was my father?" he asked.

"Your father was Darien Lauchlin."

Hearing that name made Rylan reel as if hit with a war hammer. Revulsion dripped like liquid down his nerves. Deep in his gut, his stomach clenched in nausea.

"Darien Lauchlin?" He could hardly get the words out. "No... That has to be wrong. Darien Lauchlin was a demon... A

Servant of Xerys." He almost choked. "He slaughtered thousands... mothers, babes... whole villages...."

For the first time, the Sultan moved. He leaned forward in his chair, hands gripping the armrests. Cold impatience fueled his stare. "It was war," he said, his voice low and thickly accented. "Atrocities happen. Your father fought and died so that my people could live free in a land of sunlight. To the Malikari people, your father was a hero unparalleled in history."

Rylan dropped his gaze, daunted by the force of the Sultan's glare. *Your father was a hero.* He didn't believe that, not for one minute. Never had the Kingdoms known a more heinous adversary. Darien Lauchlin had been a traitor, a slaughterer, a relentless conqueror who knew no restraint or mercy. Worse. He had wielded the power of Hell and brought it to bear against the Kingdoms' defenders. Lauchlin had been more than a butcher. He'd been demonic.

Rylan felt stunned. Unhinged. In a shaking voice, he whispered, "Prime Warden, there must be some mistake. Your information has to be wrong...."

There was sympathy and understanding in the woman's eyes. "No, Rylan. We are not wrong. Are you certain you wouldn't like some tea? Or perhaps some wine?"

"I'll take wine," he managed raggedly.

It felt like a thick fog had settled down around him, dampening his thoughts and senses. He was barely aware of the cup that was placed into his hand. He stared down at the blood-red liquid it contained. Bringing it to his mouth, he drank the wine down in a few swallows.

"How can you be so certain they're my parents?"

The Prime Warden replenished his cup. "Why don't you allow me to tell you their story? It's actually your story, Rylan."

He didn't think he wanted to hear it. He could feel the wine souring in the pit of his stomach. Chancing a glance sideways at the Sultan, he saw that the man was still staring at him, as if trying to bore into his soul.

Relenting, Rylan nodded.

Naia Seleni smiled. "Your mother and father met before Aerysius fell," she told him. "Your father was the son of Prime Warden Emelda. When he met your mother, Darien was just an acolyte. Meiran was a Grand Master, so their love was forbidden. They hid their relationship for years. But Prime Warden Emelda finally got wind of it. She sent your father to fight at the Front in an effort to separate him from Meiran."

Leaning forward, she filled his cup again with fresh wine. Rylan hadn't realized he'd finished the last cup.

She continued, "What he didn't know was that your mother was already pregnant with you. Meiran gave birth to you in secret and named you Gerald after your grandfather. Then she gave you up to a family to be fostered in the Vale."

It all corroborated the story Clemet had told him. The Prime Warden's tale seemed impossible to refute. The realization brought Rylan an acute ache of pain that burrowed deeply into his bones. There, it twisted into anger.

"Why?" he demanded. "Why did my mother give me up?"

The Prime Warden shrugged. "I suspect she was afraid the Prime Warden would react poorly to the news, perhaps even exile Darien permanently. Who can say? I'm sure your mother had very good reasons—or thought she did, at the time. She went looking for you after Aerysius fell. But your adopted mother told her you had died."

The anger he felt went cold. Then it turned, now directed at his adopted parents. They had lied. Lied to him... and lied to his mother. What would have happened if they had admitted the truth? Would he have known either of his parents? But they were dead, he reminded himself. He didn't know how his mother had passed, or when. But he did know Darien Lauchlin had died with the destruction of the Well of Tears. It was common knowledge. All of Xerys' Servants had been wiped from the world that day.

He shook his head, leaning back in his chair. "I'm sorry but... it's not every day you learn you're the son of a demon."

"You're right. Darien Lauchlin was a demon. But so was I."

Rylan's gaze snapped up to take in the face of the Grand Master who sat glaring across the room at him with smoldering eyes.

"I, too, was a Servant of Xerys," Quinlan Reis said. "But neither your father nor I had any choice in the matter. Not any real choice, anyway. We both swore our allegiance to Xerys because the only way to fight him was to serve him." He raised a finger, his face set in harsh lines. "But just because we were demons doesn't by definition make us evil. No matter what else he was, Darien Lauchlin was a man of honor. Never doubt that. He sacrificed his life so that the Well of Tears could be destroyed. If it wasn't for him, you would be living in a conquered world ruled by Xerys. And then worrying about who your father was would be the least of your problems."

Rylan looked away from the man, feeling stunned. Feeling sickened. The Grand Master's account contradicted everything he'd ever heard. Lauchlin's infamy was boundless, his legacy one of carnage and atrocity. Throughout the world, his name was synonymous with evil. Never had there been a man more reviled.

Or so Rylan had been raised to believe.

"I don't know what to say," he finally whispered. In truth, he didn't know what to feel or believe. Here were three people who claimed to know his father well. Was it possible they could be right about him? He would like to believe that.

The Prime Warden leaned forward and patted his arm consolingly. "No one can fault you for your birth. You are Gerald Lauchlin, son of Darien Lauchlin, whether you wish to be or not. But you are not alone in the world; we are here to help you and to answer any questions you may have. All three of us were very good friends with your father. If not your mother."

Rylan frowned. "Why not my mother?"

It was the Grand Master who answered him. "Your mother made some very poor choices. That's putting it lightly."

The Prime Warden rose from her chair, stroking a hand down her floor-length white cloak. She favored Rylan with a kind smile. "You must be exhausted. His Majesty has most graciously offered you a room at the palace."

They were dismissing him too soon. He hadn't gotten what he needed from them. Rylan sat up straight, shaking his head. "I don't have time to rest," he insisted firmly. "I need to find my daughter."

The Prime Warden allowed him a sympathetic smile. "We will most certainly help you find your daughter. I assure you, arrangements are already being made. We'll speak more of it tomorrow. In the meantime, retire to the palace. Get some rest."

The Sultan rose from his chair. There was no kindness in his face; only a greatly troubled look. He said to Rylan, "My servant is waiting outside. He will escort you to my coach."

Rylan nodded, feeling his hopes sink. He rose and made haste out of the room.

Ashra was waiting for him in the hallway, seated on a stool. She rose as soon as she saw him and walked swiftly in his direction. But instead of greeting him, she kept walking, passing him by and entering the room he'd just exited. He heard the door shut behind her.

Rylan stopped at the edge of the hallway and slumped against a wall, turning his mind inward in an attempt to calm his nerves. Rivulets of sweat flowed from his brow, coursed down his cheeks. The walls around him seemed to shiver and throb.

"Pardon, Great Master," said a voice.

Rylan turned, startled, to find himself staring into the face of a bearded servant attired in colorful livery. The man bowed rigidly and gestured for Rylan to follow him. "This way, Great Master."

Rylan stared after him, unmoving, his mind stuttering over the title the man had just used to address him.

Great Master.

The man had just addressed him as a mage.

Feeling dizzy, he moved to follow the servant down the tiled hallway.

8

THE SULTAN'S PROMISE

RYLAN FOLLOWED THE MANSERVANT DOWN A MARBLE STAIRCASE and out into the din of unexpected commotion. Startled, he glanced around in confusion, trying to get his bearings. He stood on the edge of a broad, cobbled road bustling with a chaotic sea of traffic. The thoroughfare led straight ahead, past long rows of sprawling, palace-like structures. Hundreds of minarets rose above the skyline, poking out between layers of graceful domes that seemed to rise and fall like the swells of an ocean. Every building looked to be sculpted of the same warm-toned blocks, each carved in intricate detail.

Rylan stood and stared around in open wonder. The only other city he'd ever seen was Auberdale, the capital of Chamsbrey, called the City of Kings. Compared to Karikesh, Auberdale seemed a ramshackle and dirty hellhole.

The Sultan's manservant opened the door to an awaiting coach and stood aside. Rylan started toward him but then paused to look around, his senses overwhelmed. The street swarmed with carriages and foot traffic. The sounds and smells were too diverse and distracting to ignore. Across the avenue, a street vendor cooking meat over a wood fire called out to him, beckoning him over. Beyond, under a green tarp, a merchant haggled over textiles with a woman swarmed by six eager children. Horse-drawn carts clattered by, boring paths through a milling population garbed in colorful shawls and knee-length tunics.

Still gawking at the tall buildings that surrounded him, Rylan climbed awkwardly into the carriage, seating himself on a cloth-covered bench within. The servant closed the door, and the carriage shifted its weight as the coachman climbed up into the box seat. Rylan parted the velvet curtains hanging in the window, eager for even a narrow view of the bustling city, as the horses started forward with the crack of a whip.

The carriage clattered along the cobbled street, then turned onto a buzzing thoroughfare bordered by tall buildings rising five or six stories that looked centuries old. Each intersection they crossed contained a tall fountain, usually multi-tiered, surrounded by blossoms. As they drew further from the center of the city, the view became greener, the streets lined with trees, the walls of the residences covered by drapes of vines and hanging baskets of flowers, until they reached a high, crenelated wall broken by a fortified gate.

There, the carriage drew to a halt. Rylan heard the driver speaking to the guards in a foreign tongue. Then, with a shout from the driver, the carriage lurched forward again, following a narrow path between manicured flowerbeds. They rattled to a stop before another wall and another gate, pausing a moment before continuing, until they reached yet another gate. And another, and another, moving through a narrowing series of concentric courtyards. Until, at last, the carriage creaked to a halt within a beautiful enclosure surrounded by tall walls and arcaded walkways.

With a squeak, the carriage door opened.

"This way, Great Master."

Rylan emerged from the coach into the bright light of afternoon. He was greeted by three servants who led him into the depths of the Sultan's palace, up a long flight of stairs, and through a winding series of corridors. Eventually, they arrived at a door that opened into a luxurious room dominated by an enormous, canopied bed. Rylan halted in the doorway, hesitant to enter. His eyes wandered around the bedchamber, taking in the woven rugs, the intricate tiles on the walls, the rich furniture and embroidered cushions. He wandered forward a few steps, then turned slowly around, amazed by the colors and patterns.

"Great Master. Please remove your boots."

Two uniformed guards entered the chamber. They moved in close, watching as he complied, then started running their hands over him, frisking him expertly for weapons. They found his dagger in short order, confiscating it without a word. They were professional about it, but they took their time and were more thorough than he would have liked. Rylan felt relieved when they left.

Another servant approached, this time, a young woman. She fished a knotted string out of a small bag and wrapped it around his waist as Rylan stood still, confounded by her attention. The string slipped up to girth his chest, then moved to measure the length of his arms and legs. At last satisfied, the woman bowed deeply and backed out the door, closing it behind her. Rylan let out a deep breath, thankful to finally be alone.

He eyed the bed and its deep layers of fabric. All he wanted was to sink down into it and fall asleep. It looked soft and comfortable. But he was filthy from the road, his shirt blood-stained. Forsaking the bed, he sat down on a cushioned sofa and leaned back heavily.

He didn't realize he'd fallen asleep until he heard a knock at the door. Rylan groaned and rubbed his eyes. Before he could get up, a manservant entered and bowed low before him.

"Great Master. His Majesty, the Sultan, requests your presence."

Rylan nodded wearily. The Sultan was the last person in the world he wanted to speak with. Despite his consideration as a host, the man was still the same tyrant who had conquered his homeland, the self-same man Rylan had spent the last two years of his life fighting to overthrow. He felt unnerved in his presence.

He rose from the sofa, nodding his head in weary acceptance, then followed the servant out of the bedchamber. The man led him down the corridor to a rosewood door with mother-of-pearl inlay. Without a word, the servant opened the door and beckoned him through. Rylan moved past him to find himself within a high-ceilinged chamber rimmed by cushioned benches, a trickling fountain in the center of the room. The servant led him across the patterned floors to another door, this one covered with gilt latticework. Without speaking, the man opened the door and beckoned Rylan within.

This time, the servant did not follow.

The grilled door closed behind him. He heard it lock.

Rylan move forward to find himself in the private chamber of the Sultan himself. Awed by the sheer grandeur of the room with its domed ceiling and enameled wall tiles, Rylan almost missed the man seated before a brazier. When Rylan's eyes fell upon him, the Sultan gained his feet with a smile.

"Thank you for coming," the man said in a deep voice flavored with a melodic accent. There was a kindness in his eyes that had been missing earlier.

Rylan felt his blood heat, a deep-seated anger kindling within him. A week ago, if he'd found himself alone in the same room with this man, he wouldn't have hesitated before putting a knife through his ribs. He still wasn't certain whether he should try. He didn't trust this man, this enemy. He let his gaze wander the room, searching for anything he could use as a weapon.

Warily, he said, "My thanks for your hospitality, Your Grace."

His host smiled. "There is no need for formalities between us. You may call me Sayeed. Please. Have a seat."

The Sultan's words confused Rylan. Why was he treating him with such courtesy? It made no sense, even if the man had been friends with his wretched father. His eyes found a gilt poker leaning against a stand beside the hearth. His gaze lingered on it as he took a seat next to the brazier.

"Would you care for arak?" Sayeed indicated a narrow bottle on the table at his side.

Rylan had never heard of arak. Some kind of spirits, he presumed. More out of reflex than desire for a drink, he said, "Sure."

With a hospitable smile, the Sultan poured two cups halfway with liquor, then topped them off with water from a carafe. He raised his cup in toast. "To destiny."

Rylan didn't move. Instead, he asked, "Why destiny?"

Without lowering his cup, Sayeed explained, "There is a saying in my culture: 'our choices define our destiny.' We alone are in command of our own fate, and no other. Not any man. Not any god. We sit in the seat of our own judgment and mete out the consequences of our decisions upon ourselves."

Warily, Rylan raised his cup. "To destiny, then." He took a sip of the arak, wincing at the strong flavor of spices and the bite of the liquor.

The Sultan drank deeply, setting his cup down on the table at his side. He said, "When I was a young man, I thought very little of my fate. The Black Lands are not like the Kingdoms— there was no sunlight, and very little joy in living. A man's future was never certain. The next day was never guaranteed, nor the next hour, or even the next second. Very few of us survived long enough to find the first gray in our beards."

He took a heavy sip of his drink, then replaced it on the table. "If you had asked me when I was a boy to name my greatest aspiration, I would have told you my one true desire was to end my life bringing death to my enemy. That craving is what drove me, every moment of my life, to seek perfection in all that I did, on or off the battlefield. Every decision I made carried me further toward that end, a little closer each day.

"Do you understand?" he asked, leaning forward. "It is not that I was fanatical or suicidal. I was merely cynical. I had every reason to be. Like the rest of my people, I had no conception that a life could be lived as an end unto itself. In a land without sunlight, it is difficult to find joy in the labor of living. That is the world I come from. The world your father helped me escape. Now my greatest aspiration is not to bring death. Instead, it is to bring peace."

A heavy silence fell between them. Rylan stared down into the flames of the brazier, feeling their heat, letting the man's words sink in deeper than they ever should have. Deep enough to make him doubt. He took another sip of his drink.

"What of you?" Sayeed asked. "What is your greatest aspiration?"

"To find my daughter," Rylan said at once.

The man nodded and then stated solemnly, "Fear not. Your daughter will be found." It sounded like a promise. The kind of promise not easily broken.

Hearing the conviction in his tone, Rylan felt a stab of hope. "You'd help me?"

"I will," the man said without hesitating.

Rylan sat stunned into silence. He could feel every truth he had ever held crumble away, slipping through his fingers like sand. For the first time in his life, he felt certain of nothing.

After long seconds, he managed to mutter, "I don't understand. I'm your enemy. So why would someone like you want to help someone like me find one little girl?"

The man gazed at him steadily for a moment. Then he drew in a deep breath and sat back in his chair. "Your father and I were more than just friends. By the end, we were brothers. We swore an oath to be united in blood, just as if we had been born of the same mother. I gave your father my pledge that, should he ever fall, I would provide for any children he might have as if they were my own—as he would have done for me. And now it seems I have failed entirely in that obligation."

A slow chill crept over Rylan's skin as he grappled with the import of the Sultan's words. Feeling suddenly weak, he said, "I don't understand. What exactly are you trying to tell me?"

Sayeed captured his gaze firmly. "When I woke this morning, I considered myself a very fortunate man. I had eight palaces, a loving wife, a beautiful daughter, and two worthy sons. I had no idea that by nightfall, that would change. Instead of two sons, I now have three. And for that, I will be forever grateful."

Rylan's thoughts stumbled to a halt. He tried to react but couldn't. He didn't have the capacity to accept or deny the gift he was being offered.

Seeing his reaction, the Sultan gave him a compassionate smile. "It is far more than duty that motivates me. Do you understand? I will take you into my house as blood of my blood, just as your father would have done for any son of mine. And I will use every resource at my disposal to help you find your daughter."

Rylan slumped back in his seat, his mind and senses reeling. He struggled to breathe through a flood of intense relief that threatened to wash him away.

"Your Majesty," he gasped. "I don't know what to say."

His host shrugged. "Sometimes the best words are those left

unspoken." He took a drink, then sat staring for a while into the flames of the brazier. At last, his smile returned, and he set his cup down on the table. "Come. I would like to show you something."

Rylan rose automatically from his chair and followed the man through a door that opened into a domed chamber with high walls covered with geometric patterns of blue and gold. Scalloped arches marched along the edges of the room. Against the far wall sat a wide throne, almost a sofa, under a golden canopy. All along the walls, under the shadows of the arcades, many small fountains trickled delicately. Rylan stared at the throne, unable to break his gaze away, his ears filled with the melodic dance of water.

Until he realized that the Sultan's attention was captured elsewhere.

Following Sayeed's gaze, he saw that the man was staring up at an oil painting hung high on the wall across from the throne. It was a portrait, rendered in bold contrasts of light and shadow, that depicted a dark-haired man of powerful counte-nance garbed in a white cloak, his hand resting on the gem-encrusted hilt of a scimitar. Rylan stared hard at the portrait, captivated by the unnerving intensity of the subject's gaze. Slowly, a tingling sensation came over him, starting behind his neck and spreading downward to his gut. He let his gaze trail down the wall, coming to rest on the sword the Sultan carried at his side.

It was the sword from the painting. Contained in the same bejeweled scabbard attached to the same belt. The buckle of the belt was gold, wrought with the image of a horse bent over backwards, as though eating its own tail. The workmanship of the buckle, like that of the sword, appeared ancient.

Rylan's eyes darted back to the portrait, his thoughts freezing to ice. "That's him, isn't it?"

The Sultan nodded. "It is."

As if compelled, Rylan took a step forward, scrutinizing the face above him. A face that, in all ways, was utterly familiar.

"He looks just like me," he whispered.

Sayeed shook his head. "You look like him."

Suddenly, Rylan felt his initial sense of awe darken and twist into something else. He reminded himself of who that man was, and what he was. He forced himself to stare into Darien Lauchlin's eyes until he felt the proper amount of revulsion. Until all he saw in that portrait was a thing of evil. Comfortably cold again, Rylan turned his back on the demon who had fathered him.

And then he remembered the oath he had pledged in the cornfield. Was it the same oath his father had sworn? Was he destined to follow in that hellish man's footsteps? No. He would never do that. But then he was reminded of his dream, of his wife assuring him that the harder he tried, the worse he would fail. He shivered with dread.

"I'm tired," he said. "I should find my bed."

"Of course." But the Sultan hesitated. Softly, he said, "Gerald. You cannot run from who you are."

The words provoked a burning slap of anger.

"My name's not Gerald," Rylan snapped, then fled the room.

9

SHARP WORDS

GIL SNAPPED CLOSED A DUSTY TEXT WITH YELLOWED PAGES AND A frayed cloth cover. He shoved it aside and drew another from the stack of books sitting next to him on the table. Holding it up, he saw it was an exhausted-looking tome with a sagging leather cover that had cracked along the spine. Gil opened the book carefully and, wetting his finger on his tongue, flipped quickly through the first few pages before shoving it aside.

"I should have let him die," he grumbled, referring to Rylan.

His own father, Kyel Archer, had fought for the Kingdoms, and had countered Lauchlin's assaults in every battle for the North. Had he known Rylan Marshall was that demon's son, Gil would have slid his own knife between the farmer's ribs.

Ashra smiled at him from across the table, where she sat with her chin cradled in her hand, ink-black hair spilling forward. "Then why are you still searching for a way to keep him alive?"

"Because someone told me I had to." Gil shoved another leather-bound book aside and grabbed the next one, flipping the cover open. He ran his finger along the first few lines of text before relegating the book to the discard pile.

"Well? Have you found anything?"

Ignoring her on purpose, he pushed the remainder of the books aside, then pulled the next stack toward him. He took the first book off the top and opened it without bothering to read the title. He flipped through the first couple of pages before deciding the book contained nothing pertinent.

Ashra cocked an eyebrow. "So you've found nothing."

Conceding, Gil gave a quick nod. "I've found too much of everything I *don't* need. One more book on symbology, lexicology, glyphology, or arcanology, and I'm going to jump out a window."

"I doubt defenestrating yourself is the answer," Ashra said, sliding a thin text toward herself with a finger. "This looks interesting."

Gil selected a much thicker tome and set it down in front of her. "Here. Try to stay occupied, so I can concentrate."

Flipping open the book, she asked mildly, "Are you ever going to actually teach me anything?"

"I am." Gil shuffled through a small pile of books before choosing one. "I'm teaching you how to sit and be quiet. If you ever get that lesson straight, we'll go from there."

The book opened to a page about a quarter of the way through, a page containing four diagrams drawn in black ink with crosshatched shading. Below the diagrams was penned a flowing inscription in strange characters. Cradling the text in his hands, Gil paced away from the table. "This is interesting. These markings look a lot like the ones on the knife."

He turned the page, then flipped back again. Behind him, Ashra rose from her seat and moved around the table, drawing up at his side. He pointed out a line of strange markings that seemed to swirl across the page. "They're similar," he said. "But I don't think they're the same."

"Are those artifacts?" Ashra asked, indicating the eight diagrams of cylindrical objects arranged in rows across the page. Each was decorated with various pictures of men and beasts, mostly battle imagery.

"I think they are," Gil said. "It says here they're relics from the lost Kingdom of Shira. What's Shira? I've never heard of it."

Ashra shrugged. Gil hadn't expected her to know; the question had been rhetorical. He looked again at the elegant script. "This isn't good news," he said slowly. "Whoever attacked Rylan had access to knowledge and artifacts we haven't even heard of. We have to show this to Naia."

He closed the book, keeping the page marked with his index finger, and headed out of the library. He heard Ashra's footsteps following behind, hurrying to catch up. They took the steps down to the ground floor and followed the tiled hallway to the end. There, the Prime Warden's secretary stopped them before they reached the door. The woman stood and slid her spectacles off her face.

Gil said, "We need to speak to the Prime Warden. It's urgent."

"Isn't it rather late?" the woman asked with an irritated look, stepping in front of them. "I'm sorry, but the Prime Warden has stepped out."

Gil drew up, frustrated. "When will she return?"

The woman retreated back behind her desk and donned her spectacles. "I wouldn't presume to know."

"Would you presume to know where she went?"

She picked up a stack of parchment and tapped it twice against the desk, straightening the papers. "The Prime Warden and her husband accepted an invitation to the palace."

"Thank you for being such a help," Gil snapped, then turned and walked back down the hallway, Ashra hurrying after him.

"Where are you going?" she gasped, catching up.

"To the palace," Gil answered, quickening his pace.

Rylan jerked bolt upright in bed. Chest heaving, he strangled a sob and glanced around frantically at the darkness. In his mind, the image of his son's charred face continued to haunt him. It wasn't fading like it normally did upon waking. He tried hard to picture Korey's face as it had been in life, giggling and happy. His son had been blessed with such an enormous heart, a capacity for love and joy that seemed boundless.

All erased. Reduced to char and ash.

He sat there in bed, trembling, shoulders shaking, until his pulse finally slowed its ragged pace. He squeezed his eyes shut, stemming the flow of tears.

He noticed he'd been unconsciously flexing his fingers, opening and closing his fist. And every time he did, the dimmest, thinnest filament of light glowed above his hand. Rylan stared down at it, uncertain what to think. At first, he couldn't make out the color of the light. For a moment, he thought it looked blue. Then red. As he flexed his hand a few more times, the light became more substantial. Purple, he decided. Like a bruise. And it was part of him.

A new and terrible part.

He held his hand open. This time, the light stayed, glowing softly. He sat scowling down at it. He knew what it was and was disgusted by it. It was mage-power. The kind of power that could cure the dying, level cities, bring down mountains, vanquish armies....

All worthless.

It hadn't helped him save his son.

It couldn't bring his daughter back.

Rylan swung his legs over the side of the bed. He sat there for long minutes, cradling his head in his hands. He sat that way until he got his breathing under control. He brought his hands up and scrubbed his eyes, then rose from the bed.

He crossed the dark room, feeling his way along, until he reached a door that led out onto a balcony. Leaving the door open, he stepped out into the cool night air and walked forward to the railing. Below was an intimate courtyard ringed by columned walkways and four high walls. A fountain gurgled in the center. A slight breeze came up, ruffling his hair, scented with jasmine. From somewhere below came the sound of distant laughter. He moved to the other side of the balcony, where there was a view of the city, visible over the walls of the palace. He stood there for minutes, his eyes wandering over the innumerable rolling domes and tall minarets.

On impulse, he raised his hand and spread his fingers in front of him. Above his palm glowed a diffuse, violet orb. Curious, he swept his hand through the air, producing an arcing trail of sparkling light. Wondering what else he could do with the light, he turned around and stared back into the bedchamber, his eyes fixated on the shadows of the floor. Concentrating, he willed them to yield.

And they did.

A thin, purple mist spread before him across the floor, casting back the shadows with a soft, ethereal light, revealing the bedchamber within. Rylan stood in the doorway, staring in fascination at his creation. He took a step forward, his feet disturbing the glowing mist. He glanced up.

Something plowed into him and hurled him sideways against the wall, knocking the wind from his lungs. Before he could react, the dark figure was already in front of him. It grabbed a fistful of his hair and cracked his head back against the tiles.

Dazed and breathless, Rylan slid down the wall. His assailant sank with him. A hand closed around his throat. A woman's voice whispered through the darkness:

"You will do as I say, or I'll speak the Word that will pierce your heart. Now. Stand up."

A focused calm washed over him. He didn't think. He just reacted. He shot his hands out, and the woman flew backward with a cry.

Rylan hadn't touched her.

He shoved himself to his feet, but the woman was already up. He caught the glint of a blade as she lunged at him. He dodged sideways, jerking the rope that held the drapes out of the wall.

The blade sliced toward him.

Rylan snapped the rope taut, deflecting the blade. He twisted the cord, catching the woman's wrist and pinning her arm behind her back. The knife dropped from her grip.

She screamed and bucked, fighting with all her might to slip the rope. He let her. When she moved to duck out of it, he tightened the cord around her neck.

The woman thrashed against him, making awful, strangling noises. The harder she fought, the tighter Rylan twisted the rope. He swung his leg over her and gripped her body between his thighs. He held her there, pinned, until her struggles weakened. The grunting became wheezing.

The chamber door crashed open. A stream of guards poured into the room.

Rylan was knocked away from the woman, the cord jerked from his hand. More guards piled in front of him, while others pinned his assailant to the floor. Panicked, Rylan scrambled forward, searching for the rope, the only weapon he could use to defend himself.

The woman lay on the floor, subdued but still breathing. She looked up at him, and for a second their eyes met. Her lips moved, and she whispered a word.

The Word that would kill him.

The impact of the spell carved through his ribcage like an axe.

Rylan's knees buckled. He fell to the ground and rolled onto his side, moaning in agony and clutching his chest. The pain was incapacitating. Hot blood ran through his fingers, pooling beneath him on the carpet. A terrible pressure constricted his lungs. He fought a losing battle for every breath.

"Stand aside!" someone bellowed.

He was vaguely aware of hands on him, rolling him over. Through bleary eyes, he made out the face of the Sultan, leaning over him.

"Do something," the man growled. "Anything!"

"There's nothing I can do," said a sad and gentle voice.

The voices were fading. The world was fading. Hands cupped his face. Then a different voice:

"Stand away from him."

A wave of anguish washed over him, and he knew no more.

10

A BLACK DAY

GIL PUSHED PAST A NERVOUS BARRIER OF PALACE GUARDS WHO, noticing the color of his cloak, dared not block his passage. The noises up ahead sent alarm bells ringing through his mind. The sounds of shouts and mayhem echoed through the maze of corridors, growing louder and closer with every step he took. Gil knew with a sinking feeling what he was walking into. And this deep within the reclusive layers of Andarapi Palace—in the Sultan's personal apartments—there was only one type of disturbance it could possibly be.

There had been another attack.

At the sight of a dozen or so guards collected in the hallway outside the Sultan's personal chambers, Ashra surged forward, panic on her face. Gil followed, rushing after her. The guards parted before him, obeying the silent authority conveyed by his black cloak. Once inside the room, he halted as if walking into a wall. Or walking into a murder.

The Prime Warden and her husband stood on opposite sides of a large dining table, where the body of Rylan Marshall was laid out, covered in blood. For long moments, all Gil could do was stand frozen, his jaw going slack. He didn't have to be told the man was dead. It was written on the faces of all the people surrounding him. Gil forced himself to walk forward, compelled by the need to confirm that knowledge with his eyes.

He moved to stand beside Quinlan Reis and looked down solemnly. Rylan's eyes were open and fixed on the ceiling, his chest still. Blood pooled on the table, pattering slowly to the floor. The Prime Warden stood with her hands clasped, her face somber. Ashra moved immediately to the Sultan's side, placing a comforting hand on his arm.

"Father," she whispered. She stared at the body on the table with vast sadness in her eyes. In response, the Sultan put his arm around her.

Gil probed his own feelings, unsure how he felt. Sadness, certainly. He hadn't known Rylan long, but he'd seemed a decent fellow. Yet deep down in some callous place inside, Gil discovered he also felt relief. He no longer had to worry about whether Rylan would choose to follow the path his demonic father had taken. At least he had lived and died a free man, and not a servant shackled to darkness. Gil was happy for that.

"Who killed him?" he asked, his voice cutting through the tense quiet.

"He's not dead," the Prime Warden responded, her voice low and hoarse.

Gil blinked. At first, he didn't believe her. He stared harder at the body on the table. There was no sign of life in it. He moved his hand to touch Rylan's arm, to feel inside him for a heartbeat. But Naia's voice stopped his motion.

"I slowed time for him," she explained softly. "He persists as he did the moment I found him. But he is only heartbeats from death. And he will die as soon as I lift the ward from him."

Gil stared at her, blinking in shock. He'd never heard of such a practice. Slowing time was something he had never considered, never knew possible; it was not anything taught at the Lyceum. He wondered where the Prime Warden had learned such a skill, but then he remembered that Naia was a former priestess of Death. Perhaps the temple was privy to secrets not widely known.

Sultan Sayeed moved forward with Ashra on his arm. "What does that mean, you slowed time?"

The Prime Warden explained in gentle tones, "It is a type of ward. Death's temple uses it to preserve the deceased before interment. Time still passes for Rylan, but very slowly. It could be years before he draws his final breath. But we cannot leave him in this state. That would not be compassionate. All I did was buy us time. No more."

Gil had always wondered about the temple's methods, how they could keep the dead preserved for the time required for a body to lie in repose. For royalty, that period could extend to months. He'd always suspected the temple used artifacts created by mages for the purpose. He just never knew how such a spell would work. Apparently, Naia did.

He asked, "Was his attacker caught?"

It was the Sultan who answered him. "She was apprehended."

Hearing that, Quin turned and addressed the guards stationed in the doorway: "Bring the prisoner here." Then he explained quickly, "Without knowing the Word, there is nothing we can do for him. We need to get it out of her. What-ever that takes."

Gil took his meaning. The Prime Warden nodded slightly. Gil was surprised Naia would agree so quickly to the notion of torture. It seemed out of character.

He glanced a question at Ashra. But she ignored him, looking quickly away. They stood silent after that; there wasn't anything more that could be done. Gil focused on the blood congealing on the table, watching it thicken and darken as the seconds wore by. Minutes later, the sound of running footsteps announced the return of the guards. Two breathless officers rushed into the room and fell upon the floor, prostrating themselves before their sovereign.

"Your Majesty, the woman is gone," the first man reported.

The Sultan's face warped into a mask of outrage. "What do you mean, *gone?*"

The officer remained bent over his knees, staring at the floor. "She is not in the dungeon—the cell door is still locked. It was never opened, this I swear. I have failed you, Your Majesty. Please take my life."

Sayeed growled like an enraged wolf. *"Leave,"* he commanded.

Both men leapt to their feet and retreated in haste, bowing as they backed out of the room. In a broken voice, the Sultan whispered, "I failed my brother." He reached down and closed Rylan's eyes, a compassionate gesture that Gil felt strange, considering he'd only known the man for half a day.

"Magic, then," the Grand Master whispered. He shook his head in obvious frustration. Removing his hat, he ran a hand through his hair before settling it back on and adjusting the brim. Then he paced away, face etched in deeply troubled lines, his shoulders hunched.

The Sultan gazed down at the body on the table. "Is he in pain?"

The Prime Warden nodded. She reached down and stroked Rylan's damp hair back from his face. "Yes. He lingers in his final moments, somewhere between death and awareness."

"Then end it."

Naia hesitated only a moment before nodding. She closed her eyes, her brow furrowing in concentration.

A spark of insight slammed into Gil, hard enough to make him flinch. "Stop!" he gasped.

The Prime Warden glanced up at him in surprise. Gil scrambled to collect his thoughts. They fluttered about in his head like butterflies, scattering in all directions. It was moments before he could gather them into words. Moments while everyone in the room pinned their stares and hopes on him.

"The Word is empowered by magic, by his Gift," Gil said quickly. "So, what if we remove the Gift from him? Wouldn't that deactivate the Word?"

Naia looked at him flatly. "That would kill him." The tone of her voice betrayed her irritation. A mage's magical legacy was inseparable from their life force. No mage could survive the removal of that Gift. But Gil hadn't meant that, at least not in the way Naia thought he did. He groped to find better words.

Quin cocked an eyebrow at him. "Isn't the whole point of this exercise to keep him alive?"

Gil scowled. He hated being the object of sarcasm. And the Grand Master's wit was sharper than most, honed to a razor's edge by a thousand years of indifference.

Gil gestured at Quin's side, where an elegant scimitar hung strapped to his waist. The sword was legendary, a magical artifact created by Quin himself. *Zanikar* was the only one of its kind, the only weapon capable of dampening a mage's ability. The blade had never been duplicated, not even by its own creator.

"Your sword is a field dampener," Gil said. "If we use it on Rylan, it would cut him off from the magic field—and maybe cut the Word off too."

Quin's face hardened. His gaze flicked down to Rylan, then slid back up to lock on Gil. His jaw worked, chewing the inside of his cheek. Finally, he nodded. "We could give it a try," he allowed. "But if we dampen him, Naia's time-slip will also stop working. We'll have only seconds to act."

"Is there a better alternative?" the Prime Warden asked. Looking around from blank face to blank face, she shrugged. "I'll heal him the moment he's dampened. Hopefully, that will be fast enough."

Quin shook his head. "That's too dangerous. If he dies, and you're touching him—"

He was right. A mage's Gift spilled out of their body upon death. If Naia was touching Rylan the moment he died, then the Gift escaping his body would rush into her and add itself to the power she already had—a lethal amount, Gil was sure.

Naia put her hand up, silencing him. "I'll be careful." She licked her lips. "All right." She moved around to the end of the table and, bending over, placed both hands on Rylan's chest. Then she looked up at the Sultan. "If this fails, I will have to let him go."

"So be it," he said, his eyes dark, his lips drawn into a thin line.

The Prime Warden nodded. Bowing her head, she closed her eyes. "I'm ready."

Quin took Rylan's arm and pushed the bloody shirtsleeve back to his elbow. Then he drew his scimitar from its sheath. Gil's palms broke out in a sweat as Quin set the edge of the blade across Rylan's wrist.

The Prime Warden said very calmly, "Do it."

At first, Gil didn't realize anything had happened. Then he saw it: the sword had moved only a fraction, yet had sliced a deep cut into Rylan's wrist. The wound gaped open, the exposed flesh white instead of pink.

"There's no blood," Ashra observed. "Is he dead, then?"

Quin sheathed his sword. "Time is catching up with him," he said, taking a step back.

Just as he finished speaking, beads of blood appeared all along the length of the gash, collecting in droplets that rolled away, running in thin rivulets. Fresh, warm blood spilled from Rylan's body onto the table, drizzling to the floor, where it spread along the grout lines between tiles.

Naia gasped, her body going stiff, as though mustering every drop of strength from every muscle on her skeleton. She remained like that, locked rigid, the knuckles of her hands turning a milky white. Her body started trembling, then shaking, as if convulsed. Quin reached for his wife, ready to knock her away. But he paused, holding his hands frozen in the air.

"Gah!" Naia gasped. She broke off contact, staggering back and raising her bloody hands before her face. Her cheeks glistened with sweat, her hair hanging in wet ropes to her waist.

"It worked," she gasped, and took a great, steadying breath.

Gil glanced down at Rylan in disbelief. His bleeding had stopped, his chest moving in a regular rhythm. His face looked peacefully asleep. Gil could hardly believe what he'd witnessed, even though dampening the Word had been his own idea.

"Praise be to the gods," the Sultan gasped, touching his fingers to his brow. Ashra slipped away from him and moved to the table, staring down in wonder into Rylan's slumbering face. She reached out and touched his arm, as though she didn't quite believe what her eyes were telling her.

The Prime Warden used a dinner napkin to wipe the blood and perspiration off her face. She said wearily, "He will survive as long as he remains dampened." Tossing the napkin down with a disdainful expression, she glanced back at Rylan. "He will never be able to use his Gift, however."

The Sultan nodded. "It is a heavy price," he acknowledged. "But worth it." He turned to his men lingering in the doorway. "Send for my Master of the Chamber. Have him bathed and cared for," he ordered. "And send for my personal physician."

"He will not be needing a physician," Naia snapped, sounding irritated. "What he needs is rest. And protection. His enemies have already proven themselves to be far more cunning than we ever suspected. And far more competent."

11

THE KINGDOM OF SHIRA

THE STAIRS BEHIND THE COURTYARD WERE OVER THREE CENTURIES old, part of the skeleton of the old manor house that had once stood in the site where the Lyceum in Karikesh had been later constructed. The manor house, like the remainder of the surrounding neighborhood, had been burned to the ground in the fires that had swept through the city shortly after the Battle of Rothscard. Like the Lyceum, Karikesh itself had been built on—and out of—the bones of its predecessor. Rothscard, as it had once been called, was no more. The Unconquerable City had been conquered and razed to the ground, and from those ashes Karikesh had risen, fresh and beautiful and daunting to behold.

The stairs beneath Gil's feet were made of flagstone darkened by the fire that had consumed the manor house. A new iron railing now encased them, ascending from out of the courtyard's thick canopy of trees. The air was humid, fed by a dozen or so fountains. The limbs of the trees bore leaves of orange and gold, ready to fall at the first hint of a gust.

Arriving at a small landing at the top of the stairs, Gil reached up and knocked on a turquoise-painted door. The door opened after only a moment, and Quin peered out, looking exceptionally different without his customary black hat. Gil held up the small, leather-bound book.

"I brought you a text," Gil said with a smile, knowing Quin's love-hate relationship with books.

The Grand Master glanced down suspiciously at the book in Gil's hand. "So you did. By all means, come in." He stepped back, opening the door wider.

Gil stepped into Quin's study, which was spacious and bright, lit by windows placed high on the walls. There was an intimate ring of red-and-gold chairs clustered around a squat table that held a variety of glasses and containers of different makes and sizes. Quin had a deep love of liquor. It was rare to find him without a glass or flask in his hand. And yet, in the eight years Quin had been his mentor, Gil had never seen him intoxicated.

"Have a seat." Quin gestured at one of the chairs, moving around the table to claim another for himself. He sat down heavily and scooped up a glass from the table.

"Whiskey?" he asked, lifting a lead crystal decanter.

Gil raised his hand. "No thank you. It's a bit early for me."

"Nonsense," Quin snorted, and poured him a glass anyway. "It's never too early. Liquor is the manure by which we fertilize our minds."

He hefted his glass as if ready to proffer a toast, then sat staring at Gil expectantly, until he followed suit. But instead of offering words, the Grand Master tilted his head back and let the alcohol slide down his throat, closing his eyes in pleasure.

"Mmmmm," he sighed, then cracked an eye open.

Gil brought his glass up to his mouth and took a sip. The bite of the liquor burned his throat. His stomach winced in protest.

Quin sprawled back in his chair, kicking a leg up and draping an elbow over the armrest. "I believe you're owed a debt of gratitude," he said to Gil. "Without you, our new friend would be decaying into compost at this moment. And if I'm right in my hunch, that would indeed be a very calamitous occurrence."

"What makes you say that?" Gil asked, braving another sip and grimacing as the whiskey ignited a fire in his belly. He choked down a wheeze.

Quin didn't appear to notice. He rubbed his fingers over the salt-and-peppered whiskers on his jaw. "As I said, it's just a hunch. It goes something like this: why would anyone want to collar or kill the son of the greatest battlemage in history? What would they be hoping to gain?"

Gil frowned. Quin had a point. He hadn't thought it out that far. "Putting it like that, it sounds like someone wants to turn Rylan into a weapon. Or stop him from becoming one."

Quin lifted his eyebrows. "It would certainly seem that way," he said and tossed back another swallow.

Gil pondered the idea for a moment. "But Rylan isn't his father," he pointed out. "Darien Lauchlin studied under the Masters of Aerysius for twenty years. When it comes to magic, Rylan knows nothing."

"Including his limits," Quin stated softly, then set his glass down. "Now let us see this gift you've brought me."

Gil handed the text to him. Quin took it and started leafing through the pages, scanning them quickly without reading a word. "What am I looking for?" he asked.

"Right here." Gil reached out and flipped the book open to the page he'd marked previously with a slender ribbon. He tapped his finger over the ink renderings he'd discovered with Ashra. "They're some type of artifacts," he explained. "Look at the script."

Quin brought out his spectacles and slid them onto his face. He held the book closer and, squinting, rotated the text first one way and then the other. "It's like the writing on the knife," he observed. "But then again, it's not."

"No, it's not. But it could be a precursor," Gil pointed out. "It says the artifacts are from the Kingdom of Shira. I've never heard of Shira, and I consider myself well-read."

Quin flipped the page, his eyes quickly scanning the text. "Shira was a great nation somewhere in ancient Zahra," he said absently. "But that was eight thousand years ago. Zahra was erased from the map by the Well of Tears." He flipped back again to the page with the cylinder seals.

Setting the book down, he stood up and pulled the knife out from under the fabric of his longcoat. Gil looked up at him in surprise. He hadn't been expecting Quin to keep the blade on his person, even though, now that he thought about it, it made sense. The weapon was much more dangerous than the other artifacts Quin usually kept around his workshop.

Lifting the knife, the Grand Master carefully studied the inscriptions in the folded steel. "I suppose it could be the same language family," he said at last, lowering the weapon. "But that's still not very helpful. All it proves is that this is a very old blade. And I somehow doubt an eight-thousand-year old Shirite was running around Karikesh last night."

He set the knife down next to the book and settled back into his seat. He brought his hand up to scratch his cheek, his eyes sliding to the side in thought. "So, who would want to kill or control the son of a demon?" he muttered under his breath. He flicked his eyebrows. "Perhaps a better question is, who would *know* Rylan is the son of a demon?"

Gil agreed; that was indeed the most important question they could be asking. According to Rylan's adopted parents, no other person alive knew the real Rylan was buried in Amberlie Grove. So if no other person knew that information... then perhaps it wasn't a person they should be looking for.

Quin unstoppered the decanter. He poured himself

another drink, then splashed some more into Gil's glass, even though it was still almost full. Gil looked at the glass dismally, thinking it might appear ungrateful if he left that much untouched. Trying hard not to retch, he forced down another swallow.

"So how are you getting along with all this?" Quin asked.

"What do you mean?"

The Grand Master shrugged. "You've been ordered to protect the son of your father's nemesis. A most disagreeable turn of circumstance, I would think."

Gil offered a wry smile. "I've been trying to convince myself Rylan's different. So far, I haven't succeeded."

Quin scooted back in his seat and crossed an ankle over his knee. "Perhaps it would help to know that both of your fathers ended up allies by the time everything was said and done."

Gil frowned. "What do you mean?"

Quin lifted his drink. "Both Kyel and Darien gave their lives to seal the Well of Tears. They died for the same cause, fighting on the same side. Never forget that."

Gil found those words hard to deny, for Quinlan Reis was right. Perhaps, at the end, both his own father and Rylan's had been able to reach some kind of understanding. It was hard to imagine. But possible.

"More whiskey?" Quin asked, lifting the bottle.

Gil blew out a long, dispirited sigh, puffing out his cheeks. "No thanks," he said. "I've had enough manure dumped on my brain for one afternoon."

He rose, then, and started toward the door.

"Gil."

He turned and glanced back at Quin.

The Grand Master advised softly, "Give Rylan a chance."

But Gil shook his head. "I don't have to. He's not a mage anymore," he said, opening the door.

Quin stopped him short with a glare and a raised finger.

"Don't make the mistake of thinking this is over," he warned. "Because it's not. Far from it."

Gil nodded once. Then he walked out the door.

———————

Rylan sat perfectly still, gazing down at the courtyard below his room's large balcony. He felt dazed, as though his mind was enveloped in a thick layer of fog. He didn't remember waking up. Or walking out onto the balcony. He thought he may have been sitting there a long time, the cool breeze fluttering the ends of the blanket that hung off him.

He closed his eyes and cleared his mind, filling his ears with the erratic sounds of the fountain below. The trickling noise of the water was easy to focus on, just loud enough to help his mind chase away thoughts that didn't belong there. He sat for minutes, concentrating on the fountain's spirited music. Or maybe it was hours.

When he opened his eyes, the sound of the fountain was still there, relentless in its melody. But he realized there was something else that was missing. Something significant. As though the life and pulse of the world had been withdrawn. Rylan stared out across the vine-draped courtyard in confusion, feeling like something of vital importance had been lost from the world.

It was the loss of the magic field, he realized. All his life, he had been able to sense the flow of the field moving through him and hadn't known it, even before the man in the cornfield had assaulted him. He'd never been able to touch it or do anything with it, but it had always been there with him, a comforting presence in his head that was so much a part of him, it was beneath notice. But now it was gone, as if it had never existed at all, and he ached for it. That sense had been taken from him entirely, and he yearned to have it back.

A breeze came up, stirring his hair. The sun was warmer and far brighter than he remembered. He turned away from it —and was surprised to find a tall guard standing behind him in the doorway, blocking the entrance to his bedchamber. Rylan stood slowly and turned to face the man, who was outfitted in the same black armor he had seen on others of his kind. The man stared straight ahead, either through him or past him, and remained unmoving.

"Excuse me," Rylan said.

Without a word, the man stepped away from the doorway.

Rylan entered the bedchamber and stood looking around, blinking. There was no sign that a scuffle had ever taken place there. The rugs were pristine, and there was no blood on the tiled floor or upon the walls. The drapery cord had been replaced, the drape itself returned to its graceful swag.

And yet, all around the room stood a ring of armored guardsmen. Looking at them, Rylan felt ill. He remembered the assault. He didn't remember how he'd survived it. But the presence of these men made him fear the Sultan had carried the notion of protecting him much too far.

"I'd like to be alone," he said.

None of the guards moved, or even acknowledged that he had spoken. Looking around the room, Rylan scanned the men's hard faces. They weren't going away, he realized. He would have to make the Sultan understand the guards would have to leave. If they didn't go, he would.

But before he went anywhere, Rylan figured he needed something more to wear than just his underclothes. He turned slowly in a circle, his eyes skimming over the bed, the two gilt chairs and matching table. Many oil lamps hung suspended from the high ceiling, and tall, golden sconces rose from the floor, holding long tapers that produced a rich, flickering light. But other than the patterned rug and the tiled hearth along the wall, the wide chamber was almost conspicuously empty: just one large, open space.

His gaze fell on the only other piece of furniture in the room: an enameled wardrobe. Rylan walked over to it and opened the double doors. Within hung an assortment of fine garments: tunics and vests, trousers and capes. New boots of rich leather. All appeared fit for a prince—certainly not for a farmer. Rylan raised his hand and ran his fingers over the detailed embroidery of a cuff.

He couldn't wear any of it. The garments in the wardrobe were all far above his station. Not only would he look like a fool, but he also didn't want to accept anything more from the Sultan. He turned and shot a resentful glance back at the guards. The eyes of the men stared rigidly back, silent and unsympathetic. Rylan clenched his jaw in frustration and grabbed a silk shirt down from its hanger. He tugged it on, then chose the most serviceable-looking trousers he could find.

He turned to a mirror mounted on the wall by the wardrobe. Moving closer, he found he hardly recognized himself. His untended whiskers had grown into a short beard, but his hair was washed, the blood cleaned from his face. Someone had bathed him while he'd lain unconscious. He shivered, finding the thought singularly disturbing.

Even more unsettling was how much he resembled the man in the portrait, the demon who was his father. Disgusted, Rylan turned away from the mirror and strode toward the door. A guard stepped forward to block him.

"You are instructed to remain here, my Lord." The guard's tone was just as rigid as his stance.

Rylan felt his blood run hot. And then cold, when it occurred to him that the guard had addressed him as nobility. He would have laughed at the situation, had it not been so infuriating.

"How long?" he demanded.

"Until you are sent for."

"So, I'm a prisoner, then." Feeling besieged, Rylan gave an exasperated sigh. At least he finally understood his role. It seemed that the Sultan was his enemy, after all. He turned away and paced back toward the center of the room, where he stood looking from implacable face to implacable face. When he couldn't stand it any longer, he turned to the guard blocking the doorway.

"Go tell *His Majesty* I demand to see him. Immediately."

The guard bowed low, until his back was parallel to the floor. "It shall be done," he said, then turned and departed. The other guards shifted along the walls, spacing themselves out and closing the gap that had been left by their companion's disappearance.

Rylan stood waiting, staring at the vine-like pattern of the rug at his feet, his eyes trailing over it. Long minutes passed, and still the guard hadn't returned. Vexed, he breathed out a heavy sigh and paced toward the balcony, just wanting to be away from the burden of staring eyes.

As he turned his back to the door, Rylan heard the latch click.

He whirled to find a man with a thick white mustache standing in the doorway, wearing a long robe and a tall red hat. The man bowed low, not quite so low as the guard had, and stood with his gaze on the floor, hands clasped in front of him.

"His Royal Majesty, Sultan Sayeed, requests the honor of your presence," he said. He motioned toward the door.

Rylan sagged in relief, moving forward to follow the old man through the doorway. But once in the corridor, he was immediately discouraged by the sight of a dozen more guards clogging the passage. Frustration tightened his gut. Jaw clenched, he followed the old man down the wide corridor to the royal chambers. The man led him to the door with the gilt grate, beckoning him through. Rylan entered and then halted at the sight of the Sultan standing in the center of the room, a golden chalice in his hand. He nodded at the old man.

"Thank you, Timur Pasha."

The old man bowed low, far lower than he had for Rylan, and backed out of the room, closing the door behind him.

Sayeed smiled warmly, perhaps even fondly. "It is good to see you hale." He motioned to two low, bench-like seats arranged on rugs before the hearth. He took the furthest one, sitting down cross-legged upon it.

Angry, Rylan stood where he was and gazed at the man harshly. "There are guards in my bedchamber, in the corridors... They follow me everywhere."

The Sultan raised his hand, indicating the long seat across from him. "Please," he insisted. He reached down at his side, lifting a bottle of wine.

Rylan hesitated a moment before complying. His eyes found the gilt poker before the fireplace. For the second time in two days, he considered using it. But if he killed Sayeed, he would never make it out of the palace alive. There would be no one to rescue his daughter. *You lucky bastard,* he thought, glaring his anger at the monarch as he took the seat across from him. If it wasn't for Amina, the man wouldn't be so lucky.

Rylan discovered that sitting on the bench-like sofa was like sitting on the floor. He sat with his legs sprawled outward but realized quickly how awkward he must look. Grudgingly, he drew his feet up under him, mirroring his host's posture.

The Sultan nodded his approval. "Surely, you understand the necessity of the guards?" he asked in his melodic baritone. Leaning forward, he poured Rylan a glass of wine.

Rylan took the glass from him, silently fuming. "What I don't understand is why any of this is happening to me. And to my son. And my daughter."

The Sultan scowled. Looking sympathetic, he said, "If I understood the source of the threat to you, then I would eliminate it. Unfortunately, I do not. All I can do is protect you. Thus, the guards."

Rylan set the wine glass down on the rug, untouched. "I can't stay here. I need to find my daughter."

The Sultan appeared to consider his words carefully before asking, "Where would you look for her?"

Rylan grimaced in frustration. "I don't know. But I'll never find her sitting here."

Stroking his beard calmly, Sayeed informed him, "I've already dispatched some of my men to Farlow, to look there for answers. They are intelligent men. I know it is difficult, but try to find peace and patience. Give my men time to investigate."

Rylan stared at him, his insides boiling with resentment. "If it was your daughter, would you have peace and patience?"

The man drew in a deep breath, then let it out again with a long sigh. His eyebrows flicked upward. After a moment's hesitation, he admitted, "No. I would not." He set his glass down and clasped his fingers together in front of him. "But I am not in your situation. You have enemies who claim they want you 'because of who you are.' Was that not their words? And why do they want you? I will tell you why: because if you have even the dimmest spark of your father in you, you have the potential to scorch the world. Do you understand what I am saying? We cannot risk your enemies gaining control of you."

His words served to fan Rylan's ire. They confirmed what he'd suspected all along—the guards were more than just protection. He was a prisoner.

"I'm not my father," he growled. "I'm not a threat to anyone. I don't know anything."

"But you could be taught," the Sultan responded firmly.

Rylan's frustration finally overwhelmed his sense of self-preservation. He surged to his feet. "So what am I supposed to do? Sit here under guard for the rest of my life? While my daughter is imprisoned somewhere? They could be *torturing her!* They could be *defiling her!* She could be dead already!"

The Sultan stared up at him, the intensity of his expression dominating even Rylan's anger. "And if she is, there is *nothing* you can do about it," he said forcefully.

He was right, Rylan realized. He sagged back down on the sofa, bowing his head. Despair gripped his heart. He was hardly aware of the Sultan refilling the wine glass he had spilled unknowingly. There was a long and heavy pause.

"Give my men time to work," Sayeed said more gently. "Trust me—they are the best chance your daughter has."

Rylan looked up at the man with contempt in his eyes. "Why should I trust you? Tell me that. The last attack happened within your own walls. How do I know it wasn't you who ordered it?"

The Sultan did not respond immediately. He sat with his eyes fixed on Rylan's own, holding him captive with a cold-as-steel glare. His face hardened to stone, and he sat still, as if locked rigidly in place.

"You are truly your father's son," he said, his voice cool and carefully controlled. "My brother was a very shrewd man. But he could also be very rash. And very arrogant."

He set his goblet down on the rug. He sat for long moments in silence, completely still, except for one finger, which he tapped absently against his cheek. After a while, he nodded as if in answer to a question, then said with a deep frown, "I will offer a compromise. From what my guards have told me, you handle yourself well in combat. They reported you had the woman subdued before they arrived, and it was only their own interference that freed her to speak the Word. This goes against my better judgment. But so long as you remain armed, you are free to come and go as you please. Do what you will with the guards who have been assigned you; henceforth, they are yours to command. I do ask, however, that you exercise great prudence and do not idly dismiss their protection."

Rylan bowed his head, feeling relieved. The Sultan was a hard man to deny and, he was discovering, a harder man to dislike. Rylan wanted to resent him, wanted that badly. But the more Sayeed spoke, the more he found himself respecting him. He seemed a man of honor, and his intentions seemed genuine. Despite every reservation, Rylan couldn't bring himself to hate him.

"My thanks, Your Majesty," he said with a feeling of relief. "I'll be prudent. But I don't have a weapon. Your men took my only dagger."

Sayeed stared down at the rug with a deep frown. Then he rose with a smile. "I think I have something." He crossed the floor to a tall cabinet and opened a drawer. From within, he withdrew a curving scimitar contained in a metal scabbard. He turned back to Rylan, proffering the sword in both hands.

Rylan stood and accepted the weapon, baring the blade. It was deceptively light, even though he had no doubt it was strong and deadly. The blade was single-edged and made of folded steel, with a dull patina of age and heavy use. It had an elegant, subtle curve that flared out toward the tip.

"This was the sword I carried when I was your father's First Among Many," Sayeed explained. "It was given to me by my own father, and it is now my gift to you. And you may also have this."

Reaching down, he unfastened the wide belt that girthed his tunic, unhooking the jeweled sword and matching dagger. Those he retained, setting the dagger on a table and leaning the sword against the wall. The leather belt with its wide gold buckle, he offered to Rylan. It was heavy, weighted with many iron rings from which different implements could be hung. Worn straps dangled from two of the rings, ready to affix to his sword's suspension. The belt looked old, although the leather was still supple.

"This was your father's war belt," Sayeed said.

Rylan stared down at the belt with a cold and ominous feeling. He bowed slightly, in a crude facsimile of the way he had seen the palace servants defer to Sayeed. "You have my thanks, Your Majesty. These are fine gifts."

The Sultan put his hand up. "Stop," he said firmly. "Do not call me 'Your Majesty.' You are family now."

An acute feeling of humility made Rylan bow his head. His eyes darted to the gilt poker leaning against the tiles of the hearth. Then he looked down at the sword and belt in his hands and swallowed heavily. Not for the first time in his adult life, he felt a profound sense of shame.

"Thank you... Sayeed," he whispered.

The Sultan reached out and firmly lifted Rylan's chin, forcing him to look him in the eyes. "Never lower your gaze," the man instructed. "Not to anyone."

Rylan nodded slowly. It was hard, keeping his eyes level when he felt so overwhelmed.

Sayeed smiled and clapped him on the shoulder. "Gird your weapon. There is an event we must attend together. I regret it will not be pleasant."

Rylan did as the man asked, wrapping the soft leather belt around his hips. It took him longer to buckle on the scabbard. "What's the event?"

The Sultan picked up his sheathed dagger and thrust it under the sash at his waist. "The execution of the guards who failed you."

12
___

THE ABSENCE OF SHADOW

GIL SAT WITH HIS ELBOWS ON THE TABLE, BLOND HAIR CLUTCHED in his fists, bent over a cloth-bound text that smelled of lamp oil and decades of dust. His eyes waded blearily across a relentless sea of words. The text was an essay on early Aeridorian languages. He flipped a tattered page and continued reading, tracking the motion of his gaze with his finger.

Until the book slid out from beneath him. A bowl of something hot slid in from his left, taking the book's place. Gil flinched as the smell of curry hit him square in the face. Across the table, Ashra cast herself down in a chair and leaned forward with her arms folded in front of her.

Gil glanced down at the bowl, then back up at Ashra. "What's this?"

"It's called food."

Gil blinked. The smell of the curry made his mouth water. His eyes narrowed suspiciously. "Why are you bringing me food?"

She smiled slyly. "It's called bribery."

"And why are you trying to bribe me?" A piece of flatbread

lay across the top of the bowl. Gil's hand slid toward it. He had to stop himself. He looked back up at Ashra and stared at her hard, waiting for a response.

The woman unfolded her arms and sat back in her seat. "Because you've been my mentor for nearly a week, and I've yet to learn one damn thing from you."

That wasn't quite true. Nevertheless, it was no reason to abstain from eating. With a grunt, Gil tore off a piece of flatbread and used it to shovel a bite of curried eggplant into his face. He hadn't swallowed the first mouthful before following it up with a second, wiping his mouth with his sleeve.

Still chewing, he remarked, "Well, this is the first time you've brought me food."

He hadn't realized how hungry he was. He'd unintentionally skipped both breakfast and lunch. The curry was delicious, but spicy. His gaze roamed the table, looking for something to drink. He didn't see anything. Either accidently or on purpose, Ashra had forgotten a very necessary part of the meal.

"So, what do you want to learn from me?" he asked, scooping another bite into his mouth.

"I want you to teach me how to be a battlemage."

He almost choked. Gil paused with a piece of flatbread halfway to his mouth, his face frozen in a look of disbelief. "What?"

Ashra regarded him with a snide expression. "I want to be a battlemage. Why else do you think I asked for you to be my mentor?"

"You... *asked*...?" The bread in Gil's hand sank slowly to the table.

"The Prime Warden didn't tell you?"

He shook his head, struggling to recall his conversation with Naia in her office. He was quite sure the woman hadn't mentioned anything about it. He admitted, "I just assumed it was her idea."

"Never assume." Ashra reached across the table and plucked a piece of eggplant out of his bowl. She popped it into her mouth, then sucked her fingers clean with a wicked grin.

Gil stared at her for a long moment in silence, waiting for his brain to catch up with the conversation. He took another bite of curry, then stared deeply into the depths of the bowl as he chewed. The spices made his brow break out in a sweat. It had to be the spices.

Taking another bite, he said, "I don't understand. You're Malikari. Your father is the Sultan. Why in the world would you want to become a battlemage?" The charter of his Order was to defend the land and its people. But Ashra came from a family of invaders, a people foreign to the land they had ravaged and conquered. He lifted his gaze, studying her face intently. The look in her eyes hardened. There was a lot of anger there, he observed. And something else as well. Was that hurt?

"This land is my home too," she said tightly. "And I want to spend my life serving it."

Gil fought the urge not to chortle. "Well, that's just bloody brilliant," he remarked, making a broad gesture with the bread. "So your father butchers half the continent, and now you just—"

Ashra raised her hand, looking furious. "*Stop,*" she commanded, her eyes scalding pools of resentment. "Are you going to teach me? Or not? Because if not, let me know, and I'll ask for someone else."

The curry was almost gone. There really hadn't been all that much there to begin with, Gil realized with a feeling of disappointment. He scraped the bread along the bottom of the bowl, chasing around the last few bits of eggplant. When they refused to cooperate, he abandoned his manners and used his fingers.

"If I have a choice about it, then I'd rather not," he said, sitting back and savoring his last bite. He doubted ridding himself of Ashra would be that easy. Regardless of who had come up with the idea, the Prime Warden had seemed very insistent that they work together. Gil couldn't think of a time when he'd ever seen Naia back down from anything.

Ashra stared at him for a moment with dead-cold eyes. Slowly, she slid out of her chair. "Then thank you for your time, Grand Master Archer," she said. She pushed her chair in with a scraping noise and started walking away.

"Wait," Gil called after her.

Ashra halted and turned back. She said nothing, just stood staring at him with a molten-lead gaze.

"Why me?" Gil asked. He was genuinely curious.

Ashra walked back to the table. She leaned forward, planting both hands on the table's surface. Staring at him hard, she said, "I told you. I want to serve this land and its people. I thought the best way to start would be to begin repairing the damage caused by our fathers. That's why I asked for you. If you and I can't learn to live with each other, then what hope do our nations have?"

Gil met her gaze and held it, looking deeply into her eyes as he considered her words carefully. Perhaps she had something, there. The war had to end at some point, and that would require reconciliation on both sides. He sucked in a cheek.

"Meet me down in the courtyard an hour before sunset," he decided, pushing back his bowl. "Bring your shadow with you."

Ashra stared at him a moment longer before a slight smile curled her lips. "It doesn't detach."

Gil returned her smile. "It will if I want it to."

Rylan squinted as he strode beside the Sultan into the glaring sunlight of the Inner Court. To his right marched an arcaded walkway that ran along the wing that enclosed the palace kitchens, evidenced by dozens of stone chimneys that protruded from the rooftops in long rows. Smoke rolled out of several of the stacks, scenting the air with smells of roasting meat and pastries.

The courtyard was full of people, all motionless. They stood in clusters beneath an oak tree of enormous girth that grew in the middle of the garden, just to the right of a three-tiered fountain. Beneath the tree was a square block made of solid marble approached by a footpath. Many men were gathered around the block to either side, heads bowed, hands clasped in front of them. Not a soul moved or uttered a sound. Only the trickling patter of the fountain disturbed the silence.

It took Rylan a moment to realize what he was looking at. He glanced at the marble slab, at last recognizing it for what it was: a headsman's block. The enormous man standing shirtless beside the tree, looming head and shoulders above the others, had to be the executioner. The eight men who formed a line along the court's brick wall were the guards who had attempted to save him from the woman's assault. They stood at attention, their faces stern but calm. They did not appear to be bound.

It was a harrowing scene, one far more disturbing than Rylan had anticipated. As their party drew to a halt under the oak tree, a shiver ran through him, making his skin crawl. It was all so eerie. The unnatural silence magnified the tension in the air a thousand-fold. A breeze came up, stirring the leaves of the tree with a rushing noise that would have gone unnoticed in any other context. Here, within the iron-clad grip of stillness, the sound of the rustling leaves took a nerve-grating toll.

Rylan looked down the line of guards waiting to be executed. The lack of terror—or even concern—on their faces was chilling to behold. His eyes shifted to the enormous, muscular body of the headsman, then down to the white marble block that shimmered in the sunlight. He glanced sideways at the Sultan.

"I don't understand," he whispered under his breath. "Your men did everything they could to protect me. So why are they being executed?"

Sayeed stood for a moment in silence. Rylan could tell from the man's frown of disapproval that he had probably committed a breach of etiquette by voicing his question. Looking around, he saw that every man in the courtyard was staring at him.

Very softly and firmly, Sayeed answered, "Our ways are not like your own. For this magnitude of failure, these men have suffered great shame and loss of honor. By facing their deaths with courage, they are absolved of disgrace and have their honor restored to them."

Rylan looked from one bearded face to the next in the long line of condemned men. He felt his stomach tighten, a knot of disgust forming in his throat. His eyes went back to the pockmarked surface of the headsman's block. "That's barbaric."

The Sultan shrugged. Leaning closer, he said softly, "To some. To others, anything less would be considered barbaric."

Which was an argument Rylan couldn't understand. His mind was still wrestling with the logic of it as one of the men standing beneath the tree stepped forward. Raising his voice, he announced:

"The executioner is ready, if His Majesty permits."

The pronouncement rang off the walls of the court, echoing vastly through the silence. There was a long pause. Then, ever so slightly, the Sultan inclined his head. The man bowed and stepped back, nodding to the headsman.

The executioner bent to unwrap a sword that lay upon the grass at his feet. When he lifted it, Rylan saw that the blade was larger than any sword he'd ever seen: six inches wide and wickedly curved, nearly as long as he was tall. As the burly man hefted the weapon, the first of the condemned guards started forward, moving on his own toward the marble block without any prompting.

Rylan stared, aghast, as the man knelt and bent forward over the block, moving his hair aside and baring his neck for the headsman. No one came forward to hold him down; the man had come willingly. The executioner moved to stand over him, positioning the blade of the wicked sword across the condemned man's neck.

Rylan's stomach tightened. He squeezed his hands into fists, looking away. "Stop," he whispered hoarsely. "Don't do this."

The Sultan's frown deepened. "Your interference brings dishonor to these men," he said in a tone weighted by disapproval.

Rylan looked back at the spectacle of the headsman, feeling dizzy. "You've a sick sense of honor," he growled. He took one last glance around the courtyard. Then disgust got the better of him. "They're your men," he said finally. "You can do what you like. But I won't have any part in it."

Aware that every face was staring at him, Rylan wheeled and stormed away, his footsteps ringing jarringly through the tension. He made his way across the courtyard to the doors of the palace. When he reached them, four black-armored guards stepped in front of him and barred his way.

Whirling, he saw that the Sultan and his retinue had followed him. Rylan crossed his arms and stood his ground, waiting for the man to approach. His anger burned hot. He had no desire to speak to the man.

Sayeed raised his hand, and the men following him halted. He stood looking at Rylan a long minute, then slowly approached, drawing up in front of him. His hand rested on the hooked pommel of the sword at his side.

Rylan indicated the guards behind him with his thumb. "You said I could come and go as I please. Was that a lie?"

The Sultan shook his head. "No. It was not a lie."

Rylan nodded, though the words did little to temper his anger. "Then let me go. I'm going to go find my daughter."

There was a long pause as the Sultan seemed to weigh his request. At last he breathed a sigh, nodding as if defeated. "Out of respect to you, I will spare the lives of the guards," he said. "They are now your men to command. If you decide to leave, I ask that you take them with you for your protection. However, it is my hope that you will decide to remain."

As he spoke, Rylan felt the anger leeching out of him. He hadn't expected the Sultan to say that. Sayeed did not seem like a man who backed down easily. Part of him still wanted to leave, to storm out of the castle, find a horse, and ride out in search of his daughter. But he had no idea where to begin looking for her. The Sultan was right; Sayeed's men were the best chance he had of finding Amina. No matter how much he hated it, he needed to remain where he was and wait for them to report back. Maybe, then, he would have at least some idea of where to begin his own search.

He licked his dry lips. Then he relented. "Thank you, Your Majesty. I'll think on it."

"That is all I can ask," the Sultan replied, and waved the guards aside.

Rylan entered the palace alone, his irritation coolly simmering. Every time he found another reason to hate the Sultan, the man did something that dismissed that reason. Like the guards—he understood that the ways of the Malikari people were different from his own, but that didn't mean he had to agree with them. Not only did Sayeed understand his position, but he had been willing to concede his own customs. He was certain the Sultan had lost face, changing his mind in front of those who served him. It was a gesture Rylan would have never expected and did not take lightly.

By the time he arrived at his own quarters, his anger had

waned entirely. He cast himself down in a chair and ran his hands through his hair. Looking up, he caught a glance of his reflection in the mirror. For just an instant, it wasn't his own image he saw there staring back at him. Instead, he caught a glimpse of the terrible man from the portrait in the throne room.

He knew it was only in his mind. Nevertheless, what he saw terrified him.

Gil looked up into the sky and saw the face of the sun slip behind a cloud. Immediately, the Lyceum's courtyard darkened, the air cooling ever so slightly. A breath of air ruffled his hair, smelling slightly of chrysanthemums. It was only a few seconds before the sun came back out again, and sunlight returned to warm his skin. On the ground at his feet, his shadow reappeared and stretched before him.

Gil smiled and, closing his eyes, reached out from within. He caught hold of the magic field's rhythmic pulse, drawing it in until it swelled like a symphony in his head. When he thought he had enough, he drew in more. And more.

Like a spider, he began spinning a web, casting out a net of magical tendrils that hung suspended in the air, surrounding him. He couldn't see his threads; they were invisible. He added more silken energy to the web, layer upon layer, until it enveloped him like a cocoon. Then he tied it off, leaving it there in place. He stared down at the ground, satisfied. His shadow had disappeared.

From across the courtyard, he heard the sound of approaching footsteps.

It was Ashra. She crossed the yard in his direction, her black cloak fluttering over an expensive-looking red dress. He watched her approach. Her eyes scanned the courtyard, no doubt looking for him. The shadow web must be working; she didn't see him. Just when she was almost upon him, Gil stepped forward into her path. Ashra ran right into him and sprang back with a startled cry.

He let the web of energy slip and, smirking, reached out to steady her. Seeing him, Ashra's face tightened into lines of anger. But the expression lasted only a moment. Regaining her composure, she crossed her arms and glared at him haughtily. "How did you do that?"

"It's called a shadow web," Gil answered. There was something about frightening her that was unexpectedly rewarding.

"How does it work?"

Gil nodded at the ground at Ashra's feet. "Look down at your shadow. Why's it there? What's making it?"

The sun was sinking low in the sky, making her shadow look thin and stretched. Ashra stared down at it for a moment, then looked back up at him blandly. "My body is blocking the sunlight."

"So, if your body is blocking the sunlight, then why isn't your shadow completely black? How can you see the ground at all?"

Ashra gestured around them. "Because other light is reflecting off everything around us. All the light isn't blocked, just what's coming in from directly behind me."

"That's right." Gil smiled. "There's light reflecting off everything around us. You can see me because there's light reflecting off me. But you can't see what's behind me because I'm blocking that light. A shadow web takes advantage of that. It absorbs the light reflecting off me, so you can't see me. At the same time, it's bending light around me, so you're seeing what's behind me. As if I were invisible."

She looked at him steadily, her eyes slowly widening in

understanding. "So a shadow web's really not made of shadow."

That wasn't entirely accurate. Gil frowned, pondering the topic. "Well, it is, but maybe not in the way you're thinking of it. All right, then. Let's try separating you from your own shadow. Hold my hand."

Ashra didn't hesitate before taking his hand. That was an improvement, at least. He stared down at her slender fingers wrapped around his own, wondering if there was a chance they could ever set their differences aside. Gil bit his lip, dismissing the thought.

He pointed at the ground. "Look down at your shadow. Don't look away."

He closed his eyes, once again reaching out to draw on the magic field. He started pulling it in, preparing to weave another web of energy more extensive than the first, one that would extend to encompass them both. He tugged harder at the field, knowing he'd need even more this time.

"You made my shadow disappear," Ashra said, sounding excited.

But he hadn't. He hadn't started weaving the shadow web yet.

Gil opened his eyes and looked down at the ground. She was right; her shadow wasn't there. It had been swallowed by another shadow, this one big enough to consume the entire courtyard. The sun must have ducked behind another cloud.

"That's not me," he said, then glanced up.

The sky overhead was choked with clouds that churned and darkened, tumbling toward the horizons. Strange lights strobed deep within their depths like many-colored balls of lightning. Gil dropped Ashra's hand, his jaw going slack. The courtyard chilled rapidly, and a gust of wind came up, whipping his cloak. In a span of seconds, a sunny afternoon had decayed into an unnerving, chaotic night.

Lightning flickered overhead, followed by a great rumble of thunder that shook his chest.

"What's happening?" Ashra asked. "Is that your doing?"

"No." Gil took a step back. And another. The sound of a tolling bell sent his thoughts racing again along with his pulse.

"Come on!" he shouted at Ashra over the rising wind. Taking her hand, he tugged her forward.

13

BESIEGED

RYLAN RAISED HIS HEAD AT THE TOLLING OF DISTANT BELLS. AT first he dismissed the sounds as just another constant noise in a city full of noises. But the bells continued, clamoring, until they caught and held his attention. Only then did he recognize them for what they were: warning bells—some kind of an alarm.

Rylan scrambled from his chair and strode to the balcony. Looking out across the palace courtyard, he saw that the sky had grown dark and brooding, the air chilled to a winterish cold. The sounds of the tolling bells came from every direction all over the city: some nearer, others farther away. Regardless, they all rang with frantic urgency. Shouts and screams rose into the air, vying for dominance with the clamor of the bells. Overhead, the dark skies rumbled with rolling thunder.

Rylan's pulse kicked up. He'd been a soldier too long to ignore the signs of impending threat. Turning, he left the balcony and crossed his chamber to the door to the hallway. The corridor outside was a chaotic turmoil of guards and servants rushing every which direction. Fighting his way upstream through the confusion, Rylan pushed toward the audience hall, his retinue of guards streaming behind him. One of his men dodged past him and walked ahead, clearing a path for him.

He found the audience hall full of people clustered together in tight nodes on the floor, nodding and gesturing as if in intense discussion. And yet, no words passed their lips. Instead, their hands moved rapidly in a kind of sign language. The Sultan sat on his throne taking reports from men who knelt before him, speaking calmly, their voices unhurried. When one man rose from the floor and backed away, the next man knelt to take his place. For a command center—for indeed that's what the Sultan's throne room had become—the large chamber was uncannily quiet and calm.

Noticing Rylan lingering in the doorway, Sayeed beckoned him forward, motioning for him to take a place beside the throne. Rylan did as he bid, lowering himself down to sit cross-legged upon a rug. The Sultan paid him no further mind, but sat listening attentively to an officer giving a quiet report that mentioned deployments and numbers far beyond Rylan's experience of a battlefield.

When the man was done speaking, Sayeed growled, "I want to know how an army that size crossed our borders and arrived at our walls without anyone noticing. How is that possible?"

Keeping his eyes lowered, the officer replied, "They came from out of nowhere, Your Majesty. They appeared from out of the air."

The bottomless scowl on the Sultan's face mirrored Rylan's own feelings. The report was absurd. If an entire army truly had arrived within sight of the city walls undetected, then the explanation was obvious: the Sultan's commanders had been entirely derelict in their duties. He wondered which Kingdom's army had managed the feat. Whichever it was, he applauded their general.

"Eighty thousand men do not just appear out of the air," the Sultan snapped. "What insignias are they flying?"

"None that are recognized, Your Majesty. This is not an enemy we have seen before."

The Sultan appeared to consider the man's words. At last he leaned forward, his fists planted on his thighs. *"Dismissed."* As the officer rose and backed away, Sayeed beckoned another man forward with a jerk of his head.

"Saddle my horse and ready my Zakai," he ordered. "I will go to see this threat with my own eyes."

"At once, Your Majesty."

Another man started forward, forestalled by the Sultan's raised hand. Sayeed looked down at Rylan. "It would seem the threats to your own life have presaged a far greater threat to us all. Do you know anything of this army that has arrived before my walls?"

Rylan looked at him and shook his head. "I don't."

The Sultan rose from his throne, straightening his brocaded tunic. "I'm going to the Lion's Gate. You may accompany me, if you desire; or not. It is up to you."

Rylan rose, uncertain what to do. He felt conflicted. If it was an army of the Kingdoms that threatened Karikesh, then his place was rightfully down there with his own people. He considered remaining behind, not wanting his loyalties challenged more than they already were. But in the end, curiosity got the better of him. He wanted to see for himself this army of eighty thousand men that had eluded detection by posted sentries—even peasants living on outlying farms. And which kingdom had fielded an army of that size, something he'd never seen in his lifetime.

"I'll come with you," he decided.

He fell in at the Sultan's side as Sayeed started toward the door. Guards and advisors rushed forward to accompany them, and they were immediately surrounded by a ring of officers in ceremonial dress, with more guards pouring ahead of them to clear the hallways. Their procession wound through the long corridors of the Sultan's palace and exited into an afternoon covered by premature darkness. They stood in the courtyard, whipped by scolding gusts, and waited for their horses to be brought up.

Within minutes, a large party of mounted soldiers arrived in a flurry of tassels and jingling tack. One of the men led a dark stallion toward Rylan and held the reins for him to mount. The spirited animal crabstepped and tossed its head with a snort, as if resentful of being ridden. They waited only long enough for the Sultan to mount before making their way to the gate. From there, their party progressed through the palace's nested series of ever-enlarging courtyards until finally leaving the protection of the high outer wall and gaining the city streets.

They emerged from the palace grounds into a chaotic scene of turmoil. The streets of Karikesh roiled with confusion and panic. Shopkeepers rushed to board up their storefronts, while street merchants worked to pile their wares into the backs of carts. Citizens fled wildly through the streets, the city guard struggling to keep order. Soldiers in formal uniforms walked ahead of their party crying, "Clear the streets! Clear the streets in the name of the Sultan!"

Black, brooding clouds hung low overhead, swallowing the daylight. Beneath them, the wind howled as it tore through the city. The panic of the citizens could be heard even above the shrieking gusts. The lantern-bearers that accompanied their party struggled against the wind to light the path ahead, the flames of their oil lamps whipped by gusts that evaded even the protection of their lanterns' colored glass panes.

They crossed a stone bridge over a wide canal into the northern side of the city. Their party continued on, winding through exceptionally narrow streets that seemed almost like tunnels bored between the high walls of residences, often covered by awnings and woven screens. Night had settled firmly over the city, even though it should have been late afternoon, and the walls around them blocked out what little ambient light there was. Without the lantern-bearers, Rylan didn't think he would have been able to see the street ahead.

After some minutes, they arrived at the Lions Gate, a tall arch warded by two broad watchtowers. The gate itself was closed and braced by enormous wood beams set at angles against it. The square in front of the gate swarmed with people: a chaotic mixture of soldiers and fearful civilians.

Guards swept forward to drive the crowd back as their party dismounted at the foot of one of the watchtowers. Rylan handed his reins to a soldier, then made his way to the Sultan's side. Sayeed placed a hand on his back and guided him forward, walking within their circle of guards into the tower. There, they took a spiraling staircase up to the battlements, where they exited to a dark and hellish view.

A strong gust seized Rylan's hair the moment he stepped out of the protection of the tower's walls and onto the crenelated roof. The air was fiercely cold, stinging his cheeks and biting his fingers. It brought with it the smell of heated oil and pitch, scents he was familiar with from his years at the front. They provoked an instant response in him, quickening his pulse and tightening his stomach.

At the sight of the Sultan, the soldiers stationed on the tower stopped all activity and inclined their heads. Sayeed ignored them, hands planted on his hips, surveying the scene. No man dared look at him, and he let them wait long seconds before acknowledging them with a nod.

The soldiers returned to their stations, while their commanding officer rose and walked forward, bowing low. "Your Majesty, a large force numbering roughly eighty thousand appeared before our gates. Their standards and insignias are unknown to us. We are uncertain of their intentions."

To Rylan, one glance over the battlements made their intentions obvious. Whatever host was down there, they were well-armed and well-armored. Their numbers stretched westward in organized units along the north wall, starting at the Lion's Gate. Rylan glanced at the Sultan and saw Sayeed's gaze roving over the host below, coolly considering. His fingers tapped absently on the jeweled pommel of the sword at his side.

"What is this?" he said.

Rylan turned his attention back to the field, where the ranks of the besieging army had parted to admit a lone man on a gray destrier. The horse moved at a lumbering walk, head down as if exhausted. Its rider was armored in field plate, his helmet shaped like a wolf's head and adorned with a long horsetail plume. In his right hand, he clutched a feathered spear, and a leather-skinned kite shield hung on his left arm. He drew his horse up just out of bowshot of the walls, well out ahead of his army, and simply waited, the wind whipping his cloak and his horse's long mane.

The Sultan's eyes narrowed as he stared down at the lone warrior below. Scowling, he ordered his commanding officer, "Send an emissary. Find out who they are and why they are here."

"Yes, Your Majesty!" The officer turned immediately and made haste to convey the order.

Rylan moved forward to a crenel and stared down at the scene, a shivering chill passing over him. He was only vaguely aware of Sayeed coming to stand at his side, hands resting on the stone of the parapet. Overhead, mounted behind them on the tower, a trebuchet creaked as its attendant crew labored to raise the counterweight.

"Do you have any idea what force this is?" Sayeed asked, just loud enough for Rylan to hear him over the wind.

"No." He shook his head, staring down at the lone rider's cloak billowing in the gale. The cloak, combined with the wolf's-head helmet, made the warrior seem fearsome and otherworldly, like a bestial spirit lured out of the wilds. The emissary sent by Sayeed's commander rode out of the lee of the wall on a black horse and made his way across the plain.

"Your Majesty," called a voice from behind them.

Rylan turned to see a group of five mages emerge from the tower's stairwell. He recognized one of them: Grand Master Quinlan Reis. None of the mages offered deference to the Sultan. Rylan wondered at that. Was the status of a mage truly equal to a ruling monarch?

"Warden Reis," Sayeed said in acknowledgement. Turning to a gray-haired mage with deep pox scars on his face, he nodded formally. "Warden Dalton."

Glancing at Rylan, Quin offered a brief smile. "It's good to see you alive," he said to him. "Now try to remain that way." He walked to the embrasure and stared down at the plain below, frowning deeply. "Were you expecting company?"

The Sultan scowled, looking deeply troubled. "No. We have no idea who they are."

"Neither do I," Quin said. He tilted his head back, holding his hat on his head as he stared up at the thick blanket of cloud cover darkening the skies. "Whoever they are, they didn't come unprepared. They brought their own mages with them."

Below, the Sultan's emissary wheeled his horse around and galloped back toward the Lion's Gate. The enemy warrior rode back in the direction he had come, quickly swallowed by the sprawling ranks of his own army. It was long minutes before the Sultan's envoy emerged from the tower steps to kneel at Sayeed's feet.

"Your Majesty," the man said in a breathless voice, addressing the Sultan from his knees. "They call themselves the Turan Khar. I had discourse with a man who claims to speak with the mouth of their Warlord. They demand our unconditional surrender and the delivery of all mages in the city into their custody. They threaten the subjugation of our populace if we fail to comply with their demands within the hour."

The Sultan bared his teeth, his eyes glinting with ire. "Let them try. They will shatter against our walls." Moving forward, he spat through the opening between merlons. The glob of spittle was quickly seized by a gale and flung backward, landing on one of the officers behind him.

"The Turan Khar?" Quin echoed over the wind, scratching the unshaven stubble on his cheek.

Rylan found himself fingering the curved pommel of the sword Sayeed had given him as he gazed down at the enemy ranks gathered below on the plain. If they had no knowledge of the foe they faced, it would be difficult to estimate their capability. More than anything, it was the thick blanket of cloud cover that brought him pause. How many mages would it take to darken the skies like that? And why would they go through the trouble?

He turned to the Grand Master, asking, "Their mages—can you counter them?"

Quin shrugged. "Perhaps. Perhaps not. It depends on how many there are, how strong they are, and what they're trained to."

The Sultan asked, "Do you know of these people—these Turan Khar?"

"No," the Grand Master replied. "But that doesn't mean anything. The older I get, the more I realize how little I actually know." He cast one last, grudging stare down at the army, then indicated the mages who had come with him. "I'm leaving you Warden Dalton and three of his battlemages to help ward the gate. I'm going to round up some more defenders." Clapping the Sultan on the arm, he turned and made his way toward the stairs, black coat billowing behind him.

They waited after that.

The unnatural night deepened and darkened around them,

the wind continuing its howling assault. Shivering, Rylan drew aside into the lee of a merlon, next to one of the mages who'd come with Quin. The man stood staring vaguely into the distance, hugging his black cloak tight against his body, his auburn hair whipping his face. Hugging himself for warmth, Rylan nodded a stiff greeting.

"What are you thinking?" he asked the mage, nodding his head to indicate the army below.

The man blinked as if waking. He ran his gaze over Rylan. "I'm thinking how much I hate the wind," he said guardedly. "Especially this wind."

Rylan agreed. There was something about the wind he didn't like either. It had a sharp edge to it that cut right through his shirt. "I don't like those clouds. They worry me."

"They worry me too," the young mage said. "Excuse me."

The man brushed past him and walked over to the far corner of the tower, taking up position there. He shot a nervous glance back over his shoulder before turning away again. The look in his eyes wasn't lost on Rylan. The man didn't like him. Perhaps he'd been warned about him. Rylan suspected few people would want to keep his company, once they found out his lineage.

Below on the plain, a low, throbbing pulse overcame the noise of the wind. Rylan leaned over the parapet to get a better view of the plain. At first, he couldn't make out where the noise was coming from. It took him a moment to realize the deep-throated rumble issued from rows of enormous drums positioned well behind the enemy lines. The throbbing cadence continued like a steady heartbeat, shaking his gut with every thunderous boom. Somehow, the minutes of waiting had grown into an hour, and he hadn't realized it. The top of the tower became a flurry of commotion as men took up positions along the battlements. Below, the drums maintained their slow, unremitting tempo, as if beating out a cadence only the gods could march to.

Until they stopped.

And the wind stopped with them.

A cold and eerie feeling curled up in the pit of Rylan's stomach. He glanced around at the other men on the watchtower, trying to gauge the situation by the looks in their eyes. What he saw frightened him. No one knew what to expect, that much was obvious. There was no trace of fear in the eyes of the officers, but there was enough concern to make his insides grow chill. He waited, watching, as the quiet dragged on for tedious minutes. The longer it lasted, the more unsettling it became. He could feel the tension in the air stretching thinner and thinner, his nerves stretching with it. His pulse throbbed in his ears, growing louder by the heartbeat.

A subtle change below caught his attention. The ranks of the army parted slightly. All along the plain, pairs of men and women were making their way forward, wading through the sea of bodies, emerging from the front lines and continuing forward a good distance. They halted just out of bowshot and formed a long, broken line that stretched the full length of the north wall. At their feet glowed a dim, gray-blue mist.

Rylan stared down at the pair nearest his own position, a man and a woman standing side-by-side. The woman wore garments little better than torn rags, her long, silvery hair hanging in matted snarls. She was young, probably still in her teens, and stood with one arm chained to the gray-skinned man who stood at her side. Both were staring up at the wall. For just a moment, Rylan felt as though their eyes met. But that was impossible; they were too far beneath him to make eye contact. He shivered, glancing sideways at Sayeed. The Sultan leaned with one arm braced against the stone of a merlon, the other hand stroking his beard. He frowned deeply as he surveyed the situation below, his eyes dark and troubled.

"Be ready," he warned his commanders.

The black-cloaked battlemages moved forward and took up positions at his sides.

"They look like slaves," one of the men observed. "Or prisoners."

The pox-scarred Warden shook his head. "That's magelight."

Rylan looked at the subtle, blue-gray mist beneath the feet of the pair standing beneath them. The light made them look ghostly. The woman's silver hair whipped about her shoulders, even in the absence of wind.

"Your Majesty," said one of Sayeed's men. "You should go down from here."

"Not yet." The Sultan peered over the edge of the wall, his eyes scanning the plain.

The long silence continued, stretching until it became unbearable. The air was still and frigid, making Rylan's breath fog before his face. Down below, the chained mages stood gazing up at the city walls, motionless, their magelight glowing softly in the darkness. The more Rylan stared at them, the more anxious he became.

A shout from behind made him flinch.

The mages beneath the walls were moving forward, lifting their hands as if holding something of great weight. Together, they tilted their heads back until they were staring straight up at the sky. Above, glimmers of red light streaked across the clouds, provoking loud crackles of thunder. More lights erupted within the cloudbank, strobing briefly like flickering torchlight. The air around them took on a strange, musty odor, like the smell of damp earth after a heavy rain. The lights in the clouds intensified overhead.

There was a sudden, crackling thunder. Then an enormous fireball erupted from the clouds and streaked over the walls with a deafening roar, trailing a crackling tail of flames and smoke behind it. It struck with force somewhere in the heart of the city, the violence of its impact trembling the ground and spewing great clouds of smoke into the sky that glowed orange against the surrounding darkness.

Screams rose from every direction as pandemonium broke loose. All along the walls, trebuchets launched flaming payloads into the attacking army. The long line of enemy mages stood their ground, chained arms raised to the sky. The clouds above flickered hellishly.

Another ball of fire shot down from the cloudbank with a thunderous roar, striking the watchtower just west of the Lion's Gate. The tower exploded in a shower of stones and men, taking a section of wall out with it. Enemy forces broke forward, spilling toward the breach, as another flaming projectile crackled through the air, striking another section of wall.

"Counter them!" the Sultan bellowed at their mages. Overhead, the trebuchet gave a creaking shriek as it loosed its payload upon the forces below.

The red-haired mage shook his head, his eyes wide and horrified. "I can't!" he shouted. "They're too powerful!"

Rylan glanced back at the Sultan, wondering what Sayeed was going to do. Another fiery projectile streaked down from the clouds, exploding somewhere behind the wall with such force that it shook the tower's foundations. Below, enemy soldiers swarmed through the breach.

"They'll be flanking our position," Rylan warned.

With a curse, the Sultan signaled his guards to retreat from the battlements and made haste toward the stairwell. Rylan moved after him, staggering as another roaring fireball impacted with the ground. The air was chokingly thick with smoke, the entire atmosphere glowing orange from the fires devouring the city. Rylan took the tower steps two at a time, following on the heels of the Sultan's party. When he reached the level of the street, he ran out of the tower and emerged into chaos. The horses they'd arrived on were gone. Groups of soldiers sprinted past them toward a melee that had overrun the square behind the Lion's Gate. There, the city's defenders were being cut down by the flood of enemy soldiers spilling over the rubble of the wall.

Drawing his sword, the Sultan started toward the thick of the fighting. But he went only a couple of steps before he drew up short. His sword sagged at his side, his shoulders slouching. He stared ahead at the slaughter, color and resolve draining from his face.

"This fight is lost," he said. He swung around to face his commander. "Order a retreat. We've lost this quarter. Withdraw to the far side of the canal!"

With one last, reproachful glare, he turned and hastened away from the flagging battle. Rylan bared his sword and, flanked by his personal guards, followed the Sultan's party as they dodged into a narrow alley. Shouts and screams jarred the night, the dance of flames casting torturous shadows on the high walls that surrounded them. Rylan followed them through an open gate and around a corner, the passage narrowing.

With a crackling rumble, a fireball streaked by low over-head, slamming into the street just a block away. Rylan was flung off his feet, his sword wrenched from his hand. The thunder of the impact rattled his brain and deafened is ears. He covered his head as fragments of buildings showered down around him. The ground trembled, and the night glowed a bloody orange.

When he dared look up, he found himself in a silent world covered in a thick layer of gray dust. He staggered to his feet, choking and sputtering, scanning the debris-littered alley for his sword. Coughing into his sleeve, he tried to shield his face from the swirling dust. He freed his sword from under a chunk of rubble, then bent to check on a man who lay unmoving at his feet. He retracted his hand quickly. The soldier was dead, part of his head caved in.

"The way ahead is blocked!" one of the Sultan's officers shouted. "We have to turn back!"

Rylan glanced back the way they had come and saw only the lights of fires.

Sayeed nodded, coughing as he stumbled forward, his face and hair painted gray with ash. Rylan waved his guards ahead, then started after the last man into a shattered alley. The path, barely wide enough for two men walking abreast, twined and twisted through a residential neighborhood. The walls of the houses were three stories high, completely cutting off the view of the rest of the city. Rylan had no idea how much of Karikesh remained standing and what had already fallen. The lights of the fires danced along the walls, smoke and dust thickening the air.

A warning shout stopped their progress.

The Sultan's men drew their swords and sprinted ahead to engage a group of enemy soldiers. Rylan started toward them but then stopped himself. Instead, he swung around and jogged back the way they had come, scanning the street behind them, making sure they hadn't been flanked. The sounds of the scuffle ended quickly. Glancing back, he saw only corpses lying in the alley where the fight had just been. The Sultan and his men were already sprinting, disappearing around a corner ahead.

Rylan started after them. But a silhouette jumped in front of him, blocking his path. The shadow stepped into the firelight, revealing features he recognized.

It was the woman who'd almost killed him.

The sight of her made him freeze, his insides chilling instantly. She took a step toward him. Gasping in shock, Rylan staggered backward, heart pounding. He scanned the alley, looking for an escape. The shadow of a doorway caught his eye, and he bolted past her toward it.

He managed only two steps before she leaped at him, knocking him to the ground. He tried rolling away from her, but she was too fast. The woman threw herself on top of him, sliding her arms under his body and clutching him tight. He bucked and squirmed beneath her, trying to fight her off.

The alley started fading. He screamed and struggled harder, but the more he fought, the more the world faded around him. Or maybe he was fading. Whichever; it didn't matter. The ground dissolved beneath him, and suddenly he was falling.

14

THE BATTLE OF KARIKESH

A BROAD STREAK OF FIRE HURLED ACROSS THE SKY LIKE A COMET, its tail a shimmering iridescence that was somehow oddly beautiful. It slammed into a nearby neighborhood with a horrendous explosion that jarred the earth and unleashed flames hundreds of feet into the air. Gil dove to the ground, summoning a shield to cover both Ashra and himself, to protect them from debris. A powerful wind raced over them toward the firestorm, feeding the flames and provoking them higher, until the unnatural night was chewed up and swallowed by their hellish glow.

Within moments, the inferno devolved into a billowing thunderhead of smoke. Gil dropped his shield and struggled to his feet. He stood gasping as an eerie silence gripped the neighborhood around them. For seconds, the silence held, its reign absolute.

And then the screams began.

Fleeing civilians spilled into the streets, their faces contorted with horror. Gripping Ashra's hand, Gil struggled against the current of frantic bodies hurling mindlessly past them. Shaken and jostled, he guided Ashra to the side of the street, where they used the protection of a building to help fight their way against the current of bodies.

Another thundering rumble shook the air. The ground beneath their feet convulsed, rattling Gil's insides. Ashra's grip on his hand tightened painfully. He willed his feet faster, dodging a stampede of fleeing civilians desperate to escape the bombardment.

A screaming woman ran past them with a bloody child in her arms. A man trailed behind her, carrying two more—one child in each arm. Gil shouted after them, but they'd already disappeared into the panicked crowd. He cursed.

Ahead, the sounds of battle rang through the quarter: bellowing shouts and the fierce clanging of weapons against armor. Within minutes, the tide of civilians stemmed, and the streets stood empty. Sounds rang hollowly off the walls of the buildings, and the air stank of smoke and blood. The sounds of the fighting grew louder. Up ahead, soldiers wearing the green and black uniforms of the city guard spilled into the streets, driven back by a vicious mob of leather-clad invaders who fought like devils. Gil stepped in front of Ashra and opened himself to the magic field, ready to strike. But there was nothing he could strike at. The fighting ahead was too chaotic, the participants too intermixed. He couldn't attack enemy soldiers without killing the men he was trying to save.

"Stay here!" he ordered Ashra and turned back toward the thick of the fighting. Drawing deeply on the magic field, he pulled in as much as he could handle, saturating himself until magical energies bled from his body, forming a glowing mist about him. Weaving a shield around himself, he strode into the melee.

A man clad in leather armor saw him and tried to drive a war hammer through his skull. Without thinking, Gil struck out with a blast of air, sending the man flying into the wall of a building across the street. Immediately, another soldier broke off from the fight and rushed toward him, swinging at him with his buckler. Gil dodged aside, hurling the man to the ground.

Seeing the color of his cloak, more men converged on him, picking him out as a high-value target. Gil drew power from the magic field and diverted the energy into the surrounding air. All around him, soldiers erupted in flames. Some dropped directly to the ground, rolling and thrashing. Others made it halfway across the street, lit up like blazing torches, before finally succumbing to the flames.

"Gil!" Ashra called from behind him.

He whirled around just in time to see a man coming at him with a sword. He lashed out with a razor-sharp gust of air, carving the man in half, both halves collapsing to the street. He looked up in shock, his eyes fixing on Ashra, as it occurred to him that she had just saved his life. He sprinted toward her.

"Come on!" he shouted, grabbing her arm. The street behind them was infested with enemy soldiers who were swiftly overwhelming the few defenders who remained. The command to retreat was raised, bellowed out over the chaos of screams and the crackling roar of flames. Clutching Ashra's hand, Gil led her toward an alleyway between courtyards, away from the thick of the fighting.

"Father!" she shouted, jerking her hand out of his grasp.

Gil looked up and found himself staring into the Sultan's bearded face. Sayeed's skin was blackened with soot and grime, his hair wet with sweat and plastered against his head. At the sight of his daughter, he strode toward Ashra and caught her up in a crushing embrace.

"I'm fine," she gasped as he squeezed her tighter. "I'm fine, Baba."

Sayeed released her and stepped back, glaring at Gil.

"What is she doing here?" he demanded. "We have lost this quarter!" When Gil opened his mouth to respond, the Sultan motioned him to silence. "Come with us!"

Clenching his daughter's hand, he started forward. "Let's go!" he shouted back to his men.

Swords bared, his guards started forward, falling in around them. They made their way down a narrow, cobbled street as burning embers drifted down around them like glowing snow. Smoke rolled over the city, saturating the air. Gil drew the fabric of his cloak over his face, but even that did little to cut the sting of the smoke in his throat.

True night had fallen by the time they reached the Canal Road. The sounds of fighting still rattled the air behind them, along with constant shouts and screams. They fought their way through crowds of civilians fleeing the North City, until they came to the bridges spanning the canal. With dismay, Gil saw that all of the bridges connecting the northern and southern halves of the city had become deadly bottlenecks. Hundreds of people clogged the bridge right in front of them, struggling to press forward. Others, forsaking the bridge entirely, were hurling themselves into the canal in an attempt to swim across.

Gil stood dry-mouthed, knowing that he was looking at a massacre waiting to happen. All it would take was one of those fire-bombs to kill every one of the hundreds of civilians struggling to cross the bridge. He glanced at Sayeed and saw his concerns mirrored in the eyes of the Sultan. He jogged over to him and gestured ahead at the milling turmoil.

"We can't get through that!" he shouted.

"We can," the Sultan insisted. He mopped the sweat from his brow with his scarf, then started winding the cloth around his head, pulling it across his face so that only his eyes showed. Which was smart, Gil figured. With this many people packed in so close, the last thing they needed was someone recognizing him.

"We'll go together," he announced, pulling his daughter close to him. He turned to his senior officer. "When we reach the other side, I charge you with guarding the crossing as long as you can." He turned to Gil and said, "Remain with them."

Astonished, Gil spread his hands. "What good do you think I can do?"

"Whatever good you *can* do," Sayeed snapped. "My men are too few, and we cannot hold all the approaches. We must stop them at the Waterfront. If we cannot, then the rest of the city will fall!"

For a moment, Gil could only look at him, too flabbergasted to respond. He was just one mage. What miracles did the Sultan believe he could accomplish? He glanced back at the fires raging in the quarter behind them. Dozens of streets emptied out of the neighborhoods onto the Promenade that ran the length of the canal, and their enemy would soon be spilling out of those streets to set upon them.

"Stop them?" he finally managed to echo, glancing from teeming intersection to teeming intersection.

The Sultan nodded, his stare penetrating. "Yes. Stop them."

Gil looked up and down the length of the canal. His stomach went sour as he realized that the only way to seal off the North City was to collapse the bridges leading out of it. A cold sweat broke out on his brow as he stared ahead at the crowded bridge that bore the weight of hundreds of civilians.

Reluctantly, he took a step toward the first bridge, wondering what it would take to bring it down. The bridge was made of a series of consecutive arches constructed of stone masonry, the roots of its thick pillars sunk deep into the bed of the canal. It wouldn't be enough to just collapse one of the arches. The engineers of the enemy would just shore it up again within hours. He would have to tear down all the arches and the pillars supporting them, all the way across.

"We could destroy the bridges," he said at last, although he really had no idea how.

The Sultan nodded. "Yes. That is the best way."

Feeling nauseous, Gil ran a hand through his sweat-damp-ened hair. "If I do that, then anyone left north of the canal will be trapped. They'll be as good as dead!"

The Sultan raised a heavy eyebrow. "Do you know of a better way?"

Gil scowled in frustration. "No. I don't."

Sayeed waved his hand, motioning his guards forward. "We will cross together. Once on the other side, I'll order my officers to station companies of bowmen along the Waterfront. That way, we can protect the crossing. You collapse the bridges. I will send my men with you."

With that, he gripped Ashra's arm and waded into the crowd of people waiting to cross the bridge. Gil moved to follow him, deferring to the guards who rushed ahead, wrestling a path through the crowd on the bridge. There were only about a dozen of them. And even though each one of Sayeed's men was worth ten soldiers of the Kingdoms, he doubted they'd be enough protection, should the enemy become serious about bringing them down.

It took half an hour to cross the bridge, which was packed so tight with people that forward motion was nearly impossi-ble. When they reached the other side, Gil followed the Sultan to a tree-lined walkway near the shore. With a curt gesture, Sayeed waved Gil forward and, nodding toward the bridge they had just crossed, growled, "Tear it down."

Gil stared at the bridge, wishing it was an order he could disobey. There were still thousands of people left north of the canal. But the Sultan was right; if they lost the Waterfront, they'd lose the entire city. Running his sleeve across his brow, he turned and started back the way they'd come, the Sultan's guards accompanying him.

He let the soldiers walk ahead of him as they made their way back against the current of civilians. Looking back across the water, he considered the congested stream of people moving onto the bridge. He turned to Sayeed's men and ordered them forward with a nod of his head.

"Clear the bridge!"

With grave expressions, the men jogged forward and, swords drawn, began pressing the throng of people back toward the center of the span, shouting and waving their weapons and, when that failed, beating people back. Gil waited until they had a small section of bridge cleared. Then he opened himself to the magic field and drew it in until he was full. He swept out with his hand.

A plume of flames erupted on the bridge and trailed ahead of the guards. Seeing the fire burning toward them, the crowd panicked and started pushing back the way they had come. Soon the entire bridge was empty and ablaze, waves of heat roiling the air above it.

Gil waited for the soldiers to return. Then, when he was sure the bridge was clear of people, he closed his eyes and filled himself with every drop of energy he could muster, until his head throbbed in pain. The air around him glowed with charged power, a halo of crackling energy. Concentrating as hard as he could, Gil reached deep inside the nearest pillar, all the way to its very core. He wrenched the pillar with his mind, twisting it violently on its foundation.

There was a terrible grinding sound, and then the pillar crumbled, raining stone into the water. Walking forward, Gil clenched his jaw and attacked the second pillar. Stone and concrete burst, and the arch gave, crumbling away. He sent his mind out to the next pillar, and then the next, collapsing one after another until the bridge was reduced to a dam of rubble clogging the bed of the canal.

Gil surveyed the devastation, licking his parched lips. His head throbbed more with every heartbeat. At last, he gave a grim nod. "Come on," he called to the soldiers. "There's four more just like it."

The soldiers stared at him with startled eyes, faces troubled. But they set out ahead of him, clearing a path.

The next bridge came down more easily, and the next was easier still. Instead of straining to wrest each pillar from its footings, all he had to do was locate the weakest joints and apply force. Inevitably, they gave. By the last bridge, the strain was starting to wear on him. His head throbbed terribly, a result of his overuse of magic.

When he had the Promenade sealed off, Gil swung around to observe the scene of desperation on the other side of the water. Caught between the water and an advancing army, the masses of panicked civilians had started flooding into the canal. He doubted many knew how to swim. Gil swore a curse, feeling physically ill. He stood there for a time, shoulders slumped, trembling in despair and weariness. He didn't look up until he heard the sound of footsteps approaching him from behind. A hand gripped his shoulder

"That will buy us time," the Sultan said, drawing up beside him. "We can only hope it will be enough."

Horrific screams traveled toward them over the water.

"Let's go." Sayeed motioned his men forward.

Ashra dropped back to walk at Gil's side. Her face was pale, her expression glassy. He took her by the arm and said reassuringly, "We'll make it through this. It's going to be fine."

She jerked her arm away and turned to glare at him in fury. "It is not going to be fine!" She motioned behind them. "Do you know how many people you just sentenced to death?"

Glancing back, he saw that much of the North City was on fire. The sight of the flames made his soul feel like rot. Around them, the Waterfront was strangely empty, with only scattered bodies telling the tale of the stampede that had passed through only moments before. A lone white dog trotted toward them but grew skittish at the smell of blood and fled. Gil looked to Sayeed, wondering what the Sultan's next command would be.

If it was up to him, he would order the city evacuated. But somehow, he doubted the man would concede so easily.

As they walked, an unnerving silence settled over the city. The glows of the fires faded, and darkness descended around them.

15

A CUP OF POISON

Rylan awoke in a cage.

Blinking groggily, he sat up and gazed around his prison. The cage was square, only slightly larger than he was tall, with thick iron bars on all sides. It sat in the middle of a long room with rock walls and a floor made of polished wood slats. The same slats made up a ceiling supported by many load-bearing posts. High up on the walls, small windows admitted only the wan glow of moonlight. Other than the cage and a few lanterns, the room was empty. It smelled overwhelmingly of lamp oil and green wood.

He sat on a thin straw pallet. There wasn't much in the cage with him; just a wood bucket for waste. Looking around at his strange and stark prison, Rylan couldn't help wondering where he'd been taken. And how he had gotten there.

He sat on the pallet, staring at the cage bars, and continued to wonder.

Minutes wore by.

Then hours.

The room was cold, and his silk shirt was too thin to keep the chill out. Shivering, Rylan curled up on the pallet, hugging himself for warmth, and waited for sleep to take him. It didn't. He was too cold, and his mind was too restless. Again and again, his son's image came to mind, and with it the relentless pangs of guilt and grief. He thought of his daughter. Was she in a similar cage somewhere? Was she even still alive? Imprisoned, he would never find her. He rubbed his eyes with a trembling hand and rolled over.

He started, flinching back.

A woman was kneeling on the floor, just outside his cage. He hadn't heard her enter. Rylan stood and clutched the iron bars. In the dim light, it took him a moment to recognize her. It was the same woman who had stabbed the Word of Command into his heart. She was wearing a pink silk robe patterned with flowers, curly brown hair spiraling past her shoulders. Her mouth was small, even dainty. So was the rest of her. Her eyes were the color of burnished copper. She sat silently observing him, fingering a stone pendant that hung from a gold chain around her neck.

Anger stirred deep within him. No matter how beautiful or exotic this woman was, she had almost killed him on two occasions. People she was associated with had murdered his son and stolen his daughter. She was his enemy. Far more so than any soldier he had ever confronted on the battlefield.

"What do you want?" Rylan growled.

The woman stared at him, unblinking. And unanswering. Her expression didn't change; it was as though she hadn't heard him. She was choosing to ignore him.

His rage smoldering, Rylan asked, "You're the one who tried to kill me. Aren't you?"

She continued to stare at him.

He gripped the bars tighter. "Aren't you?"

When she said nothing, his anger swelled.

"You are," he growled. "Why?"

No response.

"What's your name?"

Nothing.

"What is your name?"

Still nothing.

"Why won't you say anything?"

Snarling, he let go of the bars and spun away, turning his back on her. He paced away a few feet, wrestling with his anger. The anger won. He whirled back to her.

"Where's my daughter?"

No response.

"What have you done with her?"

Silence.

"Where is she?"

The woman didn't blink.

Rylan surged toward her, catching the cage bars and shaking them violently. He let out an enraged growl. "Why did you kill my son? What do you want from me? *Where is my daughter?*" Tears of frustration blurred his vision. "Speak, gods-damn you! *What do you want?*"

With a frustrated cry, he spun away and sat down on the pallet with his back to her, bringing his hands up to cover his face. He remained like that for minutes, hearing nothing but the sound of his own breathing. He focused on that noise, pinning his concentration on it until his heart slowed its furious pace.

He heard her footsteps walking away.

Then, moments later, the sound of the same footsteps returning.

Rylan drew in a long, frustrated breath, then stood and turned toward her. As he did, he noticed a bowl of rice pushed just inside the bars of his cage. He considered the woman, wondering what her intentions were.

"What do you want?"

She stared at him in silence.

Furious, Rylan kicked the bowl out of the cage, showering the floor with rice and shattering the bowl. "I don't want your damn food! *Bring me my daughter, you gods-fondling whore!*"

The woman stared at him a moment longer and then rose. Without a word, she stepped forward, bending to gather the broken bowl and the shards of ceramic that lay scattered across the floor. When she had collected all the fragments in her hand, she righted herself and walked out of the room, closing the door behind her. Rylan watched the woman exit with an acute sense of desperation. He had to get out of the cage. He had to find Amina.

He screamed his frustration at the door and shook the cage bars furiously. Neither helped to dispel his rage. He turned around and leaned with his back up against the bars, then slid slowly to the ground.

Another hour slid slowly by. Then another. Rylan lay on the mat, his mouth dry with thirst. He rolled over.

And found the woman staring at him.

She had returned and was kneeling on the floor outside his cage. Beside her sat a lacquered tray that held a steaming wooden cup. She removed the cup from the tray, setting it on the floor. With both hands, she pushed it toward him between the bars of his cage. Rylan slid over and scooped it up, raising the cup to his lips.

"It's poison."

He almost dropped the cup. Rylan lowered it from his mouth and stared down at the contents. The wooden cup was filled with a hot, clear liquid. He brought it up to his nose. There was no odor to it.

He frowned at the woman. "So, after all this, you're just going to poison me?"

It seemed unfathomable that she would have gone through the trouble of bringing him there and locking him in a cage just to serve him a cup of poison. He was about ready to throw it at her when she spoke again:

"It's been decided that you are too dangerous to let live. You will be put to death in the morning. Or you can drink the *chiri* and take your own life. Whichever you decide."

Rylan felt a hot wave of contempt wash over him. He thought again about dousing her with the poison, but he didn't want to limit his options. There were many ways to die. He shuddered, thinking of the agony the Word had inflicted on him. He didn't want to die that way.

Gazing into the cup, he asked, "What about my daughter? Are you going to poison her too?"

"We don't have your daughter."

His gaze snapped up to lock on hers. He stood there for a moment, searching her eyes deeply for confirmation she was lying. But the woman's face was stern and dispassionate. He couldn't tell whether or not she spoke the truth.

"If you don't have Amina, then who does?"

She clutched her hands together in front of her. "The Turan Khar."

Cold panic clenched his throat as he thought of the army assaulting Karikesh. "Who are they?"

"They are our enemy."

That made no sense. He frowned at the woman harder, wondering who her people were. Her skin was a creamy gold, soft and without blemish, her hair light brown, falling in tight spirals past her shoulders. She wasn't Rhenic or even Malikari. In fact, he had never seen anyone like her before.

"Why would they take my daughter?" he asked in frustration.

The woman shrugged. "They want you. It's likely they sought to lure you with your daughter."

He wanted to hit his head against the bars. "You've got to let me go," he whispered. "I've got to find her. Now that I know where to look for her—"

"No," the woman stated firmly. "Your fate has been decided. Drink the poison or wait to be executed. Whichever you prefer."

She turned and walked toward the door.

Rylan called after her, "Please! My daughter doesn't deserve this! I'm her only chance—you've got to let me go!"

The woman paused in her stride, glancing back over her shoulder at him with a look of sympathy. "I suggest you drink the *chiri,* Gerald Lauchlin," she said. Then she left, closing the door and leaving him standing there with the cup of poison in his hand.

———

Hours drug by.

He'd placed the cup in the corner of the cage near the door, protected by the bars. He didn't want to accidentally knock it over. He hadn't decided to drink it, but he hadn't decided not to. He sat staring at the cup, trying to use it as a focus to clear his thoughts. But it was just as much a poison to his mind as it was to his body. So instead, Rylan gave in to despair and let his thoughts wander where they liked, not caring how they savaged him. There was no point in fighting them any longer.

He sighed. The cup of poison was starting to look more and more like a viable option. At least he could slake his thirst. The one thing that stopped him from drinking it down was the knowledge that giving up on his own life would also be giving up on his daughter. He couldn't do that. So he lay down and closed his eyes.

———

When he awoke again, the bright light of morning glared red at him through his eyelids. He was lying on his side, his face pillowed on his outstretched arm. His head throbbed fiercely. Groggily, he sat up and turned toward the door.

And saw a dead rat lying on its side, inches away from the cup of poison.

Revolted, Rylan scrambled back against the bars. He stared hard at the dead rat. It must have drunk from the cup and died almost immediately, only steps away. He had never heard of poison that strong—strong enough to kill an animal in seconds. He wondered how long it would take the poison to work on him.

He sat on the pallet, staring at the rat. The morning was wearing on. He didn't have much time. His eyes went again to the wooden cup. He sat pondering it for a long while, wondering what manner of death they had in mind for him. Amina's face filled his thoughts. The image of the dead rat blurred and diminished in his mind.

He wouldn't drink the poison. He would fight these people until the moment his heart stopped beating. His daughter deserved no less. Miserable, he leaned with his back up against the cage bars, a knot of despair choking his throat.

He sat there for another hour. Perhaps two. Then the woman returned.

He looked up at her and asked, "What if I help you?"

The woman knelt on the floor just outside his cage, hands on her thighs. She was wearing a new mint-green robe. She stared at him without responding, her expression flat.

Feeling weak, Rylan pushed himself from the floor and stood gripping the bars. "You called me Gerald Lauchlin. That means you know who I am—who I *really* am. You brought me here for a reason. You must want me to help you. So what if I agree to help you?" Desperate, he shook his head, tears welling in his eyes. "Look. I just want to find my daughter. After that, you can do anything you want with me."

The woman lowered her eyes, a saddened expression on her face. For long seconds, she said nothing. Then, staring at the floor, she responded, "We brought you here hoping you would be different. But you are not different; you're just like your father. There is no hope for you." Her eyes met his. "You should have drunk the *chiri*. Now your death will not be painless."

She sounded regretful.

That surprised him. "Does killing me bother you?"

"Death walks hand and hand with life."

Rylan scowled; he was getting frustrated again. "Then you'll have to execute me. Because I'm not going to drink poison just to spare you getting your hands bloody." He struck out with his foot, kicking the wooden cup across the floor. It collided with the bars, spraying poison everywhere.

The woman flinched and brought her hands up to shield her face. She sprang to her feet and staggered back, looking unsettled for once. She cast him a long, disdainful glare. Then she turned and walked toward the door.

"Please!" he called after her. "Help me find my daughter! I give you my word—I'll come back and then you can kill me a thousand times! Please! I beg you! *She doesn't deserve this!*"

The woman kept walking. As she reached the door, cold despair kicked Rylan in the face.

"Amina's blood will be on your hands too!" he shouted after her.

The woman paused, one hand lingering on the doorframe. She glanced back at him.

Then she left.

This time, it was only minutes before she returned. And this time, the woman wasn't alone. Six men with swords entered the room with her, hands on the hilts of their weapons. Each man had closely shorn hair and white cotton robes that hung just past their knees. The woman stopped, but the men came forward, one holding the key to his prison.

"Move back," the guard commanded.

Rylan obeyed, edging back against the bars as the man unlocked his cage. The door swayed open with a groan, and four of the guards spilled inside. Before Rylan could react, they swung him around and pinned him against the bars. While three men held him, the other tied his hands behind his back and hobbled his legs with a rope. When they had him bound, the men jerked him around and shoved him forward, holding him up as he staggered between them. When they dragged him past the woman, she raised her hand, and the men holding Rylan halted.

"The Sensho has decided to look upon you," she informed him, gazing deeply into his face. For a long moment, her eyes searched his. Then, looking satisfied, she smiled. "Speak to the Sensho just as you spoke to me. Let him hear the love you bear for your daughter. If he deems you human, you will live. Otherwise, you will die."

Rylan slumped in relief. He still had a chance—which meant Amina had a chance. Whoever this Sensho was, he would promise the man anything he wanted. Anything. Whatever it was. Just so long as he could live to find his daughter.

That was all that mattered.

GIL TURNED AWAY FROM THE FIRES CONSUMING THE NORTH CITY, not wanting to look at them any longer. Across the canal, the Promenade was filling with soldiers of the Turan Khar. So far, they hadn't attempted to cross the water. But the respite wouldn't last forever. Soon, they would be coming. It was inevitable.

He strode back toward where the Sultan stood giving orders and taking reports from the score of officers standing around him. By their dark blue uniforms, they were Zakai, the upper echelon of the Malikari officer corps. Maneuvering through the crowd, Gil drew up at the Sultan's side, looking around the circle from one grim face to the next. It was who he didn't see that struck him.

"Where's Rylan?" he asked.

Sayeed glanced at him with weary eyes. "He is lost."

And that was that. No explanation. Blowing out a sigh, Gil ran a hand through his sweat-damp hair. There'd been enough casualties that night already. One more shouldn't matter. But for some reason it did. He couldn't tell if the emotion he felt was sorrow or relief. In the end, it didn't matter.

The Sultan told his officers, "Whatever it takes, we cannot let them cross the water. If they cross the canal, we will lose the Lower City. So we will draw our line here and hold the Waterfront, no matter the cost."

He turned to his second-in-command, a slender, gray-haired man in an elaborate uniform and a tall hat. "Erect barricades all along the Waterfront. Put every man you have along this line. Establish a command center in Murkaq Square and send criers through the city. Every man of fighting age should bring his arms and armor and join his brothers in this battle. Now go! See it done!"

The officers scattered to be about their duties, leaving Gil alone with the Sultan and his daughter. He turned and strode back toward the edge of the canal. A breeze came up, blowing sooty smoke across the water. The canal stretched broad and flat before him, its waters dark. Burning debris rode its currents, floating downstream toward the bay. To the north, fires still gnawed on the bones of the North City, casting an eerie orange glow against the low-hanging clouds that obscured the rising sun.

Not clouds, he reminded himself. Not natural clouds, at any rate.

At least the bombardment of streaking fireballs had stopped. Perhaps the Turan Khar were satisfied with capturing a large part of the city. More likely, they were just giving their mages a chance to rest before resuming their assault. Whichever, it was hard not knowing the nature of the enemy they fought or what their motivations were. Or, most importantly, their objective.

The wind rippling his cloak, Gil paced along the edge of the bank, watching the Sultan's men laboring to fortify their perimeter.

The morning wore painfully on.

The barricades grew in number and complexity, made of anything the soldiers could drag up to the Waterfront: overturned carriages, furniture, pieces of buildings; there was even a chicken coop and a dead horse piled up on one of the mounds. Gil hunkered down behind the gutted remains of a vendor's kiosk. There, a few of the Sultan's men had built a small fire, which felt good. The morning was frigid, and wisps of fog roved over the dark waters of the canal.

Quiet clung like a pall over the north side of the city, broken by the occasional nerve-chilling shriek. There was also a constant grating noise borne toward them by the wind. Gil had no idea what the sound was, but it was unsettling. He tugged his cloak around him and soon found himself nodding off.

A high-pitched screech startled him awake.

Jerking upright, Gil craned his neck and stared up into the clouds, his eyes wandering the overcast sky. A streak of motion caught his attention. He stood up, eyes tracking the small object gliding just below the clouds. At first he thought it was a bat. Only, bats didn't glide. The body of the creature was narrow and elongated, like that of a snake. It seemed to slither through the air. Another piercing shriek tensed his nerves.

His mind went immediately to the night they had left Farlow with Rylan. Some winged creature had tracked their progress from the sky, hidden in the fog. It had made a similar cry. Unnerved, he settled back down beside the fire and leaned his head against a barricade made of piled sacks of rice. He gazed up into the sky, his eyes following the creature as it criss-crossed the city in what looked like a search pattern. Perhaps it was surveilling. But that would mean it was capable of intelligent thought, which was an altogether worrisome idea.

Close to noon, Gil was startled by a shout from one of the soldiers nearby. He stood up and walked toward the edge of the canal. There, he caught sight of the body of a woman drifting by, face down, long, brown hair trailing behind. Repulsed, Gil jerked back away from the bank. But then his eyes fell on another body following the first downstream, turning slowly on the current. A few more corpses floated by. Then more. Within minutes, the waters of the Grand Canal were filled with floating human remains. Hundreds of people, murdered in the night. Dumped upstream into the canal. A warning?

No. The corpses were there to inflict terror.

The Sultan drew up beside Gil, his face frozen, his gaze moving slowly over the carnage delivered to them by the river. He stood there still for long minutes, his expression slowly hardening. At last he clenched a fist and held it up before him.

"They will pay," he growled softly. "By the gods, they will pay."

The slow procession of corpses continued as the day wore slowly on. Even after the sun had reached its zenith, the dead continue to float by: men and women alike. Children. The occasional dog.

And the afternoon brought new horrors. Across the water, thousands of enemy soldiers now milled along the bank, a writhing, disorderly mass. They carried every manner of weapon and wore a mix-matched array of armor, ranging from rags to leather to plate. It hardly seemed possible that they were part of one fighting force. He wondered if they were conscripts, dredged up from whatever far-off lands the Turan Khar had already conquered.

The sound of commotion caught Gil's attention. Across the water, a gap had opened in the mass of soldiers. Through that opening, prisoners were being led forward, struggling and screaming, perhaps a dozen in all. They were forced to their knees in a line, each with a soldier standing behind them with daggers bared. Gil wondered what kind of demands would be made for their lives.

There was a sharp, strangled cry as the first throat was slit.

Gil reached for the magic field, tugging it inside and holding it ready. But there was nothing he could do. The prisoners were beyond his range. He might be able to start a fire in their midst, but that would just kill the captives along with their assailants.

Another piteous cry, and another prisoner collapsed. A woman, this time. Gil swung away, swiping a fist out in anger. There was another nerve-shredding cry. And another. Soon all the hostages lay dead, sprawled in pools of blood. Their executioners wiped their blades clean on the backs of the people they had just murdered, then disappeared into the disorderly throng.

Minutes passed. And then the ranks of the crowd opened again. A pair of mages, a man and a woman, walked forward and stood over the remains of the dead prisoners. At their feet glowed a warm mist of magelight. They were linked together by a chain that was anchored to bands on their wrists. Even from a distance, Gil could sense the might of their combined power.

Just looking at them made him shiver. The woman had long white hair that reached to her waist. Because of her hair, at first he thought she was old. But then he realized her face was youthful, even beautiful, despite the gray pallor of her complexion. The man with her was young, with rich brown hair and golden skin. He was clothed in tattered robes made of filthy linen that looked pieced together.

For some reason, Gil thought both mages were staring at him. It was impossible to tell from that distance what the pair were actually looking at. Nevertheless, his skin prickled as he became more certain by the second that he was the object of their focus.

When the mages raised their arms, he knew they were about to strike.

Gil steadied himself, conjuring an absorption web about his body. They could still see him through it, and he them, but the web would take the brunt of any magical attack they decided to level at him. At the same time, he drew on the magic field and honed it into a weapon to attack: a two-prong spear of magic that would lance across the water and impale them both.

The pair stepped forward, lowered their arms, and peered at him intently.

Looking at them, Gil suddenly realized how beautiful they both were. He had never seen two more exquisitely made people in his life. There was a kindness to them, something tangible that he could sense even across the distance between them. A strong, enduring connection they shared with each other. They longed for others like them to include in that bond.

That's why they were looking at him, Gil realized. They wanted him to join their union. It was a lonely, achy kind of yearning, one that ignited in him a similar craving. He found himself longing for their company, wanting desperately to be with them. He knew that, beside them, he would never again know animosity or rejection. His life would be filled with the warmth of enduring love and unwavering acceptance. He would never again be alone.

He thought of how he had almost attacked them and felt instantly ashamed.

Immediately, Gil dropped his absorption web and let go of the magic field entirely. He gasped, frozen in the cold grip of dismay. Bringing a hand up to his brow, he wiped away a sheen of cold sweat. He felt flushed. Revolted. He was terrible. Despicable. There was only one thing important in the entire world, and that was protecting the two people across the water from him. He had to go to them. They needed him at their side.

He took a step toward the edge of the bank, ready to throw himself in.

And then he realized what he was doing.

"Get out of my mind!" he gasped.

He brought his hands up and clutched his head, struggling to rid himself of emotions that weren't his own, that had been placed there deliberately to sabotage his will. He grappled for command of his own mind, wrenching it back by brute force of will.

Drawing hard on the magic field, he lashed out at the two mages with all his might, striking out with a whip-crack of solid air that shot over the water, impacting with their bodies with the fury of a cyclone. The two mages were hurled backward into the crowd of soldiers behind them, mowing them down.

Instantly, Gil felt a terrible, crushing sense of guilt. He'd killed them. Two people who only desired his company, who had wanted to become his friends, perhaps even his family. Two people who would have loved him unconditionally, despite his flaws. He had murdered them....

"Are you trying to commit suicide, or are you just that stupid?"

Gil whirled to find himself staring into Quinlan Reis's face. He took a step back and stumbled, gasping in dismay as he realized where he stood. At the edge of the canal, ready to cast himself in and swim for the other side. His entire body was shaking. Aghast, he reached up and touched his face, shocked to find his cheeks wet with tears. He looked at Quin, shaking his head in confusion and shock.

"I'm just stupid," he whispered, fumbling to gather his wits about him. "They're in my mind."

The Grand Master frowned. "In your mind? How?"

"I don't know." Gil shook his head, grappling with his muddled thoughts. "But I damn near killed myself." He glanced back across the canal.

Quin led him away from the water's edge. He carried a mage's staff, a knotted piece of wood about his own height. His black coat was dusted with ash, his face smeared with grime. He walked Gil back toward the barricade the Sultan's men were still laboring to construct.

"Did you see what they did to those people?" Gil asked, his voice shaking.

Quin nodded. "I did. How an army treats its prisoners says a lot." He shook his head, biting his lip. "Expect no mercy from them. Now we know for certain that surrender is not an option."

"Surrender was never an option."

Gil turned at the sound of the Sultan's voice. Sayeed stepped between them and embraced Quin hard, clapping him on the back. He said, "We have made this city our home, and no army of man will take it from us."

Quin grimaced. "I have a feeling your resolve will be sorely tested before this is done." He lifted an eyebrow. "Do you happen to have anything to drink?"

"Come," the Sultan said to Quin.

Taking the Grand Master by the arm, he beckoned for Gil to follow. He led them back toward a tent, where he cast himself down on a rug next to Ashra, who sat leaning back against the rough wall of a building. Quin followed him to the ground, sitting cross-legged. Gil lingered on his feet, staring wearily back over his shoulder in the direction of the canal. His gaze roamed the long Promenade across the water. He wondered what had become of the mages he had attacked, if his strike had truly killed them. Part of him hoped they were dead. But another part of him hoped they weren't.

The Sultan lifted a water jug. Tilting his head back, he took thirsty gulps of the contents. He wiped his mouth on his sleeve, then handed the jug to Quin. The Grand Master took a few swallows from the container then, grimacing, handed it back.

"I need something much stronger than that to quench my thirst," he grumbled.

"If we survive this, I will treat you to all the liquor you can swallow," the Sultan replied. "Tell me, how fairs the Lyceum? Where do we stand?"

"The Lyceum hasn't been directly threatened," Quin assured him. "But we lost fourteen Battlemages in the night."

The Sultan grimaced, then muttered under his breath, "May the gods ease their souls." There was a heavy pause. Then he said, "I'm sorry, my friend, but I need you to deploy every mage you have left along the canal."

Quin reached up and scratched the whiskers on his face. He glanced along the length of the canal, his expression grim, then breathed a weary sigh. "Even stretched thin, I doubt we have enough mages to hold the Waterfront."

The Sultan shrugged. "Then give me what you have. It will have to suffice."

With that, the two men shook hands. Sayeed raised the water jug to his lips, taking a great gulp, then passed it to his daughter.

Ashra took a sip, her gaze traveling to Gil. "What happened?" she asked.

"Nothing," Gil said, not wanting to admit to the mental battle he was still wrestling with in his head. The fates of the mages he had attacked weighed heavily on him, and his thoughts kept sliding back to them. Balling his hand into a fist, he turned away.

"Bloody hell," he swore under his breath. Whatever they had done to his mind wasn't going away very quickly.

"What is that?" Quin said, rising to his feet, his attention captured on something across the bank. Moving past Gil, he strode out into the street through a gap in the barricades, walking to the edge of the canal.

Gil followed his gaze. Across the water, four women stood linking hands. Each had long white hair and ragged gowns just as gray as their skin. They stood along the edge of the canal as if waiting for a signal.

"Your Majesty," Quin called back over his shoulder. "Tell

your men it's time to earn their pay." He adjusted his hat, then started forward down the street.

"Warden!" Gil exclaimed, guessing his intentions.

Quin paused and turned back, cocking an eyebrow. "Do you have a better plan?"

Gil's mouth went dry when he saw the reckless glint in Quin's eyes. He licked his lips. "No," he admitted. "I don't."

17

SHACKLES OF IDENTITY

THEY EMERGED FROM THE BUILDING INTO A GRAY AND DREARY day. Rylan winced as a breeze full of chill moisture brushed his face. He stood on a balcony overlooking a wide valley covered in fog like a gray and frothy sea. The balcony clung to the side of a precipitous slope. The structure was connected by a wide suspension bridge to a building on an adjacent ridge, its planks painted green. Just looking at the gently swaying bridge made Rylan dizzy.

Most of the guards moved ahead of him onto the bridge, which was wide enough for two men to walk abreast. He stumbled, his stride compromised by the short rope that bound his legs. Thankfully, the bridge was much more stable than it appeared, swaying languorously beneath his feet. The planks were solid, the rope handrails fibrous and sturdy. Beneath them was only a choking sea of fog. Foliage-laden cliffs thrust upward from the mist, ringing the area like a wide bowl. Layers of buildings clung to the slopes, built on stilts that anchored them to the rocks, the structures connected to each other by protruding walkways and ambling flights of stairs.

A damp breeze came up, making Rylan shiver. Thankfully,

it wasn't strong enough to affect the rhythmic rocking of the bridge. He glanced back and saw the woman following behind, her robe rippling around her, her hair ruffled by the breeze.

They stepped off the bridge onto a walkway made of green planks. The motion of the guards' boots jarred the walkway, making it tremble beneath them. The span made him nervous —more nervous than the bridge had. There was no outside rail, nothing to prevent a tumble. Tree branches rose up from below and invaded their path. His guards simply skirted such obstacles. It seemed odd to Rylan. The walkway was dangerous enough; the least they could do was keep it clear of overgrowth.

They came to a set of stairs that climbed up to the balcony of a long building that clung to the side of the mountain. As they crested the rise of steps, the wind gusted eagerly. Rylan's guards maneuvered him through a wide door that slid open like a screen.

Within, he stood dazed, gazing around at the dim interior of the building, which was one wide-open space. Tall posts marched up and down the length of the room, carrying the weight of the second floor. The walls were made of light-colored hardwood embellished by contrasting mahogany grills and panels carved with sinuous designs. Around the edges of the room, a variety of artwork was displayed: pottery, wood and stone carvings, as well as sculptures made of a material he'd never seen before. The collection was visually stunning, set against a backdrop of opaque windows that let in the sunlight but admitted nothing of the view.

His guards led Rylan to the far end of the room, to an area defined by colorful rush mats that had been laid out in neat patterns. There, he was made to sit facing a raised section of the floor. His guards seated themselves around him on the mats, while the woman came forward to lower herself at his side.

They sat there in silence after that. No one spoke or even moved. The guards knelt with their hands gripping the hilts of their swords, as if frozen in that position. Eventually, a door in the wall slid open to admit a lone man who moved up onto the dais and, positioning himself in the center of the floor, sat cross-legged upon a thick mat. He sat still, his eyes locked on Rylan's face. For long moments, the man did nothing more than stare, his gaze never wavering.

At last, he nodded.

The woman turned to Rylan and smiled. "My name is Xiana. I am *deizu*, a mage of my people. This man is Sensho Kirwan Domeda." She motioned gracefully toward the man seated on the dais.

The man had the same milky-gold skin as Xiana. His hair and beard were gray, worn closely cropped. He had on a shimmering robe of light blue silk with gold-embroidered buttons. His frame was powerful, and he wore the hardened look of an old warrior.

"What is a Sensho?" Rylan asked, returning the man's gaze.

The woman smiled. "Sensho is what you call 'lord.' Sensho Domeda is the ruler of this region, which we call Daru." As she talked, her hands moved in flowing gestures, as though they were speaking their own language.

Rylan reminded himself that this was the same woman who had stabbed him in the chest. Keeping his eyes averted from her, he said to the man sitting cross-legged on the dais, "I'm Rylan Marshall."

Abruptly, the man slammed his fist down onto the floor, making Rylan flinch.

Xiana's eyes grew wide and her complexion paled visibly. She cast a sideways glance at Rylan, looking appalled. "Don't speak untruths in the Sensho's presence!" she gasped. "We know who you are, Gerald Lauchlin!"

Rylan gritted his teeth, reining in his anger. He stated firmly, "I was born Gerald Lauchlin. But that's not my name."

The Sensho grunted, then conferred with Xiana in their

native language. Rylan didn't understand a word of it, but the look in the man's eyes needed no translation. He saw the promise of his own death written there. He could make no further missteps.

Xiana broke off her conversation and turned to Rylan. "The Sensho wants you to explain yourself."

Rylan adjusted his posture and considered the man on the dais. The Sensho obviously understood his language. Rylan wondered why he insisted on using a translator. Looking up at him, he said, "I was separated from my parents at birth. The people who raised me named me Rylan Marshall. It's the name I grew up with. It's the only name I've ever known."

The man's gaze narrowed, and he appeared to be considering Rylan's words. After a moment, he nodded and uttered a few words to Xiana.

Brightening, the woman said, "Sensho Domeda understands. From here forward, you will be known as Rylan."

Rylan nodded his gratitude.

Smoothing her silk robe over her legs, Xiana lowered her eyes and continued, her hands flowing in graceful gestures. "But Sensho Domeda also insists that you cannot take the name Marshall. That may be the name of the people who raised you, but you are not of their lineage. To deny the name of your father is to deny yourself. And that is something that is simply not possible. From here forward, your name will be Rylan Lauchlin."

A cold and eerie feeling crept over his shoulders and shivered down his spine. Rylan dropped his gaze, unable to look at the Sensho's merciless eyes. He wanted to deny the man, to reject his logic and tell him he was wrong. That it was possible to be someone other than the man he was born. But inside, he knew the Sensho was right. He could not run from his father's legacy, however corrupt it might be.

"Call me what you like," Rylan said. "I don't care, so long as you let me go find my daughter." He looked at Xiana. "I want to know why you brought me here. And why you put that curse on me."

The old man raised his hand, commanding Rylan to silence. He shared a few brief words with Xiana. After a moment, she nodded and turned back to Rylan.

"Your name came to our attention as someone of great importance to the Turan Khar," she explained, her hands making flowing gestures as she spoke. "At first, we didn't understand why. Then we became aware of your parentage, and of the Khar's intentions for you."

"What are their intentions for me?" Rylan asked.

Spreading her hands, Xiana explained in her ever-patient voice, "The Turan Khar seek always to expand their empire. They use enslaved mages to suppress all opposition. But their last foe proved far worthier than they expected, and this defeat cost them their most powerful *deizu*."

Rylan frowned. He glanced at Domeda, then back to Xiana. "What does that have to do with me?"

Her smile broadened. "You are the son of the greatest battlemage to ever walk the earth. The Turan Khar would see you as an exquisite acquisition."

The way she said it, and with that smile, made Rylan feel sick. The coldness that already infected him started to wear away at his nerves. He began to doubt himself. To wonder if the Sensho was right: perhaps he really was too dangerous to live.

"I'm not my father," he whispered.

Xiana gifted him with another hopeful smile. "No. You could be greater."

He stared down at the worn fibers of the mat. They were soft, almost like animal hair.

"So that's why they took Amina?" he asked.

Xiana's smile faltered. "They would need a way to control

you. Your love for your daughter is beautiful and human. But it's also your greatest weakness."

He had been afraid of that. Yet somehow, his desperate mind latched onto that knowledge with hope. It meant Amina was still alive. They would need her to lure him.

"You were going to kill me," he said. "What changed your mind?"

Xiana frowned and glanced nervously up at the man on the dais. "The Sensho's mind hasn't changed. As of this moment, you still stand condemned."

Rylan nodded slowly. "Then, why are we having this conversation?"

"Because Sensho Domeda might decide to commute your sentence." Xiana's expression was compassionate. "The decision to end a life should never be made in haste, and should be only a last resort, once all other options have been exhausted." She let her hands sink to her sides.

Rylan looked at her hands, then let his gaze wander around the room. The guards who had shepherded him still surrounded them, kneeling on the floor, hands on the hilts of their swords. They had remained in that position, unmoving, throughout the entire interview. He looked past them to the long line of artwork displayed along the far wall. His attention was pulled toward the piece nearest him: a chunk of tawny, wind-sculpted stone. Not unlike the one he had brought back with him from the front, a gift from one of the men who had fought at his side.

He turned back to Xiana. "What do you want from me?"

Xiana looked away from him, her eyes going to Domeda. Their stares locked for a long moment. At last, the Sensho nodded.

Xiana turned back to Rylan and said, "We want you to assassinate the Warlord of the Turan Khar."

Rylan's breath hitched. He gazed at her in disbelief. His

brain tried in vain to sort through all the vast layers of absurdity inherent in that statement. The way she sat looking at him, face eager and expectant, made it obvious she believed he could accomplish such a feat. It was ludicrous.

Rylan asked slowly, "You realize I'm a farmer? With no knowledge of magic?"

Her optimistic smile returned. "You are the son of Darien Lauchlin. You can be taught."

Rylan shook his head. These people were crazy. There was far more to magecraft than just having the talent for it in your blood. Even he knew that. And this woman claimed she was a mage... she should know better.

But in the end, it didn't matter. If they thought he could make a difference, then let them think that. He would play along. He would do whatever it took to bring Amina home.

"And what of my daughter?" he pressed.

With a curt gesture, Xiana assured him, "To find your daughter, you must defeat the Warlord."

"She could be dead already," he protested.

Her smile drained away. "It's possible, of course," she said softly. She turned to the Sensho and asked him a question in their strange, lilting tongue. They conferred quietly as Rylan listened, his eyes downturned, focusing on the soft fibers of the mat.

At last, Xiana nodded and went silent, bowing her head. Then she said, "Sensho Domeda asks, if we let you live, how do we know you will not become the demon your father was?"

It was a ridiculous question. Rylan said, "Darien Lauchlin might have been my father, but I never knew him. He had no influence on me whatsoever. He was a Servant of Xerys. And I'm not...."

His voice trailed off.

Oh, gods...

The oath in the cornfield. When that awful man had forced

him to swear his allegiance to the God of Chaos. Had that made him a Servant, as well? Was he already following in his father's footsteps, without even knowing it? Staring at the floor, Rylan swallowed the bile that rose in his throat. Like his father before him, he had sworn his soul to Xerys. He was already the demon these people feared. He felt physically ill.

He deserved to die, he decided. But not until after he found Amina. Until then, they couldn't know. No one could know. He'd go along with them, just long enough to rescue his daughter. Then they could make an end of him. His arms tested the strength of his bonds, his fingers trembling.

Xiana said with a graceful motion of her hands, "The Sensho says you may live, as long as you are able to keep the evil of your bloodline at bay. You will learn to the best of your abilities. You will work very hard and apply all your mind and effort. And when you are ready, we will unleash you upon the Turan Khar. You will burn their Warlord to ashes and bring their Empire to its knees." She lifted a finger. "But the Word of Command I placed on your heart will remain. If at any time I feel your intentions betray us, I will speak the Word and end your life. Do you understand clearly all that I've said?"

"Aye. I do." His voice shook.

Xiana continued, "You will remain in my company every moment of the day, and never leave my side unless I ask. I will be your teacher in all things, and you will obey me in all things. Do you understand?"

"Aye."

She turned and conferred with the Sensho. Rylan tried to ignore their words, but he couldn't help wondering what they were saying. At last, Domeda barked an order. One of the guards stood up and, drawing a long dagger from his belt, moved forward and sawed through the ropes binding Rylan's wrists and legs. The rest of the guards stood and bowed. Then they formed a line and strode out of the room.

18

THE LAST BRIDGE

QUIN TOSSED HIM HIS STAFF. "WHAT DO YOU THINK?"

Gil examined the staff in his hand. It was a long piece of dense wood, possibly ironwood or mahogany. It was polished to a smoothness that felt like satin beneath his palms, and yet was ribbed with dark knots. It had a good amount of heft to it. He could feel the charged power stored within the artifact, warm and soothing to his mind. He fed a small amount of power into it. The staff glowed eagerly in response, giving off a golden radiance.

He looked at Quin in appreciation, knowing the Warden had crafted it with his own hands. "Is it a light staff?"

"It is," Quin said with a proud smile. "If something happens to me, you can have it."

"Thank you," Gil said, the offer making him uncomfortable. "I just hope it doesn't come to that."

"Let's hope it doesn't," Quin agreed. "Because if something does happen to me, you're going to be left with the job of running this war."

"Me?" Gil asked, surprised to hear Quin say such a thing.

His hand tightened reflexively on the staff as if trying to fend off the man's words.

The Grand Master grinned wryly. "Warden Dalton was always next in the long and lofty chain of command. Unfortunately, Dalton's only contribution to last night's battle was getting himself killed. Now, after Dalton, it was always a toss-up between you and Payden, at least in terms of ability. But now you've gone and made yourself the shiny, golden hero who saved the Waterfront. There's that. And there's also the unfortunate fact that Payden got himself captured an hour and a half ago."

Gil stared at him, jaw slack, his mind reeling. Dalton had been the Warden of Battlemages, the head of his own Order, and Payden had been in all his classes at the Lyceum. They weren't the best of friends, but they were more than just acquaintances. He scowled in regret, breathing a heavy sigh.

Quin extended his hand. "May I have my staff back?"

Gil nodded, handing it over. He'd forgotten he'd been holding it. He looked up into the Grand Master's eyes and saw understanding there. Out of all the Masters of the Lyceum, Quin had always been his favorite, and it was moments like this one that reminded him why. After his own father had died, he'd been raised by priests in the Temple of Wisdom. He'd spent his entire childhood in their vaults, reading all manners of arguments and philosophies. And yet, in all his life, Quin was the only man Gil thought was truly wise.

The Grand Master clapped him on the shoulder, then jerked his chin in the direction of the water. "Shall we, then?"

Quin set off down the cobbled road, Gil falling in at his side. The day was growing dim around them. Thunder rumbled in the distance. He glanced up at the clouds that hung low over the North City. They looked even darker, for some reason. Quin led him to the broken remains of the nearest bridge. Only the footings of the pillars remained above the waterline. One short section of the bridge was left intact, jutting out into the canal before ending abruptly.

"I'm going out there," Quin said, nodding at the truncated bridge. "I want you to stay here and ward me. We don't know what they're capable of, so be prepared for anything."

Gil glanced at the end of the span, a good hundred yards away. "I don't know. That's quite a distance."

Absorption shields took a lot of energy to sustain. Casting a web at that distance would strain him badly, especially if Quin met heavy resistance. It was a whole lot easier to attack with magic than it was to defend against it.

But the Grand Master only shrugged. "If we stand together, then we're a single target. Let's not make killing us too easy for them, shall we?"

Gil nodded reluctantly, even though he didn't feel good about it. He was looking at the far shore of the canal, where another pair of mages had joined the first four. They stood all in one line, holding hands, as the ranks of their army formed up behind them.

"They're coming," he said.

Quin turned to have a look. "Yes, indeed." He dredged up a somber smile. "You can do this. Your father would have been proud of you, you know."

With that, he clapped Gil on the arm and then turned toward the stone ramp leading onto the bridge. Gil wove an absorption web around Quin, his eyes tracking the Grand Master as he walked out onto the span of the bridge, the wind flapping his coat. Holding his light staff, Quin took up position at the end of the broken span. The canal's black waters stretched away to either side, smooth and flat like glass.

On the other side of the canal, a thick fog was gathering. It billowed like smoke, swallowing the ranks of enemy soldiers one by one, until only the line of mages on the shore remained visible. The fog groped at their feet, trailing past them over the ground. The mist was conjured. It had to be; no true fog could ever rise that quickly. It clung there for long, silent moments while the air grew steadily colder. Then it crept forward over the water, inch by inch, until the entire canal was consumed, and Quin appeared to be standing in the middle of a storm-gray ocean.

Across the water, the lights of hundreds of torches bloomed, hazy ochre blotches glowing from within the fogbank in a line that stretched the length of the Promenade. The lights of the torches remained stationary, steady reference points against the swirling gray mist. Gil's eyes went to the sea of fog that hung over the water, making the entire area of the canal look like a flat expanse of solid ground that stretched far into the distance. If he hadn't known it already, he wouldn't have guessed there was water below them.

From somewhere not too far away, he heard distinct splashing sounds. They were barely audible and, at first, didn't really capture his attention. But then he realized what they meant and, when he did, his blood grew chill. The fog was cover. Beneath it, the enemy was advancing across the canal.

"Quin!" he shouted.

The Grand Master glanced back at him. He nodded slightly, then turned away. Slowly, he spread his arms, staff in hand, and bowed his head. The air grew cold as Quin drew energy from his surroundings into himself. Gil looked on in amazement. He could feel the enormity of the reservoir of power Quin was amassing. His body began to glow, his skin saturated with raw energies too great to contain. They bled out of him in a red aura that thickened around him, swelling in intensity.

In one great motion, he swept the staff through the air.

A pool of flames sprang into being on both sides of the bridge, blazing and crackling. The flames quickly burned off the mist, waves of heat distorting the air above them. The pools of fire started spreading, trailing across the surface of the canal, bisecting it completely in both directions. The unnatural fog flinched back as if scorched, revealing a wide swath of water teeming with rafts loaded with soldiers.

Gil's throat clenched at the sight of them. He raised his hands and tightened his shield around Quin. Behind him, he heard shouts and the rattling of weapons as the Malikari bowmen prepared their first volley.

There was a moment of pause.

Then the air was filled with the twangs of bowstrings and the screams of dying men. Up and down the canal, rafts began exploding, the men on them hurled into the water. The dark waters churned white and then red as men flailed and struggled, lurching toward the shoreline, only to be repulsed by foot soldiers guarding the edge of the canal. Bodies began collecting in the water, floating obstacles that further slowed the frenzied men desperate to gain the shoreline.

Gil thickened his absorption web, letting it settle tightly around Quin. It was made of thin filaments of energy; nothing much. But it was strong enough to repel the few spears and arrows that were tossed at Quin from the water. And it could absorb massive amounts of energy, as much as Gil could channel. That would be the struggle. Every drop of energy the shield absorbed would have to be redirected somewhere else.

A brilliant red glow erupted from Quin's body as he arced his staff through the air, flinging water and bodies away from the shoreline. A sparkling trail of magic ribboned the air around him, shed from the glowing end of his staff. He threw his hands up, and a great gust of wind slapped the water with the force of a hurricane, capsizing the remaining rafts and dumping their human payloads into the water.

Gil glanced up just in time to see a crackling fire balls screaming through the air toward them. He intensified the shield around Quin, throwing everything he had into it. Just in time – the blazing ball of flames struck the end of the bridge with a thunderous explosion.

Gil cried out as he was hurled backward and slammed into the street with a force that almost knocked the absorption shield away from him. Shaking, he picked himself off the ground, struggling to maintain the shield. Fear gripped his chest as he walked back to the railing.

Thick gray smoke engulfed the center of the canal. It took a moment to clear, and when it did, Gil sagged in relief when he saw that Quin was unharmed. The end of the bridge remained intact. Quin pushed himself up, dusted off his clothes and, with an irritated look, raised his staff to renew his assault.

Across the canal, the line of Khar mages moved closer to the edge of the shoreline, stopping just short of the water. Together, they raised their hands. The clouds above the city roiled with thunder and flickering light. Then another flaming missile shot down from the bank of clouds, slamming into the bridge with a dragon's roar. Gil scrambled to hold his shield; it took everything he had. The amount of raw power absorbed by the shield almost overpowered him. Not knowing what else to do, he fed the excess energy into the water. Terrible, piercing screams erupted from the canal as the water nearest the bridge started boiling. Soldiers screamed and flailed, lurching toward shore. But very few reached it. They died well short of the bank, boiled to death in the bubbling water.

Lightning forked down from the sky, stabbing into the shield, sparks and filaments of light spraying out over the water. Quin raised his staff in both hands, drawing a tremendous amount of power through it, enough to make the hairs on the back of Gil's neck stand up. The staff glowed in Quin's hands, the charged energies crackling ferociously. His body drank in energy until ripples of light coruscated over him.

Then he unleashed his wrath upon the Promenade. Explosions of flames erupted up and down the far shoreline, hurling enemy soldiers and mages in all directions. The air filled with shrieks and screams.

Overhead, the skies thundered their retaliation. The clouds opened up and disgorged a barrage of lightning concentrated on the end of the bridge. Gil cried out as he felt his shield begin to fail. It was absorbing too much energy, and he couldn't channel it away fast enough. The waters of the canal boiled and bubbled, the air filling with steam. But it was too much. He couldn't handle any more.

Another crackling fireball hurled toward them from the sky.

Panicked, he shouted at Quin, "I can't hold it any longer! *Run!*"

But either Quin didn't hear him or didn't react. He stood with his arms spread, staff in hand, eyes closed in concentration. Thunder split the heavens as the smoking fireball tumbled toward them.

"RUN!" Gil bellowed.

He didn't have time to do anything but scream as the flaming missile slammed into the end of the bridge, overwhelming his shield. Flames from the explosion consumed the air around him, and he was hurled backward, his body slammed against the wall of a building. He sank to the ground, the molten air searing his throat. His vision started to dim. Feeling his consciousness fade, Gil fought against it. He gritted his teeth and pushed himself off the ground. Staggering toward the bridge, he drew up short.

The bridge was gone.

All that remained were fragments of smoldering rocks strewn across the bank. Rolling clouds of smoke devoured the air where the bridge had just been. Burning debris floated on the surface of the water, dispersed among the hundreds of bodies being borne away by the slow current.

Gil screamed in rage and grief. But all the screaming in the world wouldn't bring Quin back. He stood there for a moment trembling. Then the sounds of war cries slapped his attention back into focus. A number of Khar soldiers had gained the bank and were charging toward him.

He turned and ran, fleeing down the closest side street while, behind him, the Sultan's men engaged the enemy. The harsh noise of battle resounded as he fled through the empty streets, running until the sounds faded. Breathing hard, he staggered to a stop, bending forward with his hands on his knees.

He stood there like that for a long time, gasping and panting, his mind reeling. Slowly, he righted himself, staggering like a drunken man. He couldn't run, he realized. Couldn't retreat. He didn't know what had happened to all the others, the other battlemages. All he knew was that they weren't there, and he was all they had.

He had a duty to attend to. Even if it was the last duty he performed.

Gathering his strength and courage, Gil turned and started back the way he had come. His legs felt like lead, resisting his effort. He willed himself to move faster, until he was jogging, and then faster still, until he was running toward the sounds of battle. He rounded the last corner, emerging into the thick of the melee. Reaching out from within, he hurled the first group of soldiers out of his way, clearing a path ahead of him.

He paused for just a moment to get his bearings. Then he worked his way forward, flinging men back away from him and dropping them where they stood. He strode slowly along the edge of the Waterfront, wrapped in a fog of concentration, sweat streaming down his face. Every man who rushed him collapsed within footsteps. All along his path, soldiers erupted in flames, while others staggered away, blood running from their ears and mouths. Gil hardly noticed. They weren't men. They were just shapes, shadowy figures meant to be wrenched and distorted. He didn't pause, even when the enemy soldiers stopped attacking and started running.

The Sultan's men spilled forward, cutting down the slowest as the enemy was routed back into the water. Gil lumbered on, dazed, until it occurred to him that there was no one left to kill. He staggered to a stop and stood blinking, gazing blearily around.

Everywhere, he saw bodies. Bodies and blood. His breath hitched in his chest, his insides going numb. He turned slowly in a circle, blinking, his gaze struggling over the blood-washed street that was littered with dead. He turned toward the canal and found its waters colored red, filled with floating corpses and burning flotsam. He felt suddenly weak, his knees buckling. He caught himself on a lamp post and squeezed his eyes shut, trying to calm his ragged breath.

He stood there for a long time, perhaps minutes, waiting for his hands to stop trembling. Then, hanging his head, he strode wearily up the street in the direction of the square, to where the Sultan had established his command center. He stared at the ground as he stumbled through the streets. It was all he could do to keep his feet moving. Exhaustion bore down on his shoulders and unbidden tears stung his eyes. He had never felt more tired in his life. Even as he struggled forward, his eyelids kept sliding shut. The city around him was gray and remote, its sounds and colors muted. He observed the world as if from a distance, as though staring at reality through a shroud.

He found Murkaq Square barricaded on all sides with furniture, burlap sacks, and overturned merchant wagons. The square was abuzz with commotion that he acknowledged only groggily. Officers in green uniforms stood barking commands, while soldiers worked frantically to shore up the fortifications. In a very short time, the Sultan's forces had sealed off the square from every approach and erected a bustling command center that operated with practiced efficiency.

He found the Sultan standing in front of a large pavilion erected on the far side of the square, past the many-tiered marble fountain that was an icon of the city. Gil circled the fountain, which was still gurgling obliviously. He found Sayeed looming over a large table layered with maps, his fingers roving over the pages as he dictated commands to his officers. His face was gritty and weary, his rich tunic stained with soot and blood.

At the sight of Gil, he straightened with a look of concern and moved quickly forward, catching him by the arm. "Where is Warden Reis?"

Gil hung his head. He hesitated, reluctant to say. As if admitting Quin's death would somehow make it more real. Somehow, he worked up the courage to look the Sultan in the eyes. "He is lost, Your Highness. I couldn't save him."

Sayeed stared at him, his face slowly darkening. He let go of Gil's blood-soaked arm and brought both hands up to his brow, drawing them down over his face.

"May Isap accept his soul," he whispered, bowing his head.

19

DEIZU

THE HUT RYLAN ENTERED WAS JUST A SINGLE ROOM THAT smelled heavily of dust and resin. Two latticed windows high on the walls let in only thin streaks of sunlight that did little to warm the place. Hanging from the thatched ceiling was a variety of dried plants and meats tied to strings that twisted slowly in a breeze moving in through the windows. A small cabinet graced the far wall, the sole piece of furniture in the room. A thin rush mat and a lacquered plaque on the wall were the only decorations.

Rylan remained standing while Xiana set a wooden tray on the floor then sat down crosslegged. The tray contained two covered clay pots and two wooden spoons. She gestured at the floorboards across from her. Following her directive, Rylan sat and leaned back against the rough, dark planks that paneled the walls.

"Is your home acceptable?" Xiana asked. She lifted one of the clay pots with both hands and set it down in front of him.

"My home?" Rylan did a double take.

"Yes."

"You're giving me my own *house?*"

The woman shrugged. "You need somewhere to stay."

Rylan lifted his eyebrows. Frowning, he asked, "Aren't you concerned I'll flee?"

Xiana waved her hand dismissively. "No. There's nowhere for you to go." She reached over and lifted the lid of his pot and set it aside. "Here. I made breakfast for you," she said, and handed him a wooden spoon.

Inside the pot was a thin golden broth. Xiana reached into a woven bag she carried at her side and produced a brown egg, which she handed to him. Rylan gazed down at the egg, wondering what he was supposed to do with it. Seeing his confusion, Xiana smiled slightly. Removing another egg from her bag, she cracked it into her own pot, stirring it gently with her spoon.

Rylan stared at the raw egg swirling around in the pot, waiting for it to cook and turn white. But it never did. Curious, he dipped a finger into his own pot and made a face. The broth was lukewarm; it wasn't near hot enough to cook an egg.

"We call it *saj*. It's a traditional meal we eat daily for breakfast." Xiana leaned over and plucked the egg from his hand. She broke it into his pot, then handed him a wooden spoon and made a stirring motion.

Swirling his egg, Rylan felt his stomach twist. He didn't like the idea of eating raw egg and cold broth for breakfast every day. Xiana lifted her pot in both hands and took a sip. Rylan watched her curiously. Drinking soup right from the pot wasn't something he'd ever seen done before. Glancing at the spoon at Xiana's side, he came to the conclusion that the only purpose it served was stirring in the egg.

Xiana lowered her pot and gave him a nod of encouragement. Rylan didn't argue or complain; he was too hungry. So he lifted the pot and gulped down the broth, trying not to think about what he was drinking. He was still hungry when the pot was empty. He set it down and wiped his mouth with his hand while Xiana frowned at him. She sipped her soup daintily, taking her time, finishing every drop. Then she replaced the pots and spoons on the tray and pushed it aside.

For the first time, he noticed the robe she was wearing. It was gold and iridescent, with a dark bronze sash. It was patternless and seamless; even the weave was completely smooth. There was something about its simplicity that seemed to denote great status. She looked elegant in it.

"We must get you into the bath," Xiana said, rising from the floor. "You're filthy, and you smell." She wrinkled her nose. She went to the small cabinet and removed a folded gray robe of the same material as her own. Handing it to him, she said, "This robe is called *yori.* The material is *oki,* the silk of the whisper butterfly. A very precious material. It can be worn only by *deizu.* It's soft like moth silk but tough as armor. Take it with you. You can wear it after the bath."

Rylan received the robe and was startled by the material's texture. It was unexpectedly dense and heavy, yet luxuriously soft. He ran his hands over the fabric, marveling at the feel of it.

"Don't you have anything cotton or wool?" he asked.

Xiana stepped back and ran her gaze over him critically. *"Deizu* are forbidden to wear cotton. Except for undergarments."

Rylan frowned. "You're serious?"

"I am. Cotton is a fabric worn only by farmers and poets."

Rylan's jaw went slack. After a moment, he collected himself enough to remind her, "I'm a farmer, so I can wear cotton." He tried handing the garment back to her.

Xiana shook her head, refusing to take the robe. The look in her eyes was sympathetic. "You are not a farmer any longer. You are *deizu.* You must wear *oki.* If it bothers you, you may wear a cotton undertunic. I can have one made for you."

Rylan sighed and tucked the folded robe under his arm, grumbling, "No. I'll manage."

Scooping up her bag, Xiana gestured toward the door. "I'll show you to the bath house."

Rylan followed her out the door and down a short flight of steps, then turned to look back at the hut she had given him. It looked smaller on the outside, just four squat walls and a sloped roof made of thatch, the floor raised above the ground on short stilts. Around the hut was a small vegetable garden that reminded him of the one on his own farm. He followed Xiana down a stepping-stone path that meandered through the garden.

The hut was surrounded by woods that didn't look like any other woodland he'd ever seen. It looked denser. Healthier. Everything was much more green, from the many-layered canopy to the fern-draped forest floor. The air was cold and misty, scented with pine mixed with wood smoke from the village. They emerged from the trees onto a trail that cut through a large tract of agricultural land divided into plots. Men in loincloths and women wearing not much more stooped in the cold fields, tending their crops. They glanced up and, noticing Rylan, stared at him intently, as though he was some sort of curiosity. But as they drew near, every farmer stopped their work and bowed their heads, their gazes lowered to the ground. Their behavior made Rylan uncomfortable. He quickened his pace and kept his focus on the dirt path ahead of him.

The village itself was surrounded by a high wood-plank palisade. Xiana led him through a gate, and they made their way down a dust-paved street encased on both sides by buildings made of stone and wood. There were few people in the streets, and all stared at Rylan openly before bowing their heads in deference. Most of the men were dressed in pants and tunics, although a few wore light-colored *yori*-robes made of some type of plant fiber. All were armed. Xiana nodded and smiled as they passed, offering simple greetings.

Taking Rylan's arm, she guided him through an opening in

one of the walls. Within was a large courtyard surrounding a small house built over a steaming pool in the center. The pool took up most of the space inside the courtyard and was enclosed by a colorful garden. They followed the path around the pool and over a bridge to the building in the center. They entered the house just as a man was walking out. He gazed openly at Rylan as he passed, only barely ducking his head.

Xiana smiled. "You'll get stares," she warned him. "Everyone knows who you are. And what you are."

Rylan didn't know what to think about that. The villagers treated him with the respect people in the Kingdoms normally reserved for the nobility. In the Rhen, not even mages received such deference. The reactions of the Daru villagers made him squirm internally; he'd never liked being the focus of attention.

The small house was open in the back, the planks of the flooring meeting the waters of the pool, which steamed a thick mist into the cold air. All around the walls were hooks holding long cotton cloths. On the far end of the room, a squat fountain made of stone sat beside the pool, ringed by several stools. A constant stream of water flowed into the fountain's bowl from a pipe set above it.

Xiana gestured toward the fountain. "Remove your clothes and hang your *yori* on a hook. Then sit and wash with water from the fountain." She motioned him forward.

Rylan balked, looking back and forth between the woman and the fountain, wondering if he'd heard her right. When she crossed her arms expectantly, he shook his head. "I'm not undressing in front of you."

Xiana gave him a good-natured smile. "The bath is for everyone. It doesn't matter if you're male or female. Everyone bathes. Including you."

Rylan looked away, feeling his cheeks heat. He hoped Xiana wasn't thinking of joining him in the bath.

"Go on!" she ordered, motioning him forward.

Rylan gritted his teeth and threw the robe over a hook. Facing away from her, he struggled out of his clothes and tossed them angrily on the floor. When he stood fully naked in front of her, he looked over his shoulder to find Xiana staring at him. Embarrassment made him freeze. He trained a glare at her, hands moving to cover himself.

"At least turn your back," he growled.

She made a face. "Don't be ridiculous. In Daru, you are expected to bathe each day after the work is done. Modesty has no place among us." She waved him toward the fountain.

Dropping all pretext of modesty, Rylan clenched his jaw and crossed the floor of the bath house. He made his way to the granite stools surrounding the fountain and sat with his back to her. Cupping his hands, he started scooping water from the fountain over his head, wetting his hair.

"Stop splashing and wash," Xiana grumbled from behind him.

He scrubbed fiercely at his hair, bending to rinse it under the water from the pipe.

"Use soap!" Xiana said, the sound of her voice closer.

Even with his eyes squeezed closed, Rylan could feel her standing right behind him. He caught hold of a soft ball of soap and scrubbed it over his skin until it worked up a lather, then rinsed his body in the water stream. When he was clean, he glared up at Xiana through wet strands of hair. "Now what?" he demanded, angry and embarrassed.

The infuriating woman smiled pleasantly and gestured toward the pool. "Go soak in the bath."

Angry now, Rylan rose and stood facing her insolently. Then he brushed past her and made for the steps that led down into the steaming pool. He yelped when his toe touched the hot water, jerking his foot back.

"It's not going to boil you," Xiana laughed. "Go in!"

Grimacing, he lowered himself into the pool, moving

forward into the thick layer of mist. He had to enter the water slowly, giving his skin time to adjust to the heat. It took him awhile to submerge his shoulders. He found a ledge that served as a seat and, claiming it, leaned his head back against the side of the bath.

Xiana moved toward the pool, lowering herself down next to him on the bank. She drew her legs up in front of her and calmly explained, "This spring is the blood of the earth. It comes from deep within the mountain and has great healing powers. It is said to replenish both body and spirit."

Rylan doubted the spring had any such properties. But the hot water *was* soothing. He felt his muscles starting to relax, the tension seeping out of him. He lay with his eyes closed, his body buoyant, letting the rise and fall of his chest disturb the calm surface of the water. Almost, he could ignore Xiana's presence. Almost—but not quite. He was very aware of her there, sitting only inches away on the edge of the pool.

After minutes, she set a hand on his shoulder.

"That's enough soaking, until you are used to the heat of the water. Come out."

Rylan opened his eyes and sat up. Reluctantly, he moved toward the steps leading out of the pool. As soon as he emerged, Xiana greeted him with a towel. He dried off in front of her, then donned the gray robe she handed him with a feeling of intense relief. He looked around for his clothes.

They were gone.

"What did you do with my clothes?" he asked.

The woman gestured toward the woven bag she carried. "I have them here. They're filthy and they need to be burned." Removing the silk sash of the *yori* from the hook on the wall, she moved to wrap it around his waist.

Rylan dodged back, his cheeks flushed with anger. Even if it had belonged to his wretched father, the war belt was still a priceless piece of antiquity. He couldn't just let the woman throw it away.

"The belt's an heirloom," he snapped. "I want it back."

Xiana frowned at him, looking disgusted. But she reached into the bag and, sighing in irritation, offered the belt to him. Rylan yanked it from her grasp, holding it up and examining it for damage. Thankfully, the leather looked just the same as it had when Sayeed had given it to him. He wrapped the belt around his silk robe and cinched the gold buckle.

Xiana wrinkled her face. "Ew. That looks ghastly." Then she sighed, relenting. "But there's no rule against leather."

Feeling smug, Rylan spread his arms and turned around.

She nodded tentative approval, hands clasped in front of her. "See? You lived through it. And now you don't stink anymore." Her smile came back, a mischievous glint in her eye.

She took him by the arm and, gliding forward, led him out of the bath house and back into the garden courtyard. As they stepped onto the bridge, the sun came out, streaming light down through the clouds. Rylan squinted, bringing a hand up to shield his face. But the warmth didn't last long; seconds later, the sun dodged back behind the clouds.

Xiana looked at him. "So, tell me, what have you learned to do with your Gift?"

Rylan shrugged. He hadn't been able to do anything since Xiana's attack on him. Dampened, he couldn't even sense the magic field. "I made magelight once," he said, throwing a glare her way. "That's it. That's all I ever got a chance to learn."

Xiana ignored his look. "What color is your magelight?"

"Why?" Rylan asked, still feeling grudgeful.

Xiana said in a whimsical voice, "Some people say magelight shows the true colors of a soul.

He scowled, dismissing her claim. "It was some type of purple."

Xiana stopped walking and looked at him. "You must have a very troubled soul, Rylan Lauchlin. A dark soul. But beautiful."

She looked worried. He thought about asking her to elaborate, but then decided that he really didn't want her to. Any explanation she had to offer was probably something he didn't want to hear. Instead, he decided to steer the conversation away from him.

"What color is your magelight?" he asked.

Xiana paused, and for a moment didn't say anything. She let go of his arm.

"It was yellow."

"Was?" he echoed.

Xiana lowered her gaze to the ground. "I can no longer hear the song of the magic field," she said with an apologetic smile. "The Turan Khar captured me, along with all the rest of our *deizu*. They let me go, but first they dampened me, so I could never oppose them again. Now the only kind of magic I can use is the magic of artifacts. Like this one."

She reached up and fingered a stone pendant that hung from a gold chain about her neck. Rylan peered at it, marveling at the beauty of the stone. It shimmered with a wash of many iridescent colors, mostly pink and blue.

"It's beautiful," he said, drawing back. "What is it?"

The smile fled from Xiana's face, and she let go of the stone. "It's an imbued opal. It was given to me by a man I loved many years ago."

She didn't look old enough to have loved anyone long ago. She seemed somewhere in her late teens, but maybe she was older than she looked. The way Xiana said it made it clear that the man she spoke of was gone. Whoever he was, wherever he was, Xiana mourned his loss. Her grief weighed heavily on her voice.

"Where is he now?" Rylan asked.

"He died. A long time ago." She glanced up at him,

managing a sad smile. She started forward again, following the path back through the village.

"I'm sorry," he said, not knowing what else to say. He knew grief well. He lived with it every day. For two years, he'd mourned the loss of his wife. And now the loss of his children. It was a connection he shared with her. Somehow, it made her seem more human.

"What does it do?" he asked, indicating the stone.

Xiana's smile came back, though it was fragile and transitory. "It's what brought you here, Rylan."

She paused and nodded at a house down the road. A path led toward it marked by many lanterns made of colored glass, hanging from long poles. The tinkling sounds of distant laughter drifted toward them, along with soft music played on a string instrument he didn't recognize.

"It's a wedding," Xiana said, gesturing vivaciously. "Come, I'll introduce you."

Thinking of all the stares he'd already received, Rylan balked. "I don't think that's a good idea," he said, trying to pull away.

"Nonsense!" She caught his hand and jerked him forward.

He went with her grudgingly. They turned onto the path lined with lanterns, where Xiana stopped and looked him over quickly. Frowning, she leaned forward and adjusted his robe and pushed his leather belt lower on his waist. At last seeming satisfied, she led him down the path toward a two-story house constructed of dark wood, the windows made of some type of oiled paper covered by lattice. They entered the building without knocking. Rylan found himself in a room filled with people wearing traditional cotton robes. Both men and women were dressed in soft, muted colors.

All except one man.

Standing at the end of the room was a man wearing an exquisite robe of a shimmering white silk tied with a red sash.

He wore his long brown hair in a braid, and a well-groomed beard sharpened his jawline. Beside him stood a dainty woman wrapped in an exquisitely embroidered robe. She was young, her hair arranged in intricate braids and spirals, a band of red makeup spanning both her eyes.

All conversation abruptly died the moment they entered the room. Every face turned toward them with looks ranging from shock to adulation. Xiana led Rylan forward, the crowd parting before them, every person bowing their heads, except for children sneaking wide-eyed peeks from behind the colorful robes of their parents. Xiana smiled and said words of greeting to people as they passed by, touching hands and bobbing little bows. She stopped before the bride and groom, rotating her hands until her palms faced upward.

With a flowing gesture, she said, "This is Kodiro and his bride, Nida. Kodiro is of the royal family, the fourth heir to the Dowan of Laoni. Nida is his bride."

Rylan nodded at Kodiro, then took Nida's hand to kiss it. The moment he touched Nida's skin, Kodiro let out a furious cry. Enraged, he lunged at Rylan, knocking him off his feet. Rylan hit the floor and scrambled backward through the crowd, people screaming and dodging away from him. Panicked celebrants started spilling out the door, others backing up as far as the walls would allow them.

The groom sprang forward, cornering Rylan against a wall. He yanked him to his feet, gripping him by the collar of his robe. He started bellowing sharp, cutting words, his cheeks red, spittle flying from his lips.

Xiana leaped forward, screaming a high-pitched deluge of frantic protests. She pleaded with Kodiro, wrenching on his arm, but couldn't budge him. Undeterred, she wormed her way between them, giving Rylan the chance to slide out from the wall. The man whirled, bellowing and gesturing in rage.

"*What happened?*" Rylan shouted, trying to be heard over Xiana's screeching and Kodiro's yelling.

She turned to him, her face pale, her eyes wide and horrified. "You touched his bride!" she cried. "You do not touch a bride on her wedding day!"

Rylan's mouth fell open. He took a step toward Kodiro, shaking his head and throwing his hands up. "I'm sorry! I didn't know!"

Behind him came a sharp, metallic ring. Rylan swung around to find an old man standing with his sword drawn, the cutting edge leveled at his throat. Xiana shrieked a panicked outcry, gesturing wildly.

Everyone was shouting, the bride sobbing. Rylan stood with his hands up, keeping his attention on the sword. All at once, Kodiro threw his head back and issued an explosive howl that shook the windows. The entire room fell still. Kodiro grunted, crossing his arms. The blade remained poised next to Rylan's throat and didn't waver. Glaring fiercely at Xiana, Kodiro let loose with a string of words.

Xiana turned to Rylan, her eyebrows pinched in dismay. "Kodiro instructs me to tell you that you have sullied his bride, and their marriage is now nullified."

"I'm sorry! I didn't mean to!" Rylan gasped, spreading his arms wide in desperation.

Xiana waved her hands, cutting him off, her gaze dancing between Kodiro and himself. "Normally, the penalty for such an offense would be death."

Shocked, Rylan glanced at the blade.

Xiana went on, "I told Kodiro your life is protected by the Sensho. But he demands recompense. He asks that you name someone here to accept your punishment in your place."

Rylan's mouth dropped open. He looked at Xiana, then swept his gaze around the room, taking in the sight of the remaining wedding guests standing terrified, pressed up against the walls. He turned back to Kodiro, shaking his head.

"I can't do that!" he gasped.

In reply, Kodiro barked terse words at Xiana.

Pale and apologetic, she told Rylan, "Kodiro says if you refuse to choose someone to accept your punishment, then he will choose for you. And he will choose me."

Rylan closed his eyes, wanting to howl in frustration. This was impossible. There had to be another way. Something else he could do. He shook his head desperately.

"No. Please—tell him I beg him to forgive me!"

"*Dokh!*" Kodiro bellowed.

Xiana spread her hands. "The offense is unforgivable! You must make up your mind! Quickly—choose!"

"I can't!" Rylan growled.

The old man next to him pulled his sword back over his shoulder and took a broad step sideways, swinging around to face Xiana. Rylan dodged quickly between her and the sword.

"Tell him I've made my choice!" he shouted.

Xiana gasped, her eyes going wide. Her lips trembled. "Who?" she whispered.

Rylan balled his fists, his panic giving way to anger. Licking his lips, he told Xiana, "Tell Kodiro I choose him."

Xiana went rigid, her mouth open, her eyes unblinking. For a moment, she stood frozen, like a hare in the path of a snake. At last, she inhaled a sharp gasp. Letting out a high-pitched moan, she turned to Kodiro and relayed Rylan's words.

Kodiro's eyes narrowed, his lips curling into a snarl. His gaze snapped to Rylan, his eyes filled with molten fury. He growled something, a phrase Rylan couldn't hope to understand. Then, in one swift motion, Kodiro unsheathed his dagger and drew it across his own throat.

Rylan flinched back in shock.

Blood fountained from the deep gash in Kodiro's neck,

quickly saturating his white tunic. He stood there for impossibly long seconds, dagger in hand, his breath a harsh, bubbling gurgle. Then, at last, he staggered. He came toppling down, falling heavily on his face.

The bride screamed and kept screaming.

Xiana raised her hands to cover her eyes.

Blood pooled on the floor, spreading quickly.

Xiana shot her arm out, grabbing Rylan's hand. Suddenly, he was being propelled toward the door as terrified people fled before them. He stumbled after her into the street, past groups of sobbing and screaming wedding guests. Xiana yanked him forward, forcing him to jog to keep up with her. She didn't slow until they were out of the village. Once they were in the fields, Rylan ripped his hand out of Xiana's grasp. Drawing ragged breaths, he scrubbed his hands through his hair, feeling cold and faint.

"What did he say?" he demanded.

Xiana didn't respond. She looked too shaken. Instead, she turned back toward the village and stared wide-eyed at the rooftops. Rylan grasped her by the shoulders, swinging her back toward him.

"What did he say?"

Xiana's distant eyes locked on his. "He called you a demon," she whispered, her voice and body trembling.

20

THE SULTAN'S COMMAND

THE GOUTS OF BLACK SMOKE DARKENING MURKAQ SQUARE MADE Gil's eyes sting and water. Behind him, fires still crackled along the Waterfront and across the Grand Canal, consuming debris riding the slow currents toward the bay. The screams of dying men echoed in the near distance, along with the occasional ground-shuddering thunder of a fire strike. The square was the embodiment of organized chaos, with the Sultan's forces racing against time to both entrench their base camp and deliver men and equipment to their perimeter.

Gil stood beside Ashra next to the command tent, arms crossed, watching her father hold court over a small collection of his elite officers. The Sultan stood with one foot raised on an overturned water bucket, punctuating every command with a brusque gesture. Shadows cast by the fires roved over his features, making him look even more ominous than usual. Certainly not a man to be argued with.

He raised his hand, beckoning two of his officers forward. "Farad! Hakeem!"

The two men fell to their knees at the Sultan's feet, bowing to the ground. They remained in that posture until he motioned at them.

The first man, Farad, removed his helm with a rain of sweat-drenched hair. Head bowed and eyes lowered, he reported, "Your Majesty, we are working to fortify the Kazri Souk. As it stands, we have lost everything north of the canal. We retain only the Lower City, Your Majesty."

Sayeed bared his teeth like a rabid animal. "Give me numbers."

The second man, Hakeem, stepped forward, clutching his conical helmet in front of him. With a bob of his head, he reported, "Your Highness, the enemy has paid a heavy price for their gains. They stand now at less than half the strength they were at the outset. However, we have also paid heavily in blood. We have lost the vast majority of our brothers-in-arms. Our numbers will surely prove insufficient to hold the Lower City." There was a brief pause as Hakeem drew in a deep breath and glanced sideways at Farad. "Your Majesty, surrender is advised."

The air itself seemed to stiffen. Every man in the gathering froze, all eyes on the Sultan.

Into that great silence, Sayeed promised, "There will be no surrender."

Farad inclined his head. "As you will, Your Majesty. Your men stand ready to fight and die at your side."

"Then it is settled." Sayeed dismissed his men, then strode over to where Gil stood with Ashra. Rubbing the back of his neck, he said to Gil, "That's all for now. Return to your Prime Warden. Inform her of her husband's loss and then evacuate the Lyceum. Deploy every asset you have along our northern perimeter."

Gil didn't move. He was too shocked by the Sultan's words. "Your Majesty... we can't just abandon the Lyceum," he protested.

Sayeed spread his hands. "The Lyceum is a valuable target our enemy will no doubt prioritize. We will not be able to defend it with the numbers we have, so it makes sense to abandon it now, rather than waste resources on a battle we cannot win."

Gil understood the logic; it was a sound argument from a tactical standpoint. But the Sultan was operating off a false premise: that protecting the city had to take priority. As far as Gil was concerned, that objective was secondary to protecting the Lyceum.

"I beg to differ, Your Majesty," he said. "There's more in the Lyceum than just mages. We're talking about all of our work and all of our knowledge—artifacts, heirlooms of power, thousands of texts! We can't just let our enemy get ahold of all that! If they do, they'll have a tremendous advantage."

The Sultan merely shrugged. "Then carry those things out with you."

Gil had a hard time believing what he was hearing. Perhaps Sayeed didn't understand the magnitude of disaster the Lyceum's fall would precipitate. "Your Majesty... do you want them to have access to the transfer portals?"

Sayeed grimaced, drawing in a slow and heavy breath. His eyes wandered to the side. "No," he answered. "But neither can I keep them from our enemy. Very well. Destroy the transfer portals."

Gil took a step back, rocked to his core. He shook his head mutely, at last managing to whisper, "You don't know what you ask...."

Sayeed shot him a reproachful glare. "Of course I do."

And with that, he walked away.

Gil stared after him, his eyes loosely focused on the Sultan's back. Letting out a sigh, he stood there feeling numb, staring down at his blood-encrusted hands. With a sigh, he turned away from the command tent and started back toward the barricaded street that led eastward toward the Lyceum. The sounds of distant battle still carried over the water from the North City, but they barely registered. The noises were remote and constant, not an immediate threat. Nothing important enough to suck his attention away from the brute focus it took to stay awake. He passed through the barricade and headed down the street, only then realizing that he was being followed. He glanced back at Ashra with a frown.

"What are you doing?" he asked.

She cocked an eyebrow at him. "Going with you."

Gil scowled in dismay. He'd already led her through more danger than she had any business being in. He didn't want to be responsible for her, especially considering who her father was. The last thing he wanted was to make an enemy of the Sultan.

"You should stay here," he said.

But Ashra shook her head and smiled. "You know my place is with my mentor."

Technically, she was incorrect—that logic didn't apply to a war zone. Nevertheless, he didn't push it. He didn't have the patience or the energy to fight with her. So he decided to ignore her as he set off down the street, stepping carefully around fallen roof tiles and assorted debris that impeded his every step. Ashra walked silently at his side, every few seconds casting a concerned glance his way. She didn't say anything. But she kept the looks up for blocks, and it was getting annoying.

"I'm fine," Gil finally grumbled, hoping that would make her stop.

He turned a corner onto a side road that would take them straight to the Avenue of Elms, in the direction of the Lyceum. The buildings to either side were still intact, high-roofed structures made of dark bricks. The sounds of their footsteps echoed hollowly off the empty walls.

"I'm very sorry about the Warden," Ashra said in a sad voice. "I know he was your mentor."

Gil nodded, feeling ragged. The emotions bubbling up in his throat were unexpectedly strong. He hadn't realized how attached he'd been to Quin. They walked on in silence, Gil doing his best to ignore her by focusing instead on the relentless quiet that surrounded them. It was an eerie, unsettling feeling that should never be heard in a city the size of Karikesh. The streets were empty. From behind them, he heard distant shouts coming from the Waterfront. But from the southern neighborhoods, there was nothing but stillness, as though the city had taken a mortal wound.

The entrance to the Lyceum was only a few blocks away. The street was empty, save for a few abandoned carts and tumbled merchant's kiosks. The streetlamps were still lit; the lamplighters hadn't made their usual morning circuits. Gil couldn't help wondering if they ever would again.

The Lyceum's wide, golden dome came into view long before the rest of the building did. There were no people about, which didn't set right with his nerves. The square in front of the Lyceum was usually busy this time of day. But only leaves blown by the wind moved along the street. They ascended the wide marble steps and entered the building through an enormous arch encased by two thin towers that extended high above the roof. As they moved into the hall, two dirty and battle-weary men rushed toward him.

"Gil!" called Brinn, the taller one. "Where've you been? What word have you?"

"We're losing," Gil snapped, evading both men by turning into the hallway that led to the Prime Warden's office. He had no interest in conversation. The hallway was bustling with a flurry of people. Outside Naia's office, her secretary stood directing what looked like her own command center, waving her quill in the air as she directed people about.

When Gil made straight for the Prime Warden's door, the woman sprang in front of him. Gil halted and looked at her with an exasperated sigh.

"Look. I *need* to speak with the Prime Warden." He peered intently into her face, praying he wouldn't have to spell out his reasons in front of twenty listening mages.

The woman stared at him long and hard. Finally, with a nod, she drew aside.

Gil said to Ashra, "Wait here."

She placed a hand on his shoulder, offering him a small smile of encouragement.

Drawing in a deep breath, Gil opened the door.

He found Naia sitting behind her desk, surrounded by a cluster of men and women, all engaged in heated conversation. At first, no one noticed him. He didn't know what to do, so he stood there for a moment glancing around, trying to work up enough courage to say something. Long before he was ready, Naia glanced up and saw him.

"Where have you been?" she demanded, her voice silencing everyone in the room.

"I've been with the Sultan," he said wearily. Staring only at Naia, he addressed the others in the room with as steady a voice as he could muster, "Please excuse us. I need a word with the Prime Warden. Alone."

At the sound of his tone, the men and women gathered around her desk glanced at each other then at Naia. She peered at him hard, her eyes slowly widening as they searched his face. "Do as he says."

Without a word, everyone filed out, leaving Gil alone with the Prime Warden and her personal assistant, a small woman with a leather notebook who sat huddled in the corner. Gil glanced a question at Naia.

"It's all right," she assured him. "Priya can stay."

Her voice sounded thin and hollow, as if she had already

guessed what he was there to say. Gil swallowed, running his tongue over his lips, suddenly at a loss for words. He glanced at the acolyte in the corner. Then he stared at the ground.

Her face emotionless, Naia asked softly, "I'm not going to like this news, am I?"

Gil took a deep breath. "Prime Warden... Your husband..." He couldn't continue.

He saw on her face that he didn't have to.

Naia sat rigid, her eyes staring straight ahead at nothing.

"I'm sorry," Gil whispered, wishing there was something better he could say. He stood with his hands clasped in front of him, lingering awkwardly on his feet, watching her wrestle with her grief.

To her credit, she didn't break down.

When the acolyte rose from the chair to offer her a kerchief, Naia waved her away.

"How did he die?" she asked in a barren tone.

Gil didn't know how to answer that question. He said the first thing that came to mind. "He died a hero."

Naia looked at him, her eyes filling with unspilt tears. Nodding curtly, she whispered, "Then I'm proud of him."

She bowed her head and gazed down dully at her desk, absently chafing her hands as if trying to warm them. Gil couldn't stop staring at the motion. It was much easier to look at Naia's hands then at her face. He wanted to leave her to her grief, but he couldn't. There was still more he had to say.

Awkwardly, he cleared his throat. "Prime Warden. I'm sorry but..."

Naia looked at him, her eyes red and watery.

Gil shifted his weight, fidgeting. "The Sultan wants us to evacuate the Lyceum. He says he doesn't have the men to hold it. I believe he's wrong."

There was a long, unsettling span of silence. Naia stared down at her restless hands. Eventually, she looked up at him and said, "Then I will take your advice. With Warden Dalton gone, you're the strongest battlemage we have. And every report I've heard tells me you're the reason the Turan Khar hold half the city... instead of holding all of it. Because of those reasons, I'm naming you Warden of Battlemages in Dalton's place."

Hearing that, Gil shook his head. "Prime Warden, no. There must be a dozen people with more experience—"

Naia gazed up at him patiently. "It doesn't matter. You're by far the strongest mage we have and, so far, your decisions have been sound. I pray they continue to be."

He started to object, but Naia raised her hand, cutting him off. "You've heard my decision. Now, I'm sorry. I need a moment to myself. Please see to the defenses of the Lyceum. Do whatever you think is necessary."

Gil ducked his head. "Of course, Prime Warden."

He backed away from her desk, then turned and hastened out the door. Outside, he had to fight his way through the milling crowd of mages waiting for direction. He reached Ashra and breathed an intense sigh of relief.

Leaning into him, she asked, "Did you tell her?"

"I did," Gil said, though he didn't want to talk about it. Especially not where so many people could overhear the conversation.

"How did she take it?" Ashra whispered, her voice full of concern.

Without thinking, he snapped, "How would *you* take it?"

Ashra's eyes filled with hurt, and she looked away quickly. Gil reached out and caught her arm before she could walk away. "Look, I'm sorry," he said. "I really am. With all this, I'm not thinking straight."

"None of us are," she mumbled, her cheeks flushed. "You need to get some rest, even if it's not much. But you should try before we evacuate."

Gill shook his head. "We're not going to evacuate."

Ashra frowned. "What? You heard my father—"

"Your father's not in charge of the Lyceum," he reminded her. "Naia is. And we're not evacuating."

She glared at him hard. Then she turned and hastened away.

21

DESPERATE METHODS

THE SUN WAS GOING DOWN BEHIND THE MOUNTAINS BY THE TIME Rylan let Xiana guide him back through the door of the small hut. When she released his arm, he dropped to the floor and sat back against one of the rough, dark walls, drawing his knees up to his chest. He hardly noticed when she left. He sat there for a long time, trying to wrestle his thoughts back into focus. It was impossible. All he could think about was Kodiro's blood spreading toward him on the floor. And of the bride he'd made a widow on her wedding day.

Rylan scooted onto the rush-fiber pallet wedged into a corner and sat holding his head in his hands. A profound sadness welled up in him, tightening his throat. He thought of his son. He thought of Amina. His dead wife's image lingered in his mind, torturing him further.

His family was gone.

His life was gone.

All he had left was a boundless guilt and a terrible power he didn't understand. He was a prisoner of both, and there was no escaping either. He sat on the floor for another hour, perhaps more, crippled by despair. Eventually, exhaustion got the better of him. He lay down on the pallet and fell into a deep and troubled sleep.

He awoke the next morning to find that Xiana had returned. She entered and stooped to set down what looked like the same tray with the same clay pots. When Rylan saw the eggs come out, he wanted to groan. He rolled over on his pallet, facing away from her, and stared at the wall.

"You must eat," she said, tugging at the sleeve of his *yori*-robe.

He shook his head. He wasn't hungry, even though he knew he should be; all he'd eaten the previous day was the raw-egg broth. But he blamed her for Kodiro's death just as much as he blamed himself. He wanted nothing to do with either Xiana or her soup pots.

She tugged again on his sleeve. "You need to eat, and you need to learn," she stated firmly.

He didn't want to do either. He wanted to lay there staring at the wall until the images infesting his head went away. But he knew she wasn't going to let him do that. Irritated, he sat up and glowered at her through a tangled mat of dark hair.

They ate in silence. The soup was actually more palatable today, for some reason. Perhaps the seasoning was stronger, or maybe the broth was warmer; it was hard to say. Setting the empty soup-pot down on the tray, he leaned back against the wall and gazed down at a knot in one of the cracked floorboards. The knot had a split in it in the shape of a cross. He caught his thumbnail in the crack and worried at it absently.

"It's not your fault," Xiana said, sitting back and resting her hands on her thighs. "You had no way of knowing."

Rylan looked up at her, his anger swelling. "You're right. It's not my fault. It's yours."

She opened her mouth to speak, but he cut her off.

"You knew damn well I'm not aware of your customs. You put me in that position. That man's death is on you." He pointed at her. "Not me."

Xiana pulled in a deep breath and then nodded. "You're right. Kodiro's death was my fault. I'm sorry, Rylan. I didn't think."

His chest still felt tight with anger. He'd killed men in battle before. Many men. But this was different. Kodiro's death had been unnecessary. He searched Xiana's face deeply. It took him a minute, but at last he saw the remorse in her eyes. He'd been afraid he'd find none, but it was there, just hidden deep. That was something, at least.

"I need you to understand me," he said. "I'm here for my daughter; nothing else. No more weddings. No more baths. Hone me into a weapon as quickly as you can. And then set me loose upon my enemies."

She stared at him hard, a startled look in her eyes. Slowly, she nodded. Leaning forward, she said, "My people have a belief I'd like to share with you. We believe that everything that happens, happens for a reason. Every person you meet is someone you need to know. And you are who you are because that's who you need to be. Do you understand, Rylan? All that's happened to you, all of the trials you've faced, all of the grief you've suffered—it all means something. Everything serves a purpose. *You* serve a purpose. There are greater forces at work here than just you and me. This is all a part of it. It's what has to happen to make something far greater happen. You've been chosen for a reason. That is my belief."

She gazed piercingly into his eyes. "Are you ready to learn?"

"How am I going to learn anything, dampened?" he asked in frustration. He couldn't sense the magic field at all. Without even that meager sense, he didn't know what he could do.

Xiana responded, "I know people who can lift the damper

from you, but they are far away from here. Once you know enough, we will search them out."

He lifted an eyebrow. "And what about the Word of Command?"

"When I can trust you, I'll take you to those who can remove it," she answered, then added, "I don't trust you yet."

Of course she didn't—and with good reason. Which made him wonder how long it would take him to earn her trust. Every second he spent not searching for his daughter was a second wasted. A second Amina could be suffering. A second she could be dying.

"All right," he decided. "I'll work hard. I'll do anything you want, whatever it takes. Just teach me." He sat up and clasped his hands, ready to apply all of his concentration to the effort of learning.

"I'm not going to teach you," she said.

"What?" he asked.

Xiana trained her cold smile on him like a weapon. "The proper education of *deizu* takes years. I don't have years to teach you all that you need to learn—and neither do you."

Rylan frowned. "So, what are we going to do?"

Xiana looked down at her hands, her face fixed in tight lines, as though she were struggling hard with something—probably something about him. He hoped he wasn't on the losing side.

She looked up. "You need to become *deizu-kan*, a battlemage. And you only have days to do it. As soon as Karikesh falls, the Khar will absorb its people and move on to another city in the Rhen. I don't think you want that. We need to resort to desperate methods."

Rylan felt a cold chill creep over him, beginning at his neck. He asked warily, "What desperate methods?"

She reached up and fingered her necklace, the fiery opal that hung on its gold chain. Its colors swirled hypnotically. "I can take you to a place where you can learn all that you need to know, all at once, in a single second. But such learning comes at a heavy price."

Her words were like a crushing weight, bearing down on his shoulders. He didn't want that kind of knowledge, at any price. But he was growing desperate. Every step he took toward finding his daughter always seemed to be met with two steps back. And each step he took was progressively more impossible than the last. Exasperated, he asked, "So what's the price?"

"All that you are. And all that you have to give."

Xiana gazed at him steadily, as though scouring his eyes in search of fear. She would find none. Rylan was far too frustrated to dredge up the proper amount of anxiety he knew he should be feeling. So he shrugged.

"I have nothing to give. I don't even know who I am anymore, so I don't have anything to lose. All I want is my daughter back. Whatever that takes."

Xiana gave him a surprised look before finally muttering, "You're so naïve, Rylan." She lifted the tray and rose, turning toward the door. "I'm going to go fetch mounts and supplies."

"Where are we going?" he asked, rising after her.

"Down the mountain."

"Down into the valley?"

"Down into hell."

Xiana returned an hour later with a pair of stout mules, one a dusty brown, the other almost black. Both looked better suited to carrying baggage rather than riders on their backs. She had abandoned her *yori* for a raw silk tunic accompanied by wide-legged pants. She tossed Rylan a similar outfit and pointed toward the door of the hut.

"Go change."

He did as she bid, folding the robes he'd been wearing and replacing them in the cabinet. He then donned the new tunic and the pair of thick trousers that came with it. The earthy smell of the raw silk was overpowering, and not in a good way. Disgruntled, he cinched his belt tight, then went to rejoin Xiana in the garden outside the hut.

She looked him over sharply before issuing an approving nod. Leading one of the mules forward by the reins, she stopped in front of him. From among the gear strapped to the saddle, she withdrew a slender, curving sword and handed it to him. Rylan was surprised to find he was holding the scimitar given to him by the Sultan, taken from him when he was captured. Drawing it from its scabbard, he held it up and admired the blade, wondering why Xiana would present him with a weapon after making him a prisoner. Then he thought about it. With or without a sword, he posed no threat to her. The Word of Command was still firmly in place.

"My thanks," he said, sheathing the blade.

"Let's get moving," Xiana said.

22

THE FOLLY OF WISDOM

"Grand Master Archer?"

Gil moaned and lifted his head off the desk. At first, he had no idea where he was. It took him a moment of blinking through blurriness to realize he had fallen asleep in Quin's workroom. Wiping the saliva off his chin, he sat back in the chair and looked up at the acolyte who stood in a streak of light coming in through the doorway.

"What is it?" he asked groggily. He had no idea what time it was, although it felt like he hadn't gotten much sleep. The room was without windows, and the wood-paneled walls lent a feeling of eternal evening.

"The Prime Warden Requests a word with you," the acolyte informed him.

"All right."

As the young man left, Gil pushed back his chair, which squealed as it scraped across the floor. The sound did little for his nerves. He sat there a moment, propping his head with his hand, his elbow planted firmly on the desk. With his other hand, he groped inside his coin purse until he found the one treasure he always kept there: a white quartz rock. Absently, he fingered the rock, feeling its rough surface chafe his skin. It felt good. Cool. Just a little bit scratchy. The feel of it brought a sharp pang of nostalgia. The rock had once belonged to his father, passed to him by the priests who had raised him. It was the only thing he had left of him.

Gil let go of the rock and let it settle back into the pouch. He rose to his feet on legs that felt weaker than they should. Yawning, he raised his arms and stretched out his back. He paused for a moment to gather his wits, then left the room and walked down the stairs and through the courtyard in the direction of Naia's office.

The Lyceum was still standing, he was grateful to note. There was less confusion in the hallways than there had been. Men and women in black cloaks were still about, though fewer than before, and most seemed to be moving with some sense of purpose and direction. Naia's cold-eyed secretary greeted him with a scowl, but nevertheless let him pass without trying to stop him. Gil knocked once, then pushed open the door.

The Prime Warden looked up at him from behind her desk. She wasn't alone. Her attending acolyte sat in the corner on her stool, and along the walls stood six men and women ranging in age from middle years to the thoroughly decrepit. All were Wardens of their respective Orders. Gil noted the conspicuous absence of the Warden of Battlemages. And the Warden of Arcanists. He felt a lump form in his throat. Quin's death still rubbed his emotions raw.

"You sent for me?" he asked Naia.

She nodded and stood from her desk.

"I summoned you here to formally elevate you to the office of Warden of Battlemages." She lifted her hand, indicating the other men and women who had joined them. "I have asked the other Wardens here to serve as witnesses."

Gil looked around the ring of Wardens, feeling his skin break out in a sweat. Each one was staring at him with critical eyes. He could see the doubt on their faces, and he knew it was deserved. There were many people, older and more experienced, that the Prime Warden could have picked over him.

There were seven Orders of mages. There had been eight at one time but, of the Order of Harbingers, Naia was the last. She claimed the purpose of the Harbingers had been served with the destruction of the Well of Tears and had always refused to train an acolyte to their ways. The woman cowering in the corner holding quill and parchment served another Order, as had her predecessor.

Gil looked around the walls, from face to face, and felt unworthy to be included in such a circle. Iris Edelvar, a fiery-haired woman who led the Order of Chancellors, stared back at him from across the room, looking skeptical. To her left stood Alden Gage, Warden of Empiricists, the Order that concerned themselves with the theoretical intricacies of the magic field. Gage was a balding fellow who wore glasses and a bewildered look that was unfortunately permanent. Warden Cartwright, an ancient man with a stooped back and a skeletal face, led the Order of Naturalists, the Order chartered with the study of Natural Law. Next to him stood blonde-haired and willowy Elda Avenor, the Warden of Querers. Gil tended to think of Querers as your run-of-the-mill mages, though he knew that was doing them a disservice. The Querers went out into the world and roamed village-to-village, offering magical assistance where needed, especially healing.

He realized all the people in the room were staring at him, and he blinked. He'd forgotten the last thing Naia said. He wasn't sure what they were waiting for him to do.

"Ah... thank you," he said, hoping that was the right response. It got him some looks.

Nevertheless, Naia raised her voice and addressed those gathered, "Know that, by my will, Gilroy Archer has been elevated to the office of Warden of Battlemages. Grand Master

Archer, you are now the commander of the Lyceum's defenses. Feel free to disseminate orders as you see fit; you do not require my approval. If you need anything from me, you have but to ask. I will always be available to you, but I will not interfere with your authority unless you leave me no recourse. You are our general now. You have my blessing... and also my trust."

Gil dipped his head, feeling flustered and embarrassed. "Thank you, Prime Warden."

And then the brief ceremony was over. To Gil, it seemed rather anticlimactic.

"Congratulations, Warden Archer," said Warden Cartwright, grasping Gil's hand as he ambled toward the door. His skin felt cold and clammy, stretched thin over the bones of his hand.

"Warden Archer." Elda Avenor inclined her head as she left.

"Warden," said Alden Gage, looking just as puzzled as ever.

One by one, his new peers filed out of the office. The entire situation seemed surreal, like if he blinked his eyes, he'd find out it never happened. Soon he found himself alone with only Naia and her attending acolyte. The Prime Warden offered him a lifeless smile then regained her seat, folding her hands on her desk. Gil took the chair across from her and sat back with his hands on the armrests, gazing blankly at an oil painting mounted to the wall behind her. The light of the lanterns made the painting seem to come alive, the oil flowing across the canvas. It was some type of landscape, though one that looked foreign and utterly unfamiliar. It captured and held his attention.

"Your acolyte, Ashra," Naia began. "How far away from her Raising would you say she is?"

Gil frowned, wondering where she was going with the question. He reached up and scratched the unkept whiskers on his chin. "She has the foundations," he responded slowly. "But she hasn't received any of the specialized training necessary to take an Order."

"But does she know enough to get by?" Naia pressed.

"To get by?" Gil was confused by the question. "I'm not sure what that means."

Naia reached across her desk and lifted a feathered quill, dipping the sharpened point into an ink pot. Without looking at Gil, she applied her signature to a page of parchment set in front of her, saying conversationally, "I want her Raised to a full Master immediately. We need every mage we can possibly field."

Gil almost choked. "Ashra's not ready for a war— or even a battle!"

Naia set the parchment aside and replaced it with another. Her hand skimmed the line of cursive on the page before applying her signature with a scratching noise. "Maybe not. I wish we had the luxury of letting her develop at her own pace. But we don't." She slid another paper beneath her quill.

Gil collapsed back in his seat, all but throwing up his hands in frustration. "Can't you find her another mentor? I'm going to be too busy—"

"No, Gil." Naia set the quill down on her desk. "Ashra doesn't need another mentor. I could pick no one better suited to teach her."

She wasn't going to budge. He wanted to groan. Gil squeezed his eyes shut and sighed, collecting the scattered remains of his patience. He hadn't wanted to be saddled with Ashra in the first place, and that was before he knew he was going to be in charge of a war. He had enough to think about without having to attend to the safety of an acolyte.

But, looking at Naia's face, he realized that was simply the way it was going to be. "Then I'll do what I can," he said with a sigh.

The Prime Warden nodded. "Then it's settled. Have Ashra

prepare for the Rite of Transference. We will Raise her immediately."

Gil took that as his dismissal. He started to rise from his chair, but then stopped himself and settled back down again.

"Thank you. And again... I'm very sorry about Quin."

Naia gave him a sad smile. "Thank you. He was always fond of you, you know." Her smile disappeared. "Now, please go prepare Ashra."

He rose from his seat and, offering a curt bow, turned and left the room. He glanced sideways at the Prime Warden's secretary as he passed by her desk, noticing the woman staring after him with a look of resentment. He had no idea what he'd done to earn it. He took the stairs up two levels to the Acolytes' Residence, then wound his way through the hallways to Ashra's room. He knocked on the door and then waited. After a moment, the door cracked open and Ashra's face peered out at him. Her hair was in disarray, and she looked like she had just woken up from sleep.

"I want you to come with me," he said without preamble and stood back from the doorway, opening a path for her.

She gave him a confused look. "One moment," she said and closed the door, leaving him alone in the hallway. She emerged a minute later, tugging her cloak on over her shoulders, her hair in a messy braid.

"Where are we going?" she asked.

Instead of answering, Gil started walking down the hallway, listening to the sound of her feet as she hurried to catch up with him. He'd been thinking about the Prime Warden's question, about whether Ashra was truly ready for the amount of responsibility that was about to be thrust upon her. Despite his own reservations, he finally had to admit she was.

But there was something he wanted to teach her first. Maybe it was the last thing he would ever teach her; he couldn't be certain either of them would even be alive in another hour.

He led her up the stairs to the fourth-floor entrance of the library. Ashra stopped at the door and cast him a questioning look. But Gil didn't pause. He walked into the library ahead of her and led her deep into the warren of bookshelves and study tables, past the chess board Nat and Payden always favored, to a small alcove that housed only three rows of bookshelves.

As he led her between rows of shelves, Gil watched Ashra's eyes roving over the spines of books to either side. There were various texts of different sizes and covers: some cloth-bound, some leather. Some, too tall to be set neatly upon the shelf, were instead stacked one atop the other.

Gil stopped about halfway down and turned to her. He held out his hand, indicating the spread of books that surrounded them. "This used to be my favorite aisle in the library," he said, running his hands over the spines. "These texts have a lot to say about the philosophy and ethics of the craft. There's a lot of wisdom here. Thousands of years of thought. Thousands of words, all attempting to parse right from wrong, good from evil. And yet, if you study these books for a while, you realize that not one of them has a definitive answer. That's because there is none."

Ashra's brow pinched into lines of confusion. "What are you trying to tell me, Gil?"

It was a good question. He wasn't sure himself.

He said carefully, "I'm trying to tell you that being a mage isn't easy, and it will eat your soul if you let it. People will try to tell you there's a right and a wrong way to go about being one, but there's not. Everything is situational, and even then, half the time you'll never know if what you're doing is really the right thing."

He drew in a deep breath and fixed his stare on a lone stack of books sitting on a desk between shelves. "You're to receive the Rite of Transference today."

The expression on Ashra's face collapsed into panic.

"Today?" She gasped, reaching out to clutch his arm. "I'm not ready!"

Without looking at her, Gil said, "The Prime Warden thinks you are."

Ashra shook her head, her eyes wide and alarmed. "Why would she think that?"

Gil shrugged. "You know everything you need to know to be successful. Anything else I could teach you is merely supplemental. Everyone thinks that the moment you become a Master, you know all you will ever need to know. But that's not true. You continue to grow and learn throughout your entire life. Magic is a journey. Tonight you start yours."

As he talked, he ran his fingers over the uneven spines of the books. When he got to the end of the shelf, he looked back at her, studying the expression on her face.

"You don't think I'm ready, do you?" Ashra asked.

Was that hurt in her eyes? Or fear? He couldn't tell. Either or both would be appropriate, he supposed. Gil felt his stomach tighten. He owed her the truth.

"No," he said. "I don't think you're ready. But I'm not sure we're going to win this war. I suppose it's better to die fighting than to die running." He did his best to smile.

Ashra drew a deep breath, expelling it slowly. "I suppose it is," she whispered.

Gil glanced at the shelf next to him, his gaze coming to rest on a familiar text. He took the book down from the shelf and cradled it in his hands. Staring down at the leather cover, he felt a warm pang of sentiment role over him.

"I think this one is my favorite," he said with a faint smile.

"What is it?"

"*The Folly of Wisdom,*" he said, offering the book to her. "After my father died, I was raised by the priests of the Temple of Wisdom. They saw to it that I knew my letters and was 'properly educated,' which basically amounted to studying a bunch of old books that talked about 'classical thought.' I ate it up at the time. I thought the secret to every facet of life was contained in those books. That there was no question they couldn't answer. But looking back on it, I know now that it was all horseshit. Most of the time, there is no right answer. Just different degrees of wrong."

He watched as Ashra leafed slowly through the text. Eventually, she closed the cover and looked up at him. He removed the book from her hand and replaced it on the shelf.

"Are you ready?" he asked.

"I don't know."

Gil smiled. "Then it sounds like you are." He took her by the hand. "Come on. "Let's go get you ready to fight."

He led her out of the library and back downstairs to Naia's office. This time, the Prime Warden's secretary didn't even look up at him as he passed. He supposed there might be some perks to his new office. Smiling smugly, he opened the door for Ashra. The Prime Warden rose to her feet as they entered. Beneath her long white cloak, she was wearing a formal blue robe. A warm smile brightened her face at the sight of Ashra.

"Please come in," she said, motioning her forward. "Do you know why you're here?"

Ashra stopped in front of the desk but didn't take a seat.

"I do, Prime Warden."

Naia spread her hands. "Do you have any questions?"

Ashra glanced to Gil, looking at him for a moment before responding, "No."

"Do you know the words?"

"I do."

"Very well."

Pushing her chair back, Naia moved out from behind her desk and drew up to stand in front of Ashra. For the first time, Gil noticed she held a familiar necklace in her hands: a medallion set with a brilliant red stone that shimmered with radiant light, held by two wide silver bands that formed a collar when clasped. It was much more than just a necklace, he knew. The medallion was called the Soulstone, and it was the most precious artifact the Lyceum possessed.

Vitrus—the Gift that allowed a person to touch the magic field—could only be Transferred upon the death of a mage to their successor. For millennia, that had been the only way magic could persist. The Gift was passed from one generation to the next in discrete magical legacies that became fewer and fewer over time, until there were only a handful of mages left in the entire world.

Until Quin had created the Soulstone. The artifact was one-of-a-kind; there was no other like it. The stone harvested *vitrus* directly from the magic field itself and could Transfer it into a person. No longer did one mage have to die for another to be born. With it, Quin and Naia had managed to grow their numbers significantly. It was the one artifact Gil would never want to see in the hands of the Turan Khar.

Naia lifted the Soulstone, holding it by its silver bands. "Kneel."

Ashra dropped to her knees, bowing her head.

Moving to stand over her, Naia recited formally, "Ashra ni Sayeed, are you willing and prepared to spend your life as a guardian of the land and of its people?"

Staring at the floor, Ashra answered in a steady voice, "I am."

"And are you also prepared to accept accountability for your every action, so that your decisions be always tempered by wisdom, compassion, and humility?"

"I am, Prime Warden." There was no hesitation in her voice.

"Then stand and speak the words."

Ashra rose gracefully to her feet and, lifting her head, looked Gil in the eyes as she recited the ancient pledge, "I swear to exist only to serve the land and its people. With my life, if possible. If not, then by death."

Naia stepped behind her and drew the silver bands of the Soulstone's collar around her neck. Ashra drew in a deep breath and held it as Naia seemed to be fumbling with the clasp. It didn't take her long to get it. After only a moment, Gil heard a slight click.

Brilliant white light, brighter than the sun, erupted from the stone, forcing him backward against the wall. Ashra cried out and fell to her knees, ribbons of charged power clawing over her body like forked tongues of lightning. She collapsed to the floor, moaning and writhing as her body drank in the torrent of power delivered by the Soulstone. The light swelled, became dazzling, so brilliant that Gil had to bring his hands up to shield his eyes.

And then, suddenly, the stone went dark.

Ashra lay panting on the ground, shivering and shaking. Naia moved forward at once, kneeling beside her and removing the medallion from her neck before it could steal back the *vitrus* it had just relinquished. The Prime Warden knelt at Ashra's side and placed a hand on her comfortingly. She stroked her hair back from her face with the compassion of a mother, watching over her until Ashra's breathing slowed and her eyes fluttered open.

Naia smiled and, pulling back, said, "Rise, Master Ashra, and welcome."

Her eyes wide and watery, Ashra sat upright, still too shaken to stand on her own. Gil helped her to her feet, steadying her. Her body was covered in sweat, her hair drenched and hanging down her back, escaping her braid. Tears glistened on her cheeks.

Naia turned to smile at Gil, looking pleased. "Warden Archer, would you please excuse us? Ashra and I have some things to talk about. You're in charge of the war now, gods help us all. Please see to it that we don't lose."

Gil bowed, not knowing what to think about that.

"I'll make it a priority," he said. Turning toward the door, he managed to conjure a brief smile for Ashra. "Congratulations," he said. He waited just a moment to see if she would respond. When she didn't, he let himself out.

23

THE DESOLATION

RYLAN PUT HIS FOOT IN THE STIRRUP AND SWUNG HIS LEG OVER the mule's back. Immediately, he found himself detesting the saddle. It was made of a hard wood frame covered in bright fabric, with a high cantle and pommel. The saddle was held together by metal fittings and knobs that dug painfully into his thighs. He glanced at Xiana, wondering how the woman showed no sign of discomfort. She gave him a quick nod, then kicked her mule forward.

The trail they took led through the village streets and onto the cliffs, transitioning from hard-packed dirt onto painted wood bridges and ramps, then again to a steep path barely wide enough for the mules to walk single file. The view of the valley was obstructed by the ever-present haze that hovered over it; he couldn't tell how far up they were or how much of the trail they had yet to traverse. After an hour of plodding downhill, his back hurt from leaning back in the saddle against the hard cantle. Although it took him a while to get used to its lurching gait, in the end, he was grateful for the mule. The animal took short, steady strides, always careful where it placed its feet.

The trail switchbacked many times, and it took them hours

to finally reach the elevation of the haze. It was actually a fogbank, though it was much more brown than gray. Despite the cold, Rylan's forehead broke out into an icy sweat. In the darkness of the fog, his mind started churning, worrying that his mule would stumble or miss a step. Fortunately, the muddy fog didn't last long. The mist parted to reveal the plain below, much further away than he'd been expecting.

And much more sinister.

It took him a moment to realize what was wrong with the view. Then it came to him: there was not one hint of green in the entire landscape. Below them unfolded a flat expanse of unrelieved brown covered by more of the same filthy haze. There were scant landmarks, just a few conical hills poking up every so often from the desert's mottled complexion. The heat of the air above the plain made the view of the landscape shimmer and distort.

"What's down there?" Rylan called ahead to Xiana, not liking the looks of the terrain.

She glanced back at him with a grave expression. "I told you. Hell. Or at least as close as you'll probably ever come."

Her words made Rylan think of the oath to Chaos he had sworn, and he shuddered. The mules plodded along another two hours as the trail wound down into the foothills and the air warmed around them. Every so often, the trail became infested by chunks of crumbled rock fallen from the cliffs, sometimes caused by the passage of their own mounts. Eventually, the path widened onto an alluvial plain that sloped gradually downward between two sprawling ridges. Where the dirt began, the trail ended. Before them stretched only an infinite expanse of smooth, barren earth broken by dark chunks of lava rock that looked strewn haphazardly across the soil, giving the vast landscape a speckled appearance. There were no plants, not even one dead blade of grass.

Rylan glanced about in dismay, shocked by the sheer bleakness of the terrain. An abandoned waystation tucked up against the foothills was the only object within sight that suggested humanity had ever existed in this place.

"Where are we?" he wondered aloud.

"The Mokona Desolation." Xiana reined in her mule, falling back to ride at his side as they angled toward the waystation.

Rylan grimaced. "It's desolate, all right. How can a landscape be so barren?"

"It's worse than barren," Xiana corrected him. "It's sterile."

"Sterile? How so?"

She waved her hand, gesturing around at the bleak expanse. "The Curse your father helped lift covered this land for a thousand years—a thousand years of darkness, without one ray of sunlight. This is what remains. In the Desolation, nothing can grow. The soil is no longer fertile. It lacks seed, and any nutrients that were ever in the dirt have long since washed away. Only the Lonesome Ghosts wander these wastes."

Her words made Rylan shiver despite the heat. Glancing across the hostile terrain, he asked, "Why did you bring me here?"

She gave him a small, sad grin. "Together, we'll journey into the waste, to a place called Suheylu Ra. There, you will learn all you need to know."

"How do we get there?" he asked dismally. "I don't see any roads."

"There is no road to Suheylu Ra," Xiana answered, reining in. "Dunes and dust wander the waste and swallow any trail. There is only one way to cross the Desolation: you must learn to see and follow the lines of the magic field."

Rylan frowned. "We're dampened," he reminded her, wiping his brow. "Both of us. I can't sense the field lines, and neither can you."

Xiana made a broad, flowing gesture. "But the earth can.

There are things in the earth that are sensitive to the field lines. Sometimes the effects are profound. The Varigian Islands are a good example. They are a series of volcanoes that follow the contortion of a field line. Strange things happen there. Or the Sky Stones in Aeridor. Things like that are caused by interactions with the field."

Looking out across the Desolation, Rylan wondered again where this place was in the world. And he wondered how much more of the world there was still out there, either unknown or ignored by people of the Kingdoms.

"Why haven't I ever heard of those places?" he asked

Her hands flowing in the smooth gestures that were part of her language, Xiana explained, "Because the Curse cut off your people from the rest of the world. The societies with advanced magic were mostly destroyed, and their knowledge was lost. The weather patterns were so disturbed, the oceans were impassible. The southern hemisphere was completely cut off from the north."

Ahead of them, the waystation sat, forlorn, in the lee of a sandstone bluff, cradled by a ring of tumbled boulders. The station was little more than a dilapidated shack made of ancient, splintering wood. A small paddock stood apart from it, its fence composed of rotten boards. Old, rusted nails protruded from long cracks in the wood. The fence didn't look like it would hold against the slightest nudge from an animal. Next to the paddock, an old windmill creaked lonesomely.

Xiana climbed down from her mount. She gestured for Rylan to do the same, then opened the gate to the paddock and tied her mule to one of the wobbly fence posts. There, she unloaded her saddlebags, tossing them to the ground while Rylan stood watching her, his mule's long tail twitching against his thigh.

He started unloading his own mount. When he was done,

he turned the mule loose in the paddock and picked up his saddlebags, slinging them over a shoulder.

"What now?" he asked.

"We can't bring the mules into the Desolation," Xiana said, moving over to a low bin. She threw the cover back and pulled out an armload of hay. "There's no water out there, and the terrain's not suited to them. We'll have to walk to Suheylu Ra."

"Walk?" Rylan echoed, staring at her in disbelief.

"Walk," she confirmed. She placed the hay in a feeding trough, then dusted her hands off on her trousers. "We'll stay here tonight. In the morning, we'll set off across the waste."

They spent the night inside the small, decrepit structure, unrolling their bedrolls on the floor. The waystation creaked and groaned all night like a cranky old man, the sound of splitting wood waking Rylan up at least twice. In the morning, he woke to a breakfast of hard bread. After they ate, Xiana went out to the paddock and saddled the mules.

"I thought we couldn't ride them?" Rylan asked, walking out to join her.

"We're not going to," she responded. "But we can't leave them here either."

She tied the animals' reins to the pommels of their saddles, then opened the gate, sending the first mule off with a swat on the hindquarters. The mule bolted immediately for the cliffs, followed by the darker beast. Rylan watched them go, galloping back the way they had come toward the mountain trail.

"They'll find their way back," Xiana assured him. "They always do."

Rylan lifted an eyebrow. "So how do *we* get back?"

Instead of answering, Xiana bent to retrieve her saddlebags

from the ground. She handed him a scarf and strode for the gate, gesturing ahead. "You lead."

"I can't. I don't know where I'm going," Rylan reminded her. He wound the scarf around his head, scanning the rock-strewn plain with acute distrust. The air out there was a murky brown. It looked like the last place in the world he wanted to go.

Nevertheless, he started walking, Xiana coming along at his side with a smile on her face. He set his course for the horizon, his feet crunching on dry clots of dirt. Just as she'd said, there were no paths leading out from the waystation. He looked to her for confirmation that he was heading in the right direction. He didn't get any.

"Have you ever been out here?" he asked.

"Yes. A while ago."

"So you know the way? If we get lost?"

Keeping her gaze on the horizon, Xiana answered, "I don't know the way. It changes as the field lines wander. The path I remember no longer exists."

He frowned at the flat expanse ahead, at the heatwaves distorting the desert in front of them. "What are we going to do when I can't find it?"

She wiped her arm across her brow. "Then we die of thirst."

Vexed, he stopped asking questions. She wasn't giving any logical answers, anyway, so it didn't matter. They walked for another hour across the stone-splattered ground, until they crested a low hill made of dark, tumbled rocks. There, Rylan stopped and looked back the way they had come, discovering that the waystation and the cliffs above it were no longer visible, both lost behind the thick brown haze.

Looking down at the sharp rocks beneath his feet, Rylan realized they were standing atop a lava flow. It continued ahead for miles, in some places smothered by a thin veil of sand.

"How do I know which way to go?" he grumbled, staring

out at the vastness of the lava flow. "What am I supposed to do?"

"Keep going," she instructed. "You'll know soon."

He wondered how he would know but didn't bother to ask. Her answers were becoming progressively more vague, and he suspected that was intentional. She knew something he didn't and didn't want to share that knowledge. Which was fine. He figured he could trust her not to lead them to her own death.

Rylan took a drink from his canteen, then passed it over to her. It was filled with water from the waystation's well. The water was hot and gritty and tasted like dirt, but it did its job. She passed it back and he hung it from his shoulder. Setting his course for the horizon, Rylan started forward over the broken ground.

***

The lava flow wasn't endless.

Rylan stopped at the margin of it, where the ragged dark rocks crumbled into a mottled landscape covered by water and a thick layer of mist. It took him a moment to realize that the water stretching before them was not a lake, at least not in the sense he was used to. The plain in front of them was an enormous salt flat pockmarked by thousands of green, shallow pools. The pools were irregular in shape and bordered by winding ribbons of white salt that turned bright ochre at the margins. Above the pools hung a thick miasma that stank terribly.

Choking, Rylan turned around and started back the way they had come.

Xiana stopped and didn't follow him. "That's not the way," she said.

Rylan turned back to her, gesturing at the salt flat. "Well, that sure as hell's not the way either. So where do we go?"

Xiana set her bags down on the rocks. "This is Puna Ajaru, the Scalding Sea. We must cross it in order to reach Suheylu Ra. You will need to find a path for us through the pools."

"Through *that?*" Rylan looked out across the deadly sea of acrid mist. "We can't even *approach* those pools. Don't you smell that? That air would scorch our lungs before we took ten steps."

He scanned the plain before them with three parts dismay and one part fascination. Strange, ochre-stained mounds of salt collected in knee-high peaks emitted a noxious steam that roved in clouds over the landscape. Many of the pools bubbled like boiling cauldrons, creating a thick, foaming froth.

Xiana squatted, one hand resting on the lava rock, and pointed ahead. "The pools are acid," she said, confirming Rylan's fears. "The fog comes from holes in the ground. A large volcano lives beneath us. These rocks are the volcano's cooled blood, and the mist is its hot breath. The patterns of salt that ring the pools follow the lines of the magic field. We need to cross this plain. And the only way to do that is to follow the curve of the field lines as they wind through the acid."

"We'll die," Rylan said. He shouldn't have to tell her that. "The air will kill us long before the acid does."

She stood and looked out over the plain, her face solemn. "This is the only way to Suheylu Ra. If you follow the lines of the magic field, the poison gases will not touch us. Puna Ajaru is only dangerous if you wander off the path."

She was crazy, he decided. Either brutally insane or insanely brutal; he didn't know which was worse. He stood for a moment gazing at the rocks, coolly considering his options. They were limited. He could refuse to go forward and insist they turn back. And if she didn't listen, he could leave her there —just abandon her. Of course, that reasoning didn't take into account the Word of Command. She could activate it whenever she wanted, for whatever reason. In the end, Xiana was in charge.

He heaved a defeated sigh, running a hand through his hair. "So how do we get across?"

Xiana gestured ahead. "The fumes collect in places where the magic field is weakest. We must avoid those places and travel in the direction of the field lines. The field has a certain pattern to it, like ripples spreading across a pond. The lines travel in peaks and troughs, and you can see them echoed in the paths around the pools."

Exasperated, Rylan shrugged hugely. "How do I know what they look like?"

Xiana cracked a cynical grin and clapped him on the back. "Trial and error. So, are you ready to learn?"

Rylan glowered at her but didn't bother with a reply.

"Then let's go." Hefting her bags, she started down the slope toward the pools.

With a frustrated grunt, Rylan stumbled after her. He was already choking on fumes by the time he stepped off the lava flow onto the salt flat. The gases were noxious, scalding his throat and making his eyes water. Xiana looked at him and smiled, waving him ahead.

"Which way do we go, Rylan?"

He aimed a glare at her in frustration. "Stay here."

He moved forward carefully, his boots crunching on salt. He walked up to the edge of the first pool, then stopped, staring down at it. The water was a blurry yellow-green, the salt surrounding it white and crystalline, like snowflakes. Graceful ribbons of salt extended out into the pool in lacy tendrils. Bubbles oozed to the surface in three or four places, while a cone of salt next to him spat water and noxious steam.

Rylan held his arm over his mouth and coughed into his sleeve. He stood scanning the terrain for a pattern. But there was no pattern that he could find. The entire landscape looked entirely chaotic. Holding his breath, he picked his way forward around the margin of the nearest pool, until the ridge of salt he was walking on curved back in an S-shape.

The gases surrounding him became less dense.

"I think it's this way," he called back to Xiana. "But I'm not certain."

She smiled eagerly and moved to follow him as he circled the edge of the next pool. Carefully, keeping a keen eye on his footing, he picked his way out into the dimpled surface of the salt flat. The further he went in, the more he realized Xiana had been right. The gases dispersed and then disappeared completely from their path. His eyes stopped watering, and he drew in a deep, grateful breath. As long as they stayed on the right path, the air was fine.

"See? You're doing it." Xiana smiled proudly, although Rylan doubted he was doing much more than trusting to luck.

He worked his way across a winding ledge between two pools. When he was halfway across, the salt gave way beneath his boot and he lost his balance. Arms pinwheeling, he plunged his foot into the acid pool to stop himself from falling bodily in.

Xiana caught hold of him and hauled him back upright, gasping, "Are you all right?"

Rylan reached a hand into his boot and felt around to make sure his sock was still dry. "It didn't go through," he said in relief.

Xiana heaved a heavy sigh and shook her head. "Be more careful."

Rylan raised his eyebrows, but kept his mouth shut. He turned and started back across the narrow band of salt, working his way out further into the maze of pools. Ahead, the path forked around a broad expanse of gurgling water. He stopped, uncertain of which way to go. He took a guess, heading to the right until the air became caustic. Then he turned and worked his way back in the opposite direction, with the same result. Retreating to where he started from, he looked to Xiana for direction.

"Now what?"

She stared out across the wide, smoldering pool. Sweat beaded on her brow and ran down her face. "There has to be a way. One of these paths is the right one. What do your instincts tell you?"

"My instincts tell me to get the hell out of here." He surveyed her face for a moment, weighing her expression. At last, he concluded, "You really don't know the way, do you?"

She took a deep breath, biting her lip. "No."

"No," Rylan repeated. He swung his packs down off his shoulder and dropped them at his side. "Is this a sick joke? You got us in here and you've no idea how to get us out?"

Xiana drew herself up rigidly. "There's a way through the pools, Rylan. You just need to find it."

A strange noise, like the mournful cry of a dove, rose above the mist. Rylan glanced at Xiana in alarm. She'd heard it too; her eyes were wide and fearful, darting every which direction.

"What was that?" he asked.

She licked her lips. "The Lonesome Ghosts. If they find us here, they'll kill us."

24

PAYDEN

Gil startled awake.

He hadn't realized he'd fallen asleep. Blinking groggily, he rubbed his eyes then sat up, hands going to the papers spread out before him on the desk. He'd been reading them before he'd drifted off. He started sorting through the pages, putting them back in order, all except for one he left out intentionally: Quin's notes on the talisman *Thar'gon,* an artifact that had once belonged to his father. It had been lost when the Well of Tears was destroyed, on the day his father died. It had fallen from his hand. Where it had ended up, Gil had no idea. All he knew was that if they had that weapon now, the war would be going very differently. Unfortunately, Quin's notes contained no hints whatsoever as to where *Thar'gon* could be found.

Stretching, Gil looked around his new office. It had been Warden Dalton's office only the day before. It might be someone else's office tomorrow. But for now it was his, a good-sized room garbed in marshal décor, complete with mounted weapons, obsolete banners, and smoke-darkened tapestries. All eyesores, of course. Not that he cared.

He straightened the stack of papers and set them aside. He

was about to reach for another stack when the sound of commotion in the hallway caught his attention. Before he could react, the door banged open and three large men with swords spilled into the room. He gaped in shock as the Sultan crossed the room in two great strides.

Leaning over the desk, Sayeed bellowed, "Where are your mages? They are supposed to be protecting the Waterfront!"

Gil leaned back in his chair to get away from the man. Forcing himself to speak calmly, he responded, "I have given you as many mages as I can spare, Your Majesty. You should have received that message."

The Sultan grimaced and raised a trembling finger. Streaks of sweat dribbled down his cheeks, splashed wetly on the desk. His eyes were ringed with dark circles and had a glimmer of madness about them. Gil wondered how long it had been since the man had slept.

"There are only sixteen battlemages at the Waterfront!" the Sultan growled. "Surely, you have more than *sixteen?*"

Gil slid out of his chair and moved out from behind the desk. "Four days ago, I had forty-two battlemages. After last night, I'm down to twenty-four. That leaves me sixteen to deploy along the Waterfront and only eight to ward the Lyceum."

Sayeed made a growling noise, his lips curling back from his teeth. He spun away, striking a hand out at the air. "The Waterfront cannot be held with only sixteen battlemages!"

Gil took a deep breath, striving for composure. Then he forced the most apologetic smile he could muster. "I'm sorry, Your Majesty. We're not abandoning the Lyceum."

The Sultan barked a guttural string of Malikari at the soldiers who had entered with him. He took a step toward the door, then turned back to glare at Gil, his face a patchwork of black filth and red anger.

"I told you—it is impossible to hold the Lyceum with the resources we have!"

Gil stabbed a glare at the two men standing behind the Sultan, who looked positioned to prevent his premature exit.

"Look," he said. "I'm not asking you to spare any of your men. The Lyceum will protect itself."

Sayeed crossed his arms over his chest. "You spread your numbers too thin. Without more battlemages, we will lose the Waterfront. And if that happens, we will lose the rest of the city! A strategic retreat from this district is the only option we have." The man's stare was iron-hard and unyielding.

Gil sighed. He couldn't yield the Lyceum. But perhaps he could compromise. "I'll give you two more battlemages," he said. "But that's it. No more."

The Sultan's eyes narrowed, and he blew out a frustrated breath. Bowing his head, he scrubbed his hands over his face. "You are just as stubborn as your father."

The comment made Gil smile. "Thank you, Your Majesty."

With one last, resentful glare, the Sultan turned and stalked out of the room, his guards hastening to follow. Gil sagged against the wall in relief, looking down at his trembling hands. Sliding back into his chair, he glanced around the room, wondering if, by chance, Warden Dalton might have left a flask of whiskey behind. Dalton had always been fond of his drink, and now Gil knew why. Spotting a small decanter sitting on a shelf behind the desk, he lifted a hand toward it.

"Should we consider evacuating?"

Startled, he turned to see Naia standing in the doorway. He wondered how much of the confrontation she'd overheard. Probably all of it.

Rising from his seat, he answered, "How can we evacuate? There's too much knowledge and too many artifacts here we can't risk falling into enemy hands. There's no way we could get it all out in time."

Naia lifted a perfectly arched eyebrow. "It might be prudent to start."

She was right, Gil had to admit. He nodded in defeat. "I'll put the acolytes to work."

The Prime Warden gave him a sharp nod then left, closing the door. Gil gave the whiskey decanter a regretful look, then collected his things and walked out into the hallway, closing the door behind him. Looking up, he was surprised to find Ashra seated on a bench across from his office.

At the sight of him, she popped up and hurried over to his side. "I heard what my father said to you," she said, keeping pace with him stride for stride. "You should listen to him. He is a great commander."

"His priorities don't align with mine," Gil said, turning a corner.

"His priorities are not the issue," Ashra insisted. "If my father says we are spread too thin, then we are spread too thin. That is fact, not opinion. You must listen to him!"

"I don't need to listen to—"

A small crowd of mages spilled into the hallway, dragging two men in their midst, the walls echoing with the sounds of shouts and wailing. They stopped as soon as they saw him, letting the men they were wrestling with sag to the floor. The men were chained together, just like the enemy mages he'd confronted. At first, Gil thought they were both mages of the Khar, but then he realized he recognized one of them.

It was Payden, the man whose chess game he always liked to ruin. Payden's eyes were wide with fright, his face pale and blotchy. He clutched the man chained to him as if terrified. His companion was an enemy mage, with grayish skin and black hair, his features sharp and foreign.

"What's this?" Gil asked, starting toward them.

One of his men—Emerton— rushed forward to meet him.

"We rescued Payden, sir! But we can't get the damn chain off. It's some kind of artifact."

Approaching the two men, Gil knelt beside them. He raised his hand to touch Payden's face, but the man jerked back. The way he was staring at him, Gil didn't think Payden recognized him. The gray man chained to him whimpered.

"Is he dampened?" he asked, nodding at the Khar mage.

"Oh, yes," Emerton answered.

Gil withdrew his hand. "Payden. Can you hear me?"

At first, Payden didn't respond. He stared at him with an intensely confused expression. At last, his eyebrows netted together, and he issued a little gasp.

"Archer?"

Gil nodded. "It's me. Gil." He raised his hand again, wanting to probe the man for injury. But Payden flinched back, terror in his eyes. Gil asked, "Do you know where you are?"

Payden looked around as if seeing the tiled hallway for the first time in his life. He looked like a man just waking from a coma. "The Lyceum?"

"That's right." Gil smiled, then nodded at the gray men. "Who's your friend, here?"

"His name's Almir." Payden clutched the man next to him harder. The Khar mage was trembling, obviously terrified. He looked like an animal caught in a trap, ready to chew off its own foot. Payden stroked the man's hair tenderly.

Gil glanced back at Ashra, beckoning her forward with a jerk of his chin. Maybe a woman's gentle presence would help calm them down.

Turning back to Payden, he asked, "Is Almir dangerous?"

Payden shook his head vehemently. "No—no, he's my friend!"

Emerton said, "He's one of their mage-slaves."

Muttering soothingly, Ashra reached out and cupped Payden's face. He let her, even though he trembled at her touch.

Ashra closed her eyes, delving within him. After a moment, she released him and looked at Gil.

"I don't think there's anything wrong with him physically," she said.

Gil rose and peered down at the two chained mages, contemplating the situation grimly. Payden had been a prisoner of the enemy for two days before he'd been rescued. What they'd gotten back didn't seem like the man Gil remembered. They'd done something to him. He rubbed his eyes wearily, thinking of the way their mages had invaded his own mind from across the water. If they could do that, from that distance, he couldn't imagine what it would be liked physically linked to them.

A shout from Ashra was the only thing that saved his life.

Gil dove to the side, avoiding a lance of white-hot energy that pierced the air where he'd just been standing. He broke his fall with the palms of his hands and rolled over, scrambling upright. He reacted before he could think, hurling a thunder-clap of air back at the enemy mage.

Three men dogpiled Payden, who screamed piteously, thrashing about on the floor. The gray man lay flat on his back, unmoving. Ashra started toward him, but Gil stopped her with a raised hand. Climbing to his feet, he moved forward to examine the man himself.

The enemy mage was dead. Gil hadn't meant to kill him, but it didn't matter. His death had reduced Payden to a gibbering mess. He fought and bucked, howling and weeping.

"*You killed him!*" he screamed through his sobs. "*Why? He was dampened! It was me! Oh, gods, it was me!*"

Three men were having a hard time holding him down. Gil stared at him in disgust, uncertain what to think. This wasn't Payden. At least, not the Payden he remembered.

"Get that chain off him and get him downstairs," he growled. "Keep him warded and under guard."

"I told you, we can't get the damn thing off!" Emerton protested.

Gil stared down at Payden, already sick of his new rank, feeling his insides grow cold. "Then cut his hand off."

"You're serious?"

"Aye, I'm serious." The order twisted Gil's stomach in knots, but it didn't matter. One glance at Payden reaffirmed his decision. The man was squirming on his belly, clutching and kissing the dead man.

Gil turned and strode away, shoulders slumped. When Payden started shrieking, he closed his eyes against the sound, wishing he could close his ears as well. The shrieks faded, replaced by soul-shredding sobs and howls.

"No! Don't take him from me! Don't take him!"

Gil blew out a long, weary sigh but kept walking.

Ashra caught up to him before he reached the door. He opened it, stepping out into the light of morning, and just stood there as the door closed behind him, cutting off the sounds of Payden's suffering. He lingered there on the threshold a while, gazing out across a sky choked with smoke, the sun reduced to an orange halo. He tried rubbing the exhaustion out of his eyes, but it didn't work

At his side, Ashra said, "How could Payden have grown so attached to that man in such a short amount of time?"

Still staring out across the burning city, Gil responded, "Obviously, they did something to him."

Ashra's gaze followed his. "Let's hope with that chain off, he'll return to himself."

Somehow, Gil doubted that he would. He'd looked deeply into Payden's eyes and didn't have a lot of hope for him. He turned to Ashra. "Thank you, by the way. I think you saved my life."

She smiled softly. "I think I did. And you're welcome."

He studied her face. A week ago, he'd considered this

woman an enemy. At the time, he hadn't known what a true enemy was. He'd been a self-righteous ass, and he owed her an apology. He reminded himself to give her one later, if they lived.

Ashra at his side, he walked down the steps and out into the debris-littered street, then set his course westward toward the Kazri Souk, where his battlemages were holding their line by their fingernails. It was time to rotate some back to the Lyceum for what rest they could get. Tired mages were dangerous mages. They needed enough sleep to keep their wits about them.

They worked their way down a street lined on both sides with soldiers. Ash rained down from the sky, alighting on his cloak. More ash collected in the street like fine drifts of gray snow. Around them, the city was eerily quiet. The fighting had stopped, and an uneasy stillness chilled the air with a looming sense of anticipation.

They arrived at a small cluster of black-cloaked men and women crouching behind a hastily constructed barricade made of overturned wagons and stacked furniture. Gil was greeted by weary faces and irritated glares. Not many of them liked him, but he didn't care.

"New rule," Gil announced as he stopped in front of them. "Nobody gets taken alive. No matter what."

25

THE LONESOME GHOSTS

RYLAN STARED BACK ACROSS THE POCKMARKED PLAIN THE WAY they had come. He could only see the area right around them; after that, the gases thickened and became opaque. He saw nothing moving in the fog... until he did. In the distance, ghostly shapes manifested within the clouds of roving mist and angled toward them, their images blurry as if distorted by waves of heat.

"What do they want?" he asked. Whoever they were, they had seen them and were headed in their direction.

Xiana took a step backward, her expression suddenly fearful. "They're territorial," she whispered. "They protect their salt mines."

Which meant they probably wouldn't hesitate before killing two outsiders who had strayed into their territory.

"Come on," Rylan growled, bending to pick up his packs. "You'd better start praying, because they look like they know this place a lot better than we do." With that, he looked down and made a guess, choosing between two paths that led deeper into the fog, away from the approaching people. He caught Xiana's hand and led her after him, picking his way carefully around the margin of a pool, his feet crunching deep into brittle layers of salt.

On the other side of the pool, the gases in the air thickened again. From behind them came another mournful cry. Rylan quickened his pace, his eyes blurry with tears clawed from his eyes by the caustic fumes. He had a terribly sour taste in his mouth. He brought his arm up to his face and coughed, the action stinging his throat worse.

"This isn't working," he said hoarsely.

He could feel himself starting to panic. Pulling Xiana forward by her hand, he randomly chose a different path. Very quickly, it became apparent that it was the wrong choice. The air was scalding. Rylan hurried around the edge of the nearest pool, searching for a break in the mist. He didn't see one. Choking, he scrambled over salt-crusted hummocks and climbed onto a ridge that ran between pools.

Xiana staggered and fell to her knees, wracked in dry coughs.

Rylan glanced behind and saw the figures moving after them through the fog, much closer now than they had been before. He caught Xiana under her arm and pulled her to her feet, then struggled forward, supporting her weight. Leaning into him, she coughed into his shirt.

"You must find a path," she whispered, her voice raw and weak.

Gripping her around the waist, he pulled Xiana along with him. Together, they wound their way around green pools until they arrived at a narrow, ribboning salt path. The air there was clean. Xiana collapsed against him, wheezing and gasping. Rylan sank to his knees, desperate to catch his breath. The acid in the air had scorched his throat raw. He could hardly see through the tears in his eyes.

There was a crunching noise behind them.

Startled, he surged to his feet and turned to find a man

holding a spear standing at the edge of the pool behind them. The man was wrapped in gauzy cloth, almost like a shroud. Hauling Xiana to her feet, Rylan stumbled away, turning onto a winding path that snaked between pools. Steam erupted from a crack in the ground ahead, forcing them to change direction. Coughing, Rylan picked out a new path, glancing back for sign of their pursuer. He couldn't see him.

Xiana staggered and dropped where she stood. With a growl, Rylan lowered himself down next to her, shaking her gently. Her eyes were closed; she was unconscious. Glancing up, he saw a large group of men coming up behind them, while another, smaller group approached from the opposite direction.

Gritting his teeth, Rylan heaved Xiana over his shoulder and rose unsteadily to his feet. He took a lurching step forward then stopped. Both paths ahead were blocked by cloth-enshrouded forms. He turned slowly in place, looking from one gauzed face to the next as an intense feeling of defeat ran over him like cold water.

The strength drained from his body. He sank to his knees, spilling Xiana onto the salt. Vaguely, through the tears in his eyes, he made out the forms of men encircling them. They were speaking a harsh, guttural language he'd never heard before. Something stabbed him in the side, perhaps the butt of a spear shaft.

He raised his hands in the air.

There was a shout.

One of the men surged forward, hefting his spear and pointing it threateningly at Rylan's chest. At the same time, others closed in, leaping over pools or scurrying around the perimeter, converging from all sides. Resigned, Rylan looked up into the dark eyes of the man standing over him. He raised his trembling hands higher.

A cord slipped around his neck. It jerked him backward,

away from Xiana. The rope tightened, strangling him. He fought with the rope, twisting at the end of it. But he didn't have the strength to fight long. He collapsed to the ground, where he lay gasping on his stomach as the world darkened, the taste of blood and salt in his mouth. Someone drove a knee into his back, pinning him to the ground. Another person bound his hands.

Rylan lay still, sucking in long, rasping gasps of air.

One of their captors stooped and picked up Xiana in his arms.

"Thomak!" someone growled.

A boot kicked his leg. Rylan turned his head and stared up with bleary eyes at the enshrouded man looming over him. The man repeated the command, gesturing brusquely. Rylan didn't need a second kick to get him moving. He rose, trembling and panting, to his knees. Prompted by the threat of a spear, he struggled to his feet. A hand closed around his arm like an iron shackle, forcing him forward. Rylan complied without resistance.

He followed the line of cloth-enshrouded people, winding back through the maze of bubbling pools. To his relief, the air stayed clear; their captors knew which paths to take and which to avoid. His throat ached and his lungs wheezed; he could only breathe shallowly. Dizzy and exhausted, he staggered after the man ahead, hastened by a spear carried by the man behind.

The trail they followed rose slowly out of the acid-fed plain onto a sprawling lava flow. There, on the dark and broken rocks, Rylan's strength gave out. He stumbled and fell, collapsing forward. Dimly, he was aware of the man behind him prodding him with a spear, but he couldn't move, couldn't catch his breath. The prodding became gouging.

It didn't matter.

His eyes were closed, and he was already slipping away.

He awoke to a throbbing headache. Rylan stared, blinking, into a crackling fire that blazed only twenty paces away, showering the night air with streams of sparks. He lay on his side within a ring of people clothed in gauzy robes. They were camped around the fire, some eating, others lounging on woven mats. Still others sat in a circle across the fire from him, laughing and passing a long-stemmed pipe. The air smelled of burned dung.

With a groan, he rolled onto his back and was surprised to find himself staring up into Xiana's eyes. She bent over him and touched his face with a look of intense concern.

A hand reached down and caught him by the collar of his shirt, hauling him backward onto his haunches. He crouched, staring up into the hate-filled eyes of a brown-skinned man whose face was veiled in linen. The man barked something at him that Rylan couldn't understand. He struggled, fighting against the man's harsh grip.

"Be still!" Xiana hissed.

Rylan stopped struggling and stared into the unblinking eyes of the man who held him. The eyes hardened, and the man growled another string of harsh syllables.

Xiana said, "He wants to know what tribe you belong to."

"Tribe?" Rylan didn't dare look away from the man.

"They think you are Uratu," Xiana said quickly. "They are a people in the north with milky-gray skin."

She said something to the man in the same harsh language. The man released Rylan with a growl and, making a sharp and angry gesture, moved away. Rylan sagged back in relief.

Xiana scooted closer, leaning into him. She whispered in his ear, "They think you are a demon. I don't think they'll hurt you if you do as they say."

That startled Rylan. He glanced back at the people settled behind them, guarding them.

"What about you?" he whispered.

"They do not fear me," she said under her breath. She was looking at the ground. Not at him.

He glanced across the fire to a small group of women. One of the women wore a sleeveless robe, displaying skin mottled with patches of discoloration. Another woman pushed aside the veil that covered her face, revealing features gnarled by disease, twisted into a profile that was barely recognizable as human. Understanding shot through Rylan, followed instantly by fear.

Lepers. They're all lepers....

"Listen to me," Xiana whispered. "If you can get away, follow the field lines to the north. They will lead you back to Daru."

It took a moment for him to register what Xiana was trying to say. His eyes shot toward her. "What about your necklace? Can't you use it to get us out of here?"

She shook her head. "It doesn't work here. The field lines swirl into a vortex over this area. It blocks it."

Rylan cursed.

One of the robed men rose and walked over to stand behind Xiana. Rylan looked up into the man's veiled face, his eyes probing the shadows beneath the gauzy layers of fabric. What he saw were browless features spattered with bumps and nodules, nostrils bulbous and distended. His stomach recoiled.

The loop of a rope slipped around Xiana's neck and jerked taut. Eyes bulging, Xiana struggled as she was dragged backward toward the fire, men on all sides surging forward, brandishing spears. Rylan sprang after her with a cry, but another rope slipped over his head, tightening around his neck and holding him in place. He bucked against it, but his struggles only served to tighten the rope further. He sagged back against his captor's legs, unable to fight. He watched helplessly as they spread Xiana out on the ground in front of the fire and tied her down.

Then they started killing her.

All around the fire, men and woman scooped up rocks and started throwing them at her.

Xiana screamed when the first stone hit. Another rock struck her temple. Blood sprayed, showering the ground. The next stone cut the side of her face open, while another smacked against her ribs. Her screams didn't overwhelm the dull sounds of rocks thunking off her bones.

Rylan couldn't stand it. No matter what Xiana had done to him in the past, she didn't deserve such a horrible death. She wasn't his enemy. Not really. In her own, peculiar way, Xiana had been trying to help both their people.

He fought against the rope that held him, which tightened until he couldn't breathe. In desperation, he flailed blindly for the magic field. Of course, it wasn't there. He couldn't catch it.

Instead, he caught something else.

He pulled it in and clung to it with all his might.

The night became suddenly, inexplicably darker, almost as though a hungering shadow had gobbled up the moon. In the eerie absence of light, a sickly green glow appeared and spread over the ground. The fire's flames paled to white, all color bleeding rapidly from the world. Rylan moaned as something terrible crawled up inside him, making his skin squirm and his insides shiver.

The barrage of rocks stopped falling. Xiana lay unconscious, her face bathed in blood. The people surrounding her let their hands fall to their sides and edged backward. All the while, something cold and sinister was coiling inside Rylan. He didn't know what it was, but he could feel it filling him, tearing at his insides. Clawing its way out.

The people around him started screaming.

A cloth-wrapped man next to him groaned and wilted like a

flower, collapsing to the ground. Another man flung his hands up and danced backward, screaming, turning in circles until he fell over and lay there thrashing. Across the fire, a group of women emitted horrendous, gurgling shrieks and collapsed where they stood. Cloth-enshrouded people bolted and fled. Others toppled and lay rigid like felled trees. Those running didn't get far. They collapsed in mid-stride, then lay twitching on the ground. None got back up again.

Rylan looked on, aghast.

Eventually, there was no one left to scream.

The awful green glow leaked back into the soil, absorbed by the ground.

Xiana remained where she was, unmoving.

The people who had bloodied her lay sprawled across the ground like the victims of a god's exacting wrath.

Rylan blinked his shock away. He groped for the rope around his neck. It took him long seconds to realize it was gone. He turned to find the man who'd held him lying flat on the ground, a black and swollen tongue protruding from his leprous mouth. The rope was still clutched in his misformed hand, his face frozen in a mask of anguish.

Repulsed, Rylan scrambled over to where Xiana lay.

She was breathing. Alive. But unconscious—her head was a bloody mess from a cut on her temple. He probed the wound with his fingers, assuring himself that her skull wasn't cracked.

"Xiana." He patted her gently.

She didn't stir. Her eyes didn't open.

He didn't know what to do. She wouldn't wake up. He looked around at the carnage that surrounded them. The people who had captured them were all hideously dead. He thought about carrying her away, but then dismissed the idea. He had no idea which way to go, and he feared getting lost in the desert without her guidance. So he decided to remain there, within the grisly circle of bodies.

A terrible exhaustion stole over him. He sank down beside her. He had no idea why he felt so tired. He fought to keep his eyes open and kept jerking himself awake. At last, he gave into it. Curling up beside Xiana, he fell instantly to sleep.

He awoke to the feeling of being shaken. At first, it was just an annoying disturbance to his sleep, something he was able to ignore. But it grew insistent, at last breaking sleep's rigid grip on him.

"Rylan."

He opened his eyes and stared up into Xiana's golden face. She was leaning over him, her hands on his shoulders, the sun's brilliant aura haloing her head. Her face was crusty with dried blood, and she had a cut on her cheek under her right eye. He pushed himself upright, and gazed around in shock at the extent of the carnage that surrounded them.

Every man and woman, even children, were sprawled on the ground in gruesome poses. Their clothing was charred, their features frozen in grimaces of horror. Some had died upright, their muscles locked rigid, as though death's rigor had stolen upon them prematurely. One man's arm was thrust upward, the flesh seared away, leaving only a charred, skeletal hand.

"What happened?" he whispered, his stomach clenching in nausea. Bile rose in his throat, and he choked on it.

"I don't know," Xiana whispered, looking at him with a fearful expression on her face. "Did you do this?"

"No!" Rylan gasped, shaking his head adamantly. He didn't. He couldn't have. He was dampened—he couldn't even sense the magic field, much less use it. But he had tried. He remembered reaching out for it.

Rylan's breath caught in his throat.

Somehow, he had done this. Only, he hadn't used the magic field; he had used something else. A different power. A *darker* power. He remembered its sickening green glow, remembered it clawing its way out of him. He thought of the oath he had sworn in the cornfield, pledging his soul to the God of Chaos.

There was something terrible inside him, and somehow it had gotten out.

He shook his head in denial. Xiana pulled back from him.

"What?" she asked.

He couldn't tell her. She'd say the Word and kill him. She could never know....

A soft whimper caught his attention. Across the campfire, someone in the sprawl of bodies was still alive.

Using the sound as an excuse to escape Xiana, Rylan pushed himself unsteadily to his feet and wobbled like a drunken man over to a cluster of bodies fallen together on the ground. One of them, a woman, was moving. Kneeling beside her, Rylan rolled her over.

He jerked back with a gasp.

The woman's face was ruined. Her features were grotesquely distorted, as if they had twisted and melted, running together. What was left didn't look human.

A raw, skinless hand groped across the ground toward his.

Xiana lowered herself beside him and peered down at the woman, vast sympathy written on her face. "There's nothing we can do for her."

Desperation welled inside him, along with a cold, numbing mixture of horror and self-loathing.

"We can't leave her like this," he said. Biting his lip, he bent over her and took her head in his hands. With a powerful wrench, he snapped her neck.

Trembling, Rylan rose to his feet and stood staring down at his victim, his breath shivering in his raw throat. He looked around, his gaze traveling over the bodies hideously arrayed before him. A staggering coldness filled him as he grappled with the magnitude of the atrocity he'd committed. He'd killed men before. Men whose faces still haunted his sleep and eroded his peace.

But this... this was different.

This was evil.

"Come," Xiana urged, already limping away from him, one hand clutching her head. "We have to get away from here. Before whatever killed them comes back."

But Rylan couldn't move. All he could do was stand there hating himself, wishing he could blame these deaths on anything else. But that was impossible. The evidence of his depravity lay all around him, irrefutable.

Thinking of his demon father, he started forward, picking out a path through the carnage, tears blurring his vision.

26

THE WEIGHT OF CHAINS

GIL FELT A HAND ON HIS ARM AND FLINCHED.

He'd forgotten Ashra was there, seated next to him at the desk. Scrubbing his hand over the unshaven whiskers on his chin, he glanced up at her. She smiled back sympathetically.

"Why don't you take a break?" she suggested.

Gil drew in a deep breath and leaned forward again, rubbing his eyes. Ever since the lines had stabilized, he'd spent too much time staring at papers on a desk. Spread out before him were lists of requisitions. He'd stared at them so long, the letters had blurred and run together like wet ink. Wearily, he straightened the pages and started over again, ticking off items with a quill pen. He slid the parchment aside and gestured for Ashra to give him the next.

"This is taking too long," he mumbled. "I've got to get back out there."

"Excuse me, Warden."

Gil looked up to find Lambert, a lean man with drooping eyes, hovering in the doorway. Wearily, he motioned the acolyte forward.

"Sorry to bother you, Warden," Lambert said, taking a stiff

stride toward the desk. "It's Payden, sir. He's not eating or drinking. It's like he's given up."

That was the last thing Gil wanted to hear. He had more on his plate than he could handle already—and a war to get back to. And yet the news of Payden was disheartening.

He blew out a heavy sigh. "I've a city falling around me, and you want me to worry about one man who can barely speak his own name?" Even as he said it, he knew it was a baseless complaint. Worrying was what he did. It was his job now. And he was going to worry about Payden, too, whether or not he wanted to.

The acolyte bobbed his head. "Just thought you'd like to know, sir." He took a step backward, as if trying to retreat.

Gil put his hand up, halting him. "Where's he at?"

Lambert pointed with his thumb in the direction of the stairs. "He's still in the subbasement, sir."

Gil grimaced. He'd forgotten to have Payden transferred out of there once it became evident they weren't going to get any useful information out of him. Payden had been down there, in the dark, for four days. Gil wondered if the man was still mourning the loss of the enemy mage he'd been chained to.

"Well, that might be why he isn't eating," he grumbled.

The acolyte shook his head. "Oh, it's not, sir. Believe me, if you go look at him, you'd understand."

Gil glanced at Ashra. She was staring at Lambert with a concerned frown. Gil wondered why. She'd never deigned to socialize with Payden, or any of the other acolytes from the Kingdoms. When Payden and Gil had been Raised with the rest of their class, she hadn't bothered to attend the ceremony.

"Thank you, Lambert," he murmured.

The acolyte ducked his head and stepped back through the doorway, disappearing quickly. Gil looked at Ashra.

"That doesn't sound good," she said.

Gil bit his lip, shaking his head in frustration. "I don't have time to worry about one traitor."

"Aren't you at least curious? What happened to Payden could happen to any one of us."

She was right. He *was* curious. And that was the problem. He didn't have the time or energy to be curious. Curiosity meant he'd have to walk all the way down the stairs to the subbasement, then all the way back up again. He'd already walked miles that morning and would have to walk miles more before evening. All to find out what? Something he already knew.

He sighed, pushing aside the papers on the desk. "All right. Let's go take a look."

He shoved back his chair, the legs sliding across the floor with a terrible shriek. Ashra winced at the noise. She rose with much more grace, then paused to stretch. The strain was showing on her too. She looked haggard.

They left his office and headed in the direction of the stairs. The old manor house that had been converted into the Lyceum had belonged to one of Rothscard's original crime families. Below the ground floor was a basement consisting of networks of tunnels that extended out from the old manor's footprint under the streets into the surrounding neighborhoods. Many of the subterranean rooms were now used to house artifacts and the growing collection of mystical secrets the Lyceum had amassed.

As they descended the steps to the level of the transfer portals, the air grew steadily cooler. And cooler still when they reached the level of the first subbasement. It was an enormous chamber that had been a cistern at one time, before it had been converted to a central hub from which the network of passages branched off. It was a great, dark hall with a vaulted ceiling supported by rows and rows of pillars. The cistern was empty now, just a sprawling space that had once been packed full of items. The acolytes had been working hard to evacuate as much of the Lyceum's irreplaceable treasures as they could.

"I've always hated it down here," Ashra said, producing magelight at her feet. "If any place has ever been haunted, it's this place."

Gil silently agreed with her. He'd always avoided the subbasement too. The cistern had been drained long ago, but the air still felt humid, as though the water that had been contained here had seeped deep into the stone. The whole place had a sinister and ancient feel to it that gnawed at his nerves.

They walked through the basement until they came to an opening in the far wall. There, an iron door stood closed and bolted in front of them. Gil tugged on the bar, and it slid to the side with a fatigued groan. The door swung open on creaking hinges, revealing a dark corridor lined with bricks that smelled of mildew.

"You first," Ashra said with a smile, motioning for him to go ahead.

Gil eyeballed the corridor for a moment before stepping inside. He walked forward, Ashra's magelight swirling ahead of them, groping across the ground, until they came to a chamber lit by oil lanterns hanging from rusted brackets. There, Ashra let the magelight go.

All around the circular room were storage nooks that had been converted to cells. The air was warmer, heated by conduits that brought water up from the hot springs that existed beneath the city. As far as Gil was aware, the cells had never been used, at least not by the Lyceum. Not until now. Sweeping a glance around the room, he quickly found the only cell with its wooden door shut and barred. He moved toward it.

The key to the cell hung on an iron ring from a peg on the wall. Gil unlocked the door and used his shoulder to shove the door open, spilling light into the darkness on the other side.

The sound of a groan was the only sign that there was anyone alive in the cell. Gil hesitated, feeling suddenly guilty. By his order, Payden had been locked down there for days in the dark, for no greater crime than mourning the death of an enemy.

"Payden," he hissed into the darkness. "Do you hear me?"

For a moment, there was only silence. Then came another low groan. Gil handed the key to Ashra, then took a step inside, instantly hit in the face by an eye-watering stench that made his stomach roil. He glanced at a waste bucket in the corner. It didn't smell like it had ever been emptied.

Wrinkling his nose, he said, "Payden. It's me, Gil. I've got Ashra with me."

His announcement was greeted by the sound of quiet sobs. Gil glanced at Ashra. Then he moved forward, conjuring a dim glow of magelight that revealed the form of Payden lying on a cot, curled up in a fetal position. He was clutching his arm, which ended in a freshly healed stump. Gil moved further into the cell and knelt beside him, Ashra lingering in the doorway.

Reaching out, he touched Payden's remaining hand. "What's wrong?"

In the dim magelight, Payden's pale cheeks glistened with tears. He stared miserably up at Gil through greasy mats of brown hair. Lips trembling, he whispered, "You didn't have to kill him. Why did you kill him?"

Gil felt a hand on his shoulder and turned to look up at Ashra. She was hovering over him, staring down at Payden with an expression frozen somewhere between revulsion and pity. Gil could follow her thoughts, which had to echo his own. They'd done something to him. Something bad. He squeezed Payden's hand. His action only served to make the man weep harder.

Gil whispered, "I'm sorry."

Payden's face distorted into a grimace of immeasurable

pain. He jerked his hand away. "It was me! I did it! It wasn't his fault!" His body quaked with sobs. "Why did you kill him?"

Gil looked around helplessly, his eyes falling on a bowl of rice that had been left on the floor at the foot of the cot. He picked it up. "Here. You need to eat. Why don't you sit up, and I'll help you?"

The man only shook his head miserably, clutching his stump.

Gil set the bowl down. "Look. You've got to let him go."

Fresh tears spilled down Payden's cheeks. "I can't," he sobbed, curling into a tight ball.

Gil was growing frustrated. "Payden, you didn't know this man more than a couple of days. Why does his death bother you so much?"

Payden gasped. "Almir loved me! He loved me like no other! And I loved him! Oh, *gods,* why did you have to kill him?"

Gil squeezed his eyes shut. This was going nowhere and, besides, he'd had enough. He didn't think he could stand any more. Rising to his feet, he cast one last, regretful glance at Payden, then turned his back on him and walked out of the cell.

"Lock it," he said to Ashra, feeling defeated.

He paced across the room and waited, staring at the flickering dance of the lantern light. It was a few moments before Ashra left the cell, locking the door behind her. He saw on her face that she was just as disturbed as he was. She moved toward him with her hands clasped together in front of her, looking like she wanted to say something but couldn't find the words.

He shook his head and ran a hand over his face, feeling immeasurably weary. "He's insane," he sighed at last. He sent his magelight trailing forward into the corridor and forced his feet to move after it.

Walking at his side, Ashra said quietly, "That could be us, Gil. If we're captured. Whatever they did to Payden, they could do to any of us."

Gil glanced at her sharply. "I know."

She wrapped her arms tightly about herself. "Doesn't that terrify you?"

It did. So much so that he didn't want to admit it. They emerged from the corridor into the vast, echoing cistern. Gil paused, looking around at the long rows of pillars that marched away from them at odd angles. The effect was almost dizzying, like staring at a reflection within a reflection.

"Was he always attracted to men?" Ashra asked.

"No," Gil said. "He wasn't." He took a step forward.

The entire subbasement jolted with a terrible rumble. The floor beneath Gil bucked, tossing him off his feet. Ashra staggered and fell on top of him. The ground quaked again, and chunks of the ceiling rained down all around them. The pillar beside them crumbled, feeding the air with clouds of dust.

Rolling off him, Ashra cried, "What happened?"

Gil scrambled to his feet, choking on dust. "That had to be a fire strike."

It had to be one of the deadly fireballs produced by the Khar's chained mages. He couldn't imagine the power it would take to conjure something so devastating. All it would take was one direct hit to destroy the Lyceum. So far, they'd been lucky. But perhaps their luck had run out.

The building shuddered again, and a terrible fear clenched his gut.

"Come on!" Gil shouted. "We have to get out of here."

27

SUHEYLU RA

THEY WERE ALMOST A WEEK OUT FROM THE WAYSTATION. THE
Scalding Sea was days behind them, although they'd never
managed to escape the haze-infected sky. It hung low overhead
like a dirty pane of glass, fouling the sunlight. The temperature
soared. Every night before they made camp, they stopped and
searched for water, never finding it. The only opportunity
they'd had to refill their canteens was when the sky had thickened with thunderheads that poured rain down on top of them
in a violent downpour that lasted only minutes. Rylan scrambled to lay out a canvas tarp, using it to catch water to fill their
canteens. That was two days ago. The water was starting to
run out.

The ground they walked across was just as parched as he
was, its skin aged and cracked like old leather. They'd left
behind the sea of wandering dunes that had consumed the
landscape beyond Puna Ajaru and now crossed what looked
like a dried lakebed. Every once in a while, a lone tuft of grass
erupted from one of the cracks in the scorched clay. The first
time Rylan had come across the sight of grass, he'd almost
whooped with joy. It was a sign the Desolation wasn't never-

ending. He glanced at Xiana with hope, but only received a half-hearted smile in return.

They made camp for the night amidst a group of strewn boulders that looked out of place against the otherwise unblemished landscape. There was no kindling for fire, not that they needed one. Nights in the Desolation were warm, and they had nothing to cook. Rylan occupied his time whittling a piece of wood he'd picked up at the waystation, while Xiana lay on her side, elbow on the ground, head propped in her hand. She was watching him work, her eyes fixed on the motion of his knife blade.

Rylan held the piece of wood up to his mouth and blew off the shavings, then turned it slowly to examine his work. He hadn't set out to make anything in particular, but somehow the wood in his hand had taken on the form of a woman in a simple dress. She had no face, and he wasn't going to give her one. He wasn't that good with a knife, and he'd only mess it up. Better to leave the face blank, an empty canvas for his imagination.

"Is that your wife?" Xiana asked.

He nodded, using the knife blade to shave a little more texture into the hair. Emma's hair had been beautiful. Long and chestnut, the color of an autumn sunset. She'd usually worn it twisted into a bun, though he'd preferred it loose. He could still remember the way it smelled, like summer blossoms. Like her.

"Describe her to me," Xiana prompted.

Rylan didn't look up. Keeping the blade moving, he answered, "She was perfect. Kind, beautiful. Sincere. Full of love."

Xiana pushed herself off the ground, sitting up. "How did she die?"

Rylan swallowed, the question provoking a brief but sharp stab of pain. He started carving another fold into the figure's skirt. "She died in childbirth. I wasn't there."

Xiana's eyebrows knitted together in a look of compassion. "Where were you?"

"Fighting a damn war," he said without looking at her. He slipped with the knife, opening up a small cut in his finger. A red bead of blood swelled from the wound. He brought the finger up to his mouth and sucked it clean, then returned to his carving.

"At least your daughter survived," Xiana said. "What is she like?"

Rylan scowled. "I wouldn't know." He pressed the knife point deeply into the wood, carving out a slice. "I was discharged after two years of service in the King's army. I'd just gotten home, the day of the attack. I spent only three hours with Amina and Korey. Then my father asked me if I'd like to go into town so he could buy me a drink. I went." He shrugged. "I thought I'd have the rest of their childhood to spend with them. I was wrong. I shouldn't have gone."

Out of the corner of his eye, he saw Xiana's face fill with sympathy. He focused his attention harder on the carving. His finger had started bleeding again, and the blood had soaked into the wood, darkening the figure's breast. Somehow, the stain seemed appropriate. He blew the dust off again, examining his work. Satisfied, he sheathed the knife and tucked the carving away, then laid down to sleep with his back to Xiana.

"It wasn't your fault," she said softly.

He closed his eyes. "No. But that doesn't change anything."

They woke early the next morning and started out again across the dry lake. Eventually, the clay was replaced by sand as the terrain sloped upward into a wide plateau. A cool breeze eased their journey. It was refreshing after so many days under an

oppressive sky and a sweltering sun. When they finally reached
the edge of the plateau, Rylan stopped and looked down.

And gasped.

Below them spread a vast expanse of forest filled with oaks
and sycamores, a forest that went on forever, as far as he could
see, a continuous expanse of unadulterated green. Here and
there, man-made structures peeked out from amidst the trees.
Tall towers and rooftops, high walls and elaborate fortifications. A circular, many-spoked structure that resembled a
wheel, made of stone. An entire city lay buried beneath the
forest, which was partitioned into even, geometric patterns by
the remains of ancient roadways. An entire metropolis, long
uninhabited and thoroughly overgrown.

"What is that?" Rylan asked, nodding in the direction of the
ruins.

Beside him, Xiana stood surveying the view, her hair stirring in the breeze. "Suheylu Ra."

Rylan stared down at the landscape, feeling mildly shocked.
He'd thought Suheylu Ra was a town in the Desolation, or
perhaps just an outpost. He'd pictured something in the middle
of the waste, a place where caravans might come to trade and
rest. He hadn't been expecting an abandoned city in the middle
of a dense forest. His eyes wandered over the nearest husk of a
building that rose several stories above the canopy. Layers of
balconies ribbed its sides, and vines wandered its walls like
veins. One side of the building had crumbled away, the rubble
lost beneath the sea of trees.

"What happened to it?" Rylan asked.

Xiana's hand rose to touch the purple bruise on her face.
"Suheylu Ra was attacked by the Turan Khar."

Rylan blinked, looking out over the ruins. "The Turan Khar
did this?"

The city below had been more than twice the size of
Karikesh, and by the amount of overgrowth, it had been aban-

doned for centuries. He'd seen the Khar army and knew how devastating their mages could be, but this... this was devastation on a magnitude he couldn't even fathom. An entire civilization lay before him, erased.

"How long ago did this happen?"

"Eight thousand years," Xiana said. Before he could react, she started forward again, striding toward a dirt path that led down the side of the plateau.

"Eight thousand years?" he called after her. When she didn't respond, he hurried after her, stumbling over a rock that turned underfoot. The path was steep and made of red clay riddled with cracks and small stones.

"And why did you bring me here?" Rylan asked, catching up to her. He slipped as the dirt beneath him crumbled.

Ahead, Xiana took the trail nimbly, making her way downslope with ease. Looking back at him, she answered, "I told you. I don't have time to train you, and you don't have time to learn. In Suheylu Ra, you will find all the knowledge you need."

He didn't speak to her after that, instead focusing his concentration on getting down the hill without falling on top of her. Eventually, the dirt path led off the plateau and into a grass meadow that bordered the margin of the forest. As they walked, trees sprouted up infrequently from the grass, mostly oaks, small and sparse at first, eventually becoming taller and more frequent the further they went. Soon, they were walking within a moist and shadowy woodland.

The forest was dense, though there were many snags and fallen trees that looked like enormous bleached skeletons. The ground beneath their feet was thick with detritus; far more leaf litter had accumulated than Rylan would expect in such a forest. And there was no birdsong to be heard. The noise of the wind blowing through the branches was the only sound surrounding them.

Overhead, the tree limbs parted, revealing a stone tower

that thrust out of the ground, high into the sky. As they walked past it, Rylan saw it was an enormous monolith of fluted granite that looked scorched by an inferno. He had no idea what the function of such a structure could be; it wasn't a dwelling or any type of fortification he could imagine.

"Does anyone still live here?" he wondered aloud.

"No," Xiana answered, wiping the sweat out of her eyes. "No one can survive here. The air is contaminated."

Rylan recoiled, his eyes going immediately to the canopy of tree branches that hung low overhead. Her eyes followed his gaze.

"The further we go in, the worse it gets," she told him. "It kills anyone who lingers too long in this region. So we must hurry. A person can spend only one day here and still leave safely. And you can never come back again."

"Why not?" Rylan stared suspiciously around at the trees, a cold and eerie feeling creeping over his skin. He thought perhaps there was a taste on his tongue, something metallic; he couldn't be sure. Nervous, he spat the taste out of his mouth. A branch broke underfoot with a sharp crack. The sound made him flinch.

Xiana said, "The entire time we're here, our bodies will be absorbing the taint that is in the air. It will never leave us; we will carry it with us the rest of our lives. It won't harm us, so long as we never come back. But for anyone who returns to Suheylu Ra, it's as though they never left. A person can only survive so much of the poison. That's why each person can only come and go once in their lifetime."

With her words, the shadows of the forest somehow seemed thicker and more menacing. Rylan's eyes darted to a dull gray wall covered in vines and found himself repulsed. His lungs suddenly hurt. He could almost feel the poison in the air seeping into his body. Groping fingers of fear traced over his skin, and a cold sweat broke out on his brow.

He stopped in his tracks. "I don't want to go any further."

Xiana halted and turned toward him, scowling. "You don't have a choice. Not if you want to rescue your daughter."

His skin itched. Absently, he reached up and scratched his arm, probably harder than he should have. Looking down at the red patch on his arm, he wondered if the contamination wasn't poisoning him already.

Xiana said, "The training of *deizu* takes years. Do you want your daughter to wait years for you to learn all the things you need to know in order to rescue her?"

Rylan scowled, knowing she was right. "No."

"Then let's go. If you're worried, wrap your scarf around your face."

He'd forgotten all about the scarf she'd given him. He started fishing it out of his pack but then stopped himself, wondering how effective it would be at filtering out the contamination. Apparently, Xiana didn't think it would do any good; her own scarf remained tucked away in her pack. Grimacing, Rylan left the scarf where it was.

She started forward again, her feet crunching on dry leaves and dead twigs. They walked on in silence for a long time. He focused on the conspicuous absence of sound in the forest. There was no rustling of squirrels, no insects, nothing.

"All the animals are gone," he said, stating the obvious.

Xiana nodded. "No animal can survive here."

Ahead of them, a dark granite wall sprawled across their path, overgrown with vines. Saplings sprouted out of cracks in its sides, and the top of the wall was covered with shrubs and small trees. Xiana made toward an opening almost invisible through a thick net of vines. The passage through the wall was almost like a cave, humid and dark. It stank of water and loam.

They emerged from the cavity onto a brick-paved street lined with tall buildings. Most of the pavement was broken, and pieces of uprooted bricks were scattered across the ground. Tall trees and bushes erupted from the street and groped out of rooftops and windows, reclaiming what was once rightfully theirs.

The surrounding buildings were made of architecture that was completely foreign, all right angles and unadorned blocks of stone. They were mostly intact, though parts had given way and collapsed into the street. They had to pick their way carefully around the rubble. Rylan was careful to follow Xiana's path closely, not trusting the pavement.

"How is it possible that all this is still here?" he asked, staring in wonder at the petrified bones of the city. "Why hasn't it all just crumbled to dust?"

"Nothing decays here as it should," Xiana responded.

The buildings surrounding them were growing progressively larger, encasing them, much taller than any buildings he had ever seen before. He walked with his head craned, wondering how such soaring structures could have ever been built, much less survived thousands of years intact. Xiana turned onto a wide road that was completely overgrown. Rylan followed her, stepping around bushes and tall clumps of grass. Overhead, the sky darkened as a bank of clouds passed in front of the sun.

"Suheylu Ra was the capital of Shira," Xiana informed him. "It was the most beautiful city in the world, and also the most advanced. All built with magic. There's never been anything that could rival it. In Suheylu Ra, there were wonders you can't imagine, because you have no context. There's nothing like it that exists today."

With a proud smile that seemed out of place, she went on, "Suheylu Ra was a center of learning and the arts. This is where the first school of magic was born, and the study of the arcane reached its pinnacle, thousands of years before Aerysius or the Lyceum of Bryn Calazar were ever built. The people of Shira celebrated free thought and exploration. They hungered for knowledge and searched for it endlessly. That's how they created all of this. And that's what drew the Turan Khar."

Rylan was taken aback. "Are you telling me the Turan Khar have been around for eight thousand years? That's impossible. No empire lasts that long."

"The Khar Empire existed at the time of ancient Shira," Xiana assured him. "And now they've come back."

The tremor in her voice gave Rylan pause. He looked at her. "What do you mean, 'they've come back?'"

Xiana turned to face him, her thumbs hooked in the straps of her pack. "The Turan Khar conquered Shira, but in doing so, they doomed their own empire." She started walking forward again, turning down another road as though she knew exactly where she was going. "The Khar created a weapon that combined both magic and anti-magic. The two can't be mixed; they annihilate each other. As you see, the results are cataclysmic." She waved her hand through the air, indicating the vast expanse of devastation that surrounded them. "Anti-magic isn't native to our world, so the Khar had to get it from somewhere. They pulled it from the Netherworld."

Her words made Rylan shiver. Again, his skin prickled. Almost, he could feel the air's corruption seeping into him through his pores. "So, this anti-magic," he said warily. "Is it the same as the Onslaught?"

The Onslaught was the power of hell. The Well of Tears had been created by Xerys's Servants to harness the power of the Netherworld, and his own father had been one of them. Darien Lauchlin had been capable of drawing on that power... and now, he feared, he could too. The oath he had made in the cornfield might have made it possible. He suspected that was how he had killed the Lonesome Ghosts in the Desolation. The thought terrified him.

Xiana said, "Anti-magic has been called many things. The Onslaught. Hellpower. Dark magic. No matter what you call it, it all means the same thing. It's the magic of the Netherworld, and it's not compatible with our world. It's an instrument of pure destruction."

She led him toward a thin bridge that spanned two buildings on either side of the street. The center of the bridge had collapsed, so they had to pick their way carefully over the rubble.

As they walked, Xiana explained, "The Turan Khar opened a conduit to the Netherworld so they could harvest its magic. They called this opening *Nya-Sagaru,* the Sky Portal. Only, it wasn't just the Onslaught that came through. Xerys has many minions, and some are capable of making the crossing. The Khar weren't expecting that. Because of the way their society was structured, they were particularly vulnerable. One of Xerys' demons insinuated themselves within the ranks of the Khar hierarchy and quickly took over. Then they turned their wrath on the Kingdom of Shira and attacked Suheylu Ra."

Her gaze scanned the surrounding buildings, a far-away look on her face. "A great and powerful mage of Suheylu Ra used the Khar's own weapon against them. He combined the magic of our world with the Onslaught and used it to attack the Sky Portal. When the portal collapsed, everything that belonged to the Netherworld returned to the Netherworld— and that included the Turan Khar. The backlash killed everyone in the region and tainted the air forever." Xiana's eyes grew distant. "That was the last time the Khar ever walked this world... until now."

Looking around at the hauntingly empty city, Rylan asked, "How did they come back?"

Xiana paused and turned to him. "Recently, another portal was created and left open long enough for there to be crossover between our two worlds: the Well of Tears. Your father helped destroy it, but by that time, it was too late. The Turan Khar had already crossed." She looked down. "And now they've created a new portal."

The thought made Rylan's heart shudder in his chest. The day seemed suddenly darker. Colder. He could feel the corruption in the air needling his skin. He stood staring at Xiana, frozen by trepidation.

She took a step toward him. "Now do you understand why it's so important for you to learn all that you can, as quickly as you can? Look around you. Shiran society was far more advanced than any civilization in the world today. And yet, even they were no match for the Turan Khar. And now the Khar have set their sights on your homeland. How will your people survive?"

He stood looking at her, unable to respond. His gaze wandered the ruins that surrounded him, his ears taking in the totality of silence. Never before had he sensed such presence of death.

"They won't," he whispered.

28

A FOOL'S ERRAND

Following Ashra, Gil stumbled down the steps of the Lyceum and stopped in the middle of the street, turning slowly as he surveyed the damage to the surrounding district. The building directly across from them was on fire. As Gil looked on, part of the roof collapsed, throwing up a gush of flame and showering the street with embers. From the distance came the sounds of screams. Black smoke poured from the district just to the west.

"What happened?" gasped Ashra, gazing wide-eyed at the smoke.

"Stay here," Gil told her. "I'm going to have a look."

Ashra caught his arm, halting him. "Stop. Send some battlemages. Let them do their jobs while you do yours."

Gil's face grew instantly hot as his cheeks flushed. He opened his mouth to say something.

Before he could respond, she interrupted, "You are a commander now. That is your duty: to command. Not to run toward the front lines! Have you forgotten Payden?"

His blood overboiled. "You're my acolyte, not my mother. Let go of my arm!"

Ashra's face pinched in anger. "I'm your friend," she snapped. "And as your friend, I'm telling you you're wrong!"

A loud explosion jarred the street. Gil reached for the magic field, throwing up a glistening shield between them and the flying debris. A block away, another building collapsed, crumpling in on itself. Dropping the shield, Gil jogged forward and surveyed the damage. Many of the Lyceum's guards lay dead in the street, others moaning on the ground.

He sprinted over to the nearest injured guard and sent a flood of healing energies into him. The man gasped once then slipped quickly into the healing sleep while Gil moved to the next victim. Kneeling beside a third, he caught Ashra's hand and let her feel through him as he worked. Together, they went on to the next. Within minutes, they stood alone in the street with only the unconscious and the dead.

Gil explained, "My men can't stop the fire strikes. But I'm stronger than all of them. That's why they made me Warden. I'm going where I'm needed, and that's that."

Her dark eyes narrowed in frustration. "My father told you this would happen. You didn't listen to him. But you still can—it's not too late." She set a hand on his arm. "Tell the Prime Warden to abandon the Lyceum. Then send your mages to help my father."

Gil took a deep breath, summoning every last scrap of patience he could muster. "I'm not going to do that. Now, are you going to come with me? Or go run to your father?"

She stared at him hard. "You're a fool," she growled, her eyes glinting with ire. Looking away, she heaved a sigh. "But I'll come with you."

With a curt nod, Gil strode forward down the street, the sounds of Ashra's footsteps dogging his heels.

A crackling noise overhead made him look up. The incoming fireball was like a meteor, streaming a flaming trail behind it as it began its descent. He opened himself to the magic field, drawing it in as quickly as he could, filling himself to his limit. Then he hurled everything he had into the sky, a lance of solid air that impacted with the projectile. Flames erupted from it, but the missile remained intact, continuing its descent. His action had done something, at least: the fireball altered its trajectory just a fraction. With a crackling roar, it hurled over the roof of the Lyceum, exploding into the neighborhood just beyond.

The thunder of the impact was deafening. The entire street jolted as a massive gush of flames erupted into the air, producing thick clouds of billowing smoke. Gil looked at Ashra with an I-told-you-so glare, then set out down the street, moving as fast as he could while dodging scattered debris and chucks of buildings.

Two blocks away, they found a group of six armored mages guarding an intersection along with the last vestiges of the Lyceum Guard. They were hunkered down behind a hastily improvised barricade, while beyond them, on the other side of the intersection, a horde of Khar soldiers filled the entirety of the street. All carried poleaxes and shields, and all wore the characteristic gray faces and jutting cheekbones... all except the four pairs of linked mages who stood in the center of the intersection, ahead of the lines.

Seeing them, Gil halted, sucking in a frigid breath. Each pair of Khar mages was tethered to a black-cloaked prisoner.

"Oh, gods," Ashra breathed. "They're using them as shields."

The Khar mages stared across the intersection at them with disdainful expressions. Their captives slouched, bloodied and bruised, looking beaten in both body and spirit. Gil knew all four of them.

He felt suddenly, physically ill. A cold sweat broke out on

his brow. It took a great effort to will his feet to move forward again. He drew up beside Caster, a lanky Empiricist with a kind disposition, who had no business being on a battlefield. The man was gawking over the barricade, his hands clutching a short sword so hard that his knuckles were a creamy white. Gil crouched down next to him, the man hardly noticing.

He threw up a shield over their position then turned to Fowler, the only battlemage in the group. "What's the situation?"

"The situation is we're fucked," Fowler replied, spitting on the ground. He rubbed his bald head and then raised his hand, pointing past the pairs of chained mages to the ranks of footmen behind them. "The strikes were a diversion. While we were focused on the fireballs, their main force crossed the canal west of Kazri Souk. Where the hell were you?"

Gil cursed himself, wanting to put his fist through his own face. He swung around with a growl and paced away, fingers clenched in anger. When he turned back around, he was standing face-to-face with Ashra.

"Command," she reminded him.

She was right. He nodded.

Moving past her, he strode over to Fowler. "Take four mages," he ordered. "Keep the Khar out of the Souk." He turned to a group of men wearing the black uniforms of the Lyceum Guard. Choosing the one with the most stitched bars on his sleeve, he told him, "Split your men up between me and Fowler. Half will go with him, the other half will stay here with me."

The man turned and immediately started carrying out the order. The guards quickly divided themselves into two groups. Suddenly, every hair on Gil's neck stood on end. A bright spear of light strobed the air. The howls of agony told him what had happened even before he turned to look. When he did, he saw a dozen guards smoldering in the street.

Fowler bellowed something, and the remaining guards scrambled forward as another bolt of lightning stabbed the ground where they'd just been standing. The smell of ozone was thick in the air. Overhead, the clouds rumbled with rolling thunder. Gil looked over the barricade and saw two of the Khar mages standing with arms stretched over their heads.

The air around him heated with a terrible rushing noise. Behind, a group of guardsmen erupted in flames. Gil reinforced the shield over the men nearest him, weaving a web of light over their heads. The next stab of lightning shattered against it, making him stagger with the force of the impact.

A man across from him dropped dead where he stood. Before Gil could recover enough to summon a second shield, another man went down. Gil staggered, catching himself on the wheel of an overturned cart still hitched to a dead horse with splayed legs.

He yelled at Ashra, "Can you weave a shadow web?"

She scrambled to his side and clung to his arm. He wasn't sure if she was trying to stabilize herself or him. "I can try! I've never made one before!"

"Just do your best!"

Gil straightened, letting go of the wagon and moving toward the barricade.

He looked around for the officer he'd just spoken to and found him lying dismembered in the street. He searched desperately for the nearest uniformed guard, not caring if it was an officer or a new recruit.

Signaling a man over, he told him, "I'll draw them away from the barrier. As soon as I do, order your men through."

"I'm not in charge!" the guard protested.

"You are now." Gil swung away from the man and extended his hand to Ashra. "Come with me."

She didn't hesitate. She took his hand, moving with him toward the barricade where they hunkered down and waited.

Gil leaned forward, looking out through a gap between stacked crates. Ahead, two pairs of enemy mages stood ready to attack anything that moved, keeping their black-cloaked captives near them on short leashes. The woman on the right was Chandra Mourey, a gentle Querer who had just started a family. The man chained on the left was one of Gil's own battlemages, a tall, blond-haired man named Horton.

"We need to do something about their mages," Gil said, feeling his anger and frustration mounting. He motioned at the Empiricist squatting across from him on the other side of a wheelbarrow. "Caster!"

The man scrambled toward him on all fours, crawling up to crouch at his side. "Yes, boss?"

Gil scowled, hating himself for putting the man in the position he was going to need him in. But he didn't have a choice. "I need a diversion. Take a couple guards and head up Badek Street toward the theater. Cut around to the south and attack their flank."

Caster's face paled a bit, but he nodded gamely. Patting his shoulder, Gil sent him off and turned back to the intersection. The Khar mages lingered in the street, scanning the barricade for any target they could claim. Chandra and Horton remained chained at their sides. Chandra's eyes were fixed on the ground, a cut slanting across her face from chin to ear. Horton stood battered but defiant, his shoulders squared, his back rigid.

They lingered there for minutes at a stalemate, the Khar mages unable to attack through their shields, their own forces unable to mount a sortie because that would take them out from under the shields' protection. Gil turned around and sat with his back to the barricade, his pulse throbbing. He didn't want to look at Chandra and Horton. The sight of their faces made his stomach twist into knots.

A series of explosions rocked the square. The Khar soldiers

in the intersection screamed in outrage, then surged toward the sounds of Caster's diversion.

"Come on!" Gil cried to the guardsmen behind him. Standing, he ducked out from behind the stack of crates and stormed into the intersection.

Spears flew toward them, impacting with Ashra's shield. Gil raised his hand and drew the magic field into him until he glowed with power. The Khar mages jerked their captives back against them, directly in Gil's line of sight. He let out a cry of frustration.

"Gil!" Ashra shouted behind him. "Remember Payden!"

He didn't need her to remind him. He looked at the first black-cloaked mage directly in front of him: Chandra. She'd been kind to him at the Lyceum, had even taken care of him when he'd fallen ill with scarlet fever.

He reached inside Chandra and stopped her heart.

Flooded with rage, Gil struck out at her captors. Both mages hurled backward into the building behind them, their bodies striking brick with alarming force. A shout from Ashra made him turn. Another pair of chained mages strode toward them, pulling a Malikari captive along behind. Together, they lifted their linked arms over their heads, reaching for the sky. Webs of power crawled over them, scintillating over their bodies.

Crackling thunder clapped down from the sky. Gil put every ounce of power he could summon into his shield. The lightning strike overwhelmed Ashra's web and attacked his shield, its energies sucked in and redirected into the ground. Before Gil could recover, another pair of mages step forward, arms raised to the sky. He almost didn't react fast enough.

This time, it wasn't lightning.

It was thunder.

The air split overhead then clapped back together with horrendous force, hurling them both off their feet. Gil cried out and brought his hands up to his ears. A shrill, ringing noise stabbed through his head, like someone driving a spear into his brain. Clenching his jaw, he managed to pick himself up off the ground. He reached for Ashra, but she was already rising, shaking her head violently. A shout from behind made him turn. The soldiers who had run to attack Caster had finished their grisly work and were rushing back their way.

Gil didn't think. He just acted.

He raised his hands, striking out without thinking. The brute force of his magic impacted with the charging soldiers. Men up and down the line exploded, one after another. Blood sprayed, saturating his clothes and running down his face. Screaming war cries, more soldiers poured forward to take the place of those fallen.

Gil saw that even Ashra's help wasn't going to be enough. Not near enough. Their position was being overrun. He started mindlessly hurling magic, trying not to think of the number of people he was killing. He forced himself to imagine that the blood drenching his face was just water, that the screams of anguish were just random noise.

He couldn't keep it up.

He couldn't fool himself. Couldn't stand himself.

Reaching out, he grabbed Ashra's arm and gasped, *"Run!"*

They turned and fled back toward the barricade. He leaped over it, coming to a rolling stop on the other side. A terrible jolt rocked the street, and the world trembled. Then it erupted in chaos.

With a thunderous noise, multiple fireballs shot across the sky overhead. They impacted into the district behind them, one after another in quick succession. The area was instantly engulfed in flames, the light of day replaced by a dim, other-worldly twilight as the pouring smoke rose to block the sun.

For just a moment, Gil stood there, stunned.

Then someone bellowed, "They're attacking the Waterfront!"

He turned around, breaking his attention from the leaping flames and took in the fires consuming the Souk District just south of the Waterfront. The men he'd sent with Fowler would be caught between the spreading inferno and the canal.

He had to get there, had to get *everyone* there. Looking beyond the barricade, he saw the enemy footmen were already regrouping. Their position was untenable. If he didn't act fast—and act decisively—they would lose more than the Lyceum.

They would lose the entire city.

He shouted at the remaining mages, "Nolan! Cummings! Hold the intersection and don't give it up! Everyone else, fall back to the canal!"

"Come with me!" he shouted at Ashra and sprinted toward a side street. He could hear fighting up ahead, see men engaged in battle several blocks away. He quickened his pace, all thoughts of protecting the Souk now gone from his mind. They were losing the Waterfront.

They halted just short of the melee. The Sultan's lines weren't where he'd left them—the Canal Road had already fallen. A dozen enemy soldiers noticed their arrival and broke off from the fight, careening toward them with weapons raised. Gil turned to flee, but more soldiers poured in from an alley behind them. Within seconds, they were surrounded.

He thrust his hands out, calling on the magic field.

Nothing happened.

The enemy soldiers ringed them in but didn't attack. They stood around them in a circle, weapons raised, and did nothing. Gil turned slowly, looking from one gray face to the next, waiting for a spear or sword to take him down. His stomach twisted, and his heart stumbled in his chest. Beside him, Ashra let out a miserable groan.

Somehow, they'd been cut off from the magic field. Dampened.

He let his arms sink to his sides. He turned slowly, staring wide-eyed at the soldiers surrounding them, wondering why they didn't strike.

The ranks parted to create a passage, and through that passage, a man and a woman came forward. A pair of Khar mages, chained together with manacles on their wrists. One held a spare chain in his hand. An empty chain. Gil shivered, Payden's face filling his mind. He didn't want to end up like Payden. And he knew Ashra wouldn't want that either.

He wouldn't let that happen to her.

Gil glanced down at the dagger he wore at his side. He stood frozen, his body numb, his shoulders going slack. He looked deep into Ashra's face and saw it in her eyes: she knew what he was contemplating.

Staring back at him, she nodded. "Go ahead. Do it."

He couldn't move. Couldn't draw breath.

"Do it," she urged, her eyes hard as iron.

He moved his hand to the dagger's hilt. His muscles tensed. He closed his eyes and gathered his courage.

But he had no courage left.

He couldn't draw the dagger.

Gil saw pity and forgiveness in Ashra's eyes. She knew he was defeated. One of the Khar mages stepped forward, a dark gray man with long, silvery hair. He held up the empty chain.

"Put it on." His voice was rough, like old, hard leather.

Gil shook his head. "No."

The man's companion, a black-haired woman with blue-gray skin, came forward to stand at his side.

"You must put it on willingly," she said, smiling kindly. "It's not as bad as you think it will be. You will learn to love it."

"If you put on the chain, we will let her go," the man said, pointing at Ashra.

Gil sucked in a sharp breath, suddenly flooded with hope. "You'll let her go?" he asked, not daring to believe it.

The gray man nodded. "Yes. If you put on the chain willingly."

Gil's pulse rang like a kettledrum in his ears. He stared at the chain being offered him, overcome by a heady mixture of hope and despair. With a sigh, he let go of the dagger's hilt and extended his hand. "I'll do it. Give it to me."

"Stop!" Ashra cried, springing between him and the enemy mage. "If you let him go, I'll put it on!"

Appalled, Gil opened his mouth to protest.

"He is worth more to us." The female mage inclined her head toward Gil. "He is much stronger than you. I could feel the power in him from across the canal."

But Ashra was undeterred. "I'm the daughter of the Sultan!"

Her admission rocked Gil to the core. "What are you doing?" he gasped. *"Shut up!"*

But it was too late. To his horror, Ashra smiled. She said to the woman, "You can have two dead mages... or the Sultan's daughter on one of your chains. Which would you prefer?"

The woman looked at the man. They stared into each other's eyes for a long moment. At last, the man turned to Ashra and offered the chain to her.

"Then it is yours."

Gil wanted to scream. Or cry. Or both. "Why are you doing this?" he whispered.

Ashra smiled at him.

She *smiled.*

She turned to the woman. "First, let him go."

The female mage stepped forward, halting close enough that Gil could smell her scent, a fresh odor that reminded him of a field after a summer rain. She reached up and stroked his cheek.

"You may flee, this time," she said. "But very soon, you will belong to us. And when you do, I will possess every part of you."

Gil shuddered at her touch. He shot a panicked glance at Ashra, his heart quaking.

"Go," Ashra commanded.

He didn't want to.

But he had no choice.

29

LOCKED IN STONE

ANOTHER MISSHAPEN TOWER ROSE FROM THE CANOPY TO LOOM above them like a decrepit sentinel. Rylan stared up at it, taking in its contorted appearance, as though the stone had melted and run like candle wax. He wondered what purpose such a tower could have served. There were many like it all around the ancient city, perhaps a network of guard towers or lookouts.

He turned his attention to the wide intersection ahead. In the center was a clover-shaped fountain with many tiers of basins. To the right of the fountain sprawled the statue of a woman who looked to have just fallen there, arms thrust upward, as though trying to shield herself from something falling from above. Rylan stared at the figure as they walked by, noting its composition. It looked to have been carved from a single large clump of charcoal. It was remarkably lifelike. He could see every fine detail of the woman's dress. Looking at the statue filled him with a hollow feeling, its presence seeming to emphasize the uncanny emptiness of this place.

They walked on in silence until they came to another statue, this one seated in the center of the road, a sapling growing out of the space between its arm and torso. This time,

Rylan stopped and stared at it. He could think of no reason why someone would carve such an acute likeness and leave it sitting in such a position in the middle of a street. The longer he stared at it, the colder he felt.

He asked, "They're real people, aren't they?"

Xiana stood next to him, considering the figure. Her eyes took on a sad cast. "Yes. These are the people of Suheylu Ra."

"But they're statues," Rylan said, dropping to crouch next to the dead man sprawled in the road. He reached out to touch it, but Xiana caught his hand firmly, holding it back.

"*Don't.*"

He withdrew his hand and stood up, taking a step back. Looking around, he noticed there were more bodies scattered up and down the street. A breeze kicked up, trailing leaves across the avenue, past the petrified remains of men and women, frozen at the moment of their deaths. He looked around at the tall, abandoned buildings shadowed by the clouds. Suheylu Ra suddenly took on the aspect of an immense graveyard, listless and haunted.

Xiana took his arm and guided him forward.

When they came across the next figure, Rylan stopped and stared down at it. It had once been a woman who had died kneeling on the ground, her arms wrapped in front of her as though she had been hugging something. Or someone. On the street beneath her was a pile of dark sand.

Rylan knelt and raked his fingers through the sand, scooping some up in his hand. It was moist and cold. Gritty. He turned his hand over and let it spill to the ground. Then he rose and scrubbed his hands clean on his trousers.

"That was a person, you know," Xiana whispered, gazing at him wistfully.

Rylan winced. Looking down, he stared harder at the stone woman who knelt clutching only air, at last recognizing the horror on her face for what it was.

Shaken, he let Xiana lead him forward again. Ahead, the avenue they were on angled downhill. At the bottom of the slope, the street was covered in water, a broad pool that stretched across many blocks. The withered shells of buildings protruded from the water; in places, only rooftops were visible. In the center, the lake appeared quite deep. It had swallowed a good portion of the area. Cut off from the road ahead, they turned down a side street.

Xiana said, "In my time, Zahran mages learned their craft by making a pilgrimage to this place. Each of these statues was once a living mage who was locked in stone the day Keio Matu destroyed the Sky Portal. Their bodies were petrified... but some small part of them still exists, locked deep within the stone. Those with the Gift once came here. If you touch one of these statues, a small part of the person they once were becomes part of you. Not a lot. A few of their memories. But mostly knowledge." She stopped and looked at him. "That's why I brought you here. This is your pilgrimage, Rylan. This is where you will learn all you need to know to become what you must."

Feeling cold and suddenly weak, Rylan looked at the nearest figure. This one was a young woman shading her eyes against the glare of a sun she would never see again. He turned to Xiana, shaking off a chill he felt down deep in his bones.

"So I'm supposed to do, what? Touch one of these statues?" he asked. "And then I'll know everything they knew? That doesn't make sense."

Xiana smiled. "Magic often doesn't make sense, Rylan. You will become much greater than any Master of your Lyceum. You will become *deizu-kan,* a true battlemage in every sense, and you will have all the knowledge of ancient Shira."

He cast a worried glance up at the clouds. The breeze gusted to a wind. Clouds thickened overhead, cooling the air as the shadows fell.

"It seems too easy."

"It's not easy, Rylan." Xiana's voice was suffused with sadness and foreboding. "Trust me."

He frowned at her. "Why's that?"

"Look at me." She raised her hand and touched his face. "Remember: you are who you are because that's who you need to be." She stared at him, her eyes searching his. "Tell me, Rylan Lauchlin. Who are you?"

He opened his mouth to answer her, then realized he couldn't. He stood there feebly for a moment, unable to speak. At last, he said, "I don't know."

She leaned forward and whispered in his ear, "And that's why we're here."

Her words scared him more than she could ever know. They dredged up the memory of the oath he had sworn, the same oath his father had taken. He was terrified that oath would someday come to summarize his existence.

With a slight pressure on his back, she urged him forward. He walked automatically at her side, feeling dazed, down empty streets surrounded by buildings that seemed to sag with age and loneliness. Human figures littered the area, along with the piles of dust that seemed even more tragic. Vines hung from stone bridges, draping down to strangle their path. They walked through a thicket of shrubs and scrub grass that completely consumed the road in places. Rylan wondered how the plants could survive in this place, when every animal had disappeared. It occurred to him that maybe the animals knew better, that some instinct told them to stay away.

Xiana drew to a stop. Ahead of them reared an enormous structure that looked like a fortress, but far greater and more magnificent than any fortress Rylan had ever seen. It had several towers that soared twenty stories or more into the sky. The building looked like it had been carved from a single, dark monolith. And it was intact, its walls smooth as glass, yet riddled with gaping holes that had at one time been windows. Each of its tall towers was capped by a golden dome. Vines webbed its sides like veins, and the branches of a great tree spread from one of the windows.

"The Sanctuary," Xiana whispered, her voice choked with awe. "The birthplace of all magic. The most enlightened center of learning that has ever existed in this world."

Standing in the long shadow cast by its walls, Rylan stared up at the building with an intense feeling of trepidation, feeling none of the wonder Xiana exuded. The dark fortress looked ominous, even sinister. Perched there in the middle of the sterile and decayed metropolis, it looked like a monument dedicated to everything evil.

"It doesn't look like a sanctuary," he said.

Xiana led him toward an entrance that consisted of a narrow arch several stories tall guarded by a drape of snake-like vines. Looking down, he saw the hardware of what had once been an enormous door. But if the wood had indeed ever existed, it had long since rotted away, leaving only its bolts and hinges behind.

Rylan stopped as his feet crossed the threshold, a long shadow sliding over him. Before them gaped an enormous hall that spanned the entire length of the bottom story. Steps leading down from where they stood became submerged under water that looked like tar. There was nothing between them and the far end of the hall except that dark pool. If they wanted to go anywhere in the fortress, they would have to cross it.

Xiana strode down the steps and, without hesitation, splashed into the pool until the water rose to her waist. Then she stopped and turned back, beckoning him forward. Rylan balked. They had no way of knowing what was in that water, and his imagination was already running rampant. There could be anything down there. Anything.

"Don't worry; it's safe," she called back to him. "There is nothing alive here that can harm you."

He looked around at the ancient and brooding hall and wondered if there was even the slightest chance she was wrong. Taking a deep breath, he waded in after her.

The water was cool but not cold. The floor was mucky; it sucked at his feet, making the going harder. Drops of water fell at intervals from above, splashing down around him with soft plopping sounds, wetting the top of his head. He looked up, wondering where the water was coming from. He couldn't tell; the ceiling was stories above their heads, lost in shadow.

They came at last to the other side of the hall and climbed a short flight of steps out of the water. Rylan stood beneath an arching doorway, dripping onto a clay-packed floor. Xiana reached up and, gathering her hair into her hands, wrung the water from it. She threw the wet, heavy strands back behind her shoulders and smiled at him.

Then she took him by the hand and led him through the doorway into darkness. The shadows swarmed thickly over them. Only feeble streaks of light cast from slits high up the rear wall revealed the shape of the room they stood in. It was octagonal, rising high into one of the fortress's mighty towers. A curving stairway spiraled down into the floor, disappearing underwater. The rest of the stairs climbed the walls, corkscrewing upward. Another petrified person stood on the stairs, forever frozen between steps.

Xiana looked upward, and Rylan followed her gaze. There was nothing above them but shadows. He had no idea where that winding stair led.

"We're going up there, aren't we?" he asked, feeling no small amount of dismay.

"We are."

"What's up there?"

"The reason we're here."

She started toward the stairs, and he reluctantly followed. The steps were not steep, and they were wide, making the ascent easier. Xiana went before him, seeming unbothered by the climb. They followed the spiraling steps into the shadows of the looming tower.

High above them was a large opening in the ceiling, illuminated by a gush of light. Rylan stared up at the gaping hole as he climbed, feeling a shiver pass over him. With vast reluctance, he forced himself to keep moving after Xiana, who climbed the steps at a pace that was relentless and unforgiving. Sooner than he was ready, they had reached the top of the stairs and made the transition from stone steps into a room with a tiled floor.

Rylan stopped, letting his surroundings soak into him. They stood in a large, circular chamber in the top of a high tower. The glass of the windows had shattered long ago, leaving the room open to the elements. Another stone husk of a man stood in the center of the room, arms spread out at his sides, fingers splayed as if in pain. His head was tilted back, as though he had been staring defiantly into the face of death the moment the backlash hit him. On the floor at the man's feet was a pile of scattered sand, the kind Rylan had become all too familiar with. Another person had died there, an ancient mage whose knowledge had already been plundered.

His eyes scanned the panorama of windows. "What is this place?"

A breeze tossed his hair, smelling deceptively fresh. He wondered how much of the air's poison his body had already absorbed... and how much more he could withstand.

"This was the command center," Xiana said, walking toward one of the windows. "It's from here the Custodians of Suheylu Ra controlled the Watchers." She leaned over with her palms on the window ledge, staring out across the fallen city. A ray of light angled down from the clouds, striking the side of her face and making her hair glow as if on fire.

"What are the Watchers?" Rylan asked, moving to stand beside her.

"See those towers?" She pointed across the ruins to the nearest of the tall, fluted towers that spiked upward, forming a ring around the perimeter of the city. The upper half of each tower appeared scorched by fire. Some looked partially melted.

"The Watchers were the city's defense system. They were built to protect Suheylu Ra from any form of magical attack. Unfortunately, the Turan Khar didn't attack with magic."

"They attacked with the Onslaught," Rylan surmised.

"That's right." Xiana moved away from the window and paced back toward the center of the room, where she crossed a tile medallion depicting the image of an eight-pointed star set within a circle.

Rylan took one last look at the defeated towers, then turned to Xiana. She stopped in the center of the star, beside the effigy of the man. Raising her hand, she moved as if to trail her fingers over his stone visage but paused just short of actually touching him. She stood and regarded the figure, her shoulders slumped as if carrying a great weight.

"He is Keio Matu," she said, her eyes lingering on the statue's face with a mixture of sadness and awe. "It was he who summoned the wrath of the Watchers to abolish the Sky Portal. He destroyed Suheylu Ra in order to rid the world of the Turan Khar."

Rylan felt an eerie feeling creeping over him, like tentative fingers stroking his spine. He peered deeply at the statue's frozen face, wondering what kind of person this man had been in life. "Why did he do it?"

Xiana turned to him and shrugged. "Because there was nothing else he could do."

Rylan shook his head, unable to fathom how it could be

possible to justify the destruction of an entire city. Especially a city the size of Suheylu Ra. "I don't understand."

Xiana offered her hand to him. Rylan stared down at it for a moment before accepting it.

Gazing into his eyes, she said, "I brought you here for a reason. Keio Matu was the Custodian of the Wise Council, and also the greatest mage in all of Shira." She squeezed his hand. "I brought you here to merge with Keio Matu. Not only to inherit his magical knowledge, but also to free him from this prison he has been trapped in for eight thousand years."

30

DEFEATED

DEAD HORSES, BURNING WAGONS, AND TWISTED BODIES LITTERED the center of Murkaq Square. Spilled blood slicked the cobbles, and the fountain ran dark with it. The sun was just setting as Gil trudged past the lines of exhausted men, the black cloak on his back granting him unquestioned passage through the layers of barricades.

Murky twilight was settling in, dull with smoke and chill with mist. The flies had settled for the evening, but the birds were still at it, hopping from corpse to corpse, pecking and squawking. He'd expected the ravens, but the presence of the gulls surprised him. The seabirds were more bloodthirsty than he'd imagined, tearing greedily into flesh and driving their competitors away with raucous noise and flapping wings. As Gil wound his way toward the command tent, he found himself the object of the birds' angry scolding.

The soldiers working to clear the square went about their business with silence and efficiency, showing little sign of battle fatigue. Gil had heard rumor of the inhuman discipline of the Malikari soldiers in the field, but seeing it for himself was another matter entirely. In short order, they had cleared a wide swath of ground on the south side of the square and erected a new command tent.

Gil angled toward the pavilion, every step increasing his anxiety. He walked with his shoulders slumped and head bowed, unable to meet the eyes of the soldiers who labored around him. Shame weighed on him like a burden of lead, making every stride more difficult than the last. By the time he reached the command tent, he'd broken out in a nervous sweat, his flesh tingling with goose prickles. He avoided the stares of the guards as they stepped aside and let him pass.

It was brighter within the tent than it had been in the darkening twilight. The pavilion was spacious, lit by many lanterns scattered across the floor and hanging from cloth-wrapped posts. There was a general bustle of men and women going in and coming out, clustering at the far end around a table.

Gil immediately caught sight of the Sultan's profile, and he froze, his heart stumbling to a standstill. Sayeed stood bent over a large vellum map that hung off the edges of the table, tracing a finger across it as he gave orders to his officers. Completely engrossed in his task, he didn't notice Gil standing across from him.

Gil swallowed hard, trying to work the dryness from his throat enough to trust his voice. The attempt only served to make him choke, a sound that captured the Sultan's attention. Sayeed's gaze darted up from the map and locked on him, hardening in anger. He stood motionless for long seconds, doing nothing but staring daggers. Then he made a sharp gesture with his hands, sending every man and woman heading toward the exit. As the tent emptied, Gil withered beneath that ironstern gaze, strangled by shame.

He stood looking at the Sultan, the tension between them stretched to its thin limit.

"You ignored my command," Sayeed said softly.

Seeing the fire that burned in the depths of his eyes, Gil couldn't help feeling afraid. He stood still, trying not to think of all the ways he had failed this man. He lowered his gaze to the ground, finding it impossible to look the Sultan in the face.

"I did," he said, his voice cracking.

There was a moment's pause.

Then, "Why?"

Despair gushed through him, emptying him entirely. "I thought I was right."

He chanced a glance up and saw that Sayeed's expression hadn't changed. There were many layers of contempt in that ice-cold gaze.

"Do you still? Think you're right?" Sayeed asked.

Gil shook his head. "No."

The Sultan looked down, ignoring Gil and focusing his attention once more on his maps. The span of silence that followed informed him that he'd been dismissed.

But he couldn't leave just yet. He wasn't done admitting the depths of his failure.

"Your Majesty, I..."

The Sultan looked up at him, his gaze piercing.

"Ashra... Your daughter..." Gil swallowed heavily, summoning the very last scraps of courage left within him. "... was taken by the Turan Khar."

Sayeed closed his eyes and sucked in a deep breath that lingered for eternity in his chest before shuddering back out again. He stood still, hands planted on the map table, every muscle of his body tensed enough to snap.

"Go."

There was more menace in that one, soft syllable than Gil had ever heard in his life. He took an uneasy step backward, stumbling over his feet.

"I'm sorry. So sorry," he said. Then he turned and fled the tent.

He hastened across the square, dodging bodies and fallen weapons, slipping and nearly falling on cobbles slick with gore. He passed the flaming barricades and headed west down the street, winding through crowds of soldiers and clusters of weeping citizens.

Everywhere he looked was chaos. Men and women jogged through the streets, carrying broken children in their arms. Wives and mothers knelt beside the bodies of their husbands and sons. The sounds of weeping and keening pursued him, relentlessly dogging his steps.

Gil's eyes burned with tears that blurred his vision, distorting his perception of the confusion that surrounded him. As he approached the Lyceum, thick black smoke saturated the air, and the twilight was sucked right out of the sky, replaced by midnight. The moans of the injured and dying pursued him as he fled up the steps, putting as much distance between himself and the reality of his failure as he could. When he burst through the door of the Lyceum, some of his men, sighting him, rushed forward, shouting his name. He didn't slow his steps as he stormed down the hallway toward Naia's office.

"Warden! What are your orders?"

He had none. Anyone with eyes could see the ruin his orders had brought them to.

He thought of Ashra, and a searing pain stabbed him in the gut, then cut upward into his heart. Out of all the people he'd failed that day, it was Ashra's loss that hurt the most. He should have been the one taken away in chains. Not her.

Gil stumbled to a halt. He stood there for moments in the middle of the hallway, blinking dumbly. Then, blowing out a bitter sigh, he changed his course, making instead for the stairs and descending the steps downward to the subbasement. He crossed the cistern in haste, dodging fallen blocks and tumbled pillars, until he came to the long hallway with the circular chamber at its end. Entering the room, he slowed to a stop and just stood there, collecting the frayed bits of his faculties.

He unlocked the door to Payden's cell. Opening it just a crack, he crouched down, pressing his forehead up against the rough wood of the doorframe. He was trembling. He hadn't noticed, not until he saw he was rattling the entire door on its hinges.

"Payden," he whispered. "Payden, are you awake?"

The interior the cell was dark. He couldn't make out anything beyond the doorway. He couldn't tell if Payden was asleep or awake, alive or dead. Or if he was even there at all.

"Payden. Talk to me."

He heard a soft sound, like the rustle of blankets. A low whimper.

He opened the door a bit wider. "Please. Talk to me. They've taken Ashra."

There was a creaking noise, the sound of Payden sitting up on the cot. A shadow moved, barely visible against other shadows. But then a face emerged into the narrow strip of torchlight spilling in through the doorway: Payden. Or at least the man who used to be Payden. He crept forward until he was crouching on the other side of the door. He leaned forward, his face only inches away from Gil's.

He could smell the reek of Payden's breath and the stench of his body. The odor of the waste bucket that had never been dumped. Gil knelt in the doorway and didn't pull back. Looking at the devastation written on Payden's face was like looking into the depths of his own soul. Only, Payden had done nothing to merit his anguish.

Gil had.

"Ashra?" Payden whispered, his eyes glinting in the torchlight. He nodded fervently. "That's good, that's good." He licked his lips, his tongue worming over his mouth. "She'll be happy. She won't be needing us anymore."

Gil blew out a sigh, wondering why he was there. He didn't even know what he was looking for. Perhaps some understanding of Ashra's plight, the fate he had condemned her to. He wanted to hear that there was at least some small chance that she could be happy, even if that happiness was imagined— as if that would make some bit of difference.

But he knew it wouldn't.

He drew in a deep, troubled breath, struggling to collect himself. He asked Payden, "Do you still miss them?"

The man nodded avidly, tears collecting in his eyes. "I miss my family. I want to go back to them." He licked his lips again, making a wet noise. Gil struggled to ignore the sound, even though it made him want to shudder. It was a terrible noise, a noise that the real Payden would have never made. He looked at the man's feverish eyes and sunken cheeks, feeling pity for him.

He whispered, "They weren't your family, Payden. That's all in your mind."

The man's face crumpled into a grimace of sorrow. "People keep telling me that." He shook his head, tears spilling down his cheeks. "No matter what, it's real to me. Understand? Somewhere out there, there's people who love me. They're missing me. And I miss them. I don't care if it's only a dream—I want it back. I want *them* back. Gil... can you take me back? To live with Ashra and my real family?"

He collapsed into sobs, his shoulders heaving. Gil reached through the doorway and patted his back. He felt helpless. Not just for Payden, but also for Ashra. This was what she would be like, if he could ever get her back. A crumbled, hollow thing too brittle to stand on its own. He would never want that for her. He knew what she'd want. She'd asked him to kill her. He should have done it when he had the chance; it would have been a kindness. As he stared at Payden, Gil felt new depths of guilt settling into him. He couldn't let Ashra live like this.

A startling thought occurred to him, making him flinch. Perhaps he could save her from that fate... and at the same time strike a blow to the heart of their enemy. Perhaps, with one act, he could undo all the damage he had done.

"Payden," he whispered, his voice low and gravelly. "If I were to take you back... where would I take you?"

The man's breath caught. He glanced through the doorway at Gil with red and feverish eyes. In a quaking voice, he rasped, "You'll take me back?"

"I don't know," Gil said. "I guess I could try. But if I did, I'd have to know where it is we're going. Can you tell me?"

He swallowed, hating himself for making false promises. But he also didn't see another way. There was a chance Payden could help him find the place where Ashra was being held, and that mattered more than anything else in the world.

Payden nodded furiously, rocking back and forth and quivering. "The citadel. Can you take me there? Please? I'll do anything—"

"Which citadel?" Gil asked. There were at least four of them in the city that he could think of.

"It's the old citadel by the Lion's Gate," Payden said quickly, his voice cracking with excitement. "Please, you have to—"

Gil nodded. He knew the one. It was called the Alqazar. "I know the place," he whispered. A nervous excitement broke out all over his body, making his skin tingle.

Payden gripped the door, trying to open it. "Please, take me. Let's go now!"

Gil pushed the door closed, ignoring Payden's shrieks. He climbed to his feet, thinking of the logistics of sneaking into the North City and finding his way into a fortress where dozens of chained mages would be waiting for him. It would be a suicide venture, with very little chance of success.

He'd have to find a way to increase his odds.

"I'll go check it out," he said, rising to his feet. "Wait here, Payden. I'll come back for you." He locked the door and hung the key on its hook.

"No!" Payden screamed from the other side of the door, the panic in his voice ricocheting off the brick walls. "Please! Don't go! *Take me with you!*"

Gil forced himself to turn away. He hadn't wanted to get Payden's hopes up. "Don't worry. I'll come back."

Payden rattled the door, shaking it with all his might, making desperate moaning noises. "Don't leave me! *Please!* I want to go home! *Please!*"

The sound of his sobs was piteous. They tore Gil's heart. He turned and looked at the jolting door. He tried to imagine that it was himself in that cell, tried to imagine the pain. He went back and pressed his palm against the door. Taking the key, he unlocked it and let the door swing open. On the floor of the cell, Payden sat rocking himself, tears and snot draining down his cheeks, his red lips contorted and quivering.

"Payden," Gil said quietly. "Is there anything else you want? Anything else in the whole world that will ever make you happy?"

The man shook his head, his body shaking with sobs.

"No." The word crackled in Payden's throat. He grimaced, a look of unbearable anguish. *"I just want to go home."*

Gil closed his eyes. He couldn't stand to leave him. Not like that.

"Then I'll take you home," he whispered. Closing his eyes, he reached deep inside Payden and snapped something there, something delicate but significant.

Payden collapsed in a heap on the floor, where his body lay twitching.

Gil felt warm tears on his face as he walked away. The tears weren't for Payden, who was beyond the need for grief. His tears were for Ashra. They were derived from his own shame, and the pain of knowing that he would have to do the same for her.

Lost in a bleak and murky emptiness, he let his feet take him back through the darkness of the cistern and up the stairs, carrying him to the door of the Prime Warden's office. Ignoring her secretary, he entered without knocking.

Naia glanced up at him with a look of shock. "Gil—"

He strode forward and stopped in front of her desk.

"Consider this my resignation," he said, already turning back toward the door. "Find someone more competent."

He left the office and walked quickly back out into the hallway, striding down the corridor toward the Lyceum's main doors. He heard footsteps rushing to catch up with him, but he didn't slow.

"Gil!" Naia called after him.

He ignored her and kept walking, his black cloak billowing in his wake.

"Warden Archer!"

The authority in her voice stopped him short. Defeated, he turned back to her.

Naia strode up and stopped in front of him, a look of fury in her eyes. "What do you think you're doing?"

"I already told you," he answered. "I'm quitting."

She shook her head. "I don't accept your resignation."

Gil shrugged. "Accept it or not, I don't care. But you'll have to find someone else to do the job."

Naia rubbed her brow wearily. Her face looked more haggard than he'd ever seen it. Looking up at him, she asked softly, "What do you need from me?"

"Nothing. There's nothing you can do—I'm done. Look, I'm not my father. No matter how much everyone wants me to be, I'll never be like him. I'm no hero."

The Prime Warden drew in a heavy breath. "Neither was he."

Gil's thoughts halted. Suddenly confused, he asked, "What do you mean?"

Naia raised her chin, crossing her arms. She said, "Kyel Archer was a man who always tried to do the right thing—even if it wasn't the right thing. He made mistakes too, Gil."

Of course she was right; no man could be right all the time. But never in his life had Gil heard even one thing his father had ever gotten wrong. He disagreed softly, "Not the kind of mistakes I've been making."

"Yes." Naia said, inching closer. "Even those kinds of mistakes. That's what happens when someone becomes a leader. Greater responsibility means the mistakes are bigger. That's just the way it is. All you can do is your best."

Her words only served to fan his self-resentment. "Well, my best wasn't good enough," he growled angrily and started toward the door.

"Where are you going?" she called after him.

He stopped and looked back. "To the North City. The Sultan's in a bind; unless we can do something about their mages, it's all over. I know where they're kept now. They won't be expecting me. I'm going to kill as many as I can. If I can reduce their numbers even a fraction, it might give us a chance."

Naia shook her head slowly, her eyes thoughtful. Breathing a long sigh, she said, "Then you're going to need help."

"I'll take all the help I can get," he assured her.

She crossed her arms, clenching her jaw. "I know of a weapon that could make all the difference," she said quietly. "Against an entire army, it wouldn't do much good. But for your purpose, it would be ideal."

Gil stared at her blankly, until it occurred to him what she was talking about. "You're speaking of *Thar'gon,*" he gasped.

"Yes," Naia responded. "At one time, it was carried by your father. It only makes sense it should fall to you."

Gil's mind was reeling. His father had used the weapon to destroy the Well of Tears. But no one knew what had become of it. He said softly, "I thought it was lost."

"No," Naia said softly. "It was never lost. I know where it is. And I can help you retrieve it."

31

THE CUSTODIAN

RYLAN STARED BEYOND XIANA AT KEIO MATU'S STONE EFFIGY, cold tendrils of fear slithering down his back. He moved past her, then paced slowly in a wide circle around the figure. He tried to get a good look at the statue's face, but it was difficult. The man's head was thrown back, staring straight upward as if gazing into the face of apocalypse. His hair was unbound, hanging halfway down his back, every strand preserved in fine detail as if etched into the stone. Rylan wondered at the strange position Keio Matu had been frozen in for eight thousand years. He looked like he had been gathering himself for a feat of great courage. Or of great cowardice.

Somehow, he was supposed to form a link with this ancient man and absorb his knowledge. The very idea seemed incomprehensible, but Rylan knew better than to doubt. Such a union would make him the recipient of Keio Matu's legacy, another inheritance he hadn't asked for and didn't want. But the man before him didn't look like a demon. If anything, he looked defiant, captured in the instant he had condemned an entire civilization to death.

But was such an act not evil?

Could such a sacrifice ever be justified?

Rylan couldn't answer those questions. He shivered, feeling suddenly uncertain whether he wanted this man's knowledge. He already had one tainted legacy within him. Wasn't that enough?

"Go on," Xiana urged, taking a step back. "Touch him."

Rylan frowned, staring at Keio Matu's stone visage. "Is that it? Is there more I have to do?"

"That's it." Xiana waved him forward. "Do it, Rylan. Don't think about it. Just close your eyes and touch him."

He didn't want to.

But this wasn't about what he wanted, not anymore. This was about his daughter, about Amina. About the people of Zahra and the people of Karikesh. This was about defeating the Turan Khar and sending them back to hell where they belonged.

Closing his eyes, Rylan gritted his teeth and placed his hands on the statue.

When he opened his eyes, the sun was shining brilliantly in his face. A gentle breeze traced his skin, cooling the day to a pleasant temperature. He blinked, the glare of sunlight over-whelming his eyes. The world around him swam slowly into focus, resplendent in glorious greens and the vivid blue of a summer sky. Wind sighed through the tree branches overhead, rustling the leaves. Birdsong filtered toward him, coming from every direction. The fresh scent of roses filled his nostrils, a nostalgic scent that brought him happiness.

It was a beautiful day. A perfect day.

He turned and smiled at his beloved. She smiled back, and his heart filled with joy and desire. Ilia was the woman he loved, the woman he wanted to spend his life with. A playful breeze stirred a lock of hair over her face. She jerked her head, tossing her hair back over her shoulder where it belonged. The breeze tossed it right back, and she laughed.

He pulled her close and stroked her face with his fingers, brushing the wayward strands behind her ear. His action made her grin harder, which made his heart glad. He held her in his arms and kissed her deeply.

Gazing into her eyes, he asked, "Will you be my wife?"

At first, he thought she was going to say no. Then he saw the tears collecting in her eyes, and he knew she was his.

"Yes!" she cried, her voice full of joy and laughter.

He lifted Ilia into his arms and settled down with her on the grass. Leaning back with her on top of him, he kissed her lovingly. The scent of roses filled his nostrils, and the feel of her there, in his arms, filled his dreams for years to come. For centuries to come.

He rolled over and gazed at her breathlessly.

He produced a necklace with a radiant opal stone and drew it around her neck, then kissed her hand. She looked down, fingering the pendant.

"What stone is this?" she asked in a trembling voice.

He smiled, stroking her hair. "It's an imbued opal. With it, you can always come back to me."

Fresh tears spilled down her cheeks, her expression speaking silent words he would never hear and never forget.

The breeze sighed.

The world blurred and faded.

He held Ilia's hands and gazed into her radiant face. She wore a garland of white rosebuds in her hair, a flowing dress embroidered with a floral pattern. She was looking at him with the same expression she had the day he proposed to her.

Holding her soft hands, he pledged, "I will honor and treasure you as my beloved wife."

"I will honor and treasure you as my beloved husband." She smiled at him, all the joy in the world reflected in her eyes.

"And may death never part us."

"And may death never part us."

He drew her in and kissed her tenderly, lovingly.

The world blurred.

He made the mistake of blinking.

———

"Who are they?"

His forceful strides propelled him across the Guardian Tower's command chamber. He stopped in front of his senior officer, a white-haired man named Paru, who stood with his back against the seamless black wall, his face etched in lines of intensity. He stood at attention, staring straight ahead, legs spread, hands clasped behind his back.

In a tense but controlled voice, he responded, "The Turan Khar."

Paru's words provoked only vast confusion. The Turan Khar were not a warmongering society. They had coexisted with them peaceably for hundreds of years. They had neither the military knowledge nor the infrastructure to wage war on this scale.

"What do they want?" he demanded.

"To conquer us, of course."

Men and women milled around the command chamber. Some stood staring out the tower windows, while others, like Paru, ringed the walls and waited for orders. Below, the air surrounding the Watchers glowed with an eerie blue light he'd never seen before, the surrounding air ionized by the grotesque amounts of amassed power ready to deploy.

Another explosion rocked the Guardian tower. The Watchers flared, and beams of light shot far into the night sky, aimed at infinity. Another building, this time to the south, disappeared from existence, along with the sum of the people in it.

He clenched his jaw. "There isn't enough field strength to power that kind of weapon!"

Paru's razor-like gaze shifted to him. "Custodian. They've opened a rift. They're harvesting anti-magic from a mirror-plane."

His mouth fell open, and he stared at Paru in shock.

The world shuddered. Then it blurred and faded.

And winked back into existence.

The order to retreat resounded like a thundering hammer in his head. He staggered a few more steps before slumping forward, hands braced on his knees, panting for breath. For a moment, he just stood there, struggling to breathe through the filth in the air. Thick black smoke poured past him, heated by unnatural fires that glowed a deep crimson red. The poison smoke stung his eyes. He wiped an arm across his face, the fabric coming away stained with bloody grime.

He sucked in as much air as his lungs could draw and cried, *"Ilia!"* The sound came out barely louder than a wheeze.

She wasn't there. Men and women charged past him in mindless flight, screaming and wailing. He started limping after them.

But he stopped after only a few strides. Throwing his head back, he shouted, *"Ilia!"*

"I'm here, Keio!"

His eyes fell on her soot-darkened face, and a tidal wave of relief nearly swept him away. He sprinted toward her through the stampeding crowd and scooped her up, hugging her tight against his chest as flames the color of hell licked the sky behind them. Releasing her, he searched frantically for the best route of escape.

Before he found one, the world shuddered and faded.

He stood alone in the command chamber at the top of the Guardian Tower, looking out from one of the great wide windows. His hands, planted on the window ledge, were pale and trembling. His brain had slowed to a standstill, mired in a numbing fog that encased him like a chrysalis. Below him stretched a scarred and defeated landscape he didn't recognize.

Tall columns of smoke rose all across the plain as the cities of Shira burned. Suheylu Ra stood alone in defiance of the Turan Khar, a situation that was untenable. Already, most of his nation lay scattered and broken, his people massacred or enslaved. The Khar had a capacity for brutality that was never-ending. All the blood and tears they had already feasted on had only intensified their thirst.

He clenched his hands until his nails bit into his palms. He felt impotent, for he was. All the great knowledge and capacity of his people meant nothing in the face of the threat posed by the Turan Khar. He could only defend with the might of one world, while the Khar conquered with the fury of two worlds, combined and weaponized.

A shadow fell over him, making him shiver. He looked up in time to see a glistening, winged form slither through the air above the Guardian. The Khar's demons were already aloft, surveilling the city. Suheylu Ra was next. Very soon, it would fall.

The Khar would finish what they started... but what was next?

His own civilization lay slaughtered, its picked-on bones strewn across the continent. But there were still plenty of other nations in the world. Nations that would provide easy fodder.

It was within his power to help them, at an unthinkable price.

Unthinkable, and yet he was considering it.

Along the horizon, another city was reduced to vaporized particles.

He bowed his head.

The world blurred and wept like rain.

"There's no time!" he shouted at Paru.

"Then what would you have me do?"

He had no idea. He grimaced, gritting his teeth against the scream in his throat. He whirled away from Paru. "I'll tend the Watchers. I'll do what I can. It won't be enough, so by all the gods, get as many as you can out of here!"

Paru stood frozen for a fraction of a second longer than he should have before effecting a bow. "Yes, Custodian. We'll get as many out as we can." With that, he turned and ran, the sound of his footsteps ringing up the stairwell.

"Ilia."

His wife turned to him with despair in her eyes as she guessed his intentions. She surged forward and clutched his arms painfully. "Please don't!" she gasped. "You're the Custodian of this city! Your job is to protect!"

"*I can't,*" he growled, taking a step back and throwing his hands up in desperation. "Don't you understand? There's nothing I can do. We are defeated, Ilia!"

She grimaced, anguished tears flooding her cheeks. It was obvious she thought he was betraying her, betraying them all. What she didn't understand was that there was nothing left to betray. He moved closer, wanting to comfort her. He raised his hand to caress her face.

She flinched away from him.

The entire world shuddered as if terrified. He could hear the stone of the Guardian Tower grinding against its foundation. Striding quickly toward the window, he looked up at the darkening sky. Above the city, an enormous rift had opened and was expanding, sucking light and hope down its gullet. He'd never seen anything so monstrous.

"What is it?" Ilia cried.

It took him a moment to find the words. "It's their Sky Portal," he said. "They've summoned it here."

Her eyes widened in terror and disbelief. "How do you know?"

"What else could it be, Ilia? They use the Onslaught as a weapon. They have to draw it from somewhere."

"Anti-magic," she whispered. "How?"

It didn't matter how. He disengaged from her and sprinted back toward the center of the room. He had to bring the Watchers back online, had to get them primed and overcharged. There wasn't much time. They were already out of hope. But the rest of the world wasn't.

"I need you, Ilia. Help me wake the focus!"

Instead of heeding him, she turned back to the window. With a growl of frustration, he took up position in the middle of the room, centering himself over the eight-pointed star pattern depicted in tile on the floor. The star worked like a lens, focusing the lines of the magic field at a single point. Suheylu Ra was built in the center of a powerful vortex of magic, and the star focus could channel all that raw power.

Closing his eyes, he willed the focus to awaken and drew deeply on its power. He could feel it coursing through him, a blazing torrent of energy, far more than he could ever draw unaided. Using himself as a conduit, he directed all that energy outward toward the Watchers. Brilliant beams of magic erupted from the golden dome of the Guardian, streaming out across the city toward each of the twelve great sentinel towers, which came to life and begin to pulsate. Thin rays of light shot out from each of the Watchers, creating an elaborate web of energy above Suheylu Ra with the portal in the air as its focus.

"Keio!"

He opened his eyes and saw Ilia standing at his side, staring in shock at something behind him. He turned and looked over his shoulder.

There, at the edge of the stairs, stood a man and woman dressed all in black and holding chain-like artifacts that glowed with power. The woman was Darl, from the continent of Tur. She was beautiful in the way a crystal is beautiful, all sharp edges and smooth planes, with silvery hair and pale gray skin. The man beside her was also Darl, or perhaps one of the Sea People. His skin was a much darker gray, his hair utterly white, framing a face that was exceptionally thin. His narrow, black eyes glistened with sinister intellect.

How they had gotten past the Watchers, he would never know.

"Stand away from the focus," the man ordered as he crested the flight of stairs and moved slowly into the command chamber.

Holding the web of power as tightly as he could, Keio demanded, "Withdraw your forces, or I'll collapse your portal and send you straight back to hell."

The Darl man paused. His eyes roved over Keio, starting with his feet and moving upward to capture his gaze with a piercing stare.

"And how do you intend to accomplish that?"

The Darl's voice was strangely calm. Keio stared harder at him. There was something about him. Something familiar. He couldn't place it.

"I've primed the Watchers and aimed them at your portal. If you attack us, they'll overload. We'll see how well your portal holds up against the magic of an entire vortex flooding into it."

The Darl's expression didn't change.

The woman next to him said, "That's a very bad idea, Keio."

So they knew who he was.

He turned to regard the woman with skin the color of a corpse and eyes black and dull like charcoal. Her face was sharp and chiseled, as though she'd been carved from marble. Her expression was just as cold.

"You cannot force that much magic into a gateway stabilized by anti-magic," the man informed him in a patient, condescending, voice. "Doing so would destabilize the magic field over the entire area. The resulting backlash would contaminate everything: the air, the soil, the water, the animals."

"I'm aware of that."

He glanced at Ilia, who stood staring at him, face bloodless and slack with terror. The sight of her made his insides twist. If he carried out his threat, he'd be killing her too. He'd be killing them all.

"You're bluffing," the vile man said with a smirk, taking a step toward him. "The entire region would be uninhabitable for thousands of years. Now. My patience is wearing thin." He took another step forward. "Step away from the focus."

"I'm not bluffing," Keio assured him, even though the very words felt like a gut punch. "Your society is like a disease. I'm going to stop the spread of it here, before it infects the entire world."

He meant those words, meant them with all his soul. But then his gaze slipped to Ilia and his heart broke. She was everything to him, the brightest star in his heavens. He couldn't condemn her.

He couldn't afford not to.

There was a sudden shriek and then something knocked

into him. Hard. He lost his balance and fell to the floor, almost losing his connection with the focus. He sat dazed for a moment. Then his gaze fell upon Ilia.

She lay beside him on the floor. Dying or dead. Above her floated a shadowy wraith in the form of a man.

He scrambled toward her, taking her into his arms and holding her close, the way he had the day he proposed to her. Only, this time, she didn't hold him back. When she drew her last breath, he felt her death as his own, and a significant part of him died with her.

The Gift of magic was released from her body as she died. It flooded into him, and he screamed. He screamed until his throat was raw, then collapsed in tears.

He lay her down on the ground, then looked up at the Darl with wrath in his eyes.

Somehow, he still clung to the power of the vortex. He hadn't dropped it. And now, more than ever, he had no hesitation about using it. He rose to his feet, glaring his hatred at the vile man across the room from him. He opened his mouth, but no words came out. No words could.

The Darl extended his hand toward him. "I have no desire to see you suffer," he said in a calm and quiet voice. "If you come with me, I will take you to a place where you can be with her again. You can be with her for eternity. Come, Keio."

It was too much. He was paralyzed with pain. All he could do was stand and weep. The man dismissed his shadowy minion with a motion of his hand. Then he smiled. It wasn't a gloating smile; it was compassionate.

The smile was a mistake. The biggest mistake ever made.

With a ferocious cry, Keio drew as hard as he could on the vortex, drinking in all its terrible power and sending it back out to flood every Watcher that ringed the city.

The Darl let out an outraged cry, then disappeared.

Keio threw his head back and screamed in anguish as all

the power of an entire vortex raged through him, shredding his mind. With his last rational thought, he commanded the Watchers to overload, to direct their wrath at the portal overhead.

The last thing he saw was the sky turning a hideous, crimson red.

Then the world blurred and ran like blood.

He opened his eyes with a strangled gasp. Before him stood his beloved—whole, beautiful, alive. The sight of her made him shudder, and his eyes shed hot tears that fell like rain. He shook his head, knowing the vision in front of him was a lie. But when he blinked, she was still there, wearing the same necklace he had given her the day she had pledged to become his wife.

He reached up and touched the opal pendant, filled with an overwhelming mixture of sadness and wonder.

"Ilia," he whispered, hardly believing she was there, standing in front of him.

But the woman he loved shook her head. "No, Rylan," she whispered, her eyes drowning in sorrow. "I'm Xiana."

He withdrew his hand, suddenly uncertain. He took a step back, his gaze rising to her face, a face that looked suddenly different. But her eyes remained the same; it was her. It was his Ilia. The woman he had died loving.

"Rylan," she whispered again.

The name awakened fresh memories within him, memories that didn't seem real. Memories that belonged to another man, another life. His breath caught in his throat, and he stood motionless, clenched in the grasp of confusion and despair.

"I'm Rylan," he breathed, glancing at her for confirmation.

Xiana gave a sorrowful grin. "Yes. That's who you are."

Her words stabbed his heart. "What of Ilia...?"

Xiana stroked his face tenderly, her eyes glistening. "She's here, Rylan. She lives within me. Just as Keio Matu now lives in you."

He turned around and saw the stone figure was gone. The focus star was now covered in sand, enough sand for two such figures. A sob choked his throat. He fell to his knees and ran his fingers through the dusty grains.

He looked up at Xiana. "You've been here before," he realized. "You merged with Ilia." The words trembled in his throat. "But you said no one could come here twice. The poison in the air..."

She sank to the floor and, kneeling beside him, took his hand in hers. "This was my pilgrimage," she said, her eyes pleading his forgiveness. Reaching down, she scooped up a handful of sand. "I merged with Ilia. She gave me all of her memories and all of her knowledge. But the one thing I needed most she couldn't give me."

"What was that?"

"You. I needed you to become Keio Matu. Don't you see? Keio and Ilia were far more powerful together than they were apart—that was their true strength: their completed union. Now that you have Keio's knowledge, we can both be far greater together than we could ever be alone."

As she spoke, a terrible panic grew within him. Every second they stood there, more contamination from the air seeped through their pores. Xiana had already been to Suheylu Ra once. Rylan surged to his feet, pulling her up after him, gasping, "We've got to get you out of here."

She lifted her hand to her necklace. The same necklace he had given her all those years ago. "I'm fine, Rylan," she assured him. "I have come here twice—but I never walked back out again. I used the opal to transfer me back the last time I was here. And I'll do the same again. It will be like I only came and left once. Here, Rylan. Take my hand."

He stared at the necklace, taking in the sight of the fiery opal that shimmered with colorful iridescent. Then he looked at her face and searched her eyes deeply, desperately trying to see the woman within.

"Please, Rylan," she urged. "Please. Take my hand."

He did as she asked.

The world blurred and ran like tears.

32

THE TEMPLE OF DEATH

GIL GAZED UP AT THE SLEEK LIMESTONE BUILDING CAPPED BY A dome thick with verdigris. Its lustrous walls glistened under the bright light of the sun. Three rose windows graced the wall above the door, protected by a columned portico. Beside him, Naia stood with her arms wrapped around herself, her thick auburn hair blowing in the wind. She was gazing up at the temple with a whimsical expression on her face, like a person returning from a long journey taking in the first sight of home. He kept forgetting she had once been a priestess before becoming a mage. To Naia, perhaps returning to the temple was like coming home.

"The Temple of Death?" Gil asked. "That's where you hid *Thar'gon?*"

Naia started forward without looking at him. "Not exactly."

Frowning, Gil followed her up the temple steps and through the wide, open doorway. As they entered the vestibule, the shadows of the roof fell over them. The interior was dim, lit by many tapers that glowed from iron sconces and massive chandeliers. Beyond the vestibule, the nave was thoroughly empty, save for two rows of scalloped columns. At the far end, the lights of hundreds of votive candles flickered from the altar: layer upon layer of shelves stacked full of them, each flame a prayer for a departed loved one. Gil felt his stomach squirm at the side of them. He tried to avoid temples whenever he could. Especially this temple.

Naia paused, staring at the shrine ahead, and asked, "Would you please excuse me for a moment?"

Following her gaze, Gil realized her intent. She wanted to offer a prayer for Quin.

"Of course," he said, stepping back. "I'll wait right here."

Naia moved alone toward the shrine, walking slowly. Reaching the altar, she paused and bowed her head. She stood there for a long time, her lips moving silently, muttering the strains of a prayer. When she was done, she took an unlit candle into her hand and selected a striker from the ledge. Holding both striker and candle, she squeezed the mechanism. A spark flickered into being and went right to the candle. The wick flared briefly to life.

And then it winked out.

Naia closed her eyes and bit her lip, her face going rigid. She stood there for a moment, face scrunched in concentration. Then, drawing in a deep breath, she opened her eyes and squeezed the striker again. Once again, the candle remained unlit. This time, the look on Naia's face was one of shock. She squeezed the striker again, to no avail. She tried again. And again. Sparks rained to the floor.

Still, the little candle refused to light.

Looking shaken, Naia replaced both candle and striker on the ledge, then walked back across the nave toward Gil, arms crossed, eyes damp and red.

"Is everything all right?" he asked, concerned.

He wondered if Naia would take the unlit candle to mean the goddess had rejected her prayers for her husband's soul. He was suddenly thankful he didn't believe in the gods' divinity.

But Naia did. As she drew near him, her face brightened with a small, whimsical smile. Apparently, Naia had taken the candle's reluctance for a good sign.

"Everything is fine," she said. "Shall we go?"

Gil scratched the back of his head, motioning her forward. "Lead the way."

Smiling, Naia brushed past him and walked toward a transept that bisected the main sanctuary. The sound of Gil's boots echoed sharply off the marble floor, magnified by the high walls and towering ceiling. A spill of colored light filtered down from the many stained-glass windows set high above, each depicting a different scene from the Book of the Dead. As they entered the transept, Naia paused and waited for him to catch up.

At the far end of the room was a stairway graced with an elaborately carved railing and wide steps that sloped downward. Gil followed Naia down the staircase. Eventually, the steps ended at a long chamber with polished black walls. A stark, erratic light emanated from four large braziers placed along the margins of the room. On the far wall was a doorway with no door, just an opening into what looked like a solid curtain of darkness.

Something about the doorway made Gil shiver. It looked ominous, unnatural. He didn't like the feel of it; looking at the darkness beyond made his flesh prickle.

"Is that where we're going?" he asked, nodding toward the doorway.

"Yes," Naia answered. "This is an entrance to the Catacombs of Death."

Gil swallowed heavily. "And why are we going there?"

"Because." Naia stepped between him and the doorway, commanding his attention. "The Catacombs are where the talisman lies."

Gil peered around her at the dark opening. It looked like a

gateway to the Netherworld; not exactly someplace he wanted to be going.

"Why is it kept there?" he asked. "Why isn't it back at the Lyceum, like every other artifact we've ever found?"

Naia raised a hand to the broach that held her white cloak. "Quin and I agreed it would be safer here, kept locked away in secret, its location known only to a select few. *Thar'gon* is the most powerful artifact that exists in the world. In the wrong hands, it could be used to do great evil. But it can also be used to do great good."

Gil wondered why she hadn't produced the weapon at the beginning of the war. It could have made all the difference. Perhaps she'd been afraid of it falling into the wrong hands.

"Why would you hide it here?" he pressed. "Out of all the places in the world?"

"Because the Catacombs aren't *in* this world," Naia responded. She strolled away a few steps before turning back to him. "After your father died, *Thar'gon* changed hands a few times. Your father used it to destroy the Well of Tears, but the Well was protected by powerful magic. It killed Kyel before he could finish the job. After he fell, Quin picked it up and finished what your father began."

She paced away a few more steps. "After the Well was destroyed, Quin passed *Thar'gon* to Darien, who used it to slay Xerys' most powerful Servant. That was the last act Darien ever performed. He died shortly after. We hid the talisman in his tomb."

"So we're going grave robbing," Gil surmised.

Naia smiled. "Of a sort."

Gil stared uneasily at the dark passage. He didn't want to walk through that doorway; just the thought made him shudder. He was no stranger to temple mysteries, but there was something about that opening that made his skin crawl. He'd always denied the existence of the gods. But the darkness ahead made him doubt his convictions. With a regretful sigh, he started forward.

"Wait."

Gil halted, turning back.

"Before we enter, I must caution you," Naia said, approaching him. "The Catacombs exist partly in the Atrament. There is a chance we might encounter shades of the dead. If we do, you cannot interact with them in any way. That would break the Strictures of Death. Do you understand?"

Gil nodded, licking his lips. "I understand."

"Good. There are things in the Catacombs that will unsettle you," she warned. "I have power over most of them, so you need not fear."

"Most of them?" Gil asked skeptically. "That implies there are things in there you can't control."

"There are," Naia responded, her expression very serious. "That's why we must proceed with caution. Are you ready?"

He wasn't; he doubted he'd ever be. Nevertheless, he nodded.

"I'm ready. Let's go."

She placed a hand on his back and, with gentle pressure, urged him across the threshold of the doorway.

33

DUALITY

Rylan blinked his eyes open and stared groggily upward at the ceiling. The dark beams of wood looked familiar, although it took him muddled seconds to realize where he was: in the hut Xiana had provided for him back in Daru. He turned over and discovered Xiana lying beside him on his pallet. Her eyes were closed, her chest moving in a slow and steady rhythm, one hand curled beside her face. She looked serene. Beautiful.

Reaching out, he trailed a finger down her cheek. Then he stopped himself. He retracted his hand, mired in confusion. He didn't have those kinds of feelings for her... at least, he hadn't before. And now, he wasn't certain they were his own feelings... or someone else's.

His gaze fell upon the opal pendant on its gold chain. The way his breath caught told him that, whether he wanted them or not, those feelings were there, and they were real. It didn't matter how he'd come by them. Frustrated, he rolled away from her.

He lay staring at the walls, which were just as dark and oppressive as he remembered. Only scant streams of sunlight managed to make it past the lattice screens covering the windows. The air was frigid, moving in through gaps in the wallboards. It smelled of wood smoke from the village cookfires.

Throwing off his blanket, Rylan stood and looked down at himself. He was wearing a gray *yori* tied with a darker gray sash, though he didn't remember putting it on. The leather belt that had been his father's had been thrown carelessly in the corner. He stroked his hand down the *oki*-silk robe. His hand was filthy, the cracks and creases of his fingers etched in grime, his nails crusted with dirt. He rubbed his fingers together and watched dust rained down from them. Or was it dust? His thoughts returned to the figure that had once been Keio Matu, and suddenly the dust on his hands took on new significance.

That man was in him, part of him... infesting him. His feelings were no longer his own, and his memories were a confused tangle. He tried sorting through his recollections and was comforted to find that most of the memories were his own. Keio's seemed to have faded overnight, the way a dream fades upon wakening. Thinking of Keio made him think of Ilia. He turned to look at Xiana.

And found her awake, staring up at him.

Rylan drew back, renewed feelings stirring deep inside him, accompanied by a sharp stab of anxiety. He turned away from her, feeling betrayed by his own emotions.

She moved to sit up. Reaching out, she caught his hand. "Are you angry, Rylan?"

He pulled his hand away and scrubbed it over his whiskery face, his mind struggling to determine exactly which of the conflicting emotions in him dominated.

"I'm confused," he said at last.

She looked at him with sympathy. "It gets easier with time. I promise."

That wasn't good enough. That meant it was always going

to be like this. That it was never going to change. He clenched his fist in frustration, wishing it was possible to hate her.

"I don't know which part of me is me... and which part is him," he mumbled.

Xiana patted the floor beside her, scooting over to make room for him. He settled down next to her, leaning back against the wall. She stroked a hand through his hair. A slight smile drifted to her lips.

"I struggled with that too," she said gently. "It took me a while to realize it didn't matter. All these memories, all these feelings. They belong to me now, even if some once belonged to her. Every memory I have is precious to me. I wouldn't want to forget any of it." Looking down, she stroked his hand.

He pulled it away from her. "So, for the rest of my life, I'm going to be living with a dead man trapped inside my head? Doesn't that make me some kind of monster?"

"You're not a monster, Rylan," she said, compassion in her eyes. "Keio Matu was a great man. One of the greatest men who has ever lived."

"He destroyed Suheylu Ra!"

"He did it to protect the rest of the world!" she reminded him. "There was no hope for Suheylu Ra. He was in an impossible situation. He did the only thing he could."

Staring past her at the wall, Rylan said, "I want him out."

She gave him a look of sympathy. Leaning forward, she kissed his forehead. "I don't," she said, and rose to her feet. He saw she was wearing a pink *yori* tied with a thin sash. She stood over him with her hands clasped in front of her.

Looking down at him, she said, "Today is the day I must make my report to the Sensho, so that he may decide your fate."

Rylan had forgotten all about the Sensho—forgotten he was still technically condemned. He rose to his feet, concerned. Not that he expected Xiana to betray him. But the Word of

Command was still firmly anchored to him, and that alone made him nervous.

"What are you going to tell him?" he asked.

Xiana smiled at him affectionately. "I am going to tell him that I found nothing of your father in you. That you are a good and honorable man who does not deserve death."

Good and honorable.

He wanted to laugh at that. She was wrong.

He was neither good nor honorable, she just didn't know it. She didn't know the terrible secret he had kept from her. Remembering the people he had killed in the waste, he was suddenly confronted by an intense feeling of fear. There was much more of his father in him than she knew. So much more. Like his father before him, he had made a covenant with evil. He wondered what Xiana would think if she knew that. Or what the Sensho would think.

The part within him that was Keio Matu shuddered, sending renewed feelings of self-loathing bubbling to the surface. He shouldn't have ever tried to hide this part of him from her. This was too big, too terrible. He should have admitted it from the start. He felt suddenly terrified, the fear chilling his gut like a shard of ice.

His lips moved without him willing them to. "Xiana... I need to tell you something..."

He stopped himself. And gasped, horrified by how close he'd come to admitting he was a monster deserving death. The Sensho would execute him. Amina would never be rescued. She would spend her life as a slave of the Turan Khar. Or worse.

The part of him that was Keio Matu berated him for the thought. This was bigger than him. Bigger than Amina. Too dangerous to be kept a secret.

"What is it, Rylan?" Xiana pressed.

Looking away from her, he took a deep breath. The fear in

him was paralyzing, freezing his mind as well as his body. His mouth went dry. He was going to tell her, he realized. He was going to tell her everything. The other man within him demanded no less. Rylan opened his mouth to speak, but no words came out. He tried again, and this time his voice worked, though it was weak and ragged.

"The man who took Amina did something else to me," he said.

Xiana leaned into him and touched his hand, her face scrunched in a look of intense concern. "What? What did he do to you, Rylan?"

He squeezed his eyes shut, hating himself. "He threatened to kill my daughter if I didn't swear an oath."

"What oath?"

Suddenly, he could feel her doubt. He bowed his head, grimacing in shame. Icy sweat beaded on his forehead.

"He made me swear an oath to Chaos."

He heard her gasp. There was a long pause.

"Why didn't you tell me?" she whispered, the revulsion in her voice clawing at his heart.

He had betrayed her. Betrayed himself.

He hung his head in shame.

"I didn't tell you because I knew you'd kill me," he answered, unable to look at her. "Then Amina would be lost."

For seconds, she stood staring at him, the color draining from her face. At last, she whispered, "And why are you telling me this now?"

Tears filled his eyes. He blinked them back and didn't let them fall. "Because I understand now that Amina isn't the most important thing in the world... just in my world. I was selfish." He hung his head. "Do what you will with me."

He hardly noticed when she left. He sat back down against the wall, hugging his legs, his head bowed against his knees. They would be coming for him soon. The thought didn't scare him; it just made him sad. He sat there in confusion, wondering why he'd said anything at all. There was another man inside him now whose priorities weren't necessarily his own. He had listened to that man. And now he had failed his daughter.

He heard the guards coming up the path seconds before they burst through the door. He didn't resist as they hauled him off the floor and bound his hands behind his back with coarse rope that bit into his flesh. They dragged him out the door, a man to either side of him. He struggled to keep up with them, but it was difficult. He lurched in their grasp as they propelled him down the path through the garden.

As he walked, Rylan looked up at the sky. It was perfectly blue, the clouds wispy and fantastically white. He was glad it wasn't overcast. He was glad his last glance of the sky would be one of clear blue radiance. They dragged him through the village and onto the cliffs on the other side, to where the palace of the Sensho stood perched atop the edge of a precipice, over-looking the Desolation. The boards of the walkway groaned beneath their feet as they marched him up a ramp and out onto a rope bridge that spanned a recess in the cliffs. There, the daylight seemed brighter, making him squint. Before he was ready, the sun disappeared behind the elongated eaves of the Sensho's palace.

One of the men took him by the hair and shoved him through the doorway, pushing him toward the center of the room. He stumbled and fell to his knees. He knelt there with his arms restrained behind him, staring down at the rush mats that covered the floor. He drew in a deep breath. Then he raised his head to look up into the stern face of the Sensho.

Sensho Domeda was seated cross-legged on the dais. Xiana knelt next to him. She didn't look at Rylan, but instead kept her gaze angled downward at the mat, her expression unreadable. The guards knelt around him, hands gripping the hilts of their swords, their bodies tense with readiness. For long moments, no one moved. The Sensho sat glowering at him, his face never changing. Rylan waited for the pronouncement of his sentence, determined to accept his fate with dignity.

Unnerving seconds dragged by, stretching infinitely.

At last, the Sensho turned and grunted something to Xiana.

She lifted her gaze from the mat and looked at Rylan. With her eyes locked on his, she stated formally, "Rylan Lauchlin, you stand condemned for crimes of the blood and crimes of the soul. You were allowed one week to convince us that you were a man of better morals than your father. As your mentor, I have given my recommendation to the Sensho."

There was a slight gap of silence filled only by the sound of his own thundering pulse.

Xiana continued, "I have recommended to the Sensho that you should be allowed to live."

Rylan felt the breath gush out of him, a flood of relief that almost washed him away. He gaped up at the dais, unable to believe what he'd just heard. His head spun dizzily, and the world suddenly seemed insubstantial and surreal.

Xiana went on, "Even though you have sworn a compact with Xerys, you did so under coercion, and you had the courage to confess. This act, more than any other, has convinced me that you are a man of good judgment, who puts the welfare of others before himself. The Sensho has heard my recommendation."

Her eyes lowered again to the floor, and her voice darkened.

"Unfortunately, the Sensho does not agree. The Sensho believes that your oath to Chaos compromises your freedom of will. Because of this oath, you may be compelled to commit acts you might otherwise find appalling, and you cannot be trusted to listen to your own conscience. I am sorry, but it has been determined that you are too dangerous to live. Out of compassion, you will be executed immediately."

Rylan stared at her in shock, his mind reeling. He could

have accepted that judgment from the Sensho. But not from her. Hearing it from her, it was too painful.

And too fast.

The guards leaped up immediately and converged on him. Two fell on him from behind, their weight pinning him down. Another drew his sword and took up position over him. The image of the Sultan's men waiting to be executed flashed through Rylan's mind. Those men had been spared at the last moment. But no one was going to spare him.

"*Elantu!*" Xiana cried.

Rylan had no idea what she meant.

But Keio Matu did.

She wanted him to fight.

He opened his mind and grasped the only power available to him: the power of the Onslaught. Its sick energies filled him, defiling him. He hauled them in, then lashed out blindly.

The men holding him screamed and fell away.

Rylan scrambled to his feet, the ropes restraining him falling from his wrists. He stared about in shock, not certain what had happened, what he had done. Only one of the guards on the floor was moving. The rest lay sprawled in dark pools of sludge that once might have been blood.

Sensho Domeda remained sitting on the dais, his expression unchanged, staring unblinking at Rylan. Then he rose. Saying something Rylan didn't understand, the Sensho effected a low bow. Then he turned and descended the dais, making his way across the floor and out of the room. Rylan stood staring at Xiana, his mind reeling in confusion.

"What just happened?" he mumbled.

Smiling, Xiana came forward to stand in front of him. She took his hand. Gazing into his eyes, she said, "You just became *deizu-kan.*"

Rylan looked at her blankly. Too much had just happened. He couldn't process it all, and he had no idea what she meant.

Did they still intend to execute him? Should he be running for his life? Or begging for his death? He felt numb.

Xiana's smile deepened. She leaned forward, pressing her cheek to his and saying softly, "Go home and rest. No one will trouble you now."

"What about you?" he asked.

"I'll be along." She kissed his cheek, then pulled away, her nose wrinkling. "Ugh. Go take a bath. You stink."

He watched her walk away and disappear through a side door. Then he turned and made his way back to the main door of the palace, feeling as though he were moving in a dream. As soon as he stepped out from beneath the shadows of the eaves, the glare of sunlight assaulted his senses. It was overwhelming. Shielding his eyes, he walked out onto the wood pathway on the cliff and set his course for the village. He walked aimlessly, without thinking, not really noticing where he was going. People move past him. He didn't acknowledge them, wasn't really aware of them. He had no idea why he was still alive. All he knew was that he shouldn't be.

When he finally looked up and noticed his surroundings, he was mildly shocked. Somehow, his feet had obeyed Xiana and carried him to the bathhouse. He didn't remember deciding to go there, or which path he had come by. The shaded garden surrounding him was like a sanctuary filled with peace and tranquility. The pool misted with steam beckoned him forward.

The bath was unoccupied, which emboldened him. Moving toward the pool, he stripped and washed with soap at the fountain, just as Xiana had taught him. Rinsing, he rose and entered the bath. The water was hotter than he remembered, so he took his time, submerging himself gradually, wading in inch by inch. At last, he settled all the way down and, leaning his head against the edge of the pool, closed his eyes.

He sat there for a long time as the steam rose around him,

relaxing him. Minutes went by as the mist drifted over him. Eventually, he opened his eyes and gazed up at the thick limbs of the trees shading the spring. The leaves move slowly, rocked by a gentle breeze stirring the branches. He focused on the soft, rustling noise, letting his mind drift toward sleep.

A splashing noise jarred him awake.

Startled, Rylan opened his eyes to find Xiana standing across from him, her body naked and glistening. Her hair was wet, slicked back from her face. She waded slowly toward him, her eyes locked on his. He sat unmoving, his breath lost somewhere deep in his chest.

He forced himself to wrench his eyes away from her. She'd said it was common for the genders to bathe together, that it was just her people's way. But he couldn't do it. She was too beautiful, too desirable. The feelings of another man overwhelmed his own emotions. Unwillingly, his gaze was drawn to her naked form, captured and held there. He was unable to look away. His body hungered for her with a need he couldn't ignore.

Xiana stopped in front of him and pressed her forehead against his. He could feel her warm breath stroking his face, feel her firm breasts pressed against his chest. She stood there for moments unmoving, her eyes searching his. She smelled of roses.

Something inside Rylan broke. He pulled her close against him and kissed her lips. His hands moved over her curves, stroking, exploring, her body sliding against his. It was too much. The heat within him became a fire. It burned him raw.

He scooped Xiana up and carried her to the edge of the pool, setting her down on the deck. There, he settled down beside her and kissed her tenderly. Her soft fingers traced his skin, her breath shivering against his neck. He laid her back gently on the pinewood boards and gathered her close.

Gazing deeply into her eyes, he lost himself within her.

34

CITY OF SHADOW

THE WORLD SHIVERED AND SHIFTED.

Gil paused between footsteps, taking a moment to steady himself as his surroundings took their time to stabilize. He glanced at Naia in alarm, but the expression on the Prime Warden's face remained serene. Looking around, he saw they were in an underground passage that sloped downward in a gentle curve. The temperature had fallen drastically; he could see his breath before his face. A glowing blue mist swirled at their feet. It was magelight, and there was nothing divine about it. Just another temple mystery easily explained by magic. Feeling self-justified, he looked at Naia.

"It's cold," he said.

"It's supposed to be."

Taking his arm, she guided him deeper into the shadows of the tunnel, their feet disturbing the glowing mist. The noise of their footsteps was strangely muffled, as though the walls of the passage were porous, absorbing the noise. Shivering, Gil tugged his thick cloak tighter around himself. There were no torches on the walls; only the magelight to light their path. It cast an eerie shadowplay that danced across the stone walls. An intersection appeared ahead, where another passage crossed the one they were on. There, Naia turned, selecting the path that led to the right. As they walked, Gil became aware of an unpleasant odor that was gradually intensifying the further they went. It took him a moment to identify it: the stench of decay.

Eventually, the tunnel opened up into an enormous cavern. The sound of rushing water echoed hollowly from a distance, and Gil couldn't tell which direction it came from. Wondering how high the ceiling was, he craned his neck to look up. He didn't see a ceiling. Instead, the walls seemed to continue upward forever, never-ending.

"How far does it go?" he asked.

The Prime Warden offered a shrug. "No one knows."

Gil turned his attention to the walls. They had a strange pattern to them, like a honeycomb. Frowning, he raised his hand and pointed ahead. "What are those?"

"Burial vaults," Naia answered. "Each contains remains of the deceased."

Gil balked. Suddenly, the stench of decay seemed much more powerful. He drew his cloak over his face, sucking air through the fabric in a vain attempt to mitigate the stench. He walked faster, wanting to put a good distance between himself and the chamber with the vaults.

"Let's hurry," he pressed.

Naia complied, lengthening her stride. She led him down a path that meandered over uneven terrain toward a chasm that gaped like a ragged knife wound through the center of the chamber. Gil eyed the bridge that spanned it warily, hesitant to cross. The structure looked to be made of thin black glass and didn't seem very sturdy. Before he could object, Naia walked out onto the span, which made melodic crystalline noises as she set her weight upon it, like thousands of tinkling wind-chimes. She turned and motioned him forward.

Gil swallowed, now even more reluctant. The sound made him think the bridge would shatter like glass under their combined weight. But he followed her anyway, walking out over the chasm. A chill breeze rushed up from the depths, ruffling his cloak. Moving to the rail, he looked down, which was a mistake. Hundreds of feet below ran a dark river the color of squid ink. The air that rose from it smelled strongly of rotting death.

"That's not water, is it?" Gil asked, the stench making his stomach squirm.

"No. It's not."

He glanced at Naia uneasily. "Do I want to know what it is?"

"Probably not."

He backed away from the railing and didn't say another word until they reached the other side of the span. The Catacombs of Death were proving to be far more sinister than he had imagined. Almost, he was beginning to believe that there was far more at work than just magecraft. If magic alone had sculpted these passages, then it was a feat of industry far surpassing anything he had ever seen. They walked on a trail that paralleled the chasm, drawing closer to the burial vaults. Each vault was illuminated separately from within. Inside, Gil could see shrouded remains laid out on marble slabs. Here, the odor of decay was overwhelming.

"Gods, what a stench!" he exclaimed. "Why don't you just bury them in the ground instead of letting them go to rot?"

Naia lifted her hand, indicating the vast burial wall. "Nothing rots here. The Catacombs exist outside of time, so decomposition doesn't occur. But often corpses come to us less than fresh."

"'Less than fresh,'" Gil echoed. "That's an understatement, if I've ever heard one."

They moved through an opening in the wall that led to a dark stairwell that took them downward, emerging into another wide chamber. This one was filled with monuments and statuary, carvings of the goddess and likenesses of the deceased. Stone gargoyles guarded massive crypts, along with granite demons that seemed entirely out of place. The ground swarmed with a thick fog that moved like a slow current around the rows of sarcophagi.

He followed Naia down a narrow path through what amounted to a sprawling necropolis. Out of the corner of his eye, Gil caught sight of a flickering blue light. When he turned to look at it, whatever he had seen was gone. His skin crawled with the growing certainty that more than just magic was operating in these halls. As they left the graveyard and moved into another tunnel, he caught a glimpse of a softly glowing wight, the vague and fleeting memory of a young woman. This time, the presence lingered for just a moment before flickering out.

Startled, he glanced at Naia.

"Did you not believe me?" she asked.

"No," Gil admitted. "Every temple mystery I've ever come across has been easily explained."

"Not here," she assured him. "These Catacombs are the creation of the One True Goddess. There is magic here—don't get me wrong. But there is also holy mystery. The Atrament is very real, as is the Netherworld."

He believed her. The further they went in, the harder it was becoming to deny.

They started down another tunnel. This one smelled cleaner, the odor of rot fading and finally disappearing altogether. The air grew still, even stagnant, and warmed slightly.

Gil asked, "What made you decide to hide *Thar'gon* in the Catacombs?"

Naia responded, "At the time, Quin and I were all that was left. Every other mage had been killed—either in the destruction of Aerysius or in the wars that followed. There was no Warden of Battlemages to pass the talisman to. We decided it should be saved for future generations. This was the only place we could be sure it would be protected."

Gil shook his head. "It's never ceased to amaze me how you were able to grow the Lyceum so quickly. In two decades, you've brought us from two surviving mages to numbering in the hundreds. It's a remarkable accomplishment."

Naia smiled and reached her hand into her cloak. "We couldn't have done it without this." She withdrew the Soul-stone medallion.

"You brought it with us?" Gil stared down at the medallion, mildly shocked.

"Yes." Naia ran her fingers across the faceted stone, which gleamed with a red inner light. "I'm going to leave it here, at least for the time being. I can't imagine the danger this artifact would pose, should it fall into enemy hands."

Gil found himself in agreement. They walked in silence for a while, the glowing Soulstone illuminating their path just as much as the magelight. Eventually, they came to another inter-section. There, Naia stopped. A wrought iron gate blocked the entrance to the next chamber.

"This is it," she said.

Reaching through the bars, she struggled with the lock on the gate. She didn't have a key, and yet the lock clicked, and the gate swung open toward them just a fraction, creaking on its hinges.

Instead of entering, Naia turned to him. "Before we go further, I need you to understand something. What you will find in this room will be troubling. I'm sure you'll have many questions. Rest assured, I will answer them all later, when we have time."

The severity written on her face, and the foreboding implicit in her words, made Gil feel suddenly apprehensive. Looking past her through the bars, he asked, "What's in there?"

Very softly, Naia answered, "Your past. And also your future."

Gil looked beyond her. On the other side of the iron gate was a wide chamber that housed two structures that stood apart, on opposite sides of the room. Mausoleums, both made of contrasting marble. He remembered what Naia had said, back at the Lyceum: that *Thar'gon* had been buried with Darien Lauchlin. He stared harder at the two mausoleums, wondering which tomb could be his. Neither looked to be the resting place of a demon.

The gate shivered open wider. Gil moved into the chamber, the mist retreating from his feet. He crossed to the center of the room and there paused, standing to consider the marble tombs before him. Each mausoleum was very different. The one on the left was tall and narrow, its marble white and veined with silver. Flowers and greenery were strewn on the ground around it, all fresh. Gil felt the tugging urge to approach the tomb. He turned and cast a questioning glance at Naia.

"Go ahead," she urged, pausing well back from him.

Gil moved toward the white mausoleum with a feeling of trepidation. Stepping gingerly over the carpet of roses, he mounted the steps to the front of the structure. It looked like a small marble house with a sloped roof and a columned entry-way. Beneath the columns, there was a wall of solid marble. Above the wall, upon a triangular portico, were etched the words:

KYEL ARCHER
GRAND MASTER OF THE ORDER OF SENTINELS
BREAKER OF THE WELL OF TEARS

Gil stopped and stared at the words, feeling a paralyzing numbness slowly consuming him from his neck to his feet. He was unable to move or even blink. Unable to breathe. He stood there, locked rigid, until shock's grip on him finally relaxed its hold. He felt his entire body sag, as if all the air had been let out of him at once. Suddenly, it was all he could do to stay on his feet.

"This is my father's tomb," he said.

"It is," Naia confirmed, her voice echoing.

Feeling lightheaded, Gil forced himself to move forward, until he was close enough to touch the marble wall. But he dared not. At least, not yet. He couldn't.

"I never knew my father was here," he said. "I never knew any of this was here. Why didn't anyone tell me?" He turned back to look at Naia with accusation in his eyes. "Why didn't you tell me?"

The Prime Warden stood with her hands clasped, sympathy in her eyes. "The Catacombs are one of the Temple's holy mysteries, Gil. As a priestess, I was entrusted to keep those mysteries. I didn't tell you because you had no business knowing."

That didn't make him feel any better. It didn't justify anything. He turned his back on her and faced the crypt.

"Take your time," Naia said. "I'll wait over there."

He heard her footsteps retreating, leaving him alone with only a cold marble slab and a belly full of emptiness that felt even colder. He gazed dully at his father's name etched into the marble: perfect, thin letters chiseled by a master's practiced hand. He stared at them until they blurred.

He rubbed his eyes, shocked when his hand came away damp.

In that moment, every feeling he'd stuffed down deep since childhood came welling up: scalding anger, heartache. Loneliness and resentment. Betrayal. Every feeling a child could suffer at the death of a father came spiraling back to him like a whirlwind, and he staggered under the force of it.

He sagged against the stone of his father's crypt, pressing his cheek against the cold marble. When he closed his eyes, old memories poured into him, memories he had struggled to forget. Memories of his father hefting him in his arms, only to flip him over and tickle him until he flailed with laughter. Memories of his father's gentle smile, his smothering hugs.

He remembered the last moments he'd spent with him.

Who protects you, papa? he'd asked.

With the slightest smile, his father replied, *That's what magic's for.*

At the time, he hadn't questioned why that smile had seemed so sad. Now he knew. Because Kyel Archer had known even magic couldn't save him from the evil that was the Well of Tears. His father had known he would never be coming back but had gone anyway. He had chosen all the right words and yet had said all the wrong things.

The last words his father said to him had haunted Gil all his life: *You need to know how much I love you. And how proud I am of you.*

He was sure his father had meant well by those words, but they had been a curse that had shadowed every endeavor he'd ever attempted—because he knew he didn't deserve them. He had never done anything to make his father proud. Certainly not as a four-year-old boy. And certainly never since. Oh, he'd tried. Tried his damnedest. It didn't matter—no matter what, he always failed. He didn't have it in him to be a hero. He would never live up to his father's expectations.

Gil lifted his hand and pressed his palm against the marble next to his face, overcome by grief. But the grief didn't last long. It drained away quickly, leaving only tears of bitter anger on his face. He took a step back and stared up at the mausoleum, hating every slab of it. It was a monument to a man who'd walked away willingly from a son who loved him.

He'd never wanted his father to be a hero. He'd just wanted him to be there.

Wiping his eyes, Gil turned and crossed the rose-strewn floor back toward where Naia stood waiting for him in the center of the chamber. Stuffing his emotions back down deep where they belonged, he drew up at her side.

"Are you all right?" Naia asked, searching his face.

"I will be," he said.

There were a dozen things she could have said at that moment but, to her credit, she said none of them. Instead she lifted her hand, gesturing toward the second monument that stood on the far side of the room. No flowers graced the ground surrounding that dark tomb. Only burning candles, hundreds of them, glowing in sconces of varying heights. Gil walked forward, skirting the outside of the mausoleum, staring up at its dark gray walls, at the marble veined in bold streaks of black and white. Unlike his father's tomb, this one had an entrance. And above that entrance was a wide slab of marble with the name LAUCHLIN chiseled into the stone. When Gil hesitated, Naia nodded toward it, urging him forward.

With reluctance, he picked out a path through the burning field of lit candles. The tomb itself had no door, just an opening in the front that led to a small room that was lit by a single torch hung on the rear wall. On either side of the narrow space, two vaults were built into the walls, each covered by a slab of dark marble.

The vault on the right was inscribed with the words:

AZÁR LAUCHLIN
BELOVED WIFE

The inscription surprised him. He hadn't realized that Darien Lauchlin had ever taken a wife. The name Azár was Malikari. Whoever this woman was, she couldn't have been Rylan's mother. He turned around and gazed at the vault on the other side of the narrow chamber, this one engraved with the words:

DARIEN LAUCHLIN
PRIME WARDEN OF AERYSIUS
LAST OF THE SENTINELS

Last of the Sentinels.

Gil's mouth twisted at the words. His father had been a Sentinel—a true Sentinel—unlike the demon interred behind this slab of stone. Darien Lauchlin had lost the right to that title the moment he turned against everything Aerysius had ever stood for. He turned on his own nation, his own kinfolk—on everyone who depended on him to keep them safe. Gil stared at the hateful inscription, wanting to scrub it off the marble with his hands.

Hearing a scuffing noise, he realized Naia had come up behind him.

"Let's get this over with," he said.

To his surprise, Naia ran her hand over the polished surface of the crypt, her fingers lingering over the letters. Her dark eyes welled with sadness.

Gil was shocked by her reaction. "You knew him well?" he asked.

She smiled sadly. "Yes. I loved him very much."

Gil looked back and forth between the crypt and Naia's face.

He didn't understand; so many people held Darien Lauchlin in such high esteem. Naia, the Sultan, even Quin, all claimed friendship with a man who had done little more than rip his own society apart. How could someone as gentle as Naia love someone so evil? It made no sense.

"I'm sorry," Gil whispered, not knowing what else to say.

Naia raised an eyebrow. "Sorry that I loved him? Or sorry, as in condolences?"

It took him a moment to think about it. "I guess both," he decided finally.

Naia's smile said she forgave him, even though the look in her eyes remained distant. Trailing her hands down the polished slab of marble, she said, "Help me open it."

Gil blinked. "Open it?"

"Yes. That's what we're here for."

Gil balked, disgusted by the thought. The man inside the crypt had been dead for two decades. He'd already smelled enough moldering corpses to know that he didn't want to smell another one, especially this close.

Seeing his hesitation, the Prime Warden let out an exasperated sigh. "Never mind. I'll do it myself."

Before he could react, she depressed two buttons on either side of the stone slab. Immediately, a seam opened in the marble wall as part of the fascia slipped downward with a muffled thud. To Gil's surprise, the heavy marble slab moved easily. Naia pushed it the rest of the way to the floor without effort, revealing a cedar-lined compartment within. Reaching inside, she gave the wood panel a good tug. With a faint creaking noise, a man-sized drawer slid out of the wall. Gil took a step back in surprise.

There was no corpse. The drawer was lined with rich velvet, ready to receive a body. But the only thing resting upon it was a spiked morning star. No bones. No decayed flesh.

No corpse had ever lain there.

"I don't understand," Gil said. "If Lauchlin's not here, then where is he buried?"

Naia moved away from the drawer, turning her back to him. "There was nothing left to bury," she said softly. Looking back at him, she said, "Go ahead. Take it. It's yours by rights."

Gil turned his attention to the weapon in the drawer. *Thar'gon* had been created to be wielded by the Warden of Battlemages. His father had carried it for a time, and now, through some strange twist of fate, that duty had fallen to him. His gaze trailed over the weapon, a small sense of awe creeping over him. It was beautiful, made of polished silver that gleamed with an argent light. The haft was wrapped with black leather, the mace-like head surrounded by a thick halo of spikes.

Gil reached down and closed his hand around the haft. The moment his fingers touched it, he felt an instant connection. Like a bolt of lightning shooting up his arm and into his chest. He stood there for a moment, savoring the feel of the weapon in his hand. Then slowly, filled with infinite trepidation, he withdrew *Thar'gon* from its crypt.

"How does it feel?" Naia asked, her eyes wide and anxious.

Staring at the talisman, Gil whispered, "Terrifying."

The energy moving into him from the weapon intensified, washing over him like a swift current of warm water. It calmed him, soothed him. Filled him with a daunting sense of strength. In his hand, the talisman glowed softly.

Naia moved forward and spread the Soulstone carefully over the velvet of the drawer where the weapon had lain. Trailing her hands over the silver bands of the collar, Naia whispered, "Just for safekeeping."

35

MISLED

Xiana ran a hand over his stomach, making Rylan shiver. She lay with her head snuggled against his chest, her wet hair plastered to his skin. He pulled the covers up over her and kissed her head. His nostrils filled with the fresh scent of her, rekindling his desire.

He'd forgotten what a woman felt like.

Xiana was the only woman he'd ever lain with other than his wife. He'd expected to feel guilty, taking another into his bed. But he didn't. Somehow, Xiana felt right. Her body fit perfectly against his, the touch of her skin inspiring feelings of warmth and contentment. This was the woman he loved, the woman he'd died loving.

Rylan stiffened. Those were not his memories. Not his feelings.

And yet, somehow, they were. The feelings were real. And they weren't going away. If anything, they were intensifying. The memories that accompanied them were fading, though not the sentiment. He didn't understand, but he didn't complain. He'd forgotten what it felt like to know anything but heartache.

Stroking Xiana's soft hair, he asked, "Did you know this would happen to me?"

Her eyes closed, and she smiled softly. "I hoped."

"Why me?" He'd been thinking about that question ever since they'd returned from Suheylu Ra. She could have kidnapped any mage in the Rhen. For some reason, she had selected one with a sinister lineage she hadn't trusted from the outset.

"Because of who you are," she answered.

Because of who you are.

Those were the same words spoken by the man in the cornfield, the man who had murdered his son. A cold feeling settled over him. He lay staring up at the shadows of the ceiling, as question after question surfaced in his head, each strengthening his doubt a little more.

Her fingers stroked his chest, moving in lazy spirals.

Softly, Rylan asked. "How did you know who I am? How did you know where to find me?"

Her hand stopped moving.

For heartbeats, she said nothing. Then:

"I was told."

That was the answer he was afraid of. He pulled away from her and rolled out from under the blanket. Sitting up, he asked, "By whom?"

She rolled over onto her back and stared up at him. "By Shiro."

That name sounded familiar, though he couldn't place it. His skin shivered at hearing it. "Who's Shiro?"

Xiana heaved a dispirited sigh. She sat up, tugging the blanket up around her. She said without looking at him, "It's time you learned the truth."

"What truth?" Rylan could feel his insides tense, his heart drumming to a standstill. Real fear seeped down his spine.

Xiana gazed at him steadily. "When the Khar invaded Daru,

I was captured along with all the rest of our *deizu*. I was given to their Warlord, a man named Shiro Nagato. He is the most powerful man in their society, save only for their Empress. Before Shiro came into power, he was the apprentice of Zavier Renquist, the demon your father served... and then betrayed."

Rylan knew the name. Zavier Renquist was the infamous darkmage who had created the Well of Tears.

Xiana's expression saddened. "Zavier Renquist knew of your existence. He knew you were alive, even when your father thought you dead. He had plans for you. But your father killed him before Renquist could act on them."

Rylan dropped his gaze to the floor and sat staring at a knot in the wood. His father had unwittingly protected him from that monster. With that knowledge, Rylan was able to conjure just the slightest bit of gratitude toward the man. He realized it was probably the first and last positive emotion he'd ever feel for him.

Xiana drew away from him and leaned back against the wall. "Ever since Zavier Renquist's death, Shiro has been continuing his master's work. Part of that work involves collecting and training mages to use as weapons. The more powerful mages are highly coveted. Do you know how the tier system works?"

Rylan knew very little about magic or magecraft. He shrugged. "I just know the higher the tier, the stronger the mage."

"That's right." Xiana nodded. "But it's rare to have a mage over third tier. Very few minds are capable of handling that much power. The most powerful mages in history were sixth tier, and those you could count on the fingers of both hands. More than six tiers inevitably leads to madness. A mind cannot handle that much power. It burns a person up from the inside."

Her gaze drifted toward the windows before finally returning to settle on him. "Somehow, both Keio and Ilia were eighth tier. No one knows how they managed to survive with that much power, but they did. Only one other mage in all of history has managed to do that without going mad." She gave him a significant look.

It took Rylan only a heartbeat to take her meaning. "My father."

Xiana nodded. "And Shiro knows that. Which is why he desires you. Ilia Osan and Keio Matu were more than just lovers—they were a joined pair: two mages with souls and Gifts connected in such a way that one could draw on the strength of the other, increasing their powers exponentially. Separate, both Keio and Ilia were incredibly strong. But together... I don't know if this world has ever seen anything like them, before or since.

"So that's what Shiro Nagato means to do—he means to use us as a joined pair far stronger than any this world has seen in eight thousand years. I was the most powerful *deizu* Shiro controlled. He had me merge with Ilia... and then he sent me to find you."

The explosion of anger Rylan felt was all-consuming. It was born of hurt, the strongest kind of fuel. He surged to his feet, his vision going red. She had lied to him. He wondered what else she had lied about, and how deep the lies went.

"How could you?" he shouted at her. "How could you betray your own people—and mine?"

Raising her hands, Xiana climbed to her feet. Looking at him adamantly, she said, "Eight thousand years ago, Keio Matu defeated the Turan Khar... and I think you can do it again."

The heat within him lessened somewhat. But the pain of betrayal was still there, hanging on with a death grip. Raking his hands through his hair, Rylan paced away from her. "How? I'm dampened, Xiana!"

"Shiro doesn't know you can use the Onslaught. You have the advantage of surprise."

The pounding anger in him faltered; he knew she was right. He realized that, for the first time, he knew what a field dampener was and how it worked, cutting off a person from the magic field by wrapping a mirror-field around them. But it couldn't cut him off from his link with the Netherworld. That would take a shield made of anti-magic, something far more rare and difficult to craft.

Rylan turned away from her, his hand going to his mouth as he struggled to think it through. Her words seemed to make sense... until they didn't.

Frowning, he asked, "Why wouldn't Shiro know about my oath to Xerys? He's the one who made me swear it in the first place."

Xiana shook her head. "That wasn't Shiro."

He looked at her sideways. "If it wasn't Shiro, then who was it?"

"I don't know," she whispered.

That wasn't the answer he wanted, what he needed. He needed a name, a name he could put a face to. Someone he could blame for taking his family from him. He stood in silence for a while, stewing on the information. He paced away, raking his hand through his hair in exasperation. "So there's someone else who knows who I am... and who just *happened* to give me exactly what I need to defeat Shiro?"

Xiana folded her arms and looked at him steadily. "Yes."

He wanted to hate her. He had every reason and right to. But something inside him wouldn't let him. Not something —*someone*. Keio Matu's knowledge had come with a price. The price was that he now had to carry small fragments of the man around with him. And every one of those fragments loved Xiana with all their heart.

He sighed, giving into defeat. There could be no hating her. Whatever she'd done, she'd done it because she thought it the right thing to do. He couldn't fault her for that.

"All right," he agreed. "I'll do it."

Xiana smiled warmly, a trace of pride glinting in her eyes. "We'll do it together."

Rylan considered her smile carefully. "Answer me one question. Was there really poison in the cup you brought me in the cage?"

Xiana glanced down, her features sagging. "Yes," she admitted. "I wanted to be sure the man I would join with was human enough and strong enough to stand at my side. Had you proven to be anything less than what you are, you would have been executed."

Rylan nodded slowly. He could accept that. He caught her and pulled her to him, wrapping his arms around her and kissing her tenderly. Forgiving her wasn't a choice. It was something he couldn't help. He stroked a hand through her hair.

She pulled back from him and smiled. Turning, she walked across the room to the cabinet that sat against the far wall. She opened a drawer and produced a dark bronze outfit and, handling it carefully, held it out for him.

"I had this made for you before we left for Suheylu Ra," she said, putting the garment in his hands. "The cut is called *kamatzu*. It is worn only by *deizu-kan*."

She watched him dress, showing him the proper way of lacing the tunic up the front. From within the cabinet, she produced the sword given to him by Sayeed. Rylan pulled the blade halfway out of its sheath and held it up, feeling a surprising amount of sentiment. The Sultan had taken him in as family without hesitation, without even coming to know him. Never before had he known such generosity. Sheathing the blade, he buckled the scabbard to his belt.

Xiana smiled. "Come here," she whispered, and moved into his arms.

Rylan kissed her tenderly, sliding his hands behind her head and letting her silken hair spill through his fingers. Her warm breath sent tingles down his back. The other man within him awakened and stirred.

Too soon, their lips parted.

"Where exactly are we going?" Rylan asked.

Xiana responded, "Back to Karikesh."

"Why Karikesh?"

Xiana lifted a long knife from the cabinet and slipped it inside the folds of her *yori*.

"Because that's where Shiro is."

36

THE RESISTANCE

GIL STOOD ON A BALCONY OVERLOOKING THE WATERFRONT. THE building behind him was old, perhaps as old as the foundations of the city. Its stone walls were blackened by fire, and the entire front had collapsed, revealing a lattice of shattered rooms that now stood open to the air. Across the canal, all was quiet in the North City. The sun had set, and fires glowed randomly throughout the fallen districts, casting eerie orange glows dispersed between long swaths of gaping darkness. The screams that had echoed across the water for days had finally quieted. Only an unnerving silence remained that was somehow more chilling.

Far to the north, the massive structure the Alqazar Citadel rose high above the blue rooftops of the Andibar Quarter. The fortress's Calazi-style towers made it easy to spot, each terminating in a filigreed dome. The citadel was an enormous stronghold that warded the Lion's gate. Gil had thought it destroyed in the initial assault on the gate, but each of the citadel's four domes still soared magnificently above the city, lit by the flickering glows of the fires.

Across the canal, the broken Promenade swarmed with soldiers of the Khar. Their engineers had swiftly improvised a new bridge to span the canal. Right below him, on the southern bank, a new enemy encampment was slowly and inexorably expanding into the Malikari-held districts. To reach the North City, he would have to make it past both Khar encampments and the broad waters of the canal, which would have been impossible before yesterday.

Now he had a way.

He looked down at the silver morning star in his hand that gleamed with a soft inner light. It was a weapon unmatched by any other. While most artifacts were imbued with a single character, two at most, *Thar'gon* had been infused with at least five. It was designed with battle in mind and housed abilities invaluable to a commander. There was an amplification character that magnified the power of its wielder, as well as a motive character so powerful it had pulverized the Well of Tears. It was imbued with both light and shadow magic, giving it the ability to attack and defend at the same time—an unheard-of combination. And, perhaps most importantly, it could function as a miniature transfer portal, only one much more versatile. It could instantly transport its wielder anywhere within a short distance, just so long as the destination could be fixed as a vivid image in the mind. *Thar'gon* was also responsive in a way no other artifact had been able to imitate. It had a way of sensing its owner's physical needs and compensating accordingly. It couldn't keep a dying man alive, but it could keep him walking until his heart stopped. If the talisman had other secrets, Quin hadn't made note of them. But Gil wouldn't be surprised.

"Vergis," he whispered, tasting the Word of Command that activated the talisman's transfer spell. In his hand, Thar'gon glowed eagerly in response. Nothing happened; he wasn't thinking about a destination. But if he had been, he wouldn't be standing on the balcony any longer.

He looked out over the fallen districts to the north. The buildings across the water weren't all that far away. If he knew the interior of at least one of them well enough, he could use *Thar'gon* to transfer into one. Unfortunately, he didn't. His gaze moved further north and stopped at the dark outline of an ancient tree whose branches loomed above the rooftops of the surrounding district.

One of the parks in the Damali Quarter had a tree that was quite distinctive: an ancient oak larger than any other, with sprawling branches that writhed as if tormented, groping toward the ground like thick, moss-encrusted arms. A marker in front of the tree proclaimed it the "Alliance Oak" and claimed the tree was more than one thousand years old. There wasn't another tree like it in the city, and probably not in the world. When Gil closed his eyes, he could envision it clearly, as though he were standing right in front of it.

A slight breeze fanned his hair, smelling of smoke. He glanced up at the unnatural clouds that strobed with a murky light deep within their depths. He remained there for minutes, until he felt his resolve solidify. Then he closed his eyes and raised the talisman, holding it up as if readying for battle. In a way, he was.

"Vergis," he whispered.

The world lurched.

When he opened his eyes, Gil was staring up at the branches of the Alliance Oak, its silhouette like a convoluted fracture in the sky. Off balance, he put his hand out to catch himself. He took a staggering step forward, tripping over an exposed root. Behind him, someone shouted.

Frigid panic shot down his nerves. He was standing in the middle of an occupied district with a weapon in his hand. Another shout made it clear his presence had been noticed. Glancing around, he didn't see any people. The park appeared empty. But he could hear them. The sound of running feet echoed off the city walls.

Gil sprang forward. Clutching *Thar'gon*, he sprinted toward the street, making for a dark gap between buildings: the opening of a thin alley. He dodged into it, roughing his hands on the brick wall as he swung around the corner. Feet splashing through puddles, he dashed through the shadows of the alley until it ended abruptly at a block wall.

Gil cursed, whirling around. He listened behind him but heard nothing. There was a chance he'd slipped his pursuers, though he doubted he'd be that lucky. Frantic, he groped along the wall of the building next to him until he found a locked door.

He kicked it open and scrambled into the dark interior, almost tripping over something on the floor. Instantly, he was hit in the face with a nauseating odor. He summoned a mist of magelight that revealed dark walls streaked with darker stains. The floor was strewn with possessions and overturned furniture. Looking down, he saw that the object he'd tripped over was the prone body of a dead man.

Gil jolted back from the stiff figure as everything in the room seemed to come into focus all at once. The streaks on the walls weren't shadows at all, but dark stains of splattered blood. The body at his feet wasn't alone; an entire family had been slain here. Across the floor, the body of a woman lay slouched against a wall, her arm wrapped around a dead child. Another body lay prone in the opening to a hallway.

The smell was intense. Gil made a strangling noise and staggered into the hallway, stepping over the corpse. The hallway wasn't very long. He turned into a bedroom scattered with broken furniture. The bed had been disassembled, the mattress upturned to block the window. One of the walls had been ripped apart, creating an opening into a dark room on the other side.

He heard something from behind him: the squeak of a door.

Gil let go of the magelight and stumbled forward, scrambling through the hole in the wall. Weaving a shadow web around himself, he felt along the walls, picking his way carefully through the darkness. From the other side of the wall, he heard soft voices. Whoever they were, they knew he was there.

He shrank back against the wall, relying on his shadow web to keep him concealed. Ragged seconds scraped by. Then someone crawled through the hole in the wall and entered the room. A man rose upright, holding a lantern in front of him that cast a murky glow, revealing a small space covered by rugs and littered with filth. Another man emerged from the hole behind him.

The space was too small; someone was bound to bump into him. Biting his lip and holding his breath, Gil stepped away from the wall and edged past the man with the lantern. As soon as he was past him, he crept quietly and quickly toward the door.

The man behind him gave a shout.

Holding tight to the shadow web, Gil plunged forward. He stumbled blindly down the dark hallway until his groping fingers found a door. He fumbled with the latch, but it wouldn't budge.

Someone careened into the wall behind him. Gil kicked the door open and spilled into the street, stumbling to his knees. His pursuer burst out of the building. Falling to the ground, the man scraped up a fistful of dirt from the street and threw it at him.

Gil looked down in horror.

The dust revealed his form beneath the shadow web.

Something crashed into him from behind, slamming him to the ground and knocking the wind out of him. A man pinned him down while another grabbed a fistful of his hair, jerking his head back and pressing the sharp edge of a blade against his throat. Gil reached out from within and grasped the magic field. The man flew off him and slapped into a wall.

"Stop!" a woman's voice bellowed. "He is unchained!"

Gil surged to his feet, scrambling back away from the five people who surrounded him. An old Malikari woman moved toward him, robed in black and carrying a butcher's cleaver in her hand. The sight of her was so surreal, that for a moment all Gil could do was stare at her. She stopped within feet of him and stood examining him with shrewd gray eyes.

"What is your name?" she demanded. Her face was quilted with wrinkles, leathery and liver-spotted. Unruly snarls of gray-streaked hair defied the bun she wore at the back of her head.

Gil stared up at her, his hand clasping the hilt of the morning star. He swallowed against the dryness in his throat, muttering hoarsely, "Gil Archer."

The woman scowled harder, deepening the creases around her eyes. "And what are you doing here, Master Gil Archer?"

Gil's eyes scanned the walls behind her, searching from building to building for signs of soldiers. He couldn't believe the commotion in the street hadn't drawn any yet. He looked back at the woman, not sure what to say, or if he should say anything at all. She was Malikari, which meant she was supposed to be on his side—but that didn't mean she was.

He bit his lip and held fast to his silence.

The woman gazed at him for a moment, then eventually shrugged. "Just understand one thing, boy: whatever happens, we cannot let them have you. So I hope the reason you're here is important. If it's not, then turn around now and swim back across the water."

She stared at him harder, her fierce eyes digging into him as if trying to excavate his intentions. When he didn't respond, she tossed back her head and made a frustrated noise in her throat.

"So be it," she grumbled. "Then you will come with us."

With that, the men surrounding her converged on Gil. A man with a beard caught his arm and guided him firmly toward the side of the road. The woman fell in next to him and walked at his side.

"The streets are not safe," she snapped roughly. "Your presence here puts us in danger."

Gil resisted the desire to jerk his arms away. "I don't want to involve you," he said. "Just let me go my own way."

The woman made a *tsk*ing noise with her tongue. "Whether it was your intention or not, you have already involved us."

Before he could protest, the man holding his arm wheeled him toward an open doorway, thrusting him inside. They guided him up a damaged staircase to the third floor, then out onto a walled rooftop that had been a cooking and gathering space. They crossed the roof and climbed over the wall, then dropped down onto a narrow ledge on the other side. The man let go of him and made a short leap to an adjacent rooftop, then turned back and waved him forward.

While Gil stood staring at the street below, the old woman climbed nimbly over the wall and jumped across, continuing along the next rooftop without looking back at him. Gil bit his lip and jumped, landing hard. The man smiled and clapped him on the back. They followed the woman along in the lee of the wall, stooping forward and using the wall as cover.

A high-pitched shriek cut through the night.

"Get down!" the woman hissed.

The man pulled Gil into a crouch, shielding him against the wall. Looking up, he saw a winged creature circling above them with the wings of a bat and the body of a snake. It shrieked again, its cry like the screech of a barn owl. It dipped a wing and banked, gliding away.

The woman whispered, "You cannot trust the streets or the skies. They have eyes and ears everywhere."

Gil glanced up again, then followed her across another

rooftop and back into the interior of a building. Inside, there was a narrow hallway with many doors. The woman knocked on each door as she went by. No one answered. The hallway ended in a dark stairwell that carried them down another level. This time when the woman knocked, a man stepped out into the hallway and greeted them with a smiling face. The woman gave him a warm hug, holding him tight and patting his back.

"What word have you?" she asked, then stood listening as the men spoke at length to her in Malikari. The man's wife came out, carrying a cup of tea, which she offered to the woman. Gil stood to the side, utterly bewildered, watching the scene unfold. The gray-haired woman stood nodding, sipping her tea, the man's wife interjecting every other sentence. Eventually, the conversation came to an end. Cheeks were kissed and the teacup returned to the hands of its owner. As Gil followed the old woman down the hallway, he glanced back to see the couple still standing outside their door, smiling and waving.

"What did they say?" he asked.

The old woman answered without slowing her pace, "The corner bakery was destroyed this morning. The baker and his entire family were killed, may Isap accept their souls. That was the last bakery left in this quarter of the city. The people are frightened there will be no more bread."

Gil followed her into another stairwell. "What will they do?"

The woman shrugged. "Who can say?"

He followed her down more stairs and into another corridor, this one below the level of the street. There, she stopped and knocked on another door. It opened and a young woman appeared. A joyful smile lit up her face. She stepped forward to hug the old woman and kiss her cheek.

The man motioned Gil curtly forward. "Come!"

Gil followed her into the room, nodding his greetings at the woman guarding the doorway. The rest of their party trailed them inside and positioned themselves along the walls. Gil stopped in the center of the room and looked around at his surroundings. They were in a residence crowded with people, some looking badly injured. The smell of blood was strong in the air, as though the walls had been washed with it. The floor was layered with rugs, and a few lanterns provided an anemic light. A man slouching against a wall coughed, the sound of it wet and rasping.

The old woman guided him into the next room, which was little bigger than a storage closet. "Wait here," she said. "I will be back."

She left him alone with the bearded man who had guided him across the rooftops. For the first time, Gil realized the man was wearing a short sword strapped to his belt. He snapped his fingers and motioned for Gil to sit. Then he left. Gil sank down on the rug-strewn floor and set his weapon down beside him, leaning back against a wall. He was tired, more tired than he'd realized. He resisted the urge to close his eyes and sleep.

The man came back holding a slice of bread and a cup of wine. He sat down next to Gil, offering him the food and drink.

Gil waved his hand. "Thank you, but I'm not hungry."

"You must eat," the man insisted, stuffing the strip of bread into Gil's hands.

Gil understood. He was familiar enough with Malikari traditions to know that the sharing of food and cups was an offer of friendship. He accepted the bread with a smile of gratitude, biting into it immediately and chasing it down with a mouthful of wine. It was made of coarse grain, gritty with sand from whichever mill had ground it.

The man offered his hand. "I am Judhi ul-Calazi. It's an honor to meet you."

"Gil Archer." He clasped the man's hand and nodded back in the direction the woman had disappeared to. "Who is she?"

The man smiled. "She is Uma Halabi."

"Is she your leader?"

Judhi allowed himself a slight smile. "She is our backbone. For a week, we have been fighting to retake this quarter of the city. Many were killed on the first night of the attacks. At first, the people were afraid to stand up. But Uma Halabi gave us our spine back."

"Who was she before?" Gil asked, stuffing the rest of the bread into his mouth.

The man glanced toward the room full of wounded. "Uma Halabi is like a mother to the people of this district. Her husband was a butcher, but he was killed the night of the first attack."

"I'm sorry to hear that," Gil said. He looked up to find Uma Halabi glaring at him from the doorway. She made a brisk motion with her hand, sending Judhi out of the room with a sheepish nod of apology. The woman moved into the room and settled down next to Gil on the rug.

Drinking down the last of his wine, Gil asked her, "So, what exactly is your plan? What do you intend to accomplish here?"

The woman waved her hand dismissively. "There is no plan. We have been fighting block by block trying to retake the Damali Quarter. But the Khar have taken every district surrounding us and they have us besieged. There is no food, and most of the wells have been poisoned. We will not be able to survive here much longer, so we have no choice but to fight."

What she had already accomplished was a miraculous feat. He couldn't imagine how one old woman and a band of civilians could have held an encircled quarter, when the entirety of the Sultan's forces couldn't hold the Waterfront. More likely, the Khar had shifted their assets elsewhere, leaving Uma Halabi and her band for later; they posed little threat.

"What has it been like here?" he asked.

"The first night, when the Khar came, there was fighting in the streets and fire from the sky that brought down many of the buildings. People hid in their basements while the enemy roamed the streets, murdering everyone in sight, even those trying to surrender. The next day was worse. They brought the children out to the market square and promised to kill them unless their parents gave themselves up. When they did, they were all executed, every last one of them, along with the children they had tried to save. Since then, people have been disappearing one by one."

She sat still for a moment, her hands restlessly smoothing her skirt over her legs. At last, she asked quietly, "What about you, Master Gil? Why have you come to the Damali Quarter?"

Gil still hadn't decided whether divulging his plans to this woman was wise or rash. There were arguments to be made for both. In the end, he decided to risk it. "The Khar broke through our perimeter. They are on the verge of taking the entire city. They use chained mages to mount their attacks, and they're all but unstoppable. If it wasn't for their mages, we might have a chance."

He looked up and met her gaze. "We've learned that the Khar keep their mages in the Alqazar Citadel. So that's why I'm here. I'm going to the citadel to kill as many as I can."

Uma Halabi stared at him a long moment before flicking her eyebrows and lowering her gaze to settle on the rug. "A noble plan," she said finally. "Noble, but stupid. All you will accomplish is augmenting their ranks, when they capture and chain you."

Firmly, Gil said, "I won't be captured."

The woman's brow furrowed in doubt. "How can you be so sure?"

He lifted the talisman and set it across his lap. "This

weapon is the most powerful magical artifact we have. It can transfer me out of there in the blink of an eye."

She gazed down at the morning star dubiously. "If you are caught, then the Khar will use both you and your magical weapon to great advantage."

"I won't be," Gil insisted. "Can your people help me get to the citadel?"

The old woman shrugged. "I'm certain we could. I am also certain we won't."

"Why not?"

"Because going into the citadel would be like taking an apple from the bottom of a stack of apples. The rest of the apples will fall on you. Their mages killed thousands by calling down fire from the heavens. What do you think they will do to you?"

Gil frowned, frustrated by her doggedness. "This is the artifact that destroyed the Well of Tears. With it, I'll be just as powerful as any four or five of their mages put together."

Uma Halabi raised her eyebrows. "Then you are even more ignorant than I thought. Because they have many more than four or five mages. And when you are captured, all hope will be lost for us."

Gil grinned recklessly. "Then I guess you'd better make sure I don't get captured."

The old woman's eyes narrowed.

"Look," he said. "If I don't do this, the entire city will fall. There's no question about it. They've crossed the canal, and that was the last thing stopping them."

Uma Halabi nodded slowly. Then she gathered her robes and rose from the floor. She took a step toward the door but then paused and turned back.

"You may stay here tonight," she told him. "I'll have more food brought to you."

"Wait," Gil said, climbing to his feet. "Where are you going?"

She shot him a disdainful look. "If I'm going to help you, Master Archer, then I have arrangements to make."

"Thank you," he said to the woman's back as she left.

37

THE TURAN KHAR

"Do you trust me, Rylan?" Xiana asked.

"I do."

He trusted her as much as Keio had trusted Ilia, and that trust was never-ending. Reaching up, he stroked her face. She looked beautiful in the light of morning. The sun shone directly through one of the thin latticed windows behind her, haloing her hair. But then the sun moved on, rising above the opening of the window, and the shadows returned.

Leaning into him, she kissed his lips, at first tentatively. But then the kiss swelled into something more, something beautiful. It took on the aspect of something far larger and significant, infinitely wondrous. It promised everything he'd ever wanted, everything he'd never known he needed.

"What about their mages?" he asked, pulling back.

"If Shiro falls, then every mage under his command will lose all sense of direction and purpose."

"Why is that?"

She smiled. "Because that's how the Turan Khar operate. One mind, one purpose. All controlled by the Warlord, who is in turn controlled by the Empress. Without the Warlord's direction, all collapses. That's what Khar means. Unity. Every person in their civilization is connected to the whole."

He couldn't imagine it could be that simple, as though the Turan Khar were simply one body that could be decapitated and left to rot. He had seen their mages, seen the chains on their wrists. They certainly seemed like slaves, but even slaves had a mind and will of their own.

But she was Ilia, and he did not doubt her.

She pulled him closer, hugging him tight.

"Are you ready?" she asked softly.

He nodded.

She moved behind him. "Put your hands behind your back."

As he complied, she bent and scooped up the sash of her *yori* rope, using it to bind his wrists firmly. Tugging it tighter than he liked, she finished off the knot, then circled around in front of him and kissed his cheek.

"Close your eyes," she whispered, the sound of her voice stirring excitement within him along with dread.

Rylan caught a glimpse of Ilia's opal pendant before Xiana stepped behind him whispered the Word that commanded it. The walls of the hut around them grew thin like stretched fabric, then thinner still, until another fabric appeared behind them, this one dark and opaque. In seconds, the vision of the hut was withdrawn entirely, and a cool breeze stirred Rylan's hair.

He looked around, not recognizing where they were; it was a place he'd never been.

They stood in the center of a courtyard paved with marble tiles and bright with the morning sun. In the center was a large fountain, carried on the backs of stone-carved panthers standing in a ring. The courtyard was lined with arcaded walkways, each column elaborately scalloped. It had the look of any number of buildings he had seen in Karikesh, built in the Malikari style of architecture.

He became aware of movement around them, and realize they were not alone. In the shadows beneath the arcades stood small clusters of people, all looking at them with surprise and shock on their faces. No one moved.

After moments, a man and a woman came forward, crossing the courtyard toward them. Both wore gray robes that fluttered around them, giving them the appearance of wraiths newly emerged from the grave. The man had long black hair and gray skin. The woman who walked at his side looked Rhenic, her thick blonde hair worn in elaborate braids.

The woman halted well back from them, while the man came forward to hug Xiana and kiss her cheeks.

"Xiana..." he breathed, stepping back. "We've missed you so."

She smiled broadly and wrapped her hand around Rylan possessively. "And I've missed you, Gralish,"

"Who is this?" the man asked, frowning at Rylan's bound hands.

Xiana lifted Rylan's chin, forcing him to look at the gray man. "This is Rylan Lauchlin. He will be my other half."

The way she said it made Rylan shiver.

"Lauchlin." It was Gralish's partner who spoke. "That is an ill-omened name."

Looking at Rylan, Xiana smiled fondly "Not ill," she corrected. Her hand moved to stroke his hair. "It is a glorious name, strong with a proud legacy of magic. Rylan is mine now."

The gray man looked back and forth between Rylan and Xiana before nodding.

"Then he is ours," he decided. He moved forward and drew Rylan in for a hug, kissing his cheek. "Welcome, Brother."

His words, more than his touch, made Rylan feel soiled.

When the man drew back, he could still feel his cold lips lingering on his skin.

Xiana gestured toward the two Khar mages. "This is my family, Rylan. Your family, now. Gralish is from Ortun, a land to the north of Daru." She paused, as if uncertain how to introduce the woman.

Gralish rescued her, draping an arm around the Rhenic woman's shoulders. "This is Laira, my *iyan*."

The woman lowered her gaze demurely.

"What happened to Terrik?" Xiana asked.

Gralish did not reply. Instead, he bowed his head, sorrow darkening his eyes.

Xiana murmured, "I'm so sorry, Gralish."

"Terrik has transcended," the gray man said, and smiled through his pain. "I am very glad for him. And now I have Laira to fill my heart. I am truly blessed." He lifted Laira's hand to his lips, kissing it tenderly. Laira gave a tentative smile.

"What's wrong, love?" Gralish asked her, cupping her chin.

"He frightens me," she answered, her eyes flitting to Rylan.

The man frowned. "Why?"

She looked away again, and edged closer to Gralish, whispering, "He is a demon."

The man stepped back, his body tensing. His eyes darted to Xiana. "Is this true?"

Xiana dismissed the question with a wave of her hand. "Rylan's father served the God of Chaos. But Rylan is not like him. He is honest and kind."

She leaned into Rylan and kissed his cheek. Her lips brushed his skin lightly, traveling toward his ear and sending shivers down his spine. He closed his eyes, savoring the feeling

Gralish examined his reaction closely. At last, he nodded, seeming satisfied. "I believe you, Sister. But is he tame?"

Xiana admitted, "In heart only. He has never been chained."

The man sucked in a cheek, gazing at Rylan thoughtfully. "You must take him to the Warlord, then."

"Of course." Xiana took Rylan's arm and tugged him forward gently. "Let's go, love. I will take you to meet our father."

Rylan moved to follow her, anxious to be away from the gray man.

"Welcome home, Sister," Gralish called after them. "So happy to meet you, Brother."

The sound of his voice made Rylan's skin crawl. He hurried his pace, wanting to put a good distance between himself and the two enemy mages. He was aware of people staring at him as they crossed the courtyard. Xiana guided him by the arm around the fountain, then through an enormous, iron-shod door into the interior of the fortress.

Dark walls and fluttering shadows surrounded them. They entered a narrow hallway lit by iron lanterns that cast a dreary ochre light. The walls were etched with elaborate filigree that swirled over their entire surfaces. The dance of light across the twisting patterns was mesmerizing. Rylan walked at Xiana's side, staring blankly at the walls.

"What does it mean to be chained?" he asked.

Xiana took a moment before responding. "The chains connect two people in all ways, sealing them together as one. They also seal a person to the Unity—the whole of the community."

They turned a corner, then mounted a flight of stairs. Rylan found himself wondering if Xiana had ever been chained. Gralish had seemed to know her intimately. Had she been connected to the Turan Unity? And, if so, how had she ever escaped them?

A creeping feeling of doubt settled over his shoulders.

He asked, "Why did that man ask if I was tame?"

Xiana answered, "Because a chained mage would never harm their other half. Or the community."

They reached the end of the stairs. Before them extended a wide hallway that ended at an ominous-looking door. It was enormous, constructed of rough wood planks that looked half-rotten by the years, far older than the rest of the fortress surrounding it. The boards were pierced through with rusted bolts and secured by dark bands.

Staring at the door, Rylan pondered Xiana's words, feeling an increasing sense of foreboding. "This Shiro..." he said slowly, "is he going to try to put chains on me?"

He didn't know why he had asked that. The answer was obvious. But the doubt now chilling his insides was making it hard to think. And harder to trust.

"Yes," Xiana answered, gazing at him solemnly. "He will want you sealed to the Unity. And sealed to him."

Rylan stared past her at the door, his eyes locked on it. Shiro was behind that door. Waiting for him. He swallowed dryly. He trusted Xiana with his life. He had to remember that.

And yet, doubt gnawed at his bones.

"I'll not let them chain me," he whispered.

She squeezed his hand reassuringly, a comforting warmth in her eyes. "Are you ready?"

He nodded. He had come here to claim his daughter. There was no question that he was ready. Rylan followed her as she walked forward across the parquet floor and stopped before the massive door. Reaching up, she rapped hard upon the ancient wood.

For a long moment, nothing happened.

Then, with a shudder, the great door creaked opened just a crack. Xiana leaned forward and said to someone on the other side, "We are here to see the Warlord."

The door opened just a fraction more, revealing the thin

sliver of a man standing on the other side. A man with pale skin and even paler hair, his features narrow and jagged.

The man ran his gaze over Rylan critically. "No mage enters the Warlord's presence unbanded."

The door started to close.

Xiana thrust her hand out, stopping it.

"He is dampened. The Warlord is expecting us."

The door hesitated.

"Very well."

The menacing sound of that voice made Rylan shudder. Xiana smiled at him in encouragement, gripping him once more by the arm. With a ghastly moan, the door swung open before them, revealing a room cloaked in darkness beyond.

Rylan followed Xiana past the pale man, who closed the door behind them, cutting them off from the light of the lanterns. The room they stood in was ink-black, save for a strip of light spilling in through a doorway ahead. With a wave of his hand, the pale man motioned them toward it.

Xiana led him into the wash of light but drew up short as a pair of chained mages stepped forward, blocking their path. Rylan glanced beyond them into the room but could make out very little within. A sheer drape of red fabric hung on the other side of the doorway. Through it, he could make out only the vague outlines of wide pillars backlit by flickering flames.

Clinging to his arm, Xiana raised her chin and stated clearly to the mages blocking their path, "Brothers, please inform the Warlord that his daughter Xiana begs audience."

Rylan felt a cold shiver steal over him at her words, as all the doubt within him bubbled to the surface. He looked at Xiana and studied her face, searching her eyes for signs of betrayal. But her deep brown eyes were without emotion. He could find neither treachery nor comfort in her gaze.

Before them, the chained mages bowed together as a pair. One moved to draw the drape back, revealing a long, dark hall with a high ceiling supported by fluted columns. Flaming braziers lined the edges of the room, and rows of candles defined a path to a dais at the far end of the hall.

The mages withdrew to the side. Xiana tugged on Rylan's arm, pulling him forward. She led him into the chamber, stepping onto a crimson rug that stretched the length of the room and flowed up the stairs onto the dais. There were no windows in the hall. No tapestries or artwork of any kind. Along the top of the walls ran a band of blue tiles decorated with stylized Malikari calligraphy that wrapped around the entire room. He had no idea what it said.

On the dais, four unchained mages wearing iron bands on their wrists knelt at the foot of a throne made of human skulls. It was a grisly sight. A chilling sight. Yet, as Xiana drew him closer to the throne, Rylan's eyes were drawn solely to its occupant, a man with leathery gray skin and long white hair, whose features were more skeletal than the bones he sat upon.

As they approached, the Warlord took notice of them and turned their way. When the man's cold stare fell on him, Rylan halted mid-stride. His heart shivered to a stop. He recognized the man on the throne; there could be no other like him. It was the man from the Guardian Tower in Suheylu Ra.

The man who had murdered his Ilia.

38

THE CROSSING

GIL STOOD WITH ONE FOOT RESTING ON THE REMAINS OF A broken foundation, watching Judhi dig through a stash buried in a hole punctured in the wall of a house. The man was bent over, head and torso buried in the hole, only his legs visible. Various items came tumbling out onto the street: water sacks, canteens, scraps of clothing. With a grunt, Judhi struggled to extract himself. Rising to stand, he used his sleeve to wipe a thick coating of dust off his forehead. His thick black hair was covered with it, and his beard looked like it had been dusted with flour. He scooped up a large water bladder off the ground and tossed it to Gil, who moved just in time to catch it by the strap.

"What's all this for?" Gil asked, looking down at the water bladder.

Judhi explained, "To reach the Andibar Quarter, we must pass the Mirjaz Checkpoint." He stooped to collect the rest of the supplies he'd tossed out of the stash. "The checkpoint is very dangerous, and we must have a reason to go across. Most of the wells in this quarter have been poisoned. The only way to find drinking water is to cross into the Mirjaz District.

Most go at sunrise and return at sunset. Today, we go with them."

Gil glanced around the shattered remains of the surrounding neighborhood. Few of the houses were intact. Debris and layers of white dust filled the street, and the air was thick with the cloying smell of blood and decay. The Khar hadn't claimed the Demali Quarter yet, but it didn't look like they needed to. The neighborhood was strangled, and there was no other place for its population to go.

Judhi tilted his head back and drank deeply from his canteen. Clapping Gil on the back, he started across the street, saying, "It's time to go. The men will be ready. "

Gil walked after him down the road, picking his way carefully over the spilled remains of collapsed buildings. The street was stained dark in places where the dead had lain. In other places, the buzz of flies alluded to remains still buried beneath the rubble. Judhi led him around the corner and onto the street where Uma Halabi's residence was one of the few that remained intact.

As they walked, his companion explained, "I will tell you when we are nearing the crossing. From that point on, each of us must walk alone. If the Khar suspect we are together, or suspect we are fighters, they will kill us. We must make them believe we do not know each other, and that we come only for water."

Gil asked, "Is Uma Halabi coming with us?"

"No." Judhi shook his head. "Her face is known to them."

Gil's boots crunched on pulverized stone as they neared the courtyard entrance to Uma Halabi's home. As he opened the door, Judhi nodded at the talisman hanging at Gil's side.

"You will need to leave that weapon here."

Gil's hand went protectively to *Thar'gon's* leather-wrapped haft. "It's a magical artifact. I can't leave it behind."

Judhi frowned, his face scrunching up as he considered the

weapon. "Then you will have to find some way of concealing it. A very good way," he added.

Gil thought about it, deciding a shadow web should be enough. "No one will see it," he assured him.

Judhi grunted and called across the courtyard to a man and a woman squatting beside a pile of provisions. "Mezhar! Dija! Are you ready?"

Both stood and walked toward them, carrying an assortment of water bottles and empty sacks. Mezhar was a young man clothed in a brown tunic. His companion, a woman dressed in a man's shirt and trousers, wore her hair in a thick braid that hung almost to her knees. One side of her face was blistered and peeling. Judhi called up at a second-story window:

"Savas, you fool! Get down here! We are leaving without you!"

Motioning for Gil and his two companions to follow, he started toward the street. Before they were halfway across the courtyard, they were halted by the upstairs door banging open. Gil looked up to see a young man dressed in the robes of a cleric jogging down the stairs toward them with a clatter. Reaching them, the scraggly young man smiled sheepishly.

Another door opened, and Uma Halabi came out of the house. She moved stiffly toward them, favoring one leg. Gil walked toward her, wanting to save her the distance. When he reached her, she embraced him tightly and kissed his cheeks.

"May you know the favor of the gods," she said. She held him tightly, patting his back, then let him go. Without saying another word, she walked back inside the house.

"Let's go!" Judhi snapped.

Gil started after him, a little sad he likely wouldn't be able to repay Uma Halabi for her kindness. Looking down at the weapon at his side, he spun a web of shadow around it. The web would be useless if the guards at the checkpoint patted him down. He could only pray they didn't.

He walked beside Judhi, following Mezhar and Dija down the street, Savas distancing himself from their party. The roads were still muddy in places from a recent rain, and water drained from the rooftops to run in bloody streams toward the center of the street. They walked four blocks, their progress slowed by the sheer amount of debris that filled the road. The further they walked, the more people appeared around them, canteens and buckets in hand, until the road was somewhat crowded, everyone moving in the same direction.

Judhi drew them aside and instructed, "From this point on, we walk alone. We do not know each other. Mezhar, Dija! You act as husband and wife."

Gil looked at Judhi and nodded. They followed a steady stream of people walking toward the Mirjaz checkpoint as the sun rose into a brown, smoke-infected sky. Beside him walked a woman holding the hand of a small girl who clutched a ragdoll under her arm. Behind them came two young men who looked like brothers, both laden with water skins. One brother's head was wrapped in bloody bandages. The other's arm was missing.

Gil fell back behind them, while Mezhar and Dija dropped even further back, walking hand-in-hand. Judhi and Savas spread out as they approached the end of the street. Ahead, a thick clot of people were bunched together in a large group, waiting to clear the checkpoint. Guards in scale mail lined the intersection, waving people through one or two at a time. Behind them stood a gray-robed man with long golden hair and a longer scowl, surveying the trickle of people crossing the street. He wasn't wearing chains, which made Gil stare harder at the man. Then he saw the iron band around the man's left wrist: a bracelet that a chain could be attached to.

Ahead, Judhi reached the front of the crowd and raised his hands, turning slowly around, as one of the Khar soldiers patted him down. Another guard took the canteen that hung from a strap on his shoulder and upended it before handing it back. Judhi then crossed the street under the watchful eyes of the Khar mage, while Savas passed, unhindered, through the checkpoint.

Following the ebb and flow of the crowd, Gil moved slowly forward toward the checkpoint. Off to the side, a man had been singled out and was being questioned by a few of the guards. The man's answers grew louder, becoming sharp and panicked. Another soldier walked up behind him and, pulling a dagger from his belt, calmly slit the man's throat. The man fell to the street, where he lay gasping his last breaths into the dust.

No one in the crowd reacted.

A loud, barking command made Gil jump. Swinging back around, he realized he had reached the front of the crowd. Khar soldiers were yelling at him, motioning him forward. Shaken, he complied, raising his hands as he moved between them, his eyes on the unchained mage as he prayed to the gods they wouldn't stop to check him for weapons, as they had done with Judhi.

Another guard motioned him forward briskly, letting him by without halting him. Gil felt a dizzying flood of relief as he crossed the street, following the trickle of people moving ahead of him. He glanced back to look for the others and discovered the mage's eyes on him. He looked away quickly, fighting to keep the panic he felt off his face.

When he reached the other side of the street, he glanced at the man out of the corner of his eye and saw the mage's attention was still focused on him, his face scowling even deeper than before.

A sudden commotion behind him made him turn. Gil looked to see a group of soldiers shouting at Mezhar, while two other men dragged Dija away from him. Mezhar lurched forward, but the guards hauled him back, Dija thrashing and screaming.

There was a shout, and the guards scattered. Then a flash of light followed by a deafening crackle of thunder. Mezhar exploded, showering the square with blood. Gil ducked, shielding his head as little bits of Mezhar splattered down all around him. He gritted his teeth, swallowing hard to keep his breakfast down.

Dija shrieked horrifically.

The crowd erupted, people scattering in every direction. Gil sprinted down the street, following a stampede of people fleeing the checkpoint. He glanced behind, looking for the Khar mage. But he couldn't see him, so he picked up his pace and skittered around the nearest corner.

A hand caught his arm, using his own momentum to swing him around and slam him up against the side of a building. Gil sagged against the bricks, laboring to catch his breath. Blinking, he made out Judhi's face, its lines sharpened by shock and rage. With a growl, he began scrubbing his hands over Gil's shoulders as if frantically brushing off dust. It took Gil a moment to realize he was sweeping charred pieces of Mezhar off his clothes.

It was too much. Gil bent over and emptied his stomach.

Judhi paced away from him, right hand planted on his hip, head bowed. He swept a fist through the air, then whirled back around.

"This thing that you're doing," he growled, "It had better be worth it!"

Gil's stomach heaved again. He stood bent over his knees, one hand propped against the wall. Judhi waited only long enough for Gil's stomach to stop twisting. Then, with a grimace, he motioned him forward again. Gil spat the taste out of his mouth and followed him. They worked their way further into the district as the sun rose higher in the smoke-darkened sky. Savas found them and trailed behind, head bowed. He hadn't spoken a word the entire trip and didn't look like he was ready to start.

It didn't take Gil long to notice that the streets of the Mirjaz Quarter were very different from the district they had left. Most of the buildings were intact, and the streets had been cleared of debris. The people moving by them seemed to walk with purpose, going about normal, every-day tasks. Vendors had set up stalls along the sides of the streets, selling fruits and vegetables at outrageous prices. The neighborhoods were patrolled by soldiers wearing the same uniforms as the guards at the crossing: scale mail vests over long, wine-colored tunics, most carrying spears and bucklers covered in leather.

As they continued deeper into the quarter, it became obvious that life there had returned to some semblance of normal. Only, it was a different kind of normal than Gil was used to. Citizens went about their business silently, with great economy of movement. There were no people lingering in the street, conversing with friends and neighbors. Everyone seemed to have a job to perform, and everyone seemed singularly focused on the completion of that purpose.

They walked through an intersection that had a fly-covered corpse sprawled in the center of it. The sight was bizarre; all signs of the war had been scrubbed away from the rest of the neighborhood. Except for this one corpse that looked extraordinarily out of place. It was a woman—or had been. Flies swarmed over her, buzzing in and out of her mouth. The sockets of her eyes were encrusted with them. Judhi gave the corpse a wide berth; the smell was horrendous, and it took them many steps to escape it.

A block later, they passed a second body, this one being savaged by a dog, its snout red with blood. The animal growled at them as they passed, laying its ears back and baring its teeth. Gil hurried his steps, trying not to look. Over the next few blocks, they passed several such corpses. He didn't understand; the people had labored hard to clear the streets of any signs of war, and yet these bodies remained untouched.

"Why doesn't anyone bury them?" he asked.

It was Savas who responded. "They are traps. The Khar have ordered that the dead are to be left where they lie. If anyone tries to remove them, they are executed."

"Lower your voices!" Judhi hissed. "The walls have ears!"

Gil looked around at the surrounding buildings, suddenly nervous. There were no soldiers within hearing distance, but many of the windows were open. One of the guards down the street was staring at them hard. He shut his mouth and bit his lip. The last thing he wanted to do was get two more people killed for trying to help him.

Judhi led them around the corner, then darted through an open gate in the wall. Gil followed him into a courtyard with a well-tended garden fed by a trickling fountain. Judhi and Savas rushed forward, inspecting the courtyard thoroughly before opening the door to the adjoining house. Gil followed them inside. They moved quietly but quickly, searching every room as they came to it, until they found a set of stairs that led upward. They took the stairs to the third floor and climbed a ladder to the roof. Ducking down behind the roof's low wall, Gil followed Judhi to the northeast corner of the house. There, they squatted down, taking cover behind the wall.

"On the other side of this street is the Andibar Quarter," Judhi said. "This is as far as Savas and I can go with you. There are too many soldiers by the citadel, and there is too much risk for us. From here, you must continue alone. Come look."

He motioned Gil forward and together they looked out over the top of the wall. The house they stood on was taller than most in the surrounding neighborhood. Across a broken mosaic of rooftops, Gil could see the towers of the Alqazar Citadel only a few blocks away.

"The fortress is up that street," Judhi said, indicating a road two blocks over from the house they stood on. "Follow it north."

Gil took a moment to study the cityscape. Judhi was right; there were very few people on the streets, and most were soldiers. He would have a hard time blending in. He blew out a long sigh, finally nodding. Ducking back down, they crossed the roof and took the stairs back down to the level of the street.

There, in the courtyard, Gil turned and said farewell to his two companions. Judhi embraced him, saying, "May the gods protect you and help you find what you seek."

"My thanks for your help," Gil said. "I'm sorry about your friends. I truly am. I'll do my best to try to make their deaths count for something."

Judhi nodded but didn't respond. Savas lay a hand on his shoulder, then turned away without saying a word. Gil stood in the courtyard and watched the two men open the gate and steal back into the street. After that, he waited, giving Judhi and Savas time to put some distance between them and himself.

39

SHIRO

RYLAN STARED UP AT THE GRAY MAN SEATED ON THE SKULL throne, white-hot hatred freezing his insides. He wanted to rush forward and throttle him, to plunge his hands into his chest and rip his heart out through his rib cage. This was the man who had killed Ilia and murdered his son. Only one thing held him back: the threat to his daughter.

Amina was this man's hostage. He couldn't risk her being harmed.

Xiana dropped to her knees, bowing forward until her forehead touched the rugs, her hands beside her face. She remained in that position as the Warlord gazed down upon them with a face devoid of expression. Rylan remained on his feet, glaring his hatred.

The Warlord held his gaze.

At last, the gray man adjusted his posture and settled back into his throne.

"You may rise," he rumbled.

Xiana rose gracefully, a proud and joyous smile on her face.

The awful man folded his hands. His features were gaunt, his long, white hair worn pulled back from his face, accentuating the sharpness of his cheekbones. A slight smile touched pale lips the color of a cadaver's.

"Welcome, daughter," he said in a cruelly familiar voice. "What is this gift you have brought me?"

Xiana ducked her head and moved forward. "Father, I bring you Rylan Lauchlin, whom you know as Gerald, son of Darien Lauchlin."

The Warlord rose from his throne, and as he did, his retinue of mages scurried forward to surround them. Startled, Rylan flinched backward, but was halted by a man who reached out to restrain him.

The Warlord held his gaze as he descended the dais. He moved past Xiana without looking at her, his cadre of mages parting to admit him into their midst. He stopped in front of Rylan and stood studying him intensely.

"Do you know why you are here?" he asked.

"I came to get my daughter back," Rylan answered. He couldn't do anything until he felt assured that Amina would be safe. Nothing in the world was worth jeopardizing her. Xiana's plan would have to wait.

Assuming Xiana still intended to carry it out.

If she ever had.

Xiana walked back toward him, the ring of mages parting to admit her. She drew up and stood beside Rylan.

"Your daughter will be restored to you," the Warlord assured him. He glanced at Xiana. "Do you believe he is ready?"

"He merged with Keio Matu," Xiana reported. Reaching out, she stroked the back of her hand down Rylan's cheek, her eyes full of warmth and pride. "He has all of Keio's knowledge and many of his personal memories."

The warlord nodded. Turning to Rylan, he canted his head. "Then you know who I am."

"Shiro Nagato."

He wanted this man dead more than any enemy he'd ever

faced. He had never met a creature more deserving. It took everything he had to keep himself in check, to stop himself from striking out at Shiro with the Onslaught. But doing so prematurely wouldn't serve his goal. He needed to make sure Amina was safe first. After that, he could take as much time as he needed to make sure Shiro Nagato suffered for what he'd done.

"You have Ilia," Rylan said, nodding at Xiana. "And now you have me. You have everything you want. Now give me what I want."

Shiro Nagato looked at him shrewdly. "You want your daughter."

Rylan nodded. "Aye."

The Warlord stood staring at him, bony hands clasped together. For the first time, Rylan noticed the glowing silver band Shiro wore about his wrist. It had to be an artifact. He wondered what kind of character it was imbued with.

Shiro reached out his hand. Another mage—a woman— moved forward and handed him a set of shackles connected by an iron chain that draped from his hand. Shiro smiled down at the sinister artifact. Then he aimed that smile at Rylan.

"This is for you," he said, holding up one of the bands. "You must put it on willingly."

"No." Rylan shook his head. "Not until I see Amina." And even then, he wouldn't be wearing that sinister chain. He would be using it to strangle Shiro as he watched the Warlord's flesh melt off his bones.

Gazing levelly at Rylan, Shiro said, "Get the girl."

One of his pet mages left immediately, striding out of the room through the silk partition. Rylan felt his pulse quicken. Amina was here, somewhere within the fortress. She was alive, and they were bringing her to him. Soon, he would be able to hold and hug his baby girl. His hands trembled in their restraints.

He stared harder at Shiro, trying to probe Keio's memories to find out what he knew of the man. But Keio was buried deep within him, in a remote, inaccessible place. Sometimes his memories churned to the surface, but those times were becoming less frequent. And not when he needed them.

He felt a tugging at his wrists. Turning, he realized that Xiana had stepped behind him and was loosening the sash that bound his arms behind his back. When she drew the sash off him, he could feel the warmth of blood flowing back into his wrists. He raised his hands and wiggled his fingers, but he couldn't feel any sensation in them. Dropping his hands, he glanced at Shiro. He wanted to kill him. He *had* to kill him. The moment he saw Amina—the moment he could be sure she was safe—he would strike out and end this demon. He couldn't hesitate, couldn't give him a chance to react.

But what if he failed?

What if Shiro retaliated by killing Amina?

Rylan's numb hands started to tingle as they awakened. Soon, pins and needles were jabbing his fingers, making him grit his teeth. At that moment, the door of the hall groaned open, then quickly shut again. The sound made him flinch. He squeezed his eyes shut, his heart ice-cold with fear and anticipation. He couldn't turn around. He was too afraid to look.

So he listened, instead, to the sound of approaching footsteps that spoke with more urgency than any words he'd ever heard. The closer those footsteps came, the harder his hands trembled.

At last, after eternity, the footsteps stopped.

Rylan opened his eyes and turned around.

And found a man standing behind him, holding a little girl with a cherub face haloed by dark curls.

Rylan's heart broke open, and he gasped.

He started forward, but two of Shiro's mages caught his

arms, holding him back even as he fought against their grasp. His little girl reached out for him and started whimpering.

"Gods damn you!" Rylan shouted. *"Let me go!"*

A hand reached up and caught his chin, wrenching his head around until he was forced to stare into Shiro Nagato's eyes. The man's fingers dug deeply into his skin, squeezing harder, as he glared cold malice into Rylan's face.

"Don the chain," he said softly. "Only then will you be reunited with your daughter. Not before."

He let go of Rylan and stepped back, extending one of the iron bands toward him. The pair of mages restraining him released his arms. Sweat broke out on his brow. His insides turned to stone. He glanced at Xiana and found her looking at him, eyes moist with compassion. He looked at Amina, his mind counting his options. It didn't take him long to realize he didn't have any.

He couldn't attack Shiro. Not without risking Amina.

He felt Xiana's hand on his arm, but he didn't look at her. She had lied to him. Betrayed him. Everything she'd done, every hope she'd ever planted in him, it was all lies. False promises. Overcome by an aching hurt that stabbed deep into his bones, he dropped his gaze to the ground.

"Take it," Shiro urged. "Put it on."

He realized the Warlord wasn't speaking to him; he was speaking to Xiana.

She took the iron band from Shiro's hand and, without hesitation, fastened it to her own wrist. Rylan looked at her sadly, his heart breaking at the sight of her chained. He didn't understand how she could have done it—how Ilia could have done it. How they had both betrayed him so.

Amina started whimpering. Then crying.

Rylan's eyes blurred as he stared down at the other bracelet in Shiro's hands, the one meant for him. He knew what would happen if he put that band around his wrist. He would lose himself. The part of him that was Rylan Marshall would cease to exist.

And what would be left? He tried imagining a life lived in blissful ignorance, a life lived in contentment, not knowing anything different. Not knowing he was supposed to be someone else, another man with dreams and hopes and desires. Perhaps he could find happiness in a future with Amina and Xiana to call family, with people like Gralish and Laira to call friends. Such a future didn't sound so terribly bad. Or he could strike out and slay Shiro with the Onslaught, hoping he could carry his daughter away fast enough to get her to safety.

More likely, such and attempt would end with them both dead.

He didn't know what to do.

Everything that mattered to him was there in that room.

He remembered the words of the man in the cornfield, the man who had forced him to pledge his soul: *If you value your daughter's life, you must swear the oath. Remember the oath, and chains will never bind you.*

He looked at the chain, then back up at Amina. It wasn't much to pin his hopes on. But it was the only hope he had.

He reached out his hand. "Give it here."

The joyous smile on Xiana's face tore him apart. He didn't understand how she could be looking at him that way. Keio Matu had destroyed an entire city—the city he was charged with protecting—to keep Shiro's venom from infecting the world. And now Xiana was betraying everything Keio and Ilia had ever stood for and asking him to do the same.

He studied the rust-eaten band in his hand, contemplating it gravely. It didn't look like an object capable of destroying him. But he knew it was. Amina squirmed, red-faced and whimpering in the gray mage's grasp. Rylan turned away from her, unable to look.

Xiana smiled at him sadly. She had to know how much this hurt. And yet she was doing it to him anyway. Rylan's vision blurred. He wiped the tears off his face with the back of his hand.

Trembling, he opened the shackle and slipped the iron band around his wrist. He took one last look at his sweet baby girl, wanting her face to be the last thing he saw. She was beautiful. The most beautiful thing in an ugly world.

He closed his eyes and snapped the band shut.

There was silence.

He was no longer in the room.

He was spiraling down into a vortex, and the further he went, the more it became clear that he wasn't alone. As he twisted downward, a soothing feeling unfolded within him. It swelled inside him, chasing away all doubts and fears, replacing them with a warm sense of belonging. He knew he no longer had to bear his pains and burdens alone; there were many others with him now. He could feel them there, welcoming him with intense relief and joy. They were many. So very many. They were more than a populace.

They were legion.

Thousands of souls, some alive. Most already passed; they had transcended and become something more. Heedless, he rushed toward the beacon of their flames without sparing a thought to caution. There was no need for it. These souls were a part of him now, just as he was a part of them. They were all joined together in a core far greater than the sum of the millions that composed it. It was an essence much greater than himself, greater than everything he was leaving behind.

For the first time in his life, Rylan knew what it was like to be whole. To be complete. To be loved unconditionally, despite all his failures and faults. A feeling of security wrapped around him, and he opened himself wide to it. He let it melt and run into him. Become him. Consume him.

As his mind spiraled back into himself, he brought all that with him.

Rylan blinked as the world returned, rushing up to meet him.

The first thing he saw was Xiana. He could feel her love for him, her joy and excitement at seeing him born anew. Closing his eyes, he opened himself to her, inviting her in further than any human had ever gone. He bared his soul to her, exposing all of what he was, all that he had ever been. Every hope. Every failure. Every success and every shame. He handed it all to her.

And she accepted him completely.

He could feel her moving into him, deeper than his heart, her soul entwining and invigorating his. Until every breath, he breathed for her. With her. Through her. He was terrified. Joyous. Overwhelmed. Astounded.

Complete.

This is the way it had been once, long ago, with Ilia. The way it was supposed to be. After centuries apart, they were blessedly reunited, blessedly whole.

The Warlord stepped between them.

Looking in his eyes, Rylan felt overcome by a terrible guilt. He saw the Warlord staring back at him, gazing into that lonely place inside where his darkest secrets lay entombed. He saw the change that came over Shiro's face as he realized the truths that lay buried there. The darkness. The evil. He saw it all.

Rylan bowed his head. Shiro knew who he was: a soldier sworn to evil, a man who had been ready to turn that taint into a weapon to use against him. He could feel the weight of the Warlord's disappointment. Scalding guild heated his cheeks.

The Warlord pressed his palm against Rylan's brow. Closing his eyes, he whispered, "I forgive you, my son."

Rylan choked on an overwhelming surge of gratitude, a relief greater than anything he'd ever felt before.

The Warlord removed his hand. As he did, something snapped inside. There was an instant of terrible pain. And then a gush of magic flooded into him, filling him the way a river fills an empty basin. He could feel the magic field again. He reached out and touched it, his eyes widening in wonder.

Shiro had removed the block Naia had put on him. He'd removed the block—but not the Word. That, he'd reset. Rylan could still feel it there waiting, a wound to his heart that would never heal.

He gasped and staggered back, lurching into Xiana's arms. She caught him up, embracing him tightly. He sobbed silently, his tears wetting her face. Through the link he shared with her, he could feel the depths of love she bore for him. When they placed his daughter in his arms, Rylan broke completely. He hugged Amina against him, breathing in the scent of her hair, reveling in the feel of her soft skin.

"Papa!" she squealed.

It was the first word he had ever heard her speak.

The man who had once been Rylan Marshall stood wrapped in the arms of the people he cared most about, and that was all that mattered. He no longer had any use for his old life, his old identity. It was worthless and irrelevant.

Xiana drew back, smiling at him with joy in her eyes. "Come with me," she urged. "There are so many people who want to meet you."

Her words brought Rylan to the edge of panic. Everything was so overwhelming. His mind was already bursting with the multitudes that already occupied it. He didn't think he could handle any more. "I can't," he gasped. "It's too much...."

She smiled her understanding and kissed him softly. "Then

come. Bring your daughter. Let's get you to a place where you can fall in love with her again."

Nothing else in the world could ever make him happier. He let Xiana lead him forward by the hand, the chain connecting them hanging slack from his wrist. He hugged his daughter against him, her arms wrapped tight around his neck, her little legs clinging to his body.

He walked in a fog, his mind unable to grapple with all that had just happened to him, what was still happening. He could still sense all the others he was connected to, who were now just as much a part of him as his soul. Xiana led him through winding hallways, down long flights of stairs. The walls closed in on them, and the air cooled. Flickering candlelight added its own surreal texture to the world, making it seem as though he moved within a dream.

There was a metallic groan, and the shudder of a door opening.

Blinking, Rylan stopped and looked around, confused by what he saw.

They were in a dungeon.

A dungeon filled with people and fabric and color. It seemed so impossible; for a moment, all he could do was stand in shock, hugging his daughter close against him. Every person in the room was staring at him. Dozens of faces smiled, dozens of voices greeted him. He could feel their warmth and joy enfolding him.

The dungeon was filled with bright rugs and tapestries, colorful lanterns and gauzy draperies. The doors to the cells stood open and people moved freely in and out. It was bizarre, as though the prisoners had taken over the prison and were determined to convert their circumstances into a festive occasion.

People spilled forward, encircling them. As they did, their

emotions flooded into him. Rylan cringed back, overawed. It was too much, too soon.

"Give him some room," Xiana said, smiling. "He's overwhelmed."

Sympathy flowed toward him in waves, and the crowd retreated. But then his eyes fell on a person he recognized.

"Ashra," Rylan whispered.

She flashed him a joyous smile, and he could feel her excitement even from across the room. But she respected his need for space and kept her distance, greeting him instead with feelings of welcome and warmth.

"Come this way," Xiana urged, tugging on his arm.

Rylan followed her through a sea of people to a staircase that wound upward, spiraling into a tower. Carrying Amina, he followed her up the steps and into a circular room at the top covered in rugs, lit by the light of many candles that lined the walls.

Xiana took a seat on one of the rugs, patting the floor beside her. Rylan sank down next to her, settling his daughter in his lap. He cuddled Amina in his arms, reveling in the feel of her. Xiana leaned into him, pressing her forehead against his. She stroked her hands through his hair.

"How do you feel?" she asked softly.

Rylan gazed into her eyes, unable to break away.

"Happier than I've ever been in my life," he whispered. And it was true.

"I knew you would be," she said, and kissed him deeply.

40

ALQAZAR CITADEL

As Gil walked through the Andibar Quarter, he realized that Judhi had been right; there were scarcely any civilians about, and those that were appeared anxious about being on the streets. Squads of soldiers patrolled the avenues, and guards were stationed at every intersection. It didn't take Gil more than a block to realize he had already gathered attention. At first, he wondered why. Then he realized: every civilian on the street was engaged in some task. He was the only one that wasn't.

He couldn't just walk up to the citadel, he realized. He would need a reason for being there. At this rate, he doubted he could even reach it. He glanced at one of the guards and saw the man staring back at him. Sighing heavily, he looked away and tried to move with a sense of purpose in his stride. He turned a corner onto a side street.

Ahead of him was a cart loaded with wine casks that had become mired in a rut. Gil almost walked around it. But then it occurred to him that he had just been presented with the perfect opportunity. The driver was standing in front of the two horses hitched to the cart, tugging on the reins as if trying to pull them physically forward.

"Do you need help?" Gil asked, crossing the street toward him.

The driver looked up, his face red and wet with sweat.

"Can you push?" he gasped.

"I'll try!" Gil said, and moved around to the back of the cart.

He waited until the cart pitched forward again, then leaned into it and pushed, putting all his weight into the endeavor. Still, the cart didn't budge. Instead, his boots just started slipping. The cart lurched again, and Gil scrambled forward with it, pushing and groaning with all his might. With a jerk, the wheels came free of the rut, and the cart leaped forward. Gil lost his balance and fell, plunging his hands into the muck of the road. He struggled to his knees, his shirt and pants slicked with mud. People moving by them on the street stared at him, but no one offered to help. Gil gazed down at his ruined clothes, realizing he was attracting exactly the kind of attention he'd been meaning to avoid.

"Oh, I'm sorry!" the driver exclaimed, coming around the end of the cart. Extending his hand, he helped Gil to his feet. "Where're you headed, Brother? If it's on my way, I'll get you there."

Gil's hopes lifted. "The citadel," he answered. "If you take me there, I'll help you out if you get mired again."

"That's a deal," the driver said with a grin, clapping him on the back with a grimy hand.

Gil followed him up into the seat. With a snap of the reins, the cart staggered forward.

Amina was sleeping.

It was the most beautiful sight Rylan had ever seen. Her

plump lips were slightly open, her face peaceful, her chest moving in a slow rhythm. One little hand was curled next to her face. He stroked his fingers through her soft hair. She was bigger than he remembered.

He couldn't stop looking at her.

His mind echoed with the feelings of others that were with him now, a constant and comforting refrain. Xiana touched his hand. He didn't want to look at her—didn't want to break his attention from his daughter—but he did. She smiled at him kindly and scooted closer. Leaning over, she kissed his lips.

"You are *deizu-kan,* just as I am," she said as she drew back, her eyes glinting with pride. "We will work together, as *kaiden,* a joined pair. Everything we do, we will do together. We will share all of ourselves with each other. You will never be alone again. My heart will always be open to you. Can you feel it?"

He did. Her love flowed through the link he shared with her. He felt peace. Reassurance. All that he had lacked before, Xiana now brought him. He could sense his own feelings echoing hers. And within him, there was even more reason to rejoice: Keio Matu was finally reunited with his beloved, and Rylan felt awash in his joy.

Nothing could ever be wrong again. Everything was right.

He was whole.

Stroking his hand, she asked, "Do you know what tier you are?"

Rylan barely had to think about it; he already knew. There was a test to determine a mage's tier, and it was ironically simple. Closing his eyes, he waved his hand through the air, then opened his eyes quickly. A trail of sparkling magic lingered in the path his hand had traveled. It was fractured eight times, one for each instance of the Gift he had layered within him.

He blinked in shock. "I'm eighth tier," he said, his voice barely louder than a whisper. "Just like my father."

Xiana gave a satisfied smile. "Just like Keio Matu. We will be *Deizu-sum,* in charge of every *kaiden,*" she explained, her fingers trailing up his arm. "The weight of every life will rest on our shoulders, and the safety of the Unity will be in our hands."

The Unity. He understood the word now, completely, and all of its ramifications. It was the collection of all the people in the Empire, each connected to the other through infinite links. A collective whole, with every life touching every other life— and all those lives now bound to him. They were all-important. His own life was insignificant in comparison. Nothing else mattered; nothing could ever come close.

Not even Amina.

The thought stroked his nerves the wrong way. It was true, and yet it felt so wrong. Rylan frowned, his gaze darting to his daughter. She was still asleep, still peaceful. Her plump little fingers twitched once. Reaching out, he touched her hand.

"She's so beautiful," he murmured. "If I had one wish, it would be that my son could be here with us."

A deep, throbbing ache filled him, all the way down to his bones. An image of his son's shoe lying next to a pile of ash came to the surface of his mind and stuck there. His nerves trembled as though a sudden darkness had passed over them.

Shiro. His son.

They were somehow connected, though he couldn't remember why or how. Somehow, Shiro had taken his son away. At first, the thought made him enraged. But the feeling passed quickly. He understood. His son had been a necessary sacrifice, to nudge him in the direction of the right path, a path he would have never chosen otherwise. No matter how awful, his son's death had served a purpose. He had to forgive; he had to let it go. Shiro was his father now. And, just like any father, he loved his son enough to hurt him. Sometimes love had to be painful. Rylan understood that.

But another part of him doubted.

Korey's death hadn't been necessary... Shiro could have found another way. Suddenly, Rylan was filled with doubt. A cold, slithering feeling settled in his gut.

Chains will never bind you...

Xiana set a hand on his back, and the warmth of their connection chased the cold feeling away. Contentment settled back around him like a warm blanket, along with a great sense of peace.

"We're preparing for an offensive," Xiana said quietly, her fingers stroking his back in soothing circles. "You and I will lead the attack, as *Deizu-sum*. Together, we will bring this city into the Empire. The joy of the people will be boundless. It will be wondrous to see."

Her words provoked a stirring of excitement within him. The people of Karikesh didn't know how empty and lonely their lives were; they had never known anything different. But soon they would know a better life, and they would rejoice. Rylan was happy for them. Malikar and the Kingdoms could at last live in harmony. There would be no more cause for adversity. Every continent in the world would soon be unified, and there would be one, everlasting peace.

And yet, it pained him that so many people would have to die to achieve that goal. Perhaps it didn't have to be that way. Maybe he could do something to make a difference.

"Let me go to them," he said. "The Sultan is a good man. I'm sure I can make him understand. Then no one has to die."

Xiana smiled at him regretfully. "Death is meaningless, Rylan. The only thing that matters is the Unity. We are but transitory beings. We are here for just a moment, like a spark. We burn briefly and brightly, then we fall back into the flames. Like the spark, we are here to serve the fire; no more. That is the purpose and meaning of our lives."

"Aye." He nodded, knowing she was right.

Xiana's hand went to the chain that linked them together,

and she caressed it. "For now, you are *sayan,* the one who is led," she told him. "I am *isan,* the one who leads. Our roles may reverse someday, as you grow into your power. But until that time, I control the link."

He nodded absently. His eyes and mind had returned to Amina. He was thinking how lucky she was to grow up knowing only this. She would never know hatred. She would never know isolation or loneliness.

Only love and serenity.

"Come here," Xiana whispered, taking him into her arms. "You need rest. Lie down and sleep. I'll watch over you."

Rylan did as she asked. He lay down beside his daughter and cuddled her as he drifted off to sleep, comforted by the feel of Xiana's hand stroking his.

Gil stared up at the towers of the Alqazar Citadel and swallowed. The fortress was heavily guarded. He stood across the street, watching as soldiers inspected the wine cart before allowing it through the gate into the citadel's bailey.

He sucked in a cheek. He would have to find another way in.

With the talisman, he could transfer into the citadel if he knew what it looked like inside. But he'd never get a view of the baily from the street. Glancing up, he surveyed the row of buildings behind him and chose the tallest. He strolled up the street with his head bowed, hoping the guards wouldn't take an interest in him.

He felt an almost dizzying sense of relief when he reached the building unmolested. And his luck held: the door was unlocked. He let himself into a narrow hallway that smelled strongly of spices. The sound of laughter came from somewhere down the hall. He took the stairs up to the third floor, then found a door leading out onto a balcony. Moving toward the rail, he let out a sigh of relief.

Below was an unobstructed view of the interior of the fortress.

The Alqazar Citadel was a massive complex of courtyards and fortified structures laid out in no particular order or design. From where he stood, he had a good view of the first two courtyards. The rooftops of several buildings rolled away from him, the towers blocking his view of the rest.

The first courtyard swarmed with soldiers and supplies, smoke rolling from forges and kitchens. It would be difficult—probably impossible—to enter the fortress from there. The second courtyard was almost empty. It was encased by a series of arcaded walkways and had a distinctive fountain in the middle. Those were all the landmarks he needed. Gil spun a shadow web around himself and unhooked the talisman from his belt. He closed his eyes and fixed an image of the fountain in his mind.

"Vergis," he whispered.

The world shifted, and then the fountain appeared in front of him from out of a tilted landscape. Gil staggered, catching his balance. He stood blinking in a harsh flood of sunlight, the strong scent of jasmine filling his nostrils. There were only a few people in the courtyard, and no one seemed to take notice of him. As long as he didn't move, the shadow web was enough. He looked at a man and woman walking away from him. He could tell they were mages by the robes.

The columned walkway next to him offered enough shade to conceal him. Gil waited until he was certain no one was looking, then moved quickly beneath the arcade. He stood still for a moment, making sure he hadn't been seen. Then he looked around at the buildings that enclosed the courtyard, wondering which one housed the citadel's mages. Searching building to building would be too risky; he had to find another way.

A couple strolled past him: two women walking together hand and hand. On impulse, he moved after them. There was a good chance they were returning to their quarters and could lead him there if it wasn't too great a distance. Holding the talisman at his side, he followed them into the building and down a flight of stairs.

The floor below the main level was dark, the walls lined with old bricks. The odor of mildew clung to the air. He waited and let the two women continue down another flight, then moved quietly after them. From somewhere below rose the drone of conversation, growing louder the further he went.

At the bottom of the steps, Gil drew up.

He stood at the entrance to a large dungeon. Cells lined all four walls, and wicked-looking hooks hung from the ceiling in one corner. The room swarmed with people, sitting and standing, on brightly colored rugs or lounging on couches. They had gone to the trouble to try to make the dungeon seem livable; there were tapestries and silk partitions hanging from the roof, and curtains hung over the bars of many of the individual cells.

But nothing could disguise the fact that this was, in every sense, a prison.

He checked to make sure his shadow web was secure, then moved forward into the room. He looked from face to face, examining the natures of these strange mages he had come to kill. Some wore the gray skin of the Turan Khar, while others had olive skin of a golden hue. Some were Malikari, and others of the Kingdoms. Some of them were people he knew.

All the mages in the dungeon seemed content, even happy. They stood conversing with their peers or sharing meals, sitting in tight clusters on the rugs. Laughter came from all directions, and there was a sense of comfort and ease to the place. Gil turned around slowly, feeling a tightness in his stomach, thinking of the grim work he had come there to do.

Then his gaze fell on Ashra, and he gasped.

She sat in a corner next to a young man with long white hair and pale skin. Unlike most of the people in the room, she wore a thin chain that secured her to her companion. She was drinking something from a cup, and there was a smile on her face. To his shock, she looked genuinely happy.

Almost, he forgot why he was there. Part of him wanted to run to her and rip that chain off her arm, then use the talisman to get her out of there. But he had a duty to perform, and Ashra had to come second to that.

Unless he could accomplish both at the same time.

Wrapped in his shadow web, Gil moved further into the dim dungeon, twisting and winding through the press of bodies, until he worked his way to the corner where Ashra sat laughing at something the man linked to her had said. It was evident the two were connected by bonds stronger than the chain between them. The way the man stared at Ashra as if captivated, his fingers stroking hers, made it obvious he was in love with her... and she was in love with him. She leaned into him, resting her head on his shoulder, caressing his chest.

Gil clenched his fists in anger. He'd known she would be a prisoner in chains but, somehow, this was worse. She was a prisoner of love, just like Payden had been. And it was his fault. If he had just listened to her father, she would still be free. Despair blurred his eyes and tightened his throat as he stood thinking of all the ways he had failed her.

He couldn't leave her like this.

Gil bit his lip. He decided right then that, if he couldn't take her with him, he would do to her what he'd done to Payden. He would release her from this prison. It would be a kindness, a mercy. The Ashra he'd known would never want this. It was a betrayal of all that she was, all that she stood for. He knew that if she could, she would even thank him.

Gil looked around, taking a quick survey of the dungeon and the people in it. All of the mages surrounding him were prisoners of one sort or another. He felt sure none of them would have chosen this fate, if they hadn't had their minds and choices taken away from them. He had to release them. He had to release them all. It's what he'd come here for. Suddenly, the task he had set for himself seemed somehow less grim than it had before.

Quietly as he could, he knelt on the rug next to Ashra. He looked down at the chain connecting her to her new lover. He knew the wrist band wouldn't come off; they'd had to sever Payden's hand to remove it from him. But even if he couldn't get the band off, he could still separate her from the man who held her captive.

Gil opened his mind to the magic field and closed his eyes. He reached inside the man and cut one of the main arteries feeding his brain. The man's back went rigid and he issued a sharp gasp. He started to reach for his head. His hands never completed the motion. He dropped dead on the rug without sound or struggle.

Ashra screamed.

And she went on screaming. The room erupted in chaos.

Gil released his shadow web—it took too much concentration to keep it up. He severed the dead mage's wrist with a blade of energy that hit like an axe-blow.

Shrieking, Ashra sprang away from him.

Gil caught her chain and yanked her back.

Snarling, she started to lunge for him. But then she froze, her eyes widening in recognition.

A thunderclap of air exploded between them, hurling Gil backward. He slammed hard against the wall, and something inside him snapped. A stabbing pain pierced his chest, and he sagged down the wall to the floor.

It's a rib, he told himself. *Just a rib.*

Another ball of compressed air streaked toward him. Gil got *Thar'gon* up just in time—the air impacted with the shield thrown up by the talisman, creating a gale-force backlash of wind that lifted people and rugs from the floor and sent them flying. Other magical attacks battered against his shield: thunder and lightning, fire and air, shadow and substance.

Thar'gon deflected them all.

Ashra leaped at him, swinging her chain at his face. He couldn't react in time. The iron chain cracked him in the face. His vision exploded in a shower of sparkling light. Pain followed an instant later. He almost dropped the talisman.

Crying out, he grabbed the end of the chain and wrenched it toward him. Ashra came with it. She dove into him with her fists, snarling and clawing like a cornered animal. He tried to fend her off but couldn't; the magical shield he was holding took every drop of concentration he had. Her fists pummeled his back, her legs kicked his thighs. Her fingernails raked his face.

He couldn't fight both her and the punishing amount of magic being hurled at him—not all at the same time. So he did the only thing he could: he curled his fist into a ball and belted her across the face.

Ashra collapsed.

The magical barrage intensified. Gil clenched his jaw, throwing everything he had into strengthening the light shield, until the dungeon glowed with a white brilliance. The air itself seemed to tremble.

Someone screamed, the kind of ear-splitting shriek only made by the dying.

With a deafening *woosh,* the floor erupted in flames that rushed across the ground. Within seconds, the entire dungeon was covered by a great, fiery carpet. Gil pulled Ashra's unconscious body toward him, stuffing her behind him in the corner. He moved to stand over her, the talisman raised and spewing gouts of light.

Shrieks of agony filled the dungeon, coming from everywhere at once.

All across the floor, men and women thrashed in the flames. A few lived long enough to stagger toward the stairs, but they didn't make it. They collapsed between strides, falling like blazing logs to feed the flames. Gil threw himself back against the wall and stood there drawing heaving breaths, sweat streaming down his face from the atrocious heat. The only thing keeping him alive was the talisman in his hand. The flames only came as far as his shield and stopped as if licking a wall of glass.

When the last of the screams faded to silence, Gil lowered *Thar'gon* and let the flames die. He stood over Ashra, chest heaving, gazing around at the carnage that surrounded him. Dozens of bodies lay blackened on the floor, twisted and smoldering, in some places forming heaps of formless char.

"Oh, gods..." Gil whispered.

41

SURRENDER

Rylan screamed himself awake.

Still screaming, he jerked upright and clutched his head in his hands. An invisible fire scorched his lungs and devoured his flesh. When his breath ran out, he slumped to the floor, where he lay gasping and trembling, too horrified and shaken to react. Xiana thrashed on the cushions next to him, her back arched, hands raking over her body as if trying to beat out nonexistent flames. Eventually, she stopped and lay still, her chest heaving, tears washing her face.

It took Rylan a moment to get his wits about him enough to understand what was happening. Brothers and sisters were dead, killed horrendously. More still were dying. He could feel their suffering, their terror.

"We have to help them!" Xiana gasped, pushing herself off the floor. Her face was white and twisted.

Yes. They had to help—

Rylan scrambled to his feet, but staggered, turning back. He glanced at Amina. His daughter lay curled in a ball, whimpering and sucking her thumb. She couldn't possibly understand what was happening, but she was obviously terrified.

"Stop!" he shouted. "I can't leave her!"

Xiana looked back with disbelief on her face. She took the chain they shared in her hands and pulled, trying to draw him toward her. He knew he had to go, knew he was desperately needed.

But his daughter needed him too.

Rylan growled in desperation, torn in half between two desperate priorities. Xiana jerked harder on his chain, physically hauling him toward the door. She didn't have to pull very hard. Something far more powerful made Rylan back away from his daughter. It was the pressure of the community, conquering his will with all the grace and brutality of a god, crushing any chance of his resistance. With a sob, he turned, leaving his daughter curled on the floor, and followed Xiana toward the stairs.

Amina would be safe there. She *had* to be safe there. Oh, gods...

Surrender!

The command thundered through his head, impacting with the force of a war hammer. Rylan reeled, staggering. He shot a hand out, catching himself on the brick wall of the staircase. It took him a moment to realize that the command had come from Xiana through the link. And even then, he didn't understand what she was asking of him.

SURRENDER!

He could feel Keio Matu cringe. Rylan gasped as Xiana seized the magic inside him and wrenched it away from his control, taking it by force. Reflexively, he struggled to wrest control back, but there was nothing he could do. She was fully in charge: of his magic. Of him.

But that was the way it was supposed to be. Only one mage could control the link. Rylan didn't know how he knew that— he just knew. It was like he'd known his entire life. So he forced himself to yield, opening himself to her fully. When he did, he was bathed in a sweeping feeling of relief.

Surrender...

He understood, now, what was required of him, and he accepted it. It didn't matter who controlled his magic—or even him. What mattered was that he and Xiana work together as one, without adversity or hesitation. She reached out for his hand. He let her take it, then ran with her down the stairs.

Gil moved away from the wall toward the center of the room, stepping over blackened corpses spread across the floor like a grizzly obstacle course. More mages started filing into the chamber, emptying the dungeon's rows of cells where they had been willingly imprisoned. Their magic broke against his light shield, raining sparks and arcing forks of charged current. There were so many mages. Even with the talisman, he was being gradually worn down. There was only so much power the weapon in his hands could deflect.

He would have to try something else.

Sweeping the morning star back over his shoulder, he swung it around with all his might as if delivering a physical blow. The mages nearest him were torn apart by the force of the weapon's strike. The dungeon echoed with the screams of the living and the dying.

Gil swung the talisman again, sweeping it through the air. Bodies hurled backward, striking the walls and rebounding to the floor, where they lay limp and broken. The ground was covered with blood and char, and the air reeked of both. Gagging, Gil lurched forward, driving the remaining mages backward.

The air exploded in front of him, throwing him to the ground. He rolled to a stop against the wall, somehow managing to maintain his grip on *Thar'gon*. He struggled to stand, his vision blurring. The dungeon divided into two red-tinged images that drifted apart and then swam back together again. Disoriented, he staggered forward. Another blow struck him, knocking him to the floor, where he lay groaning.

Looking up, Gil saw a lone pair of mages walking toward him across the chamber with no trace of hesitation in their stride, as though he hadn't just killed dozens of others just like them. The sight of the pair filled him with fear, and he scrambled backward toward the corner where Ashra lay unconscious. Another powerful strike shot toward him through the air. This time, he managed to get the talisman up in time to shield himself from the brunt of it. The impact was still almost enough to knock him out. The light shield wavered, spewing sparks.

Warm liquid bathed his face, and the taste of blood filled his mouth. He was bleeding; he didn't know where from. The chained mages continued toward him, relentless. He knew he wouldn't survive another attack, even with *Thar'gon's* great strength. The two of them linked were far too powerful.

He raised the talisman defensively and used the wall to help drag himself to his feet. He blinked the blood from his eyes, freeing his vision enough to see his two assailants clearly. When he did, he almost dropped the morning star.

Rylan.

"Oh, gods..."

The sight of Darien Lauchlin's son coming to kill him froze him rigid with fear.

But only for an instant.

Gill gripped Ashra's hand, squeezing it tight.

"*Vergis!*" he cried.

The dungeon shuddered and was gone.

Rylan sank to all fours in a room full of his brothers and sisters, all dead or dying. Tears fell from his eyes, and his arms shook so hard they could hardly hold him up. He gazed around at the death surrounding him, overcome by despair. They had suffered a terrible loss.

All at the hands of Gil Archer.

He understood fully why Gil had done it. But he still despised him for it. Rylan felt each death as though it were his own, along with all the suffering that accompanied them. Shaking, he rose from the ground. Xiana threw her arms around him, her face a twisted grimace. Rylan hugged her close, weak with relief that she was unharmed, at that moment sharing more intimacy with her than he had ever shared with another individual in his life. They were joined indelibly: in magic, in life, in purpose, in tragedy. He understood her grief, for it was his own. She was the woman he had died loving, and he'd die loving her again. And again. And again—until the earth ceased to spin and the gods fell from the heavens.

Another man's thoughts. It didn't matter. He welcomed them and made them his own.

Shuddering, Xiana whispered, "Where did he go?"

"The Lyceum," Rylan responded, certain he was right.

"How could he be so powerful, unchained?"

"I don't know." All he knew was that there was nothing more they could do here. Amina was upstairs, and he needed to return to her.

As if sensing his thoughts, Xiana took hold of the chain and backed away from him, saying, "Your daughter is fine. We need to find the man who did this to our brothers and sisters."

She was right. But first, he wanted to check on Amina. He moved toward the stairs.

The chain between them jerked taut. Rylan glanced back at her.

"We are needed," Xiana pressed. "We must go *now!* We need to hunt this man down!"

"I'll come," he said, resigned. But then he caught the chain so she couldn't walk away. "Wait!" When she turned to look at him, he asked firmly, "What will happen to my daughter if I don't come back?"

Xiana's expression froze, and then it collapsed in lines of compassion. Dropping the chain, she leaned into him and kissed his cheek. "Then your Amina will be raised by the community," she assured him. "She will be cherished and cared for. Have no fear for her."

He nodded, greatly relieved. He supposed he'd already known the answer. If he died, Amina would be raised by thousands of loving parents. She would grow to be a beautiful woman with an enormous heart and enormous contributions to make. She wouldn't need his presence to thrive.

Comforted, Rylan moved after Xiana as she picked her way across the room, stepping over the burned and mangled bodies of their fellows.

Surrender.

This time, he obeyed without question, opening his heart and soul to her.

Gil lay Ashra on his own bed and crouched down at her side. Reaching out, he caressed the bloody cut on her cheek. He'd never hit a woman in anger, and the sight of the injury made his stomach wrench. It disgusted him. *He* disgusted him. Before war had come to Karikesh, he'd had no idea what he was capable of. Now he did. The events of the past week had made him conscious of the monster sleeping inside himself. He had looked it in the eyes and recognized its nature. He'd turned into the kind of man he'd always hated, the kind of man he'd sworn he'd never be.

His grip tightened on the talisman, and he healed Ashra's injury. When he opened his eyes, her skin was smooth again, unblemished. He stroked a hand through her hair tenderly. She'd be sleeping for a while. And when she woke up, he had absolutely no idea what to do with her. Standing up, he looked around. The room contained a dust-covered cedar chest that looked a hundred years old, a wobbly desk, and an iron-framed bed with a down mattress. That was all. There was nothing that could be used to restrain a person who didn't want to be there.

He moved for the door but stopped as he got a glimpse of his image in the looking glass over the washbasin. He stood for a moment staring in revulsion at himself, at the blood and soot that covered his clothes and skin. He reached up and ran a grimy hand through his sweat-plastered hair, knocking off a layer of ash.

Bending forward, he retched over the washbasin.

Nothing came up. Gil straightened, wiping his sleeve across his mouth. In the mirror, his eyes were red and scalding, just like the eyes of a madman. He scooped up the black cloak he'd thrown on the floor the previous day. Pinning it on, he looked back at Ashra. He had to leave her there. If she wasn't there when he got back, there was nothing he could do about it.

Blowing out an exasperated breath, he left the room and took the stairs down to the level of the main floor, which was swarming with people. He plowed his way through the crowd. The sight of him was enough to clear a path ahead; he wasn't sure if it was due to the look on his face or his blood-splattered visage. People saw him and backed away with looks of dismay, even people he knew well. Which was fine. No one tried to stop him or talk to him. Even Naia's secretary had the wisdom to stay in her seat when he barreled past her.

At the sight of him, Naia's jaw dropped, and she jerked out

of her seat. The advisors hovering around her desk recoiled, their faces full of shock.

"Gil..." she gasped.

Instead of responding, he glared significantly at the men and women gathered around her desk. Taking his meaning, Naia motioned them out. As they filed through the door, no one made any effort to hide their overt stares. After the door shut behind them, Gil jerked *Thar'gon* off his waist and slammed it down on her desk.

"Take this back," he growled. "I don't want it anymore."

Naia shook her head. Folding her hands on the desk, she told him, "You can't blame the weapon, Gil. And you can't blame yourself either."

He wanted to scream. He turned away from her, hands clenched at his sides, and stood glaring at the wall. "I killed a lot of them," he said, bowing his head. "But there's still more. They'll be coming."

He rubbed his eyes. "I found Rylan. And Ashra..."

His voice broke. He heard the sound of her chair scraping the floor as she rose from her seat, her soft footsteps approaching. He didn't look at her when he felt her hand on his shoulder.

"I'm so sorry, Gil."

He grimaced, clenching his teeth in despair and frustration. "They're not dead," he told her. "I brought Ashra back here. But she's like Payden. She tried to kill me." His voice was trembling. "And Rylan... they have him chained to some woman. He attacked me, and there wasn't anything I could do to defend myself. The two of them together were too damn strong."

Naia drew in a deep breath, her hand stiffening. "Poor Rylan," she breathed. "We will have to make him a priority."

Gil found himself in agreement. "He's a real threat to us."

Naia's shoulders sagged. "If he's anything like his father, I'm sure he is." She turned and walked with her head bowed back across the room.

Gil rubbed his eyes, smothered by weariness. He glanced down at the empty chair in front of Naia's desk, wanting nothing more than to cast his body down into it.

"What would you have me do, Prime Warden?" he asked, his voice full of lead.

It took her a moment to respond. "We'll evacuate the Lyceum. That way our forces can focus on what's most important. Please see to the defenses of the city, Gil. Report to the Sultan. And don't tell him you found his daughter," she added, moving for the door. She paused. "Where is she?"

"My room," he said, turning toward her. "Why? What are you going to do?"

Naia looked at him sadly. "The only thing I can do, Gil."

He threw his head back, her words punching a hole in his gut. Rage coursed through his veins like venom, chewing at his insides. If he had just listened to the Sultan in the first place, everything would be different. They would never have lost the Waterfront, and they wouldn't be on the verge of losing the entire city. Ashra would be whole and at his side, and Naia wouldn't be making her way upstairs to end what was left of her. With a defeated growl, he scooped *Thar'gon* off the desk and whirled for the door.

A thunderous explosion shook the building, knocking him off his feet.

Large chunks of the ceiling rained down on them, and he was showered by hunks of plaster.

Naia screamed.

A wooden beam struck Gil in the head, and his vision went dark. A lancing pain shot through his eyeballs, tearing a cry from his throat. He was encased in rubble. The world was black and lightless, and he couldn't tell if that was because of his injury or because it really was. He could hear Naia somewhere nearby, choking on dust. Clutching *Thar'gon*, he opened himself to the magic field and healed the wound in his scalp. A wave of enormous relief rolled over him and almost swept him away. He felt the last, tenuous threads of consciousness slipping away from him.

"Naia!" he gasped, his voice collapsing in a fit of hacking coughs.

He could hear her moving toward him, feeling her way through the debris, until at last she caught hold of a handful of his cloak. She started shifting chunks of the building off him, but the ceiling cracked sharply, raining more plaster down on them. Afraid the entire building was going to collapse, Gil clenched her hand, stopping her. She didn't have time to dig him out. And there was another way.

Holding her hand tightly, he whispered, *"Vergis."*

The darkness parted, and a thick fog rolled in to encase them. Naia was coughing, lying on her side on the ground. Gil collapsed on top of her, gasping for breath through lungs drowning in dust. He heard scattered shouts accompanied by the sound of running feet. Within seconds, they were surrounded by people. Hands gripped him under the arms, pulling him up. Someone held him upright, barking harsh words at him in Malikari. He didn't understand what was being said, but just hearing the language gave him relief. The Sultan's soldiers had found them.

Breaking free of the man who held him, Gil staggered over to where Naia lay and leaned over her. She was injured, but not badly. He healed her anyway. Then, clutching *Thar'gon*, he turned and looked back at the Lyceum, its roof visible over a row of buildings. Fire was spreading rapidly, tearing through the roof. As he watched, one of the towers collapsed in a shower of sparks. The sight filled him with panic. He raised *Thar'gon.*

"Gil! What are you doing?" Naia gasped, sitting upright.

"I'm going back for Ashra!"

He wasn't sure how, though. He had a good image of what his room looked like, and held it fixed in his mind. What he didn't know was whether that room still existed at all. But there was only one way to find out. He closed his eyes and uttered the Word of Command that activated the talisman.

The world jolted, then went black. His lungs filled with scalding smoke that choked him like a garrote. He was immediately assaulted by a blast of heat and horrifying screams. Orange tongues of hell roared violently above him, visible through the charred slats of wood that made up the ceiling. The heat was appalling.

He whirled to find Ashra balled up in a corner, clutching a wad of blankets around her. Seeing him, she screamed harder, as though the sight of him terrified her more than death by fire. He moved quickly toward her.

She flinched away from him, shrieking, "You monster! *You killed him!*"

Aghast, Gil looked up just in time as part of the ceiling broke, raining hot embers.

"Please, Ashra!" he shouted over the rage of the fire, reaching out for her. "Take my hand!"

She edged away from him. More embers showered down on them from above. The entire ceiling was close to collapse. Choking and gasping, Gil realized he had only seconds to get her out of there. If she wouldn't come, then he'd have to leave her.

"Take my hand or you'll die!" he shouted, his voice edged with panic.

Ashra snarled, baring her teeth, soot and tears streaking her face.

Gil cried out in frustration. Reaching deep inside her, he twisted something there. Ashra's mouth fell open, and her eyes rolled back in her head. He lunged for her. The moment he got his hand around her arm, the roof broke entirely.

"*Vergis!*" he choked.

42

A LOSING BATTLE

GIL STAGGERED AS BROILING AIR TRANSFORMED INTO COOL MIST on his face, the roar of the flames replaced by sounds of shouts and distant screams. He moaned against the searing agony of the burns covering his hands. Ashra lay limp in his arms, her face red and blistered, the fabric of her gown smoldering. Quickly, he healed her burns. He thought about healing his own injuries, but then thought against it. There was a chance he'd pass out, and he couldn't take that risk. He lowered Ashra to the ground gently and knelt beside her.

He looked up at the slapping sound of boots jogging toward him. The Sultan heaved himself down on the ground beside his daughter, scooping her up in his arms and draping her across his lap.

"What's wrong with her?" he growled.

"I healed her," Gil panted. "But they put one of their chains on her—she's not in her right mind."

Sayeed grimaced, then bent to hug Ashra close to him. He rocked her gently, as a father would rock his young daughter, stroking her hair. He rose with Ashra in his arms and started walking with her back across the square. The chain dangling from her arm swayed with each of his jolting strides.

Gil started after them, calling, "Your Majesty! She's dangerous!"

"She's my daughter."

"That won't matter to her," Gil whispered with a terrible, sinking feeling in his gut.

At that moment, a blazing comet arced down from the sky. An enormous fireball impacted with a nearby neighborhood with earth-shaking force. A fountain of flames erupted high in the air.

The Sultan paused in his tracks and swung back toward him. "Do you see that?" he raged from across the square. "Go do your job! Go help my people!"

With that, he lurched toward his tent with his unconscious daughter in his arms. Gil stared helplessly after them as another fireball crackled as it shot by overhead. It was so close to the ground that he ducked, throwing his arms up to shield his head.

The fireball struck the burning Lyceum. With a terrible roar, the entire building collapsed in a great gush of fire and showering embers. Flames roared, threatening the surrounding district.

Gil stood shaking his head slowly, thinking of the thousands of books that graced the shelves of the Lyceum's library. He swallowed dryly, his head murky. He willed his feet to move, but they did so only grudgingly, carrying him toward the barricade. Clutching *Thar'gon* close, he fell in with the current of soldiers swarming in the direction of the front lines.

———

Rylan strode at Xiana's side over one of the improvised bridges their engineers had erected over the canal—a feat accomplished in only a day. They walked hand-in-hand, the thin chain linking them draped from their wrists. Through that connection, Rylan could sense her gratitude that he was there beside her. Though they walked into battle, he was not afraid. He felt confident in a way he'd never felt before a fight. They had each other, a complete and perfect union. With Xiana at his side, he was invincible.

They moved at the head of a column of soldiers, two other *kaiden* of mages following behind them. Overhead, the clouds flickered with an eerie amber glow, reflecting the lights of the fires. Every once in a while, a shooting fireball shot across the night sky, a barrage meant to soften the enemy before the main offensive. The Warlord was taking no chances.

They reached the new encampment erected on the far side of the canal, and there joined the ranks of the soldiers forming up, preparing for the assault. Xiana led him to the head of the lines, where she was greeted by one of their commanders, a grisly old man with a face that looked carved from granite. As Xiana spoke with him, Rylan's attention was drawn toward a large fire burning just to the south of their position, its orange glow bathing the sky. He recognized a building next to it and was sure it was the Lyceum that burned.

He didn't want it to burn.

He brought his hands up to clutch his head against a cyclone of conflicting emotions. He didn't want to kill anyone, didn't want to see the city fall. And yet, another part of him did. He understood why their campaign had to be successful. It was for the good of the Empire, who needed the Lyceum's mages desperately, to defend itself against the hell it had unleashed by the opening of the Sky Portal. It was for the good of the people of Karikesh who, for the past twenty years, had known only instability. And it was for the good of the Kingdoms, which had been fractured in a series of wars that had lasted a thousand years. Once the entirety of the continent was under Imperial rule, then peace would reign from sunrise to sunset, from pole to pole. *Real* peace.

He felt a hand on his arm. Swallowing his emotions, Rylan looked away from the haunting glow of the fire, though its roar still echoed in his ears. Xiana's conversation with the commander had ended, and she stood looking at him with concern written on her face.

"I'm fine," he told her. The conflict within him had been resolved. Residual feelings of sadness remained, but those feelings could be dealt with. The crippling guilt had been eradicated.

Xiana nodded, understanding in her eyes. "It gets easier," she assured him, then kissed him lightly. "Every day will be a little better. I'm worried you're not ready for this yet."

"I'm ready," he said, thinking of the brothers and sisters who'd been slaughtered in their barracks.

"Good," Xiana said curtly. "Because the general is ready."

She led him toward the front of the waiting column of soldiers. They took up position in the advance guard behind a company of pikemen. There, they waited for the other *kaiden* to join them, and for the commander to give the order to march. The nervous tension of the soldiers was evidenced by the shifting of weapons and the rustling of armor. No words were spoken, and yet Rylan knew innately what all must be feeling. Even though they were on the brink of victory, they would have to cut a bloody path to it.

He looked back at the fire consuming the Lyceum, thinking how strange it was that he no longer resented the Malikari invaders who had conquered his homeland. He'd spent two long years of his life fighting them. Two long years he could have spent home with his wife and his children. He'd let a useless war rip him away from his family, and he hadn't been there when it mattered. Instead, he had wasted time and blood fighting a Sultan who had shown him only kindness.

The thought of Sayeed sent a shooting pain lancing through his heart. He'd seen Ashra in the barracks, shortly before the attack. She must be dead with all the others. He closed his eyes and searched for her through his link with the community. He couldn't feel her... and then he did. A small feeling. A small, terrified feeling. Wherever she was, she was in danger. Rylan's throat constricted.

The commander shouted the order to march, and Xiana caught his hand. He looked at her for reassurance. She smiled and kissed his hand. Then the column started forward. He walked beside her as they made their way through the center of the encampment, past rows of tents and thick forests of pickets, and onto the main boulevard that led straight into the heart of the city. The sound of their passage rattled the walls of the buildings, a growing rumble that overwhelmed the cadence of the drums and shimmied the cobbles of the street.

They advanced two blocks unhindered. Then, from out of the night, a dark cloud of arrows rained down upon them, launched from a rooftop on the other side of the street. Before Rylan could react, Xiana threw up a shield to protect them. Arrows hit the shield and exploded, sending shards of iron and slivers of wood ricocheting off the bricks of the building next to them. He glanced up at the bowmen positioned on the rooftop, ducking back behind the cover of a wall. He felt a sharp tug through the chain: the magic field was being drawn into him, through him, summoned by another's will. His first response was to fight the sensation. He had to force himself to relax, to allow it to happen without a struggle. Xiana deftly wove the sum of their mutual power into a shaft of magic that erupted from the rooftop, spewing violent jets of light. The men who weren't torn apart from the blast screamed all the way to the ground, hitting the pavement in a series of dull-sounding thuds.

Rylan shivered as he felt Xiana draw harder on him, absorbing as much of his magic as he could pass to her. The part of him that was Keio Matu reveled in the feel of the pairing. It was familiar, a tender intimacy he had shared with Ilia, though he had always been the one in command of the link. He would have to get use to the sensation of being powerless, fully at another's command. He had not been prepared for how vulnerable he would feel when the roles were reversed. Still, he trusted her with all his mind and soul.

A crackling fireball plowed into a building just a block away, bringing the whole structure thundering down in a roaring maelstrom of flames. When the noise at last settled, it was replaced by the resonating sounds of battle dead ahead: shouts and screams and the ringing clatter of weapons against armor.

Xiana pulled harder through the link. She threw up an absorption shield above them, woven of delicate tendrils of magic. Just a week ago, he would have had no idea what it was. But now, filled with all of Keio's knowledge, he felt certain he could duplicate it. Rylan watched as she expanded the shield to cover the other mages in their group. She probably could have extended it further, but that would risk it becoming too thin. When another volley of arrows plunged from the sky, they struck her shield with a clatter, like a bucket of nails spilled across an old tin roof. Most of the arrows ricocheted off; the rest snapped into bits that fell dead to the pavement.

By then, they were on the edge of the battle. A frantic melee overcame the intersection a block away, where the soldiers of their advance force had engaged the men guarding the Sultan's encampment.

Ahead, a group of Malikari regulars were attempting a sortie. They charged out from behind a series of improvised barricades, bellowing war cries at the top of their lungs, swords and spears hacking a path through the Khar assault force. Again, Rylan felt a powerful stirring as Xiana summoned the magic field through him, using him as a conduit. She waved her hand, and a pool of liquid flames erupted under the feet of the Malikari defenders. The sounds of their screams quickly drowned out the clamor of the battle. Intent on the survivors, she tried to rush forward, but Rylan balked, repulsed by the sight of so many men enveloped in flames.

Xiana looked back and smiled like a child who had just performed an accomplishment that would make her parents proud. Then she called on him again, wrenching him open and drawing magic through him painfully. This time, she wove a ball of flames that coalesced into a blazing fire strike, which she hurled into the thick of the Malikari encampment. Flames gushed high into the air as men and horses screamed and scattered, many leaping over the barricades onto the swords of their enemies.

Laughing, Xiana took Rylan's hand and *pulled,* siphoning a horrendous amount of magic through him. It was excruciating. He gripped his head, biting back a scream. She spun their combined power into a swarming mass of air that ignited as it spun, evolving into a fiery vortex that resembled a tornado. With a cry, she hurled it directly at the enemy.

The mass exploded in midair. Like it hit a brick wall. Rylan could feel Xiana's shock through the link. She drew up short, her eyes widening.

Before them stood Gil Archer, holding a silver morning star that blazed like the sun. Surrounding him a halo of gleaming light, a testament to the enormous amount of power he was drawing, too great for one human body to possibly contain. It leaked out of him in waves, distorting the air. For a second, Rylan stood still, jaw slack, just staring at him. Then it hit him: Gil had countered Xiana's strike.

And he'd done so effortlessly.

Rylan could feel Xiana's frustration. She tore more power from him, taking so much, so fast, that he staggered and almost dropped to his knees. Xiana lifted her hand in the air and made a motion like throwing a spear. A shaft of light shot out of her hand, hurling through the air. Until it reached Gil Archer's shield, where it met a violent and spectacular death.

Xiana screamed in frustration.

Gil brought his weapon around, and a wave of air sped toward them. It impacted before Rylan could get his hands up, bludgeoning him in the face and bowling him over. He lay on the ground, stunned and winded. A galaxy of stars exploded in his eyes. He rolled onto his stomach and struggled to sit up, but another blast of solid air knocked him back to the ground.

Molten fury raged through the link.

Wrenching herself upright, Xiana lifted her arms and summoned a crackling fork of lightning that stabbed down at Gil before he could get a shield up. He went down with a cry, filaments of electricity clawing over his body. Another stab of lightning spiked down, piercing him in the back.

Somehow, he clawed his way upright, getting his weapon up just in time to partially deflect a tidal wave of flames. He wavered over his feet for a moment, then fell to one knee in the center of the blood-slicked street. Half of his face was blistered, the other half covered in grime, his chest heaving.

The sight of him made Rylan wince. He could see it in Gil's eyes: the man was at the end of his strength. The realization ripped him in half.

Xiana sensed it too; Rylan could feel her eagerness through the link. With a cunning smile, she drew mercilessly on his power. Above them, a glowing web of light balled into an attack devastating enough to avenge their fallen brothers and sisters.

Gil brought his hands up, as if such an act could ward off death.

It couldn't.

Nothing could defend against Xiana's wrath. Rylan looked at her, beautiful and glorious and wrapped in power. Then back to Gil, courageous and alone and completely at her mercy. No matter what he'd done back at the citadel, Gil was a good man. Like the Sultan, he was only trying his best to help his people.

Looking into Gil's eyes, Rylan felt a cold thrust of sadness pierce his chest, more powerful and painful than the Word of Command.

This was wrong.

It was all wrong.

The Rylan Marshall he remembered wouldn't be doing this.

He made his decision in an instant—an instant that seemed to last eternity. In that moment, he ceased to be Rylan Marshall and became Keio Matu. He lived his ancient life all over again. He fell in love with Ilia all over again. He watched her laugh and cry and shudder with passion. He married her again. Made love to her again. Held her in his arms as she died again. She was the woman he loved, the woman he'd died loving. She was everything.

But Xiana wasn't Ilia.

And he wasn't Keio Matu.

A tidal wave of anguish broke over him, drenching him in emotions. Flailing wildly at the link between them, Rylan fought to turn it around, to take back control of the magic Xiana was siphoning from him. She gasped and spun around, her face twisted in anger and disbelief. She set her jaw stubbornly and wrenched on him harder. It was too much; he broke quickly. With the chain in place, she was in complete control. All he could do was watch her weave her strike with his stolen power.

But magic wasn't the only defense he had. There were other, darker forces that stirred within him, of a type that chains could never bind. He had a choice. Oh, gods, he had a terrible choice. He didn't want to make it. But if he didn't, Karikesh would fall and Gil Archer would die.

And so would Rylan Marshall.

He closed his eyes and struck out at Xiana with the Onslaught. He heard her scream, a horrendous sound that ripped his heart in half.

Reaching out, he caught her as she fell. He sank to the ground with her in his arms, staring deeply into her dying eyes. Her lips moved, and a shiver of breath passed between them. A thin streak of blood leaked from the corner of her eye, rolling down her cheek like a teardrop. She looked up at him in pained confusion.

"Why...?" she whispered.

He couldn't answer her.

He wept as she died in his arms all over again.

He could feel the moment she left him, through the link. It was like a hot knife stabbing at his soul, and he threw his head back and howled in misery. Through his link with the community, a collective outcry of horror and dismay reverberated through his mind like the outrage of a god. It was horrendous. Unbearable. The only thing he could do was hold her and grieve.

All that was beautiful in the world had been crushed by his own hands. Barely aware of a battle raging over him, he hugged her close and sobbed. He stroked her hair, as if such a gesture could make her forgive him.

But it wouldn't. All the grieving in the world wouldn't bring Xiana back. He bowed his head and sagged against her body.

A glint of color caught his eye. When he realized what it was, he grimaced in agony. Ilia's opal pendant gleamed at him from its golden chain. In a fit of rage, he tore it from her neck. He was about to cast it away, but something stopped him. Instead, he clutched it in his trembling fist.

A Malikari soldier not far from him erupted in flames. Rylan looked up and, through eyes bleary with tears, saw that the city's defenders were overwhelmingly losing. Bodies littered the street, most wearing green and black uniforms. The Sultan's men were retreating, but not fast enough. The defenders were being mowed down by a devastating assault of magic they had no hope of defending against. They were losing far more than their own lives—they were losing the entire city.

Rylan didn't realize he'd removed the shackle connecting him to Xiana until it was off his wrist. Immediately, the god-like outrage of the community vanished from his head. The relief was so vast, so intense, that he fell to the ground, gasping. He lay on the cobbles next to Xiana, panting and quivering.

A second later, he was being trampled. He struggled to rise, but a heavy boot impacted with his face. Another hammered his ribs. A body fell on top of him, crushing the air from his chest. He was cracked in the head again and again, and his vision went black.

His head throbbed in agony. He couldn't breathe, couldn't see. He struggled weakly, trying to rise. His stomach lurched. He fought his way to his feet and stood there, reeling, unable to see through the blood washing into his eyes. He wiped it away and glanced around, his vision red-stained and murky.

All around him, the Sultan's men were being pummeled by magic. Within seconds, a score of men were cut down, then another score seconds later. Everywhere he looked, soldiers exploded in flames. Others were crushed. Still others were shredded like stew meat. Rylan watched it all in abject horror. He watched until he couldn't bear it any longer.

Then he reacted.

He opened himself fully to the magic field, filling himself with as much raw power as he could draw, until it seeped from his pores. Reaching out, he flung everything he had at the ranks of the Turan Khar. Men screamed and went down. He lashed out again at the Khar forces, burning fiery holes through armor and flesh, taking down rank after rank in quick succession. He strode forward through the embattled street, carving a path paved in blood. Seeing the destruction he was weaving, soldiers broke from the fight and rushed toward him, determined to bring him down.

None reached him.

He killed and killed until there was nothing left to kill. Until he stood alone in an intersection littered with heaps of steaming flesh. Then he stopped and stood still, all his strength leaking out of him.

He looked around as slow degrees of horror crept over his skin. He turned slowly, taking in the carnage he had wrought. His stomach clenched, and he became suddenly, unbearably ill. He fell to his knees and vomited, retching again and again until there was nothing left to bring up.

Then he dropped to the street and sobbed.

The woman he loved was dead. He had killed her. His daughter was now lost to him. He had brutally slain hundreds of people who had only fought because they had no choice, because they didn't have the will or the knowledge to resist.

He wanted to die. He *needed* to die. He reached out for the magic field and wrenched it in as hard as he could. Sharpening it into a weapon, he took aim at himself.

"Rylan!"

He dropped his hold on the field.

It was Gil's voice. The battlemage was shaking him as if trying to wake him from sleep. Rylan clenched his eyes shut and hugged himself. He couldn't face Gil, couldn't face anyone.

"Rylan!" Gil gasped again, grabbing him by the arms and rolling him onto his back.

He opened his eyes and looked up through a pall of grief into Gil's blistered and grime-smeared face. He struggled for words but couldn't find any. All he could do was shake his head and weep.

"I've got you," Gil said, hauling him upright. With his other hand, he clutched his spiked weapon against him and said a word.

The world lurched.

The street disappeared.

43

TO MAKE AN END

RYLAN LOOKED AROUND, TAKING IN THE SIGHT OF A MILITARY encampment swarming with flames and commotion. Soldiers were sprinting in every direction, and everywhere he looked, wounded and dead were laid out in rows or, more often, lying where they fell. Disoriented and weak, he sagged against Gil, clinging to him desperately. It was all he had strength for.

He didn't look up at the sound of running feet. Gil steadied him, holding him upright, even though his knees wanted to buckle under his weight. He couldn't stop weeping. Xiana's pale, dead face filled his mind, haunting him from the afterlife.

"He saved me," he heard Gil say. "He killed the woman he was chained to then he just kept killing everyone. He took down an entire battalion on his own."

There was a long pause.

"Is he in his right mind?" asked a calm voice. A woman's voice.

"I don't think so," Gil said after a moment's hesitation. "I don't have time to find out."

Rylan squeezed his eyes shut, fighting against tears that wouldn't stop coming. If anything, they came harder.

"Go do what you have to do," the woman's voice said softly. "I'll do what I have to."

Another long pause.

Gil eased him down to the ground and knelt beside him, setting a hand on his back. It was a kind gesture, but Rylan took little comfort in it. He was far beyond comfort. Nothing could ever make a difference.

"Thank you," Gil said in a gruff voice. "I'm sorry. I really am."

Then he left. Rylan listened to the sounds of his footsteps walking away. Wiping his eyes, he glanced up at the woman. It took him a moment to recognize her. The Prime Warden's face was covered in soot, her hair in disarray. There was a heavy weight about her presence he didn't remember from before. She knelt beside him.

"Do you know who I am?" she asked.

"Aye," he answered, struggling to get the word out past the knot in his throat. He wiped the tears from his eyes, but they came right back. The grief he felt was incapacitating. He just wanted it to end.

Naia asked, "Do you know who you are? And what you've done?"

This time, all he could do was nod.

"Then you understand why I can't let you live," she whispered in his ear.

Her words steadied him. He felt the comforting warmth of hope. She was going to give him what he wanted, what he yearned for: a release. That was the best he could ask for. He would thank her gladly, if he could. But he couldn't; all he could do was weep.

She squeezed his hand. "Are there any last words you wish to say?"

"No." He shook his head roughly. He wanted it over. Wanted it over *now*. He couldn't stand it any longer.

"*Stop!*" a man's voice commanded. "Move away from him!"

Naia rose to her feet, stepping back. "He's too dangerous. He could turn on a whim—"

"Then I'll kill him myself!"

Strong arms were suddenly around him, jerking him to his feet. A man who smelled powerfully of blood and sweat pulled him roughly into a tight embrace and kissed his cheek.

"I thought you were dead."

It was the Sultan's voice. Rylan had almost forgotten what it sounded like. He opened his eyes and took in the sight of the man's bearded face, bloodied and bruised and mottled with grime. But underneath all those layers were a pair of brown eyes full of concern and compassion.

"Can you walk?" Sayeed asked.

Rylan nodded. He leaned heavily against him as he let the Sultan guide him across the chaotic encampment toward a pavilion on the far side. The tent was surrounded by soldiers wearing tattered blue uniforms tied with long gold sashes. Upon sight of them, two started forward, but Sayeed waved them brusquely away. When they reached the tent, he swatted back the flap and supported Rylan as he limped into the space. Rugs covered the interior, which was divided into rooms by hanging cloth partitions. Sayeed led him through the first drape of cloth, then lowered him down on a bed of cushions.

Rylan sagged into the pillows as every ounce of strength he had left his body all at once, draining out of him like water and leaving him hollow and aching. The tears threatened to come back again. He pressed his fists against his eyes, denying them.

"You are like her, aren't you?" Sayeed asked, his voice hoarse and dismal.

Like her? Rylan didn't know what he meant. He cracked his eyes open, straining to focus enough to see what the Sultan was talking about.

What he saw shocked him. He was lying next to Ashra. Her

body was so close to his, he could touch her by just flexing a finger. She lay curled on the pillows, her hands tucked beneath her chin. Her eyes were red and dim, staring straight ahead at some fixed point above his head. The sight of her brought with it a renewed sense of grief. He understood her pain, knew how excruciating it was. He reached out and stroked his fingers down her cheek, wiping away a tear.

Sayeed knelt beside him. "Is there anything that can be done for her?" he asked.

Ashra was the Sultan's daughter. No wonder Sayeed's voice sounded so weighted by defeat. For a moment, he considered softening the truth. But then he decided against it. Anything less than the truth would be a disservice to them both.

He took Ashra's hand in his, desperately wishing he could ease her suffering. Looking at the Sultan, he told him, "If you love her, then you'll let her go—let her go back to them. That's the only way she'll ever be happy."

Sayeed's face compressed into a grimace of wrath. Bringing his hands up, he shook his head savagely. "No!" he growled. "*Do not ask that of me.*"

Fresh tears spilled down Rylan's cheeks as he gazed into Ashra's tormented face. He squeezed her hand, wishing he could impart some type of strength into her. But he couldn't; he didn't have enough for himself, and certainly none to give.

He looked back up at the Sultan, wishing he had any other advice. But he didn't. Nothing else would help. Sayeed had to know that. If he wouldn't let her go, then there was only one other humane option left. He knew what he would want. What he did want.

He whispered, "If you can't let her go, then take pity on her. Don't let her suffer."

Hearing his words, the Sultan threw his head back and let out a soul-shuddering moan. He covered his face with his hands and sat in silence, every muscle rigid. He remained like that for a long time. Eventually, he drew in a deep breath and let it out again in one, great sigh.

"I always wanted a daughter," he said dismally. Leaning forward, he brushed a lock of Ashra's hair back out of her eyes. "My people have a saying: a beautiful daughter is a father's greatest joy. And also his greatest sorrow." He looked at Rylan with a bitter scowl. "What are they like? The Turan Khar?"

Rylan didn't know how to answer him. It took him a moment to formulate a reply. "They're not evil," he said at last. "In many ways, they're better than us. If you let her go back to them, she'd lead a fulfilling life. She'd know love."

Staring bitterly at his daughter's face, the Sultan stroked his hand through Ashra's raven hair. "Would she truly be happy? If I let her go?"

Rylan nodded. "Aye."

Sayeed bowed his head and rubbed his eyes. Then he sat staring at a smear of grease on the rug for a very long time, as if that single imperfection was the most important thing in the world. At length, he nodded. He leaned forward and collected his daughter in his arms and sat rocking her softly, sweetly, stroking her hair. He kissed her forehead. Then he whispered something in her ear.

At the sound of his words, Ashra stirred. She gasped, her eyes filling with life and light. She sat up and kissed his cheek, then rose to her feet, Sayeed rising with her. She wrapped her arms around his neck and hugged him fiercely.

"Thank you, baba," she said in a joyous whisper.

Then she turned and fled the tent.

Rylan watched her go. He lay in the spread of cushions, staring at the cloth partition fluttering in her wake. His spirit went with her. The rest of him remained behind, empty and broken. He wanted to go too. But he knew that he couldn't.

He looked up at the sound of a soft sob. Sayeed slouched next to him, weeping quietly into his hands. It was a sad and disturbing sight, one he had never expected to see. From outside the tent came the distant sound of dual explosions. The Sultan didn't react. Rylan wasn't sure if he'd even noticed them.

Minutes went by. Eventually, Sayeed wiped his eyes and looked at him. "What about yourself?" he asked. "Will you be able to live apart from them?"

Rylan closed his eyes, and Xiana's image came back to torture him. He had killed his love. Nothing he could do would ever bring her back. And nothing in the world would ever ease his guilt.

"I don't want to live," he said softly.

More explosions trembled the ground, this time much closer. Sayeed glanced up, his gaze wandering the mottled roof of the tent. The canvas lit up, backlit by fires that flickered for a few seconds then were gone. At last, the Sultan nodded, as if affirming some inner thought or resolution. He took Rylan's hand in his and drew it close, squeezing his fingers so hard they hurt.

"Then come with me," he said with a look of great intensity. "Fight at my side as your father once did. Let us make an end together."

Rylan looked at the strong brown fingers clasped around his own. For two years, he had brought war to this man and his people, thinking them his enemy. And yet, in the end, the Sultan was the only true friend he had left. The offer he made was a good one. A hard one, but good. It was the best end Rylan could see for himself.

He nodded weakly.

Sayeed stood and helped him to his feet, steadying him with a rock-hard grip on his arm. For a moment, Rylan felt lightheaded. He rubbed the greasy sweat off his brow, finding the strength to stand on his own.

"I'm all right," he said.

The Sultan's gaze dropped to Rylan's side, and a wistful

expression came over his face. "You still bear my sword. How has it served you?"

Rylan glanced down at the curved scabbard, feeling suddenly sentimental about it. He wished he could tell Sayeed his sword had been put to good use. It shamed him that he had surrendered to his enemy after only drawing his weapon once.

"I'm sorry, Your Majesty," he said, bowing his head. "I never got the opportunity to use it."

Sayeed nodded. Then he clapped Rylan on the shoulder. "Then let's go find an opportunity."

He walked toward the tent's exit, then looked back to make sure Rylan was following. Rylan took one last glance around the dim interior, his gaze lingering on the bed of pillows where Ashra had lain. An unexpected flare of jealousy stabbed his heart. He envied her. Gods, he envied her. He wished he could go back to them too. But for him, it wasn't that easy. Ashra hadn't killed the man she'd shared the bond with and hadn't turned against the community herself. Rylan knew he could never go back. Shiro would either kill him or chain him to someone else. Only, this time, he would make sure no amount of resistance was left in him, and the only way to do that would be to break his mind. The part of him that was Keio Matu knew that such tortures had once been practiced. And that part of him feared such a torment more than anything.

No. There could be no going back.

Rubbing the last of the tears from his eyes, he followed the Sultan out of the tent. The moment he ducked through the flap, the reality of war descended upon him. In the near distance, he could make out the chaotic sounds of battle. Explosions lit up the night just a few blocks away, sure signs that mages were still alive and active in the struggle. He thought of Gil and wondered how he was faring. Then he thought of Ashra. He hoped she could make it back, but he feared for her.

As he followed the Sultan across the square, he breathed in

the wretched smell of the camp, a heady combination of smoke, blood, and fear-sweat. In a way, it was liberating, knowing that soon he would be free of all this. His mind went to Xiana, and he even dared to hope. He would be reunited with her soon. He prayed she could find it within herself to forgive him. Perhaps, in death, Keio and Ilia could finally be united, to experience the love that had been denied them for so many centuries. He wanted to believe it was possible. He prayed it was.

As they crossed the square, a cluster of the Sultan's elite guards detached themselves from their posts and sprinted toward them. Seeing them, other soldiers followed, even wounded who could barely pick themselves up off the ground. Many were heavily bandaged, their uniforms bloodied, their armor split and dented. And yet there was no defeat in their eyes. An officer trotted forward and drew up before the Sultan.

"Rally what men you can find who can still hold a weapon," Sayeed ordered. "Fall back to the palace. We will cover your retreat."

The officer rose from the ground, a look of dismay on his face. Before he could protest, the Sultan ungirded the gem-encrusted sword and its matching dagger from his hips, handing them over.

"Give these to my son," he said as the officer relieved him of the weapons.

The man's face paled, but he asked without objection, "Which son, Your Grace?"

The Sultan scowled. "Whichever son survives."

A blazing fireball shot down from the clouds, pummeling a building directly to the east. Officers started bellowing commands and, within seconds, the encampment was being mobilized to withdraw.

Sayeed placed his hand on Rylan's shoulder. "We'll form a rearguard and make our stand over there," he said, pointing toward a cluster of barricades and pickets that blocked off the north side of the square from the approaching streets. "It will be just the two of us, along with my personal guard. Are you agreeable to that?"

Rylan nodded absently, his gaze lingering on the series of barricades ahead. Although he could tell some work had been put into them, they wouldn't be enough. He wondered how long the Sultan expected the rearguard to hold the square—and why he wanted to. Any number of officers could have covered the retreat. It didn't make sense that Sayeed would risk himself. Perhaps to lend fortitude to his men. More likely because he knew the fight was already lost. Looking around at the numbers of brutally injured standing and holding weapons, Rylan thought that might be the case.

"Do they speak to you, these people of the enemy?" Sayeed asked. "Can you still hear them?"

Rylan looked at him, surprised not only by the questions, but also by his own reaction to them. A great, aching emptiness clenched his middle, threatening to squeeze more tears out of him. "Not anymore," he whispered.

The Sultan nodded, looking thoughtful. "How did you escape them?"

Rylan thought back on the answer to that question, an act that only brought more hurt. He felt the tears run down his cheeks. He didn't try to stop them. All he could see was Xiana's face, and the pain of betrayal in her eyes. He clenched his jaw and balled his fists, his whole body shaking. He glared at the meager defense offered by the barricades, thinking death could not come soon enough.

"When my son was killed, there was a man," he said slowly. "He told me that if I valued my daughter's life, I had to swear an oath to Xerys."

Sayeed gasped.

"What else would you have me do?" Rylan asked contemptuously. "I pledged myself to the same godsdamned devil my father did. So that's how I did it. Their chains couldn't bind that part of me. I used the power of hell to kill the woman I was shackled to, and then I took their damn chain off my wrist and threw it away."

The Sultan listened to him with a look of shock. *"Ishil'zeri!"* he exclaimed. "You truly are your father's son!"

The statement hit Rylan like a punch in the throat, for it was true. "I know," he said, hating himself.

Sayeed reached out and caught Rylan behind the head, gripping his hair in an iron fist. "Look at me!" he growled, his voice coarse with anger. "Your father was not evil, and neither are you! Darien Lauchlin was the most courageous man I have ever known." He let go of Rylan, but the fierceness didn't leave his eyes. "Never be ashamed to be like your father. Do you understand? Be proud."

Rylan nodded, wishing he could believe him. Almost, he thought he could. The Sultan had surprised him by defying his expectations from the outset. Instead of a tyrant, Rylan had found him to be honorable. Even admirable. Not the cruel dictator he had been led all his life to believe. Perhaps it was the same with his own father. Perhaps Darien Lauchlin really was the hero this man kept claiming him to be. He hoped so.

Another battery of explosions shook the square. Another nearby building collapsed. Rylan staggered, his chest vibrating. Sayeed grabbed his arm and pulled him toward the breastworks. Ahead, the sounds of the battle grew more frantic. Before they reached the barricade, Rylan could already see the futility of it all. The Sultan's men were far outnumbered, their position untenable.

Sayeed pulled him down behind a fortification that was little more than a pile of burlap sacks bulging with potatoes. From there, they ducked into a confined space that projected out into the street, bordered by crates and occupied by eight other men, all wearing the blue and gold uniforms of the elite guard. When Sayeed entered the bastion, the men acknowledged his arrival with dips of the head, but that was all. Anything more would announce his value as a target. He shouted something in Malikari to a man with a leathery face who looked like he might be in charge. Rylan turned his attention to the sounds of battle on the other side of the barrier, uninterested in hearing the reports.

When Sayeed was done giving directives, he crouched down beside Rylan, setting a hand on his back. "They are preparing to assault us directly," he said. "Their numbers are far superior, so we will surely be overrun. The best we can hope for is to slow them enough to cover the retreat."

Rylan listened to his words without reacting; the situation was what it was—which was why he was there: to make an end, as the Sultan had put it. Looking around at the other men hunkering behind the barricade, he realized they were all there for the same reason. The thought made Rylan sad. Most looked like good men, men who didn't deserve to die. Unlike himself.

Two more explosions jarred the ground, and fire erupted from a redan out in front of their position. Soldiers engulfed in flames rolled on the ground or threw themselves mindlessly over the breastworks.

"Here they come!" someone shouted.

The air was suddenly filled with the cries of men and the loud rattling of arrows striking helms and shields. There was an explosion. Close this time. The ground heaved, hurling Rylan off his feet, pieces of the street raining down to batter him. He rolled over, scrambling onto his elbows. The man next to him fell over dead, and so did the next one. The man after that was just a boy, who looked at him with tears in his eyes.

"Is it going to hurt?" he whimpered.

"No," Rylan whispered.

The word barely left his mouth before the boy tumbled

backward in a spray of blood. Rylan gazed sadly at the still figure, glad the arbalest's bolt hadn't made a liar out of him. He turned to find Sayeed lying on the ground, a crossbow quarrel protruding from his chest. His officers rushed to form a frantic ring about him.

Rylan reacted without thinking. He scrambled forward and crouched at the Sultan's side. With a twisting motion, he worked the bolt out from between Sayeed's ribs and flung it away. Then he placed both hands on the Sultan's chest and sent a potent mixture of healing energies burrowing into the wound. He closed his eyes, feeling the flesh beneath his fingers start to mend, the wound shrinking and then closing entirely. When he opened his eyes, the Sultan was unconscious but alive.

He couldn't stay that way, or he wouldn't be alive very long. Rylan smacked his cheeks, shaking him hard to bring him back to his senses. Sayeed startled awake with a great gasp, hands groping at his chest. He blinked his eyes in confusion, looking up at Rylan groggily. The ground shook again, rocking their position. Rylan hauled Sayeed upright, supporting him with a hand under his arm.

"Your Grace, they're breaking through!" someone shouted.

Rylan glanced in the direction the man pointed, to the other side of the intersection, where an explosion had breached the barricade. A group of city regulars were fighting a losing battle to defend the breach but were dropping faster than they could be replaced. Rylan transferred Sayeed's weight to an officer and started toward the breach, weaving a light shield as he walked. A barrage of arrows peppered the ground around him, others ricocheting off his shield. Ahead, enemy soldiers overran the breach, hacking through the last of the struggling defenders. Rylan threw his hands up, and fire erupted beneath their feet.

Men screamed and ran, trailing flames after them. Most

collapsed to the ground after only a few steps. The others he brought down individually. His chest tightened from the ache of knowing he had just sent more brothers to their graves. These could have been men fighting to defend him. They should have been.

But their deaths weren't on him. They were on Shiro.

The street erupted in front of him, and then every building surrounding the square seemed to explode all at once. He was knocked off his feet by the concussions, the noise so deafening that it trembled his bones. He couldn't hear after that, nothing but a high-pitched tone that whistled in his ears. It took him long seconds to recover, for the debris to settle. Then another barrage of flaming missiles rained down on the city, shuddering the ground and thundering the air.

Rylan hauled himself to his feet and looked around. Behind the breastwork he'd abandoned, the ground was on fire. Dead men lay everywhere, some burning, others not. Enemy soldiers poured through gaps in the barricade, quickly overwhelming the defenders that were left. He didn't see any sign of Sayeed. He trudged forward, fists balled, looking out at the world through bleary eyes that had seen too much.

"Back!" one of the last remaining officers shouted. "Move back!"

The man's head snapped around as a crossbow quarrel plugged him in the mouth. He flopped to the ground, where he lay twitching. Rylan turned away. He strode forward, hurling fire at the advancing men. Behind him, more Khar soldiers spilled into the square through multiple gaps in the breastworks. Rylan finished off the last of the soldiers in front of him, then glanced behind to find the entire square overrun.

A hand caught his shoulder, and he whirled, reaching for the magic field. He recognized the Sultan an instant before he would have killed him.

"What can you do?" Sayeed demanded, nodding behind

them to where enemy soldiers had engaged the last of his rearguard.

"There's too many," Rylan said. "And they're too mixed in with our own men."

"Damn our own men," the Sultan growled. "Burn everything."

And so Rylan did. Dropping the magic field, he reached instead for the Onslaught, drawing the tainted energy into him and then hurling it outward at the fighting. An explosion of green fire erupted in the midst of the square, eviscerating bodies and dousing the ground with boiling blood. The soldiers who survived fled and ran. He realized the Sultan was staring at him, a mixture of wonder and disgust written simultaneously on his face.

A large group of men raced toward them from the other side of the square. Rylan closed his eyes and drank in the Onslaught, saturating himself. Before he could release it, something plowed into him, tossing him to the ground like a ragdoll. He landed on his back and lay there stunned, his breath lost somewhere in his chest. He reached for the magic field.

It wasn't there.

Startled, he fumbled blindly for the Onslaught.

It, too, was gone.

Rylan froze. Somehow, they had found a way to chain that part of him too. He heard a crunching sound beside his face. Looking up, he saw a man looming over him in layers of black robes, a bone-handled dirk thrust through the sash at his waist. Rylan let his gaze wander slowly upward. When at last he got a look at the man's face, he winced in shock.

Shiro Nagato stood over him, arms folded across his chest.

44

WARLORD

GIL HAD FALLEN BACK TO THE PALACE ALONG WITH THE BULK OF the Sultan's forces. Now he paced nervously along the wall-walk, watching the lights of explosions flaring in the distance. They came slowly at first, then all at once, one after another in quick succession, until they climaxed in a crescendo of flames and ground-shaking thunder. When the barrage finally stopped, all was still and silent, save for a smoke-fed breeze. The city of Karikesh had fallen with a gasp. He drew in a long, shuddering breath, knowing the enemy would soon be upon them.

What was left of the defending army had withdrawn with him to the palace. The gates remained open, admitting a panicked flow of people flooding in from the surrounding districts, seeking refuge from the enemy advance. They would find none. He'd seen the size of the Khar offensive force and had experienced first-hand the capabilities of their mages. He knew that all the palace's intricate fortifications wouldn't be enough.

Andarapi Palace had been built for a siege. The grounds had been designed in a series of concentric courtyards, each with its own fortified wall. There were five courtyards in all, and each wall would have to be breached before the palace itself could be taken. Under any other circumstance, the Sultan's palace would be a bastion of refuge, virtually unconquerable. But not before this army. Their linked mages would simply pummel them with fire strikes until they submitted.

He glanced across the courtyard to where the Prime Warden stood waiting, watching events unfold from the safety of a guard tower. The Outer Court below them was lit by many bonfires and bursting with terrified civilians. They had seen the climactic bombardment of fiery missiles, and they knew what it meant. The influx of refugees was quickly becoming unsustainable, the street in front of the gate overrun by a panicked horde.

Another explosion shook the palace, this time much closer. He looked up and down the length of the wall, at the battlemages he'd stationed along it, and felt a sinking dread. They were the only battlemages left, just the five of them. And when they were gone, there would be no others. Gil nodded at the man nearest him, a grizzled old warrior with a tattooed face named Cort. The mage spat a wad of leaf-juice out the side of his mouth and did nothing to acknowledge him.

"Warden."

Gil turned to find three men drawing up behind him. Two were Zakai, the Sultan's elite guard. The other was a man with a closely trimmed beard, a little younger than himself, wearing a richly embroidered tunic—not exactly battlefield attire. Probably a noble's son, by the look of him. Gil frowned at the man as he approached, not having the time or patience for nobility.

"Warden Archer," the young man said, inclining his head. For all his rich costume, he looked patently terrified. "My name is Selim. Please tell me how to instruct my men, so that their efforts can best support your mages."

Gil stared at him for a moment, frowning as he studied the young man's face. Selim's hair was wavy and shoulder-length, his nose prominent in a way that served his face. It was his eyes, more than anything, that Gil recognized. He'd seen those eyes before. This was the Sultan's son.

"Well met, Selim," he said.

While the man fidgeted with his high collar, Gil glanced back down at the street below the gate, where the bedlam was becoming a crisis. The courtyard on the other side was full; there was no place to stuff any more people. Not that it mattered.

"Man the outer wall lightly," he said. "We'll let them take it, then stop them at the Second Court. Let's pack them in here between walls, as thickly as we can. Once they're pinned, we can take our time about killing them."

The prince paled visibly, looking even more nervous than he had moments before. "What would you have me do with the people in the Outer Court?"

"Evacuate them to the inner wards," Gil told him.

Beads of glistening sweat had broken out all across Selim's brow. His gaze darted to the crowd below, then back to Gil. At last he nodded, puffing out his cheeks with a heaving sigh. "We'll have to close the gate, then."

With that, the prince turned and strode away, flanked by his retinue. Gil watched him as he took the stairs down from the battlements and descended into the roiling courtyard, his senior officers raising the cry of, "Close and bar the gate! Clear the ward!"

Rylan looked around the circle of men and women and felt torn physically in half. Many of them were mages who had shared the bond with him. He knew them all, if not their names, and knew them well. They were all beautiful souls with generous hearts. He longed for their forgiveness and their companionship. He yearned for the chain they had bound him with, that linked him heart and mind to the community. Now he was cut off from them, and the agony that brought was unimaginable. The only emotions he felt were his own, and that isolation was devastating.

He knew it was deserved. He had killed Xiana, his *desan,* along with dozens—if not hundreds—of others. He could already see his fate clearly written in the eyes of Shiro's unchained mages standing across the circle from him. Their hatred of him was unmistakable and unbearable. Rylan couldn't face them; he had to look away. He would end his own life if he could and spare them the trouble. But he could not. Somehow, they had shielded him not only from the magic field but also from the Onslaught. He was helpless, completely at their mercy. His life and death were now in Shiro's hands alone.

The Warlord moved toward him and took Rylan's face in his hand. His long-nailed fingers squeezed his cheeks, digging painfully into Rylan's flesh. His eyes were like a black abyss, and they sucked him down. Within those eyes, he saw his own damnation, full of suffering and torment and every torture in between. Terrified, he tried to look away, but the iron strength of Shiro's fingers denied him even that mercy. The Warlord increased the pressure until Rylan moaned, then pulled sharply away, retracting his hand. He moved back into the center of the circle, to view both Rylan and Sayeed at the same time.

"I'm sorry, Father."

Ashra's voice. Startled, Rylan turned as she squeezed between him and Sayeed, kissing her father's cheek as she brushed past. She continued on into the center of the circle and there went to her knees before Shiro. Eyes lowered, she offered him the empty chain still attached to her wrist. The Warlord didn't take it. Instead, he gestured behind him. Ashra obeyed, assuming a place in the circle of mages between two who welcomed her with a tight embrace.

The Warlord issued a nod, and another man stepped forward: one of the mages of Shiro's inner circle, an old man of golden skin and thinning gray hair, who wore a gray *yori* robe. A mage of Xiana's kin, Rylan supposed. All of Zahra's mages had been captured by the Turan Khar. He wondered how long ago that had been.

The unchained mage went to stand before Sayeed. "You are the Sultan?"

Sayeed nodded. "I am."

The mage motioned with his hand to indicate his master. "You stand in the presence of Shiro Nogato, Warlord of the Turan Khar. If you kneel and pledge fealty, your life will be spared."

Sayeed looked at the Warlord. "No."

He spoke the word firmly, without hesitation, his face showing no sign of fear. Nor did he show sign of malice. He stood straight and still, a proud man, but not an arrogant one. He gazed calmly straight ahead, his eyes pinned on something behind Shiro. Rylan followed Sayeed's gaze and realized he was looking at his daughter.

"Father..." Ashra said softly, tears gathering in her eyes.

Rylan opened his mouth, wanting to beg him to reconsider. Shiro was not a man of mercy. But one look at the Sultan's face stopped him from objecting. In Sayeed's eyes, he saw a strong sense of peace and purpose that reminded him of why they were there in the first place: to make an end. He realized this was the end the Sultan had chosen for himself.

Shiro turned and stepped out of the ring. As he did, two unchained mages came forward and, taking Sayeed's arms, walked him out to the spot the Warlord had just relinquished. They left him there, alone, in the center of the circle, facing his weeping daughter. Rylan's breath caught. He knew what was coming. He didn't want to watch, but he couldn't look away.

Somehow, Sayeed conjured a loving smile for his daughter. And then he burned.

"That's the last of them!" Qoyle shouted.

Gil looked down at the Outer Court, relieved to find it finally emptied. All the civilians had been successfully evacuated to the palace interior, freeing the outer bailey to be used as a kill zone. Hundreds more civilians were trapped in the street on the other side of the gate, clamoring and pounding and bleeding to get in. They were trapped between a closed gate and an advancing army, and they knew it. There were mothers down there with children. It didn't matter. He didn't dare open the gate.

A sustained droning sound came from somewhere in the distance, softly at first, then rising gradually. He had no idea what it was. It sounded like a dozen gusts of wind howling through the city streets, each gust with its own eerie tone. The noise kept growing, multiplying, adding additional layers, until it seemed to be coming from every direction, reverberating throughout the city.

All at once, thousands of screaming people came pouring out of the side streets, smashing into the crowd already gathered in front of the palace gate. Chaos ensued. At the same time, a barrage of fire strikes streaked down from the sky, taking out whole buildings. One slammed into the street a few blocks away, sending a rush of broiling air gushing toward the palace. Another strike tore a portion of the castle wall apart, hurling burning men and smoldering stones into the street. The immensity of the noise was deafening. For seconds after, there was silence. No one moved.

Then the screams began. Terrified civilians erupted from the ground and lunged for the gate, jostling their way forward or climbing over each other, pounding and clawing their hands bloody on the portcullis.

Gil brought the talisman up and drew in as much power as he could. He flung a shield over the people battering on the gate. That was as good as he could do; the shield was stretched as thin as he dared. Anymore, and it wouldn't take a direct hit.

The screams intensified. Khar soldiers were gathering at the far end of the street, waiting for the bombardment to stop before engaging. Gil felt suddenly ill, his stomach wrenching. Off to the side of the street, the burned body of a boy dangled from a tree limb. Below his feet, hundreds were being trampled or crushed. He couldn't stand the sound of their screams.

He called down to Selim, "Open the gate! Let them in!"

There was no answer. He looked down to where the prince and his guards had been standing and saw nothing but a pile of rubble. He wanted to scream in frustration.

"*Open the godsdamned gate!*" he shouted to anyone who could hear.

For a moment, nothing happened. Then the wall he stood on rattled with the turning of winches, as the portcullis was raised. A crowd of thousands rushed the opening, some squirming under the portcullis even before its teeth were a foot off the ground. Up the street, enemy soldiers had already engaged the rear of the crowd, cutting down the slowest while driving the panicked masses before them. Soon there was a bottleneck of people struggling through the gate. Those in the front of the mob couldn't move fast enough to keep up with the weight of the crowd crushing them from behind.

Another fireball arced down from the sky, this one aimed directly at the gate. Gil redirected his shield at the last moment. The blazing missile exploded above him, scorching the air. The recoil sent him hurling backward, slamming into the stone merlon behind him. Before he could recover, another fire strike was already inbound.

The Khar mages weren't aiming at the gate, he realized. They were targeting him.

Picking himself up, he raised the talisman over his head.

"*Vergis!*" he shouted.

Rylan staggered over to Ashra, catching her in his arms. He turned her away from the sight of her father's smoldering body, cradling her against him as she sobbed into his chest, her whole body shaking. Tears gathered in his own eyes. He had seen too many good people die. Too much horror, too much of it committed by himself.

"Move back," the unchained mage commanded.

The rest of Shiro's entourage backed away, leaving Rylan alone with Ashra in the center of a new, expanding ring. They were preparing to kill him, he realized. To immolate him the way they had just executed the Sultan. Only, it wasn't just him they intended to kill. They had left Ashra with him in the center of the circle.

He shoved her away from him as hard as he could, propelling her toward the outside of the ring. But the people there caught her and pushed her right back to him. Ashra fell to the ground at his feet, clutching her knees against her. Raw panic shot through every nerve in Rylan's body.

"No, not her!" he yelled, moving between Ashra and Shiro's mages. "She's done nothing! *Please!*"

The Warlord stared at him. Then he turned his back. Removing a pair of black leather gloves from within the layers of his robe, he wriggled his hands into them as he strode away from the circle.

Rylan took a step toward the unchained mage, throwing his

hands up. "Please! All she wants is to go back!" The gray-haired man stared at him expressionlessly. Desperate, Rylan called after Shiro, "*Take her back!*"

The Warlord paused. He looked at Rylan.

"No," he uttered.

All the strength left him, all at once. He dropped down beside Ashra, trembling in fear, tears gathering in his eyes. He wrapped his arms around her as she curled tight into a ball on his lap, her shoulders quaking. The chain fixed to the shackle on her wrist trailed across the ground, the empty band lying next to his hand. To Rylan, there was something symbolic and sad about that image. She shouldn't have to die like this. Not like this. Not alone.

She didn't have to, he realized.

He scooped up Ashra's chain from the ground and snapped the empty band around his own wrist.

He gasped, suddenly filled with a bottomless comfort. He shivered and closed his eyes, basking in a flood of compassion and warmth. The force of it swept him away, and suddenly he was adrift, floating on a calm, wide sea of peace. And Ashra was there, riding the current beside him, accepting him, welcoming him in. He was content. Neither one of them would have to die alone.

And then a new sensation woke within him: a new power that coursed into him through the link, filling him completely. When he recognized it, he quivered with excitement and hope. It was Ashra's connection to the magic field; she was unshielded. And, through the link, her power was his to command. All he had to do was take it.

The unchained mage raised his hand, eyes narrowing in concentration.

Rylan reacted. He struck out with every drop of power he could summon through the link. The Khar mage spun away, fanning blood everywhere. The knife-sharp blast of air that sliced him in half continued past him, cutting down others gathered behind him. Some struggled to rise, but Rylan lashed out again with Ashra's power, and this time he expanded the strike to encompass the entire ring of people that surrounded them. Blood and bodies collected in the street.

Panting, he fixed his gaze on the only man left standing.

The Warlord regarded him with a smoldering glare. Almost, Rylan thought he saw a smile. Then Shiro's lips moved, uttering a single word:

"*Nachiro.*"

Rylan winced as an invisible knife stabbed him in the chest and started tearing him open. The pain buckled his knees, driving him to the ground and wrenching a cry from his lips. It was like something clawing and biting its way into him, burrowing through his ribcage. It wrapped around his heart and *squeezed*. He couldn't breathe. His lungs were on fire, his mouth filling with blood. Frantic, he lashed out at the spell with Ashra's magic, but the Word wasn't his to command. It was unstoppable, relentless

Ashra let out a raw shriek, the most painful noise he'd ever heard.

He rolled over onto his back, struggling against the spell, gasping and scrabbling for a few more seconds of life. It didn't do any good. The pain undid him, ripping him apart. He didn't have the breath to scream.

Vaguely, he heard Ashra sobbing. Through the link, she could feel everything he felt. And he could feel her pain as if it were his own, her horror at watching him wheeze his last gasps beside her on the ground.

And it wasn't just Ashra's pain he felt. The whole of the community was reacting to his death, a collective outcry of sorrow and dismay. As the world darkened and his consciousness faded, Rylan experienced the sensation of drifting away, drifting toward something bigger, something aware. He melted into it, becoming one with it.

He entered the Unity.

And suddenly, he knew.

The Khar were not their enemy.

They were a people enslaved by Shiro. An entire society, imprisoned for thousands of years and compelled to serve a single demon. The same demon who stood glowering above him, a silver bracelet glowing from his wrist. It was that artifact that controlled them all: the `san. Whoever controlled the A'isan controlled the Empire.

And that was the answer.

Rylan used the last of his strength to pass control of the link back to Ashra.

She struck out ruthlessly at Shiro, launching a razor-sharp gash of air that sliced across his neck. Blood gushed in jets from the opening in his throat, and the Warlord sank to his knees with a look of shock on his face.

Ashra struck again, cleaving his head off.

Rylan felt the Warlord's death through the link: an instant of startled fury that lasted less than a heartbeat. And then the collective outcry and confusion of an entire civilization suddenly stripped of purpose. Rylan smiled, filled with a boundless sense of relief. He kept that smile on his lips as he faded from the world.

"Don't!" Ashra cried.

He felt her hands on him. Then a shocking wave of heat tunneled into him, attacking and dismantling the Word of Command. Rylan stared up at her as his breath returned to his chest. He lay gasping on the ground, feeling his flesh knitting back together, straining to understand what had just occurred.

"How...?" he wheezed.

Ashra shook her head, her eyes moist. She held up her arm. On her wrist was the *A'isan*, shimmering with argent power.

"They told me how," she whispered. Holding his eyes, she unclasped the glowing band and released it from her arm. With a trembling hand, she offered it to him.

"They want you to have it," she told him in a small voice.

"Me?" he whispered. He didn't understand.

But then it dawned on him: they didn't want him. They wanted Keio Matu. It was a wise choice. He accepted the band from her and lay still, just holding it for a moment, rotating the silver manacle, letting it catch the light. It felt soft, like satin. Not like any metal he had ever felt. And it was warm, almost as though it were a living, breathing thing with its own vitality. It pulsed in response to his touch, as though urging him to put it on.

He didn't want to.

The sound of a distant explosion rattled the street. His brothers and sisters were still obeying the last command of their Warlord, still calling down fire strikes upon the palace. The sound rocked his bones. More people were dying.

They didn't have to. He could stop it, stop the entire war. All he had to do was put on the A'isan. But if he put it on, he might never be able to take it off. He glanced helplessly at Ashra. She looked back at him with tenderness and compassion in her eyes. She understood what he was struggling with. At every level.

"Go ahead," she urged. "It was meant for you."

Rylan knew she was right.

He snapped it on.

Gil stood alone before the palace gate, three pairs of Khar mages stalking up the center of the street toward him with purposeful strides. Behind them came an entire assault force.

He was the only thing between them and the gate, and Gil knew he wouldn't be enough.

All around him, the city burned. A block away, the trees lining the street were ablaze. Beyond them, fires gnawed at a row of houses. The outer walls still stood, but the flames had engulfed the insides and could be seen licking out the windows and devouring the rooftops. Burning embers showered the street, drifting down like hellish snow.

The Khar mages stopped yet twenty paces from him and just stood there, one pair ahead of the others. The man facing him had a pale gray face and silver hair. He was lashed to a flaxen-haired woman of the Kingdoms. They both stood regarding him with emotionless faces that masked their intentions. The robes they wore were the same as all the others, and yet they carried themselves differently, as though they were officers, or even nobility.

The two exchanged glances. Then, linking hands, they approached him warily. Gil stood his ground, unsure of what to do. With the talisman in his hands, he could hold his own against the six of them together. But he couldn't defend against the army behind them. If they wanted to take him out, there was nothing stopping them. He kept his weapon raised and ready, shifting his weight over his feet.

The pair of mages halted only paces away. The man was younger than he'd thought, perhaps his own age. If it wasn't for the gray skin that made him look like a cadaver, he might have been handsome. The woman he was chained to clung to his arm, looking just as fearful as Gil felt.

The man inclined his head stiffly. "We are here at the command of our Warlord," he said. "To offer our surrender."

Gil's jaw went slack in shock, *Thar'gon* sinking to his side. He glanced behind the two mages at the size of the force behind them, wondering if the man's words were just a taunt. Their mages outnumbered his, and their fire strikes had already breached the palace walls. In all ways that mattered, they had already won.

He asked skeptically. "Why would you surrender?"

"Because that is the order."

Which made no sense. Gil shook his head, struggling to understand what was happening.

Ahead, the lines of soldiers parted to admit another pair of chained mages through their ranks. At first, Gil was so shaken by the gray man's offer that he didn't pay much attention to the new pair. But then he noticed all the soldiers bowing their heads and backing away diffidently as the man and woman passed. The gray-faced mage in front of him at last stepped aside, allowing him a good look at the two who approached.

He almost dropped his weapon.

The sight of Rylan and Ashra, chained together, made his mouth go dry.

They stopped in front of him.

Ashra gave him a weak smile. Her cheeks were no longer wet with tears. She looked renewed. Invigorated. Her raven hair fluttered before her face, played out by a breath of smoke-fed air. Beside her, Rylan stood with a strength of presence he'd never had before. He wore a gleaming silver band on his arm that radiated power in visible waves. He stared at Gil a long, silent minute before finally acknowledging him with a nod.

Gil looked back and forth between the two of them, wondering if he'd lost his mind. "What's going on?" he asked gruffly.

It was Ashra who answered him. "We killed the Warlord. Rylan replaced him."

Gil glanced at the gleaming band on Rylan's arm. Then his eyes shot back to the man's face. "You replaced him?" he echoed, licking his dry lips.

"For now," Rylan clarified. He shrugged casually. "Until the Empress decides otherwise."

Gil didn't know what to make of that. It was too much to digest, all at once. He decided to take it step by step, one thing at a time. Address the most fundamental questions first. Breathing a long, steadying breath, he asked Rylan, "So what are your intentions?"

Rylan glanced behind him at the gathered army. "I've ordered a withdrawal from this city," he replied evenly. "And from this continent."

Gil nodded, his mind still reeling. He fumbled for the next question. But the sound of a scuffing noise broke him off from his thoughts. Turning around, he looked back to find the Prime Warden standing behind him, her face looking haunted. She drew up at his side and took his arm.

Naia considered Rylan and Ashra with a cautious gaze. After moments, she asked, "When will they be back, Rylan?" She stared intensely into his face, waiting for a reply

Rylan blinked. Then he looked at her. "I don't know," he answered, his eyes distant. "Their Warlord was a demon. The invasion was his inception. As for the Empress... I can't speak for her, but I hope to convince her otherwise."

Upon hearing his words, Naia's frown deepened. She let go of Gil's arm, a grave expression on her face. "You're going with them? Why?"

Rylan shrugged. "Because my daughter is with them." He lifted his arm with its gleaming silver band. "And they need me," he said with a slight, whimsical smile. He glanced at Ashra, looking at her fondly. He kissed her cheek.

Rylan turned to Gil. "Here," he said. "She belongs with you."

He reached out and released the band from Ashra's arm. Her eyes opened wide, and she gasped. She glanced at Rylan, then stared down at her naked arm. Her expression slowly changed, evolving from disbelief into wonder before collapsing into sorrow. She took a step back and stumbled away, careening into Naia's arms. She clung fiercely to the Prime Warden, sobbing into her shoulder.

Gil whirled back to Rylan, anger chewing his bones. "If you're going to release her, then release her mind! Otherwise, it's just cruelty."

Rylan smiled. "She'll be fine," he assured him. "She just lost her father, and she's been through a lot. But her mind is hers, and hers alone."

With that, he unhooked the band that had held Ashra's chain from his own arm, letting it fall to the ground. He stared down at it, a saddened look on his face. Then he nodded, as if in answer to an unspoken question. Breathing a sigh, he turned and walked back the way he had come.

"Rylan!" Naia cried.

He stopped and looked back at her.

"Don't go!" she urged, taking a step toward him. "You're not one of them. Please, Rylan. Try to remember who you are!"

Rylan smiled back at her, the lights of the fires reflected in his eyes. "I do remember who I am," he assured her. "I also remember who I was. That's why I have to go back."

With that, he strode away. As he walked, he pulled something out of his coat. Some type of stone dangling from a slender gold chain. He brought the stone up to his lips and kissed it.

As he walked, he started to fade. Within seconds, he was gone.

The pairs of mages he had come with nodded their heads and turned away, walking back down the street through the drifting smoke and eerie lights cast by the fires. Gil stared after them a moment and then turned to Ashra, still cradled in Naia's arms. He set a comforting hand on her shoulder. To his surprise, she looked up and offered him a fragile smile. It was weak and timid, but it was there.

When he looked back, he saw that the street was empty.

They were alone. The entire Khar army had disappeared, the silence they left behind resonating off the walls. Gil gazed ahead in shock, then squeezed his eyes shut, relief pouring into him countercurrent to the strength pouring out. He staggered.

"What now?" he whispered.

"Now?" Naia responded. "Now we rebuild."

THE END

GLOSSARY

acolyte: apprentice mage who has passed the Trial of Consideration and sworn the acolyte's oath.

Aeridor: lost continent somewhere in the Southern Hemisphere.

Aerysius: ancient city where the Masters of Aerysius once dwelt. Destroyed when the Well of Tears was unsealed.

Almir: mage of the Khar.

Alqazar Citadel: fortress in Karikesh that wards the Lion's Gate.

Andarapi Palace: royal palace in Karikesh.

anti-magic: the magic of the Netherworld. Variously known as the Hellpower, the Onslaught, and dark magic.

Archer, Gilroy: sixth tier Grand Master of the Order of Battlemages.

Archer, Kyel: father of Gil Archer. The man who destroyed the Well of Tears. (deceased)

artifact: heirloom of power that has been imbued with magical characters or properties.

Ashra ni Sayeed: daughter of the Sultan of the Malikari Empire and acolyte of the Lyceum of Karikesh.

Atrament: the realm of Death, ruled by the goddess Isap.

Auberdale: capital city of Chamsbrey.

Avenor, Elda: Warden of Querers.

Black Lands: what was once Caladorn, now a sterile wasteland.

Catacombs: place of burial that exists partly in the Atrament.

chiri: alcoholic beverage made from antherberries.

Curse, the: term used to describe the darkening of the skies and earth of the Black Lands.

dampen: to shield a mage from sensing the magic field.

damper: an object that has the ability to dampen a mage from sensing the magic field.

darkmage: a mage who has sworn loyalty to Xerys.

Daru: Nation on the continent of Zahra.

Death's Passage: *see* **Catacombs.**

deizu: a mage.

deizu-kan: a Battlemage.

deizu-sum: the most powerful of mages.

Desecration, the: the apocalyptic event created by the Well of Tears.

Dija: woman of Uma Halabi's band.

Desolation: *see* **Mokona Desolation**

Domeda, Kirwan: Sensho of Daru Provence.

Edelvar, Iris: Warden of Chancellors.

Emmery: former Kingdom of the Rhen that was conquered by the Malikari.

Empress: ruler of the Turan Khar.

Farlow: town in Chambsbrey near the city of Auberdale.

field lines: currents of the magic field.

Gage, Alden: Warden of Empiricists.

Glen Farquist: holy city in the Valley of the Gods.

Gralish: mage of the Turan Khar.

Grand Canal: canal that bisects the city of Karikesh.

Grand Master: any Master of the forth tier or higher.

Guardian Tower: ancient focus of magic in Suheylu Ra.

Halabi, Uma: woman leader of a resistance group in the Damali Quarter.

Hellpower: *see* **Onslaught.**

Hopkins, Pat: mage of the Lyceum.

isan: in a *kaiden* pairing, the mage who controls the link.

kaiden: a pairing of mages accomplished by linking their power through a chain-like artifact.

Karikesh: capital of the Malikari Empire.

Kingdoms: free nations of the Rhen that are not part of the Malikari Empire.

Kateem, Khoresh: infamous Emperor who united all of Caladorn under a singular rule before the Desecration.

Kazri Souk: the world's largest market in Karikesh.

Kelson, Gayle: the Rector of Acolytes at the Lyceum of Karikesh.

Kodiro: the fourth heir to the Dowan of Laoni.

Laira: woman of the Rhen, partner of Gralish.

Lauchlin, Darien: the Last Sentinel of Aerysius. Conquered the Northern kingdom of Emmery to create the Malikari Empire. Former Servant of Xerys. *(deceased)*

Lauchlin, Emelda: former Prime Warden of Aerysius. *(deceased)*

Lauchlin, Gerald: father of Aidan and Darien Lauchlin, forth tier Grand Master of the Order of Sentinels. *(deceased)*

Lonesome Ghosts: various tribes of the Mokona Desolation.

Lower City: portion of the city of Karikesh south of the Grand Canal.

Lyceum of Bryn Calazar: ancient school of magic in the nation of Caladorn that was destroyed in the Desecration.

Lyceum of Magic in Karikesh: school of magic founded after the destruction of the Well of Tears.

Malikari Empire: Empire formed after the conquest of the Rhen by the people of Malikar.

mage: a person with the ability draw power from the magic field.

magelight: magical illumination that can be summoned by a mage that takes on the signature color of the mage's magical legacy.

magic field: source of magical energy that runs in lines of power over the earth.

Master: any mage; more specifically, a mage of the first through third tiers.

Marshall, Amina: daughter of Rylan Marshall.

Marshall, Clemet: father of Rylan Marshall.

Marshall, Emma: wife of Rylan Marshall who died in childbirth (deceased).

Marshall, Korey: son of Rylan Marshall.

Marshall, Lena: mother of Rylan Marshall.

Marshall, Rylan: farmer and former soldier.

Matu, Keio: Custodian of the Wise Council of Suheylu Ra.

Mezhar: member of Uma Halabi's band.

Mokona Desolation: desert on the continent of Zahra formed by the Desecration.

Murkaq Square: large central gathering area in Karikesh.

Natural Law: law that governs the workings of the universe that can be strained by the application of magic, but never broken.

necrator: demonic creature that renders a mage powerless in its presence.

Netherworld: realm of Xerys, God of Chaos.

Nogato, Shiro: Warlord of the Turan Khar.

North, the: the Northern kingdoms of the Rhen, including Emmery, Chamsbrey and Lynnley.

North City: portion of the city of Karikesh north of the Grand Canal.

oki: the silk of the whisper butterfly.

Onslaught: the corrupt power of the netherworld, also known as the Hellfire.

Orders: different schools of magic among the Masters of Aerysius and the Lyceum of Bryn Calazar.

Osan, Ilia: mage of ancient Shira, wife of Keio Matu.

potential: the ability in a person to sense the magic field.

Prime Warden: leaders of the Assembly of the Hall of either Aerysius or the Lyceum.

Priya: the Prime Warden's acolyte.

Promenade: area of Karikesh just north of the Grand Canal.

Puna Ajaru: a large volcanic caldera filled with pools of sulfuric acid. Also called the Scalding Sea.

Raising: Rite of Transference, during which an acolyte inherits the legacy of power from another mage.

Reis, Quinlan: former Servant of Xerys, now the husband of Prime Warden Naia Seleni and Warden of Arcanists.

Renquist, Zavier: ancient Prime Warden who created the Well of Tears.

Rhen, the: portion of the Southern Continent south of the Black Lands.

Rhenic: common language spoken throughout the kingdoms of the Rhen.

Rite of Transference: *see* **Raising**

Rothscard: largest city and former capital of the Kingdom of Emmery; renamed Karikesh by Sultan Sayeed the Conqueror, who made it the capital of the Malikari Empire.

Sanctuary: birthplace of magic in ancient Shira.

Savas: member of Uma Halabi's band.

sayan: in a *kaiden* pairing, the mage who submits.

Sayeed ibn Alborz: Sultan of the Malikari Empire, known as Sayeed the Conquerer.

Seleni, Naia: former priestess of Death, now the Prime Warden.

sensho: ruler of Daru Province.

Sentinels: an extinct order of mages that was chartered with the defense of the Rhen. Sentinels swore an Oath of Harmony to do no harm.

saturation: Battlemage tactic of overloading with magical power in anticipation of creating an enormous discharge of force.

sharaq: ancient system of honor code of the Malikari people.

Silver Star: ancient symbol of mages, indicative of the focus lines of the Circles of Convergence.

Servant of Xerys: darkmage who has pledge fealty to the God of Chaos.

Shira: ancient fallen nation on the continent of Zahra.

Sky Portal: a portal to the Netherworld created by the Turan Khar.

Soulstone: ancient artifact created by Quinlan Reis as a storage receptacle for a dying mage's legacy.

Suheylu Ra: fallen city of ancient Shira.

Tanisar corps: legions of highly disciplined elite infantry units of the Malikari Empire.

temples: various sects of worship. Each temple is devoted to a particular deity of the pantheon.

Thar'gon: magical talisman that can only be wielded by the Warden of Battlemages .

tier: additive progression of levels of power among Masters. The higher a Master's tier, the greater that person's ability to strain the limits of Natural Law.

transfer portal: portal capable of transferring a person from one location to another instantaneously.

Transference: process by which an acolyte inherits the legacy of power from another mage, resulting in the death of the Master who gives up his or her ability.

Tur: the northernmost continent.

Turan Khar: the combined peoples of the Empire of Tur.

ul-Calazi, Juhdi: member of Uma Halabi's resistance group.

Valdivora: sword once borne by both Darien Lauchlin and the ancient conquerer, Khoresh Kateem.

Vale of Amberlie: long, narrow valley in the North of the Rhen.

Valley of the Gods: valley where exists the holy city of Glen Farquist.

vitrus: the Gift that allows a mage to touch the magic field.

vortex: cyclone of power where the lines of the magic field superimpose and become vastly intense.

Walsh, Payden: fith tier Battlemage of the Lyceum of Karikesh.

Warden: the leader of one of the magical Orders.

Warden Cartwright: Warden of Naturalists.

Warden Dalton: Warden of Battlemages.

Warlord: mage in charge of the armies of the Turan Khar.

Watchers: stone towers that formed the defense grid of Suheylu Ra.

Waterfront: area of Karikesh just south of the Grand Canal.

Well of Tears: well that unlocked a gateway to the Netherworld. Created by Zavier Renquist and destroyed by Kyel Archer and Quinlan Reis.

Withersby, Meiran: Prime Warden of Aerysius.

Word of Command: a word that, when spoken in proximity, activates a spell.

Xerys: God of Chaos and Lord of the Netherworld.

Xiana: mage of Daru Provence.

yori: a type of robe.

Zahra: continent in the northern hemisphere.

Zakai: officers of the Tanisar corps that form their own distinctive social class.

Zanikar: magical sword and artifact created by Quinlan Reis.

THE PANTHEON

Alt: God of the Wilds
Athera: Goddess of Magic
Deshari: Goddess of Grief
Dreia: Goddess of the Vine
Enana: Goddess of the Hearth
Isap: Goddess of Death
Om: God of Wisdom
Xerys: God of Chaos
Zephia: Goddess of the Winds

THE ORDERS OF MAGES

Order of Arcanists: order of mages chartered with the study and creation of artifacts and heirlooms of power.

Order of Architects: order of mages chartered with the construction of magical infrastructure.

Order of Battlemages: order of mages chartered with martial applications of the magic field.

Order of Chancellors: order of mages chartered with the governance of the Assembly.

Order of Empiricists: order of mages chartered with the theoretical study of the magic field, its laws and principles.

Order of Naturalists: order of mages chartered with the study of Natural Law.

Order of Querers: order of mages chartered with practical applications of the magic field.

Order of Sentinels: extinct order of mages chartered with watching over and protecting the Rhen in a manner consistent with the Oath of Harmony. Replaced by the Order of Battlemages.

Order of Harbingers: extinct order of mages chartered with maintaining watch over Athera's Crescent.

ACKNOWLEDGMENTS

Thank you to my teachers. They are the reason why I'm here, writing this note. For Scott Peterson, who entered my story into the San Bernardino County Writing Celebration when I was in the eighth grade. For Glen Taylor, who took me to Europe with his tour group, where I fell in love with Moorish architecture. For Mr. Kelly, who fostered my love of nature. For Erin Christopher, who forced that love down my throat (said lovingly). For Dr. Skillman, who taught me to love plants. And, most of all, for Jennifer Mather, whom I wanted to be like when I grew up.

Printed in Great Britain
by Amazon